Once Again...,
The Once Trilogy, Vol. 2

Once Again…,

Bryan Ó Muimhneacháin

Paladin Books
2022

Once Again... is a work of fiction. Names, places, and incidents are products of the authors imagination or are used fictitiously.

First Printing: 2021

ISBN: 978-1-7334083-6-3

Paladin Books, LLC
PO BOX 574
St. Clair Shores, Michigan, 48080

www.oncestories.com

v2

Dedication

For those who believe

That stories about heroes

matter.

And of course...,

Always and forever,

For my wife.

Contents

Foreword

There was a boy, a long time ago. He told himself stories to get through the night.

He grew older. As he did, he left a lot of the stories behind. Life, it seemed, was more imminent than stories.

But there were whispers. And through the ups and downs of living, the stories would tickle the back of the man who had been the boy.

And finally, through catastrophe, the stories broke through.

Maybe that's all just a little more real than it should be in the forward to a book about heroes and villains. As before, maybe it's just for the thrill of the adventure and the soaring joy of heroics that you came. That's fine too.

But the man who was once the boy has heard the whispers. And the stories have come back...

Once Again...,

CHAPTER ONE

— DANA —

“Well, this just feels stupid,” I grumbled as I swallowed the dark brown ale and put my mug down with an audible thud.

The wiry rogue to my left cocked his head and gave me a noncommittal shrug of one shoulder. He took yet another swallow of his own ale, draining it while I looked around at the press of patrons crowded into the pub and shifted uncomfortably in my seat. There wasn’t anything wrong with my chair, of course. There were, to put it simply, too many people fitted in too little space for my preference. That’s not to say that the pub was particularly small; in fact, it wasn’t. The main room was a large yet simple affair, with ample open space laid out in the shape of an ‘L.’ The floor consisted of flagstone pieces, mortared together with hard clay, and its workmanship belied a history that seemed more illustrious than the building’s present use. On the inside corner was a large stone hearth that rose unbroken to the underside of the building’s roof some fifteen feet above. Openings were facing both branches of the room, with all the appropriate hardware for warming pots and sundries, but there was no fire this evening. The warm humidity of the midsummer day still lingered, and the throng of bodies milling about only amplified it. A sticky, damp breeze wafted in from the windows on the outside walls, but it offered little relief. I felt a trickle of sweat work its way down from the nape of my neck to the center of my back, and it unquestionably was not helping my already sour mood. I sipped my ale again, draining the last of the malty liquid from the cup. It wasn't cold exactly, or even notably cool, but it somehow implied a form of relief from the heat. I looked around again. We had lost sight of our companion shortly after we had settled in at our table, as he had left by the time we had gotten the same drinks that we were both now finishing. Kelly had left his mug behind, though, and it remained beside me on the table, lighter only by one or two sips that he had taken before leaving.

"He's doing it again," I grumbled.

"So you shouldn't be surprised. What's the big deal? This place seems decent. Not that it has to be for us to have a good time," said Denis. He waved his hand at an angle and caught the eye of the overworked barmaid. He began an exaggerated pantomime of pouring and drinking an invisible ale. This was his chosen way to ask for another round.

"Oh, I know that," I said, choosing not to acknowledge his performance, "It's this. *This.* It's what he always does.

Any minute now, he'll show back up with some local that just so happens to need help. Again."

Denis shot me a considering look as if now deciding to evaluate how seriously to take my irritation. "Okay, that may be true…," he began.

"It is, and he leaves us out of it every time," I growled.

"So, this is bothering you a lot, hunh?" Denis said. He sounded surprised, and his tone was now more severe. The barmaid arrived much more quickly than I would have expected, considering the number of patrons she was serving. She sat three full mugs on the table and then paused, her eyes resting on Kelly's nearly untouched drink to my right. For a moment, she hesitated, uncertain if she had made a mistake. I pulled two of the three fresh ales closer to my side of the table, settling my hand on one and grouping the other two beside me. She seemed to relax, reassured again that she had not misunderstood Denis's peculiar act from moments before. She was a young thing, I could see; it was unlikely that she had seen more than fifteen summers. Yet, she obviously took her work seriously and nodded at us with exemplary professionalism before she quietly slipped away into the crowd.

Denis had continued unabated; the only evidence that he had even noticed her coming and going was that he swapped his empty cup for the third of the full ones. "Why's it bothering you so much all of a sudden? I mean, it's been three years. It's not like it's something new."

"It's not all of a sudden, I've asked before. But you said it yourself just now— three years. I haven't pressed, but I'd like to know what he's doing. We've gone over hill and valley and sea and storm. By now, wouldn't you think he'd have explained it to us? And like I said, it's not like I haven't asked. But every time I do, he says—"

"'Don't worry about it,'" Denis mumbled, "He says that to me too."

"Exactly," I said, finding that the acknowledgment only fueled my frustration rather than abating it.

"You aren't wrong," he said, giving me another tiny shrug. "He does keep too much to himself. And, like I said, I've asked, too, once or twice. He does seem to have a..., a source he's using somehow. And, sure, I'd like to know what it is."

"Absolutely," I said, perhaps too triumphantly.

"Great Spirits," he said in mock amazement, "did you just agree with me?"

"I did, which makes me wonder if I should be drinking this second ale," I said, giving him a sly smile.

"Must be that you've become more insightful," he observed.

"I don't know. I think it's unlikely you've started to be wiser. Or maybe my standards have dropped," I said. We gave one another a grin.

Denis continued after another sip, "But what it comes back to for me is this, Dana. Really, what's the harm? The things we do – they're always things that matter, and we're always well cared for afterward. Should we care?" I watched the crowd as he spoke, and his words became distant as I found myself wondering when Kelly would resurface. He noticed my distraction and fell silent until I turned back to face him.

"It is what we decided to do," he added.

"Look, the *what* of our life is fine. Amazing, even," My mind presented a montage of faces and places from our travels, and it was almost enough to stop the whole discussion in its tracks. After a moment, though, the heat and discomfort brought me back to the present. "But that's not the problem," I continued, "It's the *how* of it all that I don–," I stopped mid-word as the crowd parted briefly, and I caught sight of Kelly. He was at the far end of the more extended branch of the room, standing at the far end of the bar that stretched down that wall. Beside him were two other men I didn't recognize. The first one was short, stocky, and dressed more formally than most of the crowd, with a dark blue waistcoat over what I believed began the day as a white shirt. He was nervously mopping his bald head with a small cloth and nodding rapidly. The other man was tall – or at least slightly taller than Kelly – and dressed in long black robes. He wore his thick brown hair pulled back in a ponytail long enough to disappear into the hood hanging on his back. As I watched the three men, I was struck suddenly by how very similar the latter looked to Kelly. Had I not known better, I would have taken them for brothers.

But how true is that? I wondered abruptly. *Do I* really *know better?* The thought swirled around my mind even as the crowd closed in again, blocking my view.

"Hey. Hello? Dana?" Denis was talking. "You still there?"

I looked at him, though it took a moment to bring my focus back. A look flashed across his face, and I saw he knew something had thrown me. "What? What happened?" he asked.

I opened my mouth to tell him when the black leather-clad figure of Kelly emerged from the crowd and approached our table, accompanied by the small bald man I had seen with him moments before. Casually, he took his seat next to me, where his ale sat. The newcomer sat nervously down beside Denis. There was no sign of the robed man, which irked me anew. Denis and I considered the newcomer for a moment as Kelly settled into his seat. He looked briefly at the two mugs in front of him. Then, with only a slight hesitation, he slid the slightly fuller one across the table as if that had been his intent all along. The guest accepted the mug with a nod.

Kelly gestured to the man and said, "Denis, Lady

Dana, this is Conseiller Alfre Monague. He's the town selectman – basically, the mayor – of Gretchville," Conseiller Monague partially stood, performed two awkward half-bows both to Denis and to me, accompanied them with mumbled greetings, then sat and mopped his brow again. He followed with a nod to Kelly and a thirsty appraisal of the mug of ale. He lifted the drink but paused with its edge almost touching his lip. He looked at me again as if seeing me for the first time, then slowly and with great effort put the mug back down.

"So, you don't like ale?" Denis asked, sipping from his mug with an explicit flourish.

"I was wait-een for the lady," he said with a nervous clearing of his throat. His accent was thick, and while I was sure I remembered hearing something like it in the Imperial court, it was for me obscure enough that I couldn't place it. He was not as short as he had initially looked, though still much less tall than my companions and me. Height is something I notice first very often, as my own is so often the subject of discussion. He was, however, portly, with a kind of solidity to him that gave him an air of strength, even while it amplified the impression that he lacked for height. For what was probably the twelfth time since joining us, he mopped the sweat from his forehead. The warm and humid weather was not to his comfort, I could see, and on that, if nothing else, we agreed. I had had my fill of it as well. I gave him a gentle smile.

"Not at all, sir," I said, "There is no need to stand on propriety just now." I waited again. Looking from me to Kelly and then to Denis in turn – as if verifying it was acceptable to all – he slowly brought the mug back to his lips. When it got there, though, he took a generous mouthful, swallowing it and finishing with a sigh. He closed his eyes as he let the drink ease down his throat, doing much more to calm him than to cool him. I noticed Kelly looking at me with a look of acknowledgment, if not amusement. I curled my lip into a half-grin and shrugged my shoulder before I sipped my drink once again. Kelly knew I had strong feelings about such displays of what – for want of a better term – I will call 'mock sophistication' outside of the royal courts. There, a blooded gentleman would not dare sip his drink until all the noblewomen at the table drank first. It was fitting. But that was a different time and place, and I had no intention of participating in such pretense in a tiny rural public house.

The ale, though, was doing its work on Monague. I was glad for this, and though it took until he had nearly drained the mug before he spoke again, the Conseiller appeared much calmer. He leaned in toward the table; his tiny cloth now retired to a pocket on his breast.

"I can't believe our good fortune, your arrival in our town like this just now," he said. He looked back and forth between the three of us, spreading his attention evenly.

"Fancy that," Denis muttered, shooting a quick look at me. I twitched.

"It's been 'orrible; just 'orrible, and we've nowhere to turn," Monague continued unabated, "what with all the recent troubles down south, we are isolated 'ere."

Kelly nodded knowingly. I looked at Denis, and he returned the look. We shrugged; clearly, neither of us knew anything about any 'troubles down south.' But, once again, it seemed Kelly had some bit of information that we didn't. My irritation fluttered back.

"No army, no militia, nothing," the selectman was saying to Kelly's sincere nods. The more he nodded, the more the selectman spoke. I thought that it worked like shaking the last bit of grain from a bag. "And then, just the other night, almost an entire family – poof. Gone. Only the father and the son were left, although that is no mercy. They are in such a bad way from their wounds that they have not woken since."

I gave him a narrow-eyed glare. "A whole family? You mean to say, children?"

He gave a violent nod as he spoke. "And they weren't the first. I now believe we have lost dozens of people. All ages."

Denis cocked his head. "'Now believe?' How long has this been going on?"

"A few weeks," his eyes strayed down to the table as he

spoke, “maybe a month or two. It is ‘ard to tell. At first, we – that is, I – believed it was that people were only leaving. It ‘appens ‘ere; this is not one of the old settlements such as you find up in Yorch. Even those down south in Gladia are more established. ‘Ere, there are mostly migrants, moving from one to the other, north or south. Some little few stay and try to make a life ‘ere; our land is cheap and can produce if enough work is put in, so they think they ‘ave a chance. And some do, though most do not. My point is, I didn’t notice at first. I can’t know for sure how long it has been happening.” He retrieved his handkerchief from his pocket and wiped his head again.

Kelly’s expression had shifted. His eyes were unfocused as he stared off into the depths of the room without seeing. “Wildlife, maybe?” he said, “Have to be something significant, though. There is the Ederland forest down south. It’s pretty far, but it wouldn’t be impossible.”

“No sir,” Conseiller Monague said, roused at the mention of Ederland, the evil jungle in the northern reaches of Gladia, “There are many settlements in the lands in between that ‘aven’t been affected as we ‘ave. And no one ‘as seen anything in the fields and marshlands between ‘ere and there, either. I ‘ave made many inquiries, monsieur.” He was glaring at Kelly as if offended at the suggestion that he hadn’t thought of it. There was a pause, but the selectman realized that his need was too great to hang on his pride. He let the matter drop with another swallow of his drink.

"Hill-folk then," concluded Denis, adding, "ugh."

"We'll see what we can find," Kelly said. And that was that. Monague drained his mug, thanked us again, made some vague reference to a reward, and finally turned and left.

Kelly looked at Denis and me and said, "So tell me. If you were a bunch of mountain-dwellers, why would you risk coming down to civilized areas—,"

I raised an eyebrow.

"— partially civilized areas," he corrected, "to steal townsfolk and farmers, heavy on the women and children?"

"Slaves," Denis said quickly, giving voice to the obvious.

"That would seem to be the reason," I said, "It's the only thing that explains all of it. It isn't traffickers, or they wouldn't leave strong men and boys behind. Men are useful for hard work, sure, but they're more challenging to keep contained. And likely, that isn't the major need, either. Children have value as they can be trained and do light things right away, and they're easier to control. The women are for...," the words caught in my throat.

"Making more hill-folk," Denis said. He waved to the young barmaid, signaling for one more pint.

A gurgled noise came out of my throat at that. The outline of the situation in Gretchville was becoming more apparent, and my stomach had started turning. I felt my teeth begin to grind unbidden.

The barmaid came a moment later and handed the drink to Denis. Kelly and I both waved off her silent offer of another, and I passed her enough coin for our bill. This accomplished, I asked, “So, where do we go from here?”

We looked at Denis. He put his mug down and looked back and forth between us.

“What? Why do you two always look at me like that?” he said, a mock offense in every syllable.

“Because you’re very good at thinking the way lowlifes think,” Kelly said.

“Very good,” I echoed, “That’s quite true.”

Denis blew air out of his mouth across his tongue, producing a ‘*P-p-p-p-t*’ sound. We waited for another moment.

“Okay, do we have a map of the area or anything?” he said, his mind already in pursuit. “We need to find any low valley passes that might lead from the vicinity of the town up into the mountains. If they’re slipping away so fast that they’re not seen, it can’t be on foot, and that means they’ll need wagons for the victims.”

“See?” Kelly said, “I told you that you were good at this, kid.” He reached into a pouch and produced a roll of paper, spreading it out on the table. I leaned in to find that it was a hastily drawn map of the area around Gretchville, sketched and annotated in a hand I didn't recognize.

"Where did—?" I started.

Kelly shrugged off my question with a glance and a shrug, turning his attention to the map. Denis was already scanning it, his eyes narrow and his brow knit. If he was interested in the map's origin, he gave no indication. I, however, sipped on my beer as my earlier frustration came crashing back. It was now, though, amplified by my absolute disgust at the kidnappings. Minutes passed, with the only sound being the background noises of the pub. Then, finally, Denis looked up.

"All right. Come on, let's go rescue some children," he said as casually as if he were discussing the weather. Kelly nodded, seemingly satisfied, and rolled up the map.

We had all stood and started for the door when it happened. The frustration that I had been wrestling with all evening finally bubbled over, and I grabbed Kelly's arm, turning him toward me and squaring myself at the same time. "This is enough," I said, the words bursting forth.

"Hunh?" he looked at me, confused.

Denis had stopped a pace away, watching.

"No more," I said, surprising even myself with the intensity in my voice. I glanced at Denis before I looked Kelly in the eye and continued. "We're – well, I am – done with all of this. All the secrets. The way you seem to know – practically everywhere we go – that we will find someone with a problem. The private information only you seem to have. That damnable map!" I gestured toward the rolled paper still in his hand for emphasis. "Done," I finished, with my voice flat and cold.

Kelly's face was almost blank, though I believe there was perhaps just a twinge of guilt. "I don't..." he started, but with no conviction.

"You do," I said. "Another example. Who was the other man at the bar? The one with you and Monague earlier?" My tone grew louder and more intense as I spoke.

He kept my gaze but remained silent. Denis watched the exchange at what was, for him, a comfortable distance away as a heartbeat passed. Then two. The noise of the bar had faded to nothing in my ears.

"Fine," I said, finally releasing his arm, my voice quiet again. "Let's go save the slaves. But that's it for me. I can't keep being led around blindly. So this time is the last time." I turned and brushed out of the bar, leaving them both behind.

"Well, it was intense," Denis said. It was the first thing he had said about the exchange in the pub since it happened. None of us had mentioned it, actually, and over the ensuing two days of our search, we spoke exclusively about the task at hand. It was the least comfortable we had been together in three years.

"Shhh," I hissed at him. He glanced back over his

shoulder to give me a knowing look. We were lying on our bellies on a grassy hill overlooking a shallowed valley. A thicket of shrubbery arched partially over us and around the hilltop, providing an abundance of cover.

"Well, it was," he said, his voice was now quieter, but it did not indicate a change of subject. I gave a quick nod as if to tell him to turn around, and, after favoring me with a bit of a glare, he rolled back flat again. He dropped his head down and sighted down the length of Kelly's black crossbow, which he held propped up on a small stone in front of him. Off in the middle distance, yards away from the leaves that hid us, a cluster of three ramshackle wagons sat in a half-circle around a small campfire. The wagons were simple affairs, ten-foot squares of planking with workaday wheels covered over with canvas tenting. The three of them were chained in series one to the next. The last one on the furthest end was in turn affixed to a small carriage and from there to four stout horses. The campfire area was inhabited by four large, unkempt men seated around the fire, eating some of what appeared to be a thin soup from a small cauldron they had suspended above the flames. Several piles of equipment sat scattered around, giving evidence that they had just broken up camp.

"We don't know yet if those are our...," Denis started but broke off as one of the men stood and walked to the last wagon. At first, I couldn't tell what it was, but something had emerged from beneath the canvas tenting. As we watched in silence, the man unfastened the corner of the tenting and roughly flipped it back. The late afternoon sunlight flooded the back of the wagon to reveal a cluster of people, women and children mostly, chained together and scrambling away from the sudden opening. The protrusion – which I could now see had been a child's arm – slipped quickly out of sight as the man waved his hands and said something to them that was lost to the distance.

"Oh, well, fine then," Denis said, resignation in his tone, "but I'm still not done with the other discussion."

I patted his shoulder and whispered, "I know. Honestly, I was a little surprised by it too. But we'll have more time to talk about it later. After we're finished."

"Yeah," he said, lining his eye back up to the sight of the crossbow, "After we're finished."

We watched in silence for several minutes. "Four," Denis said quietly, his typical bluster now vanished like a wisp of cloud. "Roustabout armor, and not heavily armed."

"Fifteen in that wagon, give or take. If I had to guess, there's probably the same in all three. Forty-five in total, maybe?" The words tasted bitter. I don't like slavers.

"They've probably camped here while they made their collections, and now they're heading back up deeper into the hills," he said. It made sense. Using the maps, Denis had found a few paths where wagons could pass more deeply into the wilds and hills that filled the land between Gretchville and the mountains to the northwest. It had taken us almost all of the intervening two days to find this camp, and it seemed like we were just in time as they appeared to be packing up to go.

"We almost missed them," I whispered. "How unfortunate for them that we didn't."

Denis was now stock still, his eye keen down the length of the crystal-tipped crossbow bolt. I looked around carefully, my hand on my rapier, but we remained alone and, as best as I could tell, unseen. Below, the man was again saying something to the captives in the wagon. The words remained lost to the breeze and distance, but the result was apparent as they cowered further back against the far side. He flipped the canvas back down and secured it again before turning back to the fire.

"What is he waiting for?" Denis mumbled.

Despite our disagreement, I felt a grin tickle the corner of my mouth as I thought about Kelly. I knew what was coming. "He's waiting for all of them to be in a cluster around that fire."

As the fourth slaver settled back down by his companions, we heard a sound from a short distance off to our right. Hoofbeats and the rustling of leaves rose along with the noise of a bellowing shout until finally, in a burst of motion, a magnificent brown and blonde stallion burst from a nearby copse of trees, bearing straight down on the little campsite at lightning speed. On its back, Kelly crouched with one hand in the horse's mane and the other waving his black longsword over his head. He shouted and howled an incoherent battle cry, and the four men around the fire froze in confusion and a sudden pulse of fear.

"Now," I said. Instantly came the high-pitched 'ping' of the crossbow as Denis sent the crystalline bolt down into the camp. It disappeared into the horse's rigging at the caravan's front, any noise of its impact lost in the uproar from our friend.

"Done," Denis said, "let's go." He bounded up from where he lay in a single motion and ran toward the camp. I followed with my sword in hand.

The four slavers had finally realized what was happening and were now drawing their weapons but hadn't quite gotten them in hand before Kelly and Locksley were on them. The stallion bolted and jumped straight over the campfire as Kelly dove from his back, careening into the two closest men and toppling them into a heap before he rolled away and came up to his feet. One of them, we could see, remained still on the ground while the other clambered up and readied a thick quarterstaff. The other two slavers, the one to my right being the one we had witnessed threatening the captives, turned to support their partner.

Of course, in all the action, they had not noticed Denis

and me. We arrived together, and in well-worn habit, I went to the one on the right while he went to the left. I was within striking distance before my prey reacted. He had only started to turn my way when I jammed the hilt of my sword into the soft of his neck. He crumbled as he fell backward, clutching at his ruined throat. I looked in time to see that Denis was on the other, coming in a low roll under his target's awkward axe swing. The twin daggers in his hands flashed too fast to follow, slicing across the back of the other's ankles as he rolled past. The man dropped to the ground as if pushed down by an invisible hand. I momentarily wondered if he would ever walk again. Then I remembered the people in the wagons and decided I didn't care.

Kelly was dueling with his opponent, calmly deflecting the thick quarterstaff's thrusts without attacking in return. The result was that, with each swing, the slaver grew angrier and more feral.

"Come on, Kel. Quit it," Denis said.

"Fine, fine," Kelly sighed, rolling his eyes as if bored. The slaver veritably burst with rage at the practiced nonchalance of their exchange. He stepped back first and then charged with a spittle-filled howl. Kelly altered his stance as the man rushed at him. The fight was about to be over.

The slaver swung his staff with all the power of his fury. Had it hit, it would have been enough to pulverize any target's head whether they had a helmet on or not. Of course, I knew it wasn't going to hit. Kelly sidestepped at the last possible moment, and the only thing in the space where the staff struck was the sharp edge of the wicked ebony longsword. It cleaved through the three-inch-thick pole as if it were water, sending the top four feet flying away. A victim now of his momentum, the slaver lost his balance in the absence of an impact. He tumbled to the ground, the remaining stump of the staff falling out of his hand. He rolled over and found Kelly standing over him and pressing the edge of the longsword to his throat.

"Hee-yah!" A voice came from the direction of the carriage. We turned together to see another figure from the far side of the wagons scrambling up into the driver's seat of the carriage. He snapped the reins to drive the horses forward.

"Five of them," Kelly said to no one as he held his blade in place on the fallen man's throat.

"I saw four," Denis said with a shrug.

"Me too," I said, shoving my gasping opponent over toward the rest.

"Yeah, me too," Kelly sighed.

The horses lurched forward as the reins snapped, but the carriage and the driver seat didn't move. Instead, the horses went off at a run, heading in different directions. The latching joint that had held them to the carriage – the final resting place of Denis's bolt – sheered apart like paper as they rushed forward, freeing them from the rigging. The slaver, not believing – or possibly not understanding – what was going on, was jerked forward by the reins wrapped around his arms. His body bounced along the ground as he clawed to remove the line that bound him to the animal.

"Should we go get him?" I said.

Kelly had rolled his captive over and used the man's belt to secure his hands. "It should be fine," he said.

I looked up in time to see Locksley, having come back around toward us in a broad, full circle, gallop up alongside the fleeing horse. At first, he matched the other's pace but then began to drop back. The other horse, still dragging the fifth man, slowed to stay beside him, and in moments, the two came to a stop aside one another. The slaver lay motionless several feet behind, his arm still tangled tightly in the reins. Locksley took a step or two back and stood next to the unconscious figure as if on guard.

"Of course," Denis said as he dragged the slaver he had hobbled over to where Kelly and I were now standing. "Oh, stop it, you whiner," he said to the man as he left him on the ground near his companions. The man gave a childlike whimper, all the while clutching at his ruined ankles. "You'll be fine," Denis said over his shoulder as he came to stand by me, "Maybe a limp. Probably a limp. Anyway, just be quiet."

Denis and Kelly finished securing the five men while I went to the wagons. One by one, I drew back the canvas and revealed the occupants. I spoke as gently as I could, but the terror they had experienced seemed to have settled in, and most of them just stared at me blankly. Using a set of keys that I had taken from one of the kidnappers, I gently unlocked their bindings. The locks – and indeed the chains, to be honest – were of poor quality. They would have been simple to defeat by anyone with proper training. I had finished releasing those on the first two wagons and headed to the third when I realized that the freed victims were all but gone, having run off and disappeared into the tree line. I took a breath to call after them, but the evident futility of it turned that breath into a heavy sigh.

"Don' worry, lassie." A woman's voice came from the cluster of people remaining on the third wagon.

"We would have offered them a ride back to their families," I said without turning, the resignation evident in my voice. I would have had no idea which of the twelve people in the little cart I was addressing, but as I turned, there was a shuffling of the bodies, and eleven people backed away from a tall, older woman in a worn blue dress at the far end. I say older, but I mean only 'older than I,' and her life had distinctly been one that multiplied those years beyond their actual number. She was prematurely gray-haired, though it was thick and long and bound in a braid that hung over her shoulder. Her face was creased with the lines of a life lived, the deepest ones drawn around her eyes where laughter had left its footprints. I would have been more surprised at the slavers taking someone like her, but there was a light in those eyes that was clear even from the several feet that separated us, making the question gratuitous.

"They don' need a ride, missus," she said, straightening up to fill the space left as the others had moved away from her. "They just needed the freedom to run. You and your boys seem to have given them that. Gratitude." She bowed her head deeply.

"Shh, witch," said one of the other women. I snapped her an angry look, and she recoiled.

"Don' pay them any mind, lass," the first woman said. She gave no visible indication that she had even heard the comment and indeed seemed not troubled by it.

The gray-haired woman cocked her head a little and considered me carefully, then flashed a smile that proved that I had been right about the creases around her eyes. "But if you could get these last chains off, it might make the whole experience just a touch better for everyone, yes?" She wiggled her leg, and the chain still affixed to it clattered on the floorboard.

"Oh, of course," I said, my anger disappearing like a soap bubble popping. I opened the locks as I had on the other two platforms – even on the woman who had so recently been the subject of my ire. Within moments the captives had run off much the same as the previous ones had, shepherding their children and scurrying away as quickly as their legs would take them. Shortly, I was alone except for the woman in the corner. She quite casually remained sitting where she had been, gently rubbing her ankles where the chains no longer were, and I saw no indication that she was planning to move.

"I'm not sure how I feel about them just running off," I said absently as the last of the former prisoners disappeared out of sight beyond the trees. "I feel responsible for them."

"Sure, you do," Denis said, approaching the wagon from the direction where he and Kelly had been up until then managing the captured slavers. "You always do when we help someone," he continued, looking briefly toward the woman and back to me without pausing, "You spent too much time around noble-folk. Always thinking they have to solve everything."

The woman laughed to herself at his words. She stood up as casually as could be and walked over to the wagon side. Without saying anything, she then extended her hand expectantly. To my surprise, and probably to his own, Denis offered his hand in return without hesitation. More, once she had his hand in hers, she leaped over the short side of the wagon to the ground with a grace that belied her apparent age.

"Sorry," Denis said with the realization that he'd just been a gentleman by mistake, "but what is happening right now?"

"You're a good boy, laddie," she said, releasing his hand and patting his face. A muffled snort of laughter escaped me before I caught it.

"Ma'am," I said. I hopped off the cart and came to stand with them, "May I ask your name?"

"You may," she said, spinning in my direction with enough of a twirl that her blue dress flared slightly. "I am Eryth Erantress. I'm a," she looked up into the sky as if considering her words, "a healer, by trade. Likely that's why I was in that cart with all the mommies and babies."

Denis looked at her carefully as if she were some new kind of creature that he'd never seen up close. Eryth turned back to him and returned the look, squinting her eyes a little and scanning him up and down. I realized that she was mocking him, even as she was genuinely appraising him. She finally released the squint and smiled at him.

"Well, lassie, you keep pretty company," she said, giving me a wink.

Of course, Kelly chose precisely that moment to walk over to us, undoubtedly wondering what had been keeping us. He saw Eryth and stopped, bowing his head in a brief but courteous nod.

Eryth turned to me, her eyes open wide. “So *much* pretty company. How do you manage it?”

“I—,” I started, though I wasn’t sure what came next. Kelly spoke up quickly, rescuing me from the awkwardness.

“Madam,” he said, with all formality and gentility, “are you well?”

“Oh my,” Eryth said, placing her hand on her chest in a dramatic pretense of being flustered, “we have a real eastern gentleman here, do we?”

Kelly gave a sidelong look toward Denis, who shrugged.

“Don’t look at me,” he said, jutting a thumb in my direction, “She’s the one picking up strays.”

“Now, now, laddie,” Eryth said, more seriously than she had been up to now, “I don’t expect eastern manners from you, but there’s no need to be impolite.” She turned back to Kelly as she spoke, “I’m sure his lordship here would never be so—,” she stopped abruptly, her eyes wide. She was staring at Kelly with an expression I couldn’t place. I followed her gaze, realizing only then what had caught her attention. She was looking at the ebony longsword still in his hand.

“That,” she said, waving her hand toward the sword. “Boy, do you know what that is you carry?”

Kelly had seen her lock her eyes on the sword as well. He began to sheath it before she had even spoken again. “I do," he said, stepping closer, "and it appears you have some thoughts on it."

She looked him steadily in the eyes for a moment, breaking only for a cautious glance down to the sheathed blade. Then she smiled, her eyes lighting back up in the way they had been before, and she bowed low.

"This is a day of marvels," she said as she straightened back up, the broad smile still on her face. She turned, taking each of the three of us in for a moment before she stopped and faced me again. "Could an old woman be privileged to take a ride back to Gretchville with three such impressive and handsome heroes as yourselves?"

I looked at Denis and then at Kelly, and silently we reached an agreement. I nodded to Eryth, and if it was possible, she brightened even further.

"Wonderful," she said, "Where would you have me?"

Kelly stepped forward with his hand extended. "Would you be comfortable enough on the driver's bench of the cart? I assure you these men won't be a problem."

"Tish-tosh," she said, "I wasn't concerned about that at all. I expected you'd want me in the back to be true. Riding with you in the front is more than I hoped. I haven't caught your name as yet, my lord, but I am Eryth."

"Kelly," he said as she took his arm, "Just Kelly. Come over here and rest for a moment while we get everything packed up." The two of them walked toward the remains of the camp, where Kelly left her beside the smoldering fire.

"What in the world is she about?" Denis said, stepping up closer to me with his voice low as they walked away.

"I have no idea," I said, watching them, "but one of the other prisoners called her a witch. She says she's a healer, and that's why the hill people took her."

"That's not a witch," Denis said, "First, there's no such thing. People who say that they are usually are just trying to cheat the stupid. And there's more to her than that."

Kelly returned, a grin plastered on his face as he looked at each of us. "Well, you do make interesting friends," he said, folding his arms.

"I like her," Denis said, looking from one to the other of us. "What? I'm not saying I know exactly *why*, and I'm not suggesting we simply trust her; I'm not either of you two for crying out loud. But you're right; she's interesting."

"You like her because she said you were 'pretty,' dungeon rat," I said.

"Only proving that she is a person of clear insight and discernment," he replied.

"Sure," I said, as we started toward the wagon laden with the five slavers, "but for someone who pretends to be so suspicious, you fold pretty fast when someone makes you blush."

"That's not the point," Denis said.

"Of course, it isn't," I said, stepping over to him. I

reached up and tousled his unruly hair as if he were a child. "You don't care at all. You're just pretending." I took the tone of a mother talking to her child. He swatted my hand away and gave me a look before we both broke into laughter.

"And that's a point for the lady," Kelly said.

"You two are a pain in my arse," Denis grumbled without any real ire.

"Another life goal achieved," I said.

The ride back to town took much less time than the trip out, as we kept to the road rather than repeating the serpentine, overland pattern that we'd followed during our search for the kidnappers. Kelly and Denis fashioned a makeshift linkage for the carriage to replace the one that the crystal-tipped bolt had destroyed. The clear crystals, Kelly had explained once, when treated with heat and another oil, could cause metals to rot and rust in moments, and that was what we had used to prevent the kidnappers from escaping. Now, they had affixed a crude but effective wooden catch in its place and placed two horses – mine and the one we still had from the slavers – in harness. Kelly drove the cart with Eryth beside him, Denis rode a little ahead on his mount, and most significantly of all, I rode Locksley in the rear position. From there, I could watch our captives, though the truth was that I needn't have bothered. They sat vacant-eyed and disheartened in the wagon. It all worked out well for me, as it gave me the all too rare opportunity to ride the great stallion. Locksley seemed, to me, to be walking more gingerly as if he were my host and was trying to make my trip more comfortable.

We arrived back in the tiny village and turned the captives over to the town's counsel-men who, it appeared, also served as the local constabulary. Conseiller Monague thanked us profusely, telling us that word had spread that many of the captives had already been seen very near their homes. He promised that there would be a reward ceremony the following day and also that, for tonight, we would be given the best rooms at the inn, a sizeable, unpretentious building that stood not far from the tavern. The innkeeper, who was the father of our young barmaid and, we were told, brother to one of the women we'd rescued, declared that we would eat free for life in his establishment. We protested appropriately but ultimately agreed to accept their hospitality, and so we headed toward the inn. After a few steps, though, a thought struck me. I stopped and looked around, catching Denis's attention.

"What?" he said, stopping just ahead of me.

"She's gone," I said, giving the dispersing crowd one last survey, "Eryth. She's not here."

Denis looked around now, as well. "Hunh," he said, in a failed attempt to seem interested.

I gave him a look, but with a shrug, he turned and

continued on his way. I followed, slowly and reluctantly. I couldn't have said then why I found her disappearance so aggravating. Perhaps I would have blamed it on the already bitter feelings I had that still carried over in me from the previous days. What I would learn later that evening, though, would prove instead that I was merely prescient.

A gentle tap at the door of my room roused me from a dreamless sleep. Instinctively, my hand went to the hilt of my blade next to the bed even before I called out.

"Who's there?" I said, blinking the sleep from my eyes.

"Kelly," came the quiet reply. The door muffled the voice, but I knew the sound instantly. "May I come in for a moment?"

I stood, grabbing the ample, if not quite soft, night robe provided for me along with the room. Wrapping it around myself, I opened the door to find Kelly, his arms folded behind him and an unreadable expression on his face. I stepped back, allowing him to enter, and he stopped just inside the door frame.

"I want to say some things to you," he said, "and to do some of that, I need you to come with me. Denis already went on ahead."

I eyed him, "What are you talking about?"

He looked down for a moment gathering his thoughts,

and then back up at me, his gray-blue eyes steady on mine. "You said some things the other day that... that have stuck with me. The worst one being that you intended to leave."

I dropped my eyes for a moment. "I did," I said flatly.

He nodded. "First, I want to tell you that I understand that. I have not been as open with you – or Denis, if it comes to it – as you expected. Or as you deserved," he said. He dropped his eyes again and continued, "I understand, and if you feel you need to go, that's up to you."

I felt a pit in my stomach. Truthfully, it had been there since the night in the pub, but now it yawned open and threatened to swallow me. I opened my mouth to speak, but he held up a hand tentatively. I waited.

"Secondly, I want to say that I'm sorry. I should have told you more. For all we've been through over the last three years – even just how we came together originally – well, I shouldn't have held so much back. Old habits or not; you are my friends, not just my companions. And stay or go, that changes starting now. Come with me, and I will tell you what you want to know starting tonight. No more secrets. After that, you can decide what you want to do."

He looked at me with a withering earnestness. I felt my shoulders slump, and I looked down and away from those eyes. I sighed.

"Get out," I said.

He tensed. "What?"

"Get out so I can get dressed, and we can go wherever you're talking about going," I said, looking back up at him with a smile. "I don't want to leave you two, you idiot. But you can't keep me – us – out like that."

He utterly failed to suppress his smile, "Let's fix that," he said, "I'll wait in the hall."

I followed Kelly out of the quiet inn and down the worn lane that led out of town. He was walking a couple of paces ahead, keeping a brisk pace despite the still oppressive humidity. The night brought cooler temperatures, but the air remained thick, giving everything a slightly damp sheen. Kelly's black armor almost glistened in the increasingly distant torchlight from behind us. I considered him as we walked, a contemplative mood having taken me since he had come to my room. He stood tall and straight, without the stoop that many men developed. It reminded me of Julea, of course. Both she and her mother paid almost obsessive attention to their posture. It wouldn't have surprised me if it was that which first drew her to him. Not to negate his other attractions. His hair was closer cut than when we first met three years ago; it wasn't short precisely, but just less unruly. It was a concession to our nomadic life; he preferred to maintain his grooming, and the shorter cut was more manageable. He made no sound as he walked, and I wondered – for perhaps the thousandth time – how he managed it on a gravel path and in full armor.

"Here," he said suddenly and broke to the right onto a narrow path. It led to a group of trees that seemed like darkness given physical form. Then, without hesitation, he stepped into the branches and vanished. I hesitated, finding my hand reflexively on the hilt of my sword.

"Come on, just follow me. I've got you," Kelly's disembodied voice beckoned from the blackness.

I tentatively stepped forward, and the shadow swallowed me. One step. Two. Then on the third, the ground that should have been beneath my foot wasn't, and I tumbled forward. A surprised yelp broke free from my throat as I fell, but I immediately found myself caught in his firm, leather-clad arms. My feet scrambled to find the ground again, and when they finally did, I saw that we were down a few feet from the path behind us. We were also bathed in the light of a hidden campfire. I turned to look at Kelly as he let me go, reassured that I had my footing again.

"What is this? Where are we?" I said, scanning the scene. Several feet away, a small fire burned low with a dim yellow-orange light at the center of a small clearing. Three logs were visible, forming makeshift seating around it, and on the nearest sat Denis. He turned and tossed me a casual wave.

"Hey," he said, "I had even odds that you would tell him to bugger off. Glad you decided not to." With a wink, he turned back toward the fire.

"Have a seat," Kelly said, moving around from behind me and pointing at the end of the log near Denis. The fire seemed to be burning only for light and to drive off the insects that plagued the whole south in the depths of summer; it burned low and without significant heat. I walked over and sat, noticing just then a fourth figure in the little clearing sitting on the furthest log. It sat enshrouded in black cloth robes, with a black hood pulled low. Kelly came over alongside me, taking off his baldric and resting it and his sword beside him. He leaned forward, his elbows on his knees as he looked from me to Denis in silence for a moment.

"Look, this is her thing...," Denis said, obviously uncomfortable.

Kelly smiled. "No, kid, this involves you both. I owe you both this, even if you don't need it. It's about trust," he nodded to me, "I do trust you both. So, I should tell you both the truth."

Despite the earlier reassurances, hearing those words made my stomach tighten again. 'Telling us the truth' was only so crucial now because he hadn't been, and that was still raw for me.

"First things first," he continued, "I am sure that by now, you've both concluded that our..., er..., adventures weren't random. It wasn't like we were finding trouble wherever we went by coincidence."

Denis snickered and kicked at the dirt. "The hardest part was pretending that I didn't notice you were slipping off and spending time with people like that guy," he said, pointing toward the black-cloaked figure that hadn't spoken yet.

I looked at him. "You knew about him? You never said anything."

Denis shrugged dismissively. "Of course. The first time I saw our boy here chatting with a guy in black robes was a few weeks after we left Lochhaven three years ago. It was right before we broke up that bandit guild south of Claire. I made the connection then."

Kelly was watching him steadily. "I'm surprised you didn't say anything," he said.

Another shrug from Denis. "If it started to seem like we were being played, I would have done something about it. As it was, there was never a reason. I figured you'd talk about it if you wanted to," he said.

I glared at him for a moment before turning back to Kelly. Something about Denis's trust – his willingness to go along without the answers I demanded – stung me with guilt. Kelly caught me staring and continued. "The monks – the ones that healed me and taught me about the gems – they're very focused on keeping those secrets. They are the ones that convinced me of the danger if I'm to be true. And they're active in that belief. They have a network of emissaries throughout the known lands who are constantly watching for anything that indicates that the knowledge has gotten out."

I pointed toward the black-cloaked figure. "Him," I said.

"One of many," Kelly said, nodding. "Some of them move from place to place, listening for things that sound unnatural. Some live quiet lives in towns or cities where there have been unusual events in the past. But they're always there, and they hear everything."

"But we've never seen any weird gem-stuff," Den said, his head cocked in curiosity, "I mean, other than our own weird gem-stuff."

Kelly shook his head. "That's true. But they hear of other things too, occasionally even by accident. I've asked them to tell us about things like that."

I looked at the cloaked figure. He – and I only knew it was a 'he' because Kelly hadn't corrected me before – sat still as a stone, his face still covered by the hood. "And you didn't want Kelly revealing your existence to us," I said to him. The figure nodded slowly.

"God's teeth, Finn," Kelly said in sudden exasperation, "Would you take the bloody hood off and act like a person? You're not fooling anyone."

The shrouded figure unfolded his arms and tugged

back the black hood, revealing a man about my age with a cherubic smile and dark eyes. I immediately recognized him as the man that had been with Kelly and Monague at the pub.

"Finn?" Denis said, looking at Kelly.

"Den, Dana; this is Finn O'Seachnasaigh. He is...," Kelly paused and gave him a look.

"His friend is what," Finn said, finishing the sentence whatever Kelly had meant to say. "More, as it comes to it. Saved yer man's life too," he said, the smile turning somewhat self-satisfied.

I looked over to Kelly. He had been watching Finn but then turned to face Denis and me. "He's not lying. It was Finn that found me half dead...," he said.

"More'n half, lad," Finn added.

"... And brought me to the monks," Kelly finished.

"I love that ye call 'em 'monks.' The ol' boys would love t' hear that," Finn said with a laugh.

"Wait," I said, focusing on Kelly, "forgive me. Are you now telling me – us – that for three years, we've been led around by some..., cabal that conspires to keep the gem's powers secret? And that this man is the one that brought you to them originally?"

Kelly nodded soberly, but Finn suddenly spoke up.

"Easy there, missy," he said with some heat, "I've not 'led ye about' at all. I've just passed along things I've heard to yer man here. He's not under any obligation to the ol' boys or me."

Kelly held up a hand and said, "Finn, it's okay. She's got a right—,"

Finn cut him off and continued. Gone was the cherubic smile, his face now a hard mask, "And, yes, I did get him help when I came on his broken self out in the Talte. But I've not asked for a single thing for m'self. Or for the boys. Only what he's offered to do. I believe you've seen some benefit yourself there, lass. So maybe pull back on the judgment, eh?"

I stood and faced Finn squarely, the pent-up frustration in my mind now gaining a form. The form's name was 'Finn.' "Your mouth seems to be talking over our discussion. If stopping it is a problem for you, I will gladly help," I snarled.

"Dana," Kelly said, standing up.

Finn stood, his robes flipping back to reveal dark leather armor and a sheathed short blade. "Y're welcome to try," he said stoically.

A voice came from behind him in the darkness. "I can't leave you young people alone for a moment, can I?" A woman stepped out of the shadows and into the dim light. She wore a dark-blue dress that appeared almost black in the yellow-orange glow of the fire. It was cut off the shoulders with billowing sleeves and a skirt that angled down from knee height on her left to touch the ground on the right. A brown leather corset that matched her high boots completed the ensemble, and a long silver braid hung over her left shoulder as she walked certainly around the log and placed a firm hand on Finn's chest.

"Eryth?" I said.

After a moment of holding her hand on his chest, Finn backed up and sat back again on the log. Eryth turned to face me with a broad smile and sparkling eyes.

"Lady Dana Lunavale, I am delighted to see you again," she said, bowing elaborately. I returned the gesture, my irritation evaporating into a cloud of confusion.

"Master Denis," she said, giving him a short nod. I looked to see Denis nod in return. I also noted that he was replacing his daggers in their sheaths. At what point he'd drawn them, I hadn't seen. But that wasn't terribly surprising.

Eryth turned to Kelly and curtsied gracefully. "And of course, Lord K—,"

"Ah," Kelly stopped her, "just Kelly, remember?"

She crossed the distance between them and threw her arms around him in a tight embrace. They spoke quietly to one another for a moment, and then she returned to the far log and settled down by Finn.

"Lady Dana," she said, her tone sincere and honest, "I should apologize to you personally. So many of what I'm sure would seem to you as 'lies' are my fault. I'm the one that told Lo–, er..., Kelly, to keep his peace these years. I did not know you two save as an Imperial loyalist and a..., what was the phrase?" She looked at Denis curiously.

He sighed and rolled his eyes. "I think you mean 'dungeon rat,'" he said.

"Just so," she said, the twinkle in her eye seeming to sparkle just then intentionally. "I should have known he wouldn't choose untrustworthy companions." She smiled at Kelly.

Kelly smiled at her and nodded an unspoken thank you, and then he looked at me. "Obviously, you see by now that Eryth and I know one another. What you don't know is that it was she that directly saved my life. I owe her, well, everything," he said.

"Posh," she said with a brushing motion of one hand.

"In any case, Finn got word to me about the kidnappings, and then he told me Eryth was among them. So, we came here," he continued.

"Y'd have come anyway, lad," Finn said, "I know how ye are."

Kelly shrugged a shoulder. "Anyway. When we found them, we found her among them. We pretended we didn't know one another, but I had to talk to her first. I told her about how you were feeling, Dana, and she said that if I trusted you, I should trust you."

"Poetical," Denis said.

"So here we are," Kelly said. He was looking at me now intently, trying, I knew, to read my feelings from several feet away. Which, if it came to it, was not as unlikely as it sounded. It had worked before. I looked at him in return. Of all the people I had known in life or could imagine knowing, we three had come to have a connection. And I knew him as well as he knew me. Did I really feel that any of this changed that? I thought, and then I did the thing I rarely do and listened to my heart.

"You were dumb," I said, prompting a snort of laughter from Denis.

Kelly smiled sadly. "Yeah," he said.

I stood and stepped toward him, where he met me halfway. I grabbed him and hugged him as he returned the embrace.

"Stop that," I said into his ear.

"Okay," he said quietly, "Never again."

We stood like that for what I believe was exactly the right amount of time before breaking the embrace and sitting down again.

"Well, that's a sight," Finn said. He smiled at me, I returned it, and our earlier friction dissipated.

"How come I don't get a hug?" Denis said.

"I will hug you later," Kelly deadpanned.

"Okay, but it better be a good one," Denis said, kicking

at the dirt in a mock show of disappointment.

"You three are adorable," Eryth said, leaning her head on her hands and watching the interchange with interest. "But come, we have a bit of business," she said, straightening up so that she was sitting almost regally on the log.

"Aye, that we do," Finn said, looking for a long moment at Kelly and then at me.

"Problem?" Kelly asked.

"Depends on who y' are," Finn said. It was plain that he was taking the lead in whatever it was that was coming next. He turned to Kelly and said, "Y' recall I told ye about the Archduke of Preskia, yeah?"

"I do. Assassination is what you told me," Kelly replied, shooting an apologetic glance at Den and me.

"That was the way of it. It caused no small bit o' trouble for Gladia; make no mistake. Rocked the throne there; it did. It seems that the ruling family – the Olindons, that is – it seems they've got things steady again, but it was dodgy for a good bit," Finn said. The Kingdom of Gladia, not many days travel south from Gretchville, was the most extensive and most civilized of the southern lands, the only nation on the peninsula it occupied. The Olindons had been on the throne there for generations, though each city-state – Preskia being one – had its local rulers. More significantly, the nation is a longtime ally of Yorch, almost a sibling, really. Many of the finest soldiers in the Empire are actually from the Talhas tribes in northern Gladia. That included the personal bodyguard of Princess Julea Niconnal bar Ardallah, heir to the throne of Yorch, the woman who was dear to both Kelly and me.

"If it's stable," Kelly was saying, shaking me out of my reverie, "what's the problem?"

Eryth smiled and looked at Finn, who leaned back as she took the lead. "There is no problem, laddie. We're not coming to you with a problem to solve just now," she said.

"Then what are you on about?" Denis blurted impatiently. The night had been more than enough for him already.

"It's an opportunity," Eryth said, her smile undimmed, "Gladia has stabilized, and King Adam has it in mind to reassure his allies. So, he hosted a conclave. A celebration of unity, of sorts. But the point is – the Empress and her daughter were in attendance."

I felt my eyes go wide as I turned to Kelly. For a moment, he didn't move, then he turned to me, and though I could see his resistance to it, there was a spark in his eyes.

"Now, we know that Gladia proper; being an ally of Yorch; isn't safe territory for you," Eryth continued, her hand held out as if to slow the lines of thought that it was clear had already swept Kelly and me away.

"Blackcrow," Finn said, and the single word snapped us both back to reality.

“Then I guess I don’t see the point of this,” Kelly said.

“Real nice,” Denis said, “getting my friends all fired up and then—,”

“Shush,” Eryth said impatiently to him. She turned back to us, “They left Seoda harbor a few days ago; you couldn’t get there if you wanted to. But they will be stopping for supplies in a day or two. In Euticha.”

“The *independent* city of Euticha,” Finn said with emphasis.

No one spoke for a long time. Kelly stared at the fire, and I stared at Kelly, and Denis stared at us both. In time, Eryth and Finn stood up and moved away from the fire. She stopped beside Kelly and put her hand on his shoulder. Neither said anything. Then she gently patted him before she and Finn disappeared into the darkness, leaving us alone.

“So,” Denis said when the silence had lasted too long, “we’re skipping the party tomorrow, right?”

CHAPTER TWO

— AERYK —

As I've come to know it, the sea is both a dear companion and a harsh taskmaster. Edword says that is why we know that the sea is a woman, though I have a personal belief that he has a skewed point of view. Not because I have had tremendous success with women, of course, but because I know his dalliances have mostly been of a particular type. In any case, my life at sea has borne out at least one thing. For any pain and suffering doled out by the taskmaster, on the days she chooses the hat of the dear companion, she instead is capable of lifting your spirits beyond your expectations.

The *Midnight Wind* made her way west, with a steady blow from the southeast, the sun brightly aflame in the summer sky, and a run of dolphins in a game of chase off the starboard bow. I watched them for a bit before I turned back to the helm. The sailor who had been at the wheel for some time gave way as I took the station, snapping a casual, offhand salute to me before disappearing down the steps from the quarterdeck. I surveyed the horizon, took my bearings with the compass and the sun, and laid my hand steady on the wheel.

For most of three years, the ship had been my home, and I made no secret of my affection for her. But in truth, it was here, upon the deck and at the helm, that I was indeed where I felt most like I should be in the world. I pulled the scarf from my head and ran my fingers through my hair before replacing it. I hadn't initially taken to wearing the scarf on my head – I've never liked hats of any kind – but the hot sun and the sea had taught me its value. And perhaps some humility as well, as I learned that the alliance of the two could lay a man low as surely as a sword blade. But it had also hardened me, turned my skin a deep tan, and given me a life I would never have imagined.

"Mr. Puppy!" The booming voice of Captain Edword Ribald echoed from the main deck well before he climbed the steps and into view. He paused as he topped the stairs and gave me a stern look.

"Aye, Cap'n," I said, neither meeting his eyes nor taking my hand off the wheel. 'Mr. Puppy' was a name that had attached itself to me early in my tenure at sea with the pirates. Edword had referred to the crew as 'sea-dogs,' and I asked where that term originated. He explained that it was just an old expression that sailors used, that he had no idea why, and that I shouldn't worry because, at that point, I was no more than a 'sea-puppy.' This explanation was, of course, said in full view of much of the crew. Thus, from that point on, they began to refer to me as 'the puppy.' I had expected – or hoped – that as I worked my way into becoming a full-fledged member of the crew, the moniker would fade. But, instead, even when the same crew duly chose me as quartermaster of the ship, I remained 'the puppy.' Edword had, though, demanded that his new second-in-command be afforded appropriate respect. Consequently, I became 'Mr. Puppy.' It was at first somewhat humiliating, if I'm honest, but the result was that as the 'sea-puppy,' the men saw me as one of their own instead of an outsider. The whole experience did more to teach me the ways of a pirate crew than any single other event.

"How's our course?" the captain said, coming closer and dropping to a more conversational volume and tone. Edword was over six feet tall, dark-skinned, and festooned with long braided hair that seemed both unnatural and yet perfectly suited to him. He was, I had come to believe, also carved out of stone. In some three years at sea, I had never seen him tired – or even slowed – by the physical hardships of either sea or battle. He stood next to me now, looking out at the horizon, his left hand resting on the hilt of the jeweled long-sword he had carried since we'd met.

"Steady and clear," I reported, "and no hint of a change on the horizon. Honestly, cap'n, the *Wind* could almost take herself back west without our help in these conditions."

Edword watched the horizon for another moment, then turned to me. "I ain't sure she couldn't under any conditions thrown at her," he said. The *Midnight Wind* was his imagination made real, and he believed in her more than he believed in any man. Of course, the secrets that lived below decks made her particularly special, but even they weren't the source of his confidence. It was pride, and I had to admit that it was an appropriate pride. "Belay that, anyway," he said then, a new expression on his face as he considered me. "we'll be back toward your home waters here soon. Wondered what your course might be."

"I'm not sure I understand," I said.

"We been gone a while. Long ways from yer home. Wondered if that made ye think about what you once decided you *weren't* when you chose to be what you *are*. Wondered too if maybe you'd be thinking on going ashore," he said. He looked at me, the subject now hanging above us like the smoke from a freshly lit fire.

It was true. The way of it was that we had not been near my old homeland since I had come aboard. Even before we struck out east across the Great Ocean, we had spent a goodly amount of time – all of that time, in fact – away from my father's holdings in Lochhaven. And we had seen much since that might quite understandably make a man long for home – to 'go ashore' – and leave the sea behind. I considered what he said, chasing down the future possibilities in my mind much as I'm sure my captain had done before coming to me. There was no real hope that I'd be welcomed back home, to be sure. Presuming my father was still alive – and I knew that undoubtedly he was, as he was far too ornery to have died – he would yet hold me in contempt, time be damned. But that didn't matter, I realized. The truth of it was that no kind of welcome would have tempted me to leave my post. The sea had become more my home than I could have imagined, and I wasn't abandoning it.

"You'll not be rid of me any time soon, cap'n," I said, turning back to the horizon.

Edword nodded, the great mass of braids bobbing as he did. He, too, turned back to the sea. "Fine day to sail," he said after a moment.

"Aye, sir," I replied. And we stayed like that until we heard the words from the crow's nest that changed our course and, ultimately, our future.

"Smoke!" came the call, "Off the port! Ten o'clock!"

We glanced at one another before Edword went to the port rail, scanning the distant horizon off the bow. I held the *Wind* steady on her course, and though I craned my neck and squinted, I saw nothing. The bright sun reflecting off the calm waters all but blinded me as I tried to catch a glimpse of the reported smoke.

“There!” Edword suddenly said, pointing just to the left of where I had been looking. A small gray-black smudge faintly marred the blue skyline. Had I not been looking for it, even the captain’s assistance wouldn’t have made it distinct to me, but as it was, I could make out a plume of smoke rising from what should have been the deep open waters of the Great Ocean.

“Helmsman to the quarterdeck,” I called into the small brass horn just to the port side of the steerage pedestal, knowing it would carry my voice belowdecks. I had become, if the crew was to be believed, capable enough a pilot to guide the ship – as long as the circumstances remained mundane. Myself, I’d grown to feel confident that I could be trusted in all but the worst storms as well, having had excellent training and more than a bit of experience. But I knew my limits. In case of real adventure or severe storms – the infamous ‘Triangle Blows’ that plagued the Great Ocean around that time of year come to mind – there were men far more skilled than I on board. When given a choice, it was best to trust such men and stow your pride. Moments passed until I was then relieved by one such expert helmsman. I turned and stepped over to Edword, who had remained at the rail, watching the plume of smoke as it swirled and spread in the distant sky.

“Recent,” he said in typically taciturn fashion. “Whatever is there is still burning.”

"A ship?" I asked.

"Lots of smoke for a ship," he said. His tone hinted that his words were more indicative of his thinking aloud rather than of his responding to me. "Take us in, quartermaster," he said abruptly, "and rouse the men."

"Aye, sir," I said. And that began a sequence of events that had become second nature to me over the months and years. I barked orders to the helm to come about and guide the *Wind* to the mysterious smoke. I then shouted to the lookout to inform me at once of any changes. Grabbing the brass horn, I called for all hands to fall in and then headed down to meet them. Moments later, I joined the assembled crew on the main deck. I turned and stepped up onto a small raised platform toward the aft, not far from the helm above. It gave the assembly a decent view of me as well as enabling the helmsman, who obviously couldn't leave his post, to hear me from where he was atop the sterncastle. I cleared my throat and addressed the crew.

"We've no idea what we've seen," I said, looking over the hardy crowd of sailors. There were new faces, as there always were, but many more were familiar to me. These had been my shipmates for much – if not all – of the time I'd served under Edword. Some caught my eye and gave me a wry grin – a sign of support and knowledge that their 'sea-puppy' had grown up. "Likely, there is nothing there of threat or value," I continued, "but the captain would rather not have us caught with our britches low. I'll take these twelve with me," I said as I gestured to a small cluster of the men to my right. "We'll look into anything that the captain feels needs closer inspection. The rest of you make ready the launchers below deck and rig her to move if we need to move. Let's get to work," I finished.

There was a general shout of agreement, in which I heard a few clear calls of "Aye, Mr. Puppy," before they broke up and went about the practiced ritual of preparing the *Midnight Wind* for battle or flight as the need arose. I went into the sterncastle and therein to my cabin. I retrieved my staff and added my light but sturdy leather armor to my livery. The leathers were standard issue for the crew, designed to be light enough for wear at sea or even in the water, even as they afforded reasonable protection from a blade. Returning to the deck, I surveyed the men as I walked the distance toward the bow. This wasn't a crucial exercise for me – the crew acted almost as a single being when adventure was afoot – but I felt it the responsibility of my office to appear as if I were evaluating them anyway. Despite the detour, I was shortly up the steps to the foredeck and came to the railing on the bow where I joined Edword. He, too, had added a leather-armored vest to his garb, though as ever, his arms remained bare. Without a word, we watched the distant gray-black smudge draw closer.

Time passed. Our new course forced us to tack into

the wind to reach the source of the wispy cloud, delaying us and stirring a kind of frustrated anticipation in the captain and me. For his part, Edword paced back and forth along the foredeck restlessly, whereas I repeatedly called for reports from the men to verify their preparations and our readiness. The men answered me each time with more or less tolerance; the truth of the matter was that once we were prepared, there was nothing more to do.

An interminable amount of time passed, but finally, we came upon the object of our curiosity. Despite our long approach, there was still a significant amount of smoke rising from the area, though it appeared that the tide had spread the source over a more considerable area than the more distinct cloud we had first seen implied. The wind, which had seemed to strive to push us away, now carried the majority of that smoke to our port as we approached, and that was beneficial for us. We could see acutely the scene from which the black haze rose. Some number of indistinct black lumps were bobbing and swirling in the gentle tide before us across an expanse that was large but still less than half a league across. We dropped sail as we approached the nearest, and it was soon close enough to the side of the *Wind* that Edword and I could scrutinize it from our position on the bow. Gnarled, charred wooden shafts rose at wrong angles from a partially submerged ship's hull floating just below the water's surface.

"They were ships," Edword said, "Merchants, I'd say." He pointed at where, in the closest clump of wreckage, the remaining pieces of the hull could be seen. Its supports were collapsed but still visible, clinging to the unburned wooden corpse of the ship beneath the surface; these were a clear sign of the reinforced hold of a cargo ship. "But what burns the top off a ship and leaves the bottom?" he murmured, leaning heavily on the railing.

"Why's the water steaming?" I said, having just put my finger on what was making the scene feel eerie to me. Edword looked over, and I gestured to the water near the ruined husk. A light mist of steam rose all around the wreck to a distance of some six to ten feet.

"Ain't right," he muttered.

The *Wind* continued onward through the debris, each of the carcasses in various stages of the same sort of carnage. We saw the same scene repeatedly, steaming water filled with debris and jetsam and fragments of charred fixtures floating free in the remains of the ships where they had served.

"No bodies," I said quietly, halfway between an observation and a question. The longer we looked, the more the scene troubled me. There was something surreal – unnatural and yet somehow resonant that I couldn't as yet put my finger on.

"And no cargo," Edword replied, his eye keen on each

of the wrecks as we passed by, “nothing floating, nothing stuck in the remains.”

“That doesn’t make sense,” I said.

“You ain’t wrong. How do you burn down a ship so fast that the bottom of the hull isn’t scratched but still manage to carry the cargo off?”

“Were they unladen?” I offered, knowing even as I did that such would make no sense.

“Why attack an empty fleet? Easy to tell the difference. They sit higher in the water,” Edword shrugged a shoulder. “Trust me. I know how you pick a target. Might be that would explain how those remains look.”

“How is that?”

“Small. Whatever burned them, it burned them down to the waterline, and if they had cargo, that line would be higher. There would be more left,” Edword said as if it were the most obvious thing in the world.

We watched the wrecks in silence as I thought for a moment, then realization began dawning in my mind. “No bodies. They surrendered,” I almost whispered.

“Aye,” Edword said, coming to the same conclusion, “and why not? No cargo to fight for. I reckon at least most of them surrendered. Whoever did this seized all hands, then took an’ destroyed every last ship.”

I studied the nearest wreck again while the thought sank in. Someone had attacked an empty fleet and taken the crew, then destroyed the ships – ten, by my count – in some...,

I straightened bolt upright as if I'd been struck. Edword looked at me sharply.

"I've seen this before," I said, my voice barely above a whisper, "and so have you."

Edword squared to me and gave me an intense look. "Come again?" he said.

Images of the past filled my mind unbidden. I saw again as Kelly and I climbed aboard a rickety fishing boat alongside a handful of soldiers in the harbor of Clemons. We meant to rescue Princess Julea Niconnal of Yorch – ironically from the man beside me, the man who was now both my captain and my friend. So much had happened since, and still more had changed, but this memory wasn't about the changes. In my memory, I saw Kelly pouring oil on the deck of that boat, oil that when set alight burned with an unnatural green flame. Of course, as I came to know, it wasn't just oil he'd used; it was oil treated with the infernal gems known as Kelian emeralds – a thing that I now number to be among the most dangerous materials in the world. Our gambit back then had succeeded with the princess's rescue when we caused both that small boat and the flagship of her pursuers to be engulfed by a wicked, unnatural fire precipitated by those gems. That flagship was the ship Edword had been captaining, which we found out not long after.

"Clemons," I said, recalling to his mind as directly as I could the memory of the incident.

Recollection and realization flashed together across his face in an instant. "Kraken's blood," he cursed. He looked at me sternly, and I knew his mind immediately.

"Helm!" I called to the quarterdeck, "Reverse course! Get us out of here!"

The helmsman began to spin the wheel, and I started off to my station above when Edword's voice roared from behind me.

"Belay that! Helm to port!"

I stopped in confusion and turned back to the captain. He, though, was glaring off to the south, where the far side of the field of wreckage had drifted. Returning to the rail, I followed his gaze into the middle distance. There, a large smoking flotilla of debris – the largest patch in sight – floated uneasily in the quiet sea, smoking heavily. At first, I couldn't see why we were heading toward it, but in one quick flash, it became apparent. At the waterline, a small figure floated, with one hand fixed on the charred husk and the other splashing in the water with all its might.

A survivor.

"Crew to the launch!" I called, and the twelve men I had selected earlier moved immediately to the davit, where they made ready one of the small launches stored there. I ran the few steps to where I'd left my staff and turned to go. Edword stepped into my path, and I stopped before him.

"Wits about ye," he said, clapping my shoulder with his hand, "Get in and get out. I want to be away from this graveyard." I gave him a short nod before I hurried off to the launch.

Shortly, my small crew and I were lowered to the water, and the men were hard at the oars while I knelt in the bow. The sea retained its abnormal quiet for us, and we made rapid progress to the vessel's smoldering husk. The closer we drew, the more the acrid smell of the still-burning timbers burned our noses while random swirls of smoke clouded our eyes. Even more, I began to feel, even at some distance, a wash of heat coming off the debris and the sea around us. I wondered just how hellish the smoke and heat were for our survivor, bobbing unprotected in the eerily steaming sea. Then, just yards off from the wreckage, I saw her. For a brief second, I caught sight of her bright but terrified light-brown-eyes looking toward us before her hand slipped off the blackened wooden strut that had kept her afloat. Steaming blue water pulled her under, dark-brown hair quickly disappearing in the white foam.

I leaped, without thought, dropping my staff in the bow of the boat and knifing into the water off the port side in a practiced dive. The water was hot, which I expected, though I absently thought about just how intense the uncanny flames had to have been to warm the water around the wrecks for so long. Swimming in my armor was second nature to me now, as it was one of the things that Edword expected of his crew, and I was at the woman's side in a very few short strokes. I dove, found her flailing arms in my hands, and with great effort lifted her back to the surface. As we broke out into the air, both she and I gratefully and desperately filled our lungs. I rolled onto my back – my arm around her waist to keep her head above water – and paddled with my other arm back toward the launch until we were close enough for the men to get a rope to us and pull us aboard. Gently, they eased the girl down into the boat as I climbed up over the opposite side and sat wearily on the closest bench.

"Take us back," I instructed, and once again, the crew took to the oars, spinning the small craft around and pushing us back to where the *Midnight Wind* waited. I coughed for a moment, clearing away the small amount of seawater that always seemed to find its way into my mouth when I swam. That accomplished, I crossed over to where the girl lay. She was young, twenty at most, and the harshness of a life at sea had not yet taken from her the freshness of youth. Her recent experiences, though, had taken their toll, her brown hair a muddled clump that hung on her shoulder. She seemed confused and afraid, and it was clear that the faces of the hardened sailors around her were not doing anything to alleviate that feeling. On top of that, at any movement, great spasms of coughing wracked her petite form and made her breathing labored. Thus, though now safe, she seemed on the edge of panic.

"Hi," I said as I approached her slowly and from an angle where I could be sure not to startle her. Another strange face, even a friendly one, suddenly popping into her vision, would do nothing to calm her. It is also creepy.

She curled away from me, so I stopped while still a foot or two away, hoping to give her the solace of space. Unfortunately, such was no mean feat in the narrow hollow of the launch, and I wound up crouched awkwardly in front of her. She eyed me warily.

"We're not going to hurt you," I said as kindly as I knew how. '*As I knew how*' was, sad to say, a tremendously limiting factor. I have been told – by my shipmates of all sources – that speech should do more than say words. There is a need for passion, warmth, sensitivity, even anger, and a host of other things. I can say without fear of argument that when a crew of pirates tells you that you need to show more emotion when you speak, you should allow for the possibility that you are, in fact, in need of assistance. In any case, I said the above as kindly '*as I knew how,*' and waited for her response.

She pulled more into a ball and away from me, initiating another bout of coughing.

Damn.

"*Wind* is on the starb'rd, Mr. Puppy," said one of the men, "She looks ready t' receive us."

"Bring us in," I said, casting him a glance over my shoulder. I felt as the men change the rhythm of their strokes to move us closer to the mooring ropes as I looked back at the girl. To my surprise, she had unclenched moderately from her recoiled pose and was looking at me with curious brown eyes.

"Puppy?" she asked, her voice so quiet that I nearly missed that she had spoken at all.

I shrugged my shoulder slightly and carefully curled the corner of my mouth in a grin as I nodded.

"I'm Candice," she said. Her voice remained quiet, but the panic that had lived behind her eyes seemed abated somewhat.

"I'm Aeryk," I said. She looked at me, and after a moment, I affected the grin again. "But it seems like 'Mr. Puppy' will work just as well," I concluded with a sigh.

Did she just smile? I thought as the shadow of one passed over her lips. *Look at me, lads! I'm comforting.*

"You're safe now," I said, returning to business. "Just rest. We can talk later." I thought about pressing her with some questions, but I could see that the boat was nearly back on its moorings, and we would be interrupted shortly. Besides that, judging by the intermittent coughing she was doing, she would need to recover some before that opportunity would present itself. I stood up and turned from her, intentionally not moving away. Her trust was tenuous, I knew, and leaving her alone in the crowd of sailors at this point could lose me the advances I had made.

The launch wobbled and rocked convulsively as it was pulled back into its bay, where it came to rest with a stout 'thud.' Each jostle the small boat endured was joined by the sound of a wet cough from the girl behind me. However, once we settled, I turned back to Candice to find her quiet and observing me closely. Without moving either closer or further away, I offered her my hand. She leaned forward hesitantly, wobbling as she did, but ultimately reached out and took my hand in hers. Another fit of coughing took her as she stood, and though she doubled over with the spasms, she never released her grip. I thought to pat her back or offer some other kind of assistance but instead waited while she again got her breathing under control, lest I accidentally frighten her. Finally, she calmed and wearily stood up straight. I looked at her and made an effort to look sympathetic. Then I tilted my head slightly to the boat's side. She nodded and followed as I led her off the launch and onto the *Midnight Wind*. She held my hand tightly and leaned on it consistently to steady herself as we made our way to the deck where Edword was waiting for us. He gave the girl a quick look, and I knew he had taken in every detail that he felt was worth noting in that single glance.

"Survivor, cap'n," I said, stepping a bit ahead of her without releasing her hand. Edword, I knew, cut a rather striking figure, and I had seen him cause hard men to fall back. It seemed best to me to insulate Candice from that first impression. "We found her barely hanging on to the last wreck," I finished.

Edword looked at me with the same searching look he had given her before he spoke. "What'd she see?"

I opened my mouth to tell him that we hadn't gotten to that yet when a tiny but steady voice from behind me spoke up.

"There were ships, sir," Candice was saying, "not from our parts; if you take me, Captain, sir."

Edword shot me a glance, and I stepped aside. She looked at him steadily if timidly, her hand still tightly holding mine.

"Y' saw them well?" he asked.

She nodded, a ghost of what she had seen clouding her expression. She took a breath to continue when another frenzy of coughing burst forth, doubling her over and causing her to lean into me.

"Too much o' the sea," Edword said calmly as she slowly recovered. "Take an' put her in my cabin. Let her rest up; we can hear her tale soon enough."

"Aye, sir," I said and, Candice leaning hard against

me, I led her off to the captain's cabin as the *Wind* came about and resumed our original course.

It wouldn't be for several hours after we had left the wreckage far behind us, and the helm had us once again firmly on a course for the western lands of home, before Edword met me up on the quarterdeck. I had stationed myself there, relaying orders to the crew and serving as the second eyes for the helmsman. The sun was lower in the western sky by that time, and our course toward it was no longer the smooth and joyful one of the early afternoon's. A stiff west wind pushed at us now, forcing us into the zig-zag pattern that allowed us to continue ahead, though it felt like three steps taken for each one forward. To our two o'clock, thick black clouds hovered, ever threatening to drop onto us with one of the Great Ocean's infamous 'Triangle Blow's.' The sailors told stories of storms like that – storms that would pluck a ship right from the ocean and leave her and her crew somewhere else. Somewhere in another place, another sea, another world.

Sailors tell stories.

Edword stood several feet away and said nothing. He watched the early sunset and the hovering storm clouds in silence with me for a long time. Finally, he turned around and leaned against the rail, facing me.

"You coming to talk to the girl?" he said. He was

asking, not telling, but that didn't mean it didn't matter.

"Might be a storm there," I said, "I thought maybe—"

"That one's gonna miss us," he said, cutting me off with a dismissive toss of his head, "and I want to hear her tale."

I gave the helmsman a nod, and he returned it. It was a bit of a topic among the crew, Edword's strange kinship with the weather and the sea. His surety that the storm would miss us was as good as a guarantee, and no man on the crew doubted it. Well, almost no man. I wasn't always sure. I'd only been aboard three years, though, and an authentic crewman for much less, so perhaps it was just that I wasn't used to it yet. Whatever the case, his assurance fundamentally meant to every other man and boy aboard that we'd see no storm, and therefore I was free to go with him.

"Call me if there's a change," I said quietly to the helmsman. Trusting Edword was one thing; being sure was another. Plus, not saying it loud enough for him to interpret it as doubt counted as at least two more.

"Aye, Mr. Puppy," the helmsman said in the same low tone. I turned and followed Edword down the steps.

A few moments later, we entered the small structure amidships, where the captain's cabin rose from the main deck. I stopped as I came in, remembering the first time I'd seen the room three years ago. In my mind's eye, I saw

Princess Julea telling Edword that everything was fine when we all knew that her bodyguard, our friend, had just been skewered with an arrow. I saw also that same friend, Lady Dana, standing weakly in the doorway, leaning on Kelly when she should have been a dead woman. And I felt again the pain inside from thinking all of that had been my fault. The room itself hadn't changed much, though three years of being lived in had lent it more of a feeling of someone's home than the more impersonal feel it had back then. Before she even had her name. The large table in the middle of the first room stood now draped with several worn maps and charts that had not been there when the ship was new. The room was also adorned with the personal items that Edword considered acceptable for those he invited into his office area. That second door led to his personal space, I knew; the room where whatever arcane thing Kelly had done to save Dana's life had happened. I had no call or desire to see that then, nor had I in the intervening years. Candice stood beside the chart table to my left, having risen from a small bench behind her when we entered. There was fear in her eyes again on seeing Edword, but as she turned to me, the fear seemed to melt, and she smiled.

"Mr. Puppy!" she said excitedly, rushing over to me.

Edword's face remained unreadable, but I was sure that he would have comments for me later. And that they would be uncomfortable. And that the crew would be there.

I took her outstretched hands in mine and redirected her gently, finally putting my hands on her shoulders. "How are you feeling?" I asked — there was no point in trying to talk with her if she would be hacking her way through it.

"I'm bee-tar," she said, and for the first time, I heard her accent, immediately helping me place her.

"Gueldrelanne," I said, thinking of the traders that had come to Claire from the southern kingdom.

"*Oui,*" she said, a smile flashing across her face. It was alien to the haunted expression she had before, and for a brief moment, her natural beauty flashed through.

"What's your name, mademoiselle?" Edword said. I looked over and saw him half sitting with one hip hitched up on the chart table and his arms crossed. He unmistakably knew Gueldrelanne as well.

Candice looked past me to the pirate. "I am Candice Durand. I am a daughter of Phillipe Durand, master of the *Brandy Diamond* and owner of the Western Imperial Commerce Enterprise," she said proudly. Then her eyes clouded and became unfocused. "Or I was before he was taken from this world today," she continued slowly, her voice now haunted.

She seemed to wobble a bit, and I pointed toward a nearby chair, where she sat with a sigh. She stared listlessly ahead for a moment, and I could imagine the events of the day bubbling up in her mind again. I took a step back and sat in another chair – not too close, but not so far that I'd seem distant. She finally glanced over at me with a look I took for gratitude, which gave me a sense of validation for my approach.

"Can you tell us what happened?" I said, leaning forward with my elbows on my knees. Edword was many things, but comforting wasn't one of them. Unfortunately for Candice, that meant that the role of comforter fell to me, and as I have suggested, it is not a particularly natural one for me. Nevertheless, I made a great effort to keep my voice gentle and asked, "How did you come to be alone in the ocean like this?"

Candice looked down as she spoke as if reliving the tale as she told it. "Under contract, we embarked from the harbor of Euticha to retrieve a shipment of teas and herbs from Cinniuint in the Empire for resale. This one run would have paid our expenses through the winter. My father called in all of the ships – put all of the other contracts on hold just for this one. With all twelve of our fleet, we left immediately from our port for the north."

"We?" Edword asked.

Candice seemed to bristle a little, and there was a glimmer of fire in her response that made me wonder just what she had been like before the catastrophe. "*Oui*, monsieur pirate," she said, "I served as my father's first mate on the *Diamond*. Does this surprise you?"

Edword watched her without reacting save for a leisurely shake of his head. I knew he was giving her careful consideration, though. He was used to people recognizing what he was, of course, but few of them were women who were barely more than children and also first mates in merchant fleets.

"Once at sea, we saw the signs of the storms – *Le Vent Triangulaire* – and knew we had to plot a course around them," she continued, sparing Edword her glare and looking over to me as she spoke. "I had us turn out to sea with hope that they would pass either very fast to the north or very slowly to the south."

"Gamble," Edword said, though his tone was more of admiration than criticism. She noticed the shift and looked back at him with acknowledgment.

"Perhaps," Candice continued thoughtfully, "and unfortunately, we'll never know whether I'd have won that wager. It was taking the course out to sea that brought us to where you found—," here she paused, correcting her unspoken narrative before finishing, "me."

She looked down again, her unseeing eyes inspecting the floor. I looked at Edword; my unvoiced question of whether this was a wise time for the interview was met only by his implacable gaze. I turned back to the girl. She was staring straight forward, and her voice had gone cold as if she were relating a story from someone else. "The *Diamond's* lookout saw them first – five small blemishes on the blue-gray horizon. Before we knew it, though, they were in front of us. They moved too fast. Too fast to be real, but they were real. My father said there were no colors, but I saw a red flag on the lead ship. There were no markings on it, but it was there. I see it very clearly in my memory. They wanted to intercept, it was certain, and we assumed they were pirates. But we were bare. It made no sense; it would have been clear to anyone that our holds were empty. So my father sent the order to strike our colors and await boarding, and we were hoisting the whites when it happened," she trailed off at the end, even the impassive recital of the events becoming hard for her.

I waited a moment for her to collect herself before I asked the obvious.

"What happened?"

She stared fixedly at the floor as she spoke next, her voice barely above a whisper. "Three of their ships – every other one – had turned broadside to us. Then they…, there was a sound: a screeching, something like glass on glass. Then lightning hit one of our ships. But it came from them, from one of the three pirate ships. And it came straight on. It didn't bend or branch, the way natural lightning would, but it was straight. The ship that was hit just…, just stopped being a ship. There was a blue flame, and then there was no ship. No crew. Nothing but fire on the water. Blue fire." Her eyes had become sunken as she spoke, and when she looked up, there were tears on her cheeks. Edword handed me a white handkerchief, and I passed it to her. She dabbed at her cheeks for a moment, then continued, twisting the cloth in her hands as she spoke.

"My father, he... he dragged me to the rail on the far side of the deck. He looked at me there. He didn't say anything. He just looked for a moment. Then he shoved me, and I fell over the railing and into the water. I..., I don't know what happened after that. There were waves and sound and more blue light above me. I swam back toward the *Diamond* – I could still make her out somehow from under the water when there was a light that blinded me and a wave that spun me around and drove the air from my chest. All I could do then was try to go up, and eventually, I did; I got to the surface and...," She trailed off again.

I looked at Edword only to see him staring hard at me. Parts of the story sounded very familiar and very like our suspicions.

"I was yards away from the ship," she said suddenly, bringing us back to her story, "and all I could see was that our fleet was just gone. There was blue flame and smoke and the stench of burning and nothing else. I swam; I didn't know what else to do. I swam toward what remained of my life, but I had to stop; the water was so hot, it burned to swim in it. I fought to stay afloat until I couldn't do it anymore, and then I went to the wrecks despite the heat and the pain."

"And that's where we found you," I said. I said it because I suddenly felt like I'd say anything to make it so that she could stop.

"*Oui*," she said, looking up at Edword and me in turn. "And then when you arrived, I thought I was dead for certain, though I knew I couldn't stay in the water either."

"Wait," Edword said, "why did you think you'd be 'dead for certain'?"

"I saw your ship approach," she said fearfully, looking back and forth between us as if we were missing the most obvious thing in the world. We waited.

"This ship is one of the ones that attacked us," she said.

I looked at my captain, and he at me, and a horrifying clarity struck us both simultaneously. I felt my jaw working soundlessly even as Edword's eyes narrowed, and every muscle in his arms went taut.

Candice was watching us nervously. "You are the pirate known as Edword Ribald, *oui*?" she asked.

Edword nodded. "I am, and this is my quartermaster, Aeryk Escrios. But mademoiselle, I assure you, neither we nor any of ours attacked you."

I looked at her as she turned to me. "I swear to you, it wasn't us," I said.

She looked back and forth between us as

understanding wrestled with trauma in her mind. “But the ships? They were so much similar,” she said.

“That,” Edword said through a growl, “is very much a problem.”

It was sometime later. I couldn’t say how long. I stood with the wheel in my hand, guiding the ship toward the setting sun where I knew we were heading. In the meanwhile, my thoughts went in directions I didn’t see as clearly. Edword and I had moved Candice into one of the cabins beneath the sterncastle, where she promptly fell asleep. I watched her for a time, mostly to make sure that sleep took hold and that she wasn’t instead about to shock herself awake. With what she’d been through, I would not have been surprised either way. I had seen some of the men aboard this very ship – hardy sailors with decades at sea under their belt – go from sleep to sitting bolt upright in a cold fever sweat after one near-death experience or another. The fact that the young girl we’d rescued didn’t react that way was either a testimony to her exhaustion or her constitution. I was unsure which, but in either case, I stayed until I was convinced she was hard asleep. Thus assured, I came out on the deck, dismissed the helmsman, and settled into my home place to be alone with my thoughts.

The sun sat kissing the horizon, casting an orange-yellow glow on the distant edge of the sea, when Edword came up the stairs and stood beside me. He said nothing for a long time as, once again, we silently brooded together while watching the sea.

"Blood in the sky," he said finally and jutted his chin to the north. There, the dimming light of the sun now had red mixed into its warm orange hues.

"Storm coming," I said.

"North still," he muttered, "but this one'll come for us."

I waited.

"But that ain't the only storm," he finally said.

I looked over at him. "You think the girl's story means more than just a random raid," I said, leaving it open enough to seem like a question though it actually wasn't.

"Only one place a ship like the *Wind* comes from," he said. His face was still expressionless, but there was a growling steeliness under his words.

I thought for a moment, watching the sea again. I wanted to say that what Edword was suggesting wasn't possible. I wanted to say that there was no way that other ships like the *Midnight Wind* existed. That there was no connection between her and the attack on Candice and her father's ships. But then I remembered the last time I was certain about something so significant. It was three years ago, and it culminated in the most significant blunders of my life. Consequently, I bit back the denial and instead said,

"What about the fire?"

Edword stepped closer and turned to face me fully. He had a way of waiting until he was sure I was engaged in the discussion properly before he did the same. I had now apparently passed the threshold, and so he continued in earnest.

"Think on it," he said, "there's only one place in the world that knows even a few of the *Wind's* secrets that ain't up here," he said, tapping his head.

I furrowed my brow, but his reasoning was solid. "They couldn't know everything," I acknowledged, "but the base design could still exist in other hands."

"'Course they don't know everything," Edword growled, "*Wind* is one of a kind. Most of what makes her special is still my secret. But there were plans, and shipwrights and workmen were doing the work. Even the treatment on her hull had to be done by craftsmen."

"What about the fire?" I said again.

"Seals the deal, Puppy," Edword said. "Who knows about the weird stuff?"

I snorted. 'Weird stuff' had become Edword's phrase of choice whenever the subject of Kelian stones or green flames or indestructible black swords or preternaturally fast ships came up. It was his way of coping with the fact that neither of us – none of us if it came to it – really felt like we understood how the world worked anymore.

"That's a brief list, cap'n," I said, "I count us; our friends; the hermits in the Crushed Lands; the Empress of Yorch...,"

"And the king in the north. The king of Sargeaux," Edword finished, "Willm."

I nodded. We had learned the actual name of the man that had betrayed both Edword and me shortly after I set sail with the pirates three years ago. Edword's first order of business back then was a one-man blockade of the kingdom north of my old home. Ship after ship fell to us as we harried both warship and merchant ship alike. Then, abruptly, his ships stopped coming, and so we moved on, content to be a shadow and a threat in the minds of their sailors. But it was on one such raid that our prey had yielded up the name of our enemy. The merchant captain told us that he was under the flag of King Willm Steinhargh, the new master of what he now called the Kingdom of Sargeaux. There was another name he had for which our little band had been responsible. One that we also heard from that same sailor.

"Steelclaw," I said.

Edword looked at me as if he had eaten a lemon. "Hate that name," he said.

I continued, "Let's guess that's true; it sure seems the most likely of all the options. What's he doing with this little fleet of his? Why attack a fleet of empty merchant ships?"

We thought for a while before, with great effort, the

captain spoke, and when he did, there was undefinable darkness behind his words that gave me pause.

"What's the one thing went missing after the attack?" he said.

I thought for a moment. "Candice?" I offered.

Edword shook his head and leaned closer. "Close. You're almost there."

I thought again. Empty ships. But Candice had survived in the water, so...,

"The men," I said.

"Aye. The men. If they'd meant to kill everyone, there'd have been more than just the girl in the water. They took seasoned sailors from almost a dozen ships. Why you reckon they did that?"

My mind whirled. "Ransom, maybe?" I guessed, grasping for an answer.

Edword leaned back and folded his arms. "You still not dirty enough, Pup. Let me help. If you going to fight someone, you know the best place to be standing? Behind his best friend."

In an instant, the horrifying truth crashed into me in an almost physical impact. "He took dozens of men who all come from Euticha...," my voice trailed off.

"Get there faster, mister," Edword said, his pretense of patience now gone.

"They're a shield," I said as I felt the blood draining

from my face, “He’s going to attack the city.”

CHAPTER THREE

– JULEA –

"Princess Julea Niconnal bar Ardallah!"

The deep voice boomed out over the foredeck and shook me out of my reverie. Since the journey to Lochhaven that changed my life, I have often found that open water puts me in a reflective state of mind. My thoughts seem to spin out and away from the present, into either the past or, occasionally, even the future. At the moment in question, it happened to be the future that had seized me, and I was deeply lost in the concerns of our imminent return to the Great City when the sound of my Talhas bodyguard's call brought me back. I looked down at where my hands tightly gripped the finely wrought steel railing of the foredeck in an effort to replant myself in the present, sighed, and then turned around. A proper mountain of a man stood several feet away, looking at me with a mixture of respect and carefully restrained irritation. He wore a dark gray uniform, consisting of a heavy leather vest that was fastened across his chest by six wide leather straps and gold buckles, all of which seemed to be doing yeoman's work to contain his heavily muscled form. Dark brown leather pauldrons were buckled on each shoulder, and around his neck hung two golden chains, denoting his rank. A brown belt crisscrossed his waist, but where others would wear a blade, his belt was empty. There was no missing the handle of his massive axe peeking over his shoulder, though.

"Good morning, captain," I said to him pleasantly, though I was sure to be loud enough for the nearby crewmen of the Imperial vessel to hear as well. Raising one's voice to a noblewoman was poor form, and raising one's voice to the Imperial heir could potentially be seen as treasonous. Best to ally any concerns.

Captain Rohb O'Laird came forward and took a knee before me. We both well knew that such a display was an unnecessary honor, and it was clear that he was tacitly apologizing for his tone. I gently patted his shoulder – which felt much like patting a horse's flank – and turned back to the sea as he rose.

"Sorry," he said quietly, stepping up beside me, "courtly etiquette has always been a problem for me."

"That is not new information," I said, smiling up into his kindly, if embarrassed, face.

"I should know better by now," he said with a shrug.

"You are an excellent warrior, a loyal guardian, and a good friend," I said, "I shouldn't worry if you have some rough edges. In truth, I wouldn't want you any different. You keep me grounded."

"Thanks," he said, then corrected, "I mean, thanks, your Imperial Highness."

"Ugh," I said, poking him with my elbow, "Dana told you to say that, didn't she?"

"To say so either way could be seen as breaking a confidence, couldn't it?"

I smiled, "I suppose. Now then, in any event, what was it you came here so rudely to say?"

"Your mother, ma'am," he said, "I was sent to bring you to her."

I dropped my head and let out a sigh. "Any idea what she wants?" I asked.

Rohb waited until I lifted my head back up and looked at him before he answered. "Nothing she specifically told me," he said.

"But...," I prodded.

"But she seemed somewhat dispirited to hear that you were out on the deck unaccompanied," he said, casting me a sidelong look.

"She didn't attempt to blame you, did she?"

Rohb shrugged, "Not as such. But *I* was asked as to where you were and why I had allowed you to be there."

My head dropped again. It seemed to be more comfortable to deal with my mother with my head down.

"So, I should probably go see her," I said.

Rohb, judiciously, said nothing.

I straightened, taking a moment to straighten my head properly and roll my shoulders. I took another moment as well to survey my clothes. I had violated the rules of etiquette on any number of occasions when it came to Her Imperial Majesty, but as this time it could somehow reflect on Rohb, I thought it best to have a care. I considered my dress – white-silver with a lace overlay on the skirting. The top covered my shoulders, though it left my arms bare, while the neckline dipped low. A matching silver corset with white stitching completed the gown, and I wore matching silver and white gloves contrasted with a black choker to complement the look. My secret, such as it was, was the black working boots I wore that were hidden by the lace-trimmed fabric. *What she doesn't see doesn't matter,* I thought rebelliously.

"Very well, let's go see her," I said with a sigh. Rohb offered his arm, and I reached up and took it as we turned away from the ocean and headed toward the stern where the cabins were.

Where Empress Ardallah waited for me.

The Imperial ship *Fenris* was a colossal fortress of a vessel and the largest ship in the Imperial fleet. Her entire reason for existence was the transport and protection of the Imperial presence. As such, no expense or luxury had been spared in her construction. Three huge masts rose from her main deck with a fourth smaller mast on the foredeck. In the stern, there were three floors stacked beneath the quarterdeck. Nearly every inch of the space inside was designated for the royal family and the household. My personal quarters were on the second level to the starboard side, and the entirety of the top floor was the private domain of the empress herself. The lowest level, however, was where Rohb and I would find my mother waiting. It held a largish chamber she used for audiences with the officers of the ship or other guests. Two of such naval officers stood at the door, and they bowed their heads at my approach.

"The Princess Julea to see Her Imperial Majesty," Rohb said. The guards nodded and pulled at the chamber doors, and they swung open to either side, allowing us within. The interior floor of the chamber was two steps lower than the doorway, leaving the ceiling some twelve feet above us and giving the room a fantastic feeling of openness that was remarkable for the interior of a vessel at sea. The walls were mostly whitewashed and trimmed with the gold, silver, brass, and marble that was the hallmark of Imperial fashion. Opposite the doors were large windows mounted inside of what looked like fine metal caging. These allowed a broad view of the sea where the wake of the giant ship churned whitecaps in the water behind us. Each of the individual glass panes was mounted on hinges, and many of them were swung open. Thus the smell of the sea permeated the air. Numerous tables, storage cabinets, and miscellaneous fixtures were fitted around the perimeter wall, fastened in place in the manner of such things at sea. However, the dominant feature in the room was a white circular platform opposite the door and nearer the windows. It was covered with a circular black rug decorated with the large golden wolf's head – the symbol of the empire. On this, two couches and a high-backed chair were fastened with clamps to the platform, forming a formally arranged conversation space. On the chair sat a striking ivory-haired woman in a glistening white dress trimmed with silver and gold: Her Imperial Majesty Ardallah Niconnal bar Morrisia; my mother.

"Portable throne," I said under my breath as we came down the stairs into the room. Out of the corner of my eye, I watched as Rohb fought mightily to suppress a grin.

"That will be all, captain," said the empress just as we had stepped down into the room. She was carefully studying a small sheaf of papers in her hand and had not looked up as she issued the dismissal. Rohb nodded to her anyway, glanced at me before he nodded formally to me as well, and turned back to the doors. I watched him leave over my shoulder and waited until I heard the latch shut once again before I turned back to Her Imperial Majesty. She was now looking up at me, the papers on her lap.

“Oh, don’t give me such a look,” she said with a dismissive wave of her hand. I noted her choice of the personal pronoun and wondered at it. It seemed, then, that this was to be an informal conversation. She waved me forward as she took the papers from her lap and set them on the small table to the right of her chair, pausing a moment to adjust them into a neat stack. I crossed the room, stepped up onto the platform, and sat on the couch to her left, amazed at how something like the small action of stepping onto that platform gave me an almost palpable feeling of entering her presence. “You really can’t expect to have your personal guard around for matters of state, Julea. That is not why we have them,” she continued after I sat.

“The captain is a friend, mother, not just my guard,” I heard myself say, though I realized the foolishness of it immediately.

“Your penchant for befriending servants of the throne will only cause you strife, daughter,” she said, “I assure you of it.” There was a heaviness to her words, and part of me considered it. For a moment, I considered asking her. *Had she experienced something that made her think that way?* I wondered though it seemed almost impossible to contemplate. Ardallah had always been more an institution than an individual – more *empress* than *mother* even – and imagining a past where she wasn’t like that was akin to picturing a walking fish.

"I shall take that into consideration, mother," I said instead, with almost no convincing enthusiasm.

She looked me over, very much aware of my silent dismissal of her counsel. She was tall and willowy, though without the delicateness that such would have indicated on a lesser person. Her eyes were dark but gleamed with an overwhelming sense of intelligence and attention. Her sharp features and high cheekbones hinted at a foreign lineage rather than to the native blood of Yorchians, though she never spoke of it. In the past, some had been brave enough to inquire and had been censured without hesitation. Her skin was nearly as pale as her dress and were it not for the tiny imperfections brought on by age, she appeared as nothing less than a living, breathing statue of ivory. Her expressionless gaze watched me for just a moment longer than was comfortable before she spoke again.

"You were found on the deck, I understand," she said.

"I was. I enjoy the sea air."

"A feeling I share. I, however, prefer to enjoy it from here, away from the crew," she said, gesturing minutely at the open windows.

"I don't mind," I said, tilting my head in a tiny shrug.

"Of course, you don't," she said with a gentle sigh. I recognized the disappointment in her voice; I had actually inspired that tone often enough that I now saw it as an indicator that I had done something worth doing.

She turned her attention to the papers, smoothly drawing the top sheet off and handing it to me. “This is our letter of appreciation to King Adam Olindon for his hospitality this past week. It is the word of the royal court, of which you are a prominent part. Read it over and sign it below my name,” she said.

I accepted the paper and did as she bade me. It was composed of effulgent words of praise for the hospitality we had received in Gladia, several passages regarding the illustrious history of the alliance between our nations, and a general statement of commitment to maintain that alliance in the future.

“This is a very politically heavy thank-you letter,” I said, glancing back to her.

“Aren’t they all?” she said.

I stood and reached over to retrieve the quill from the table to her right. Her hand shot out, surprising me as she took the rest of the papers off the table before I had gotten close. I gave her a look, but her impassive face merely met my gaze before glancing down to the pen. I cautiously picked it up and returned to my seat, where I scribbled my signature on the page.

“And what do you think of our visit south?” she asked as I wrote.

“What do I think?” I asked, surprised at the question.

“Indeed. One day you will be called on to handle

affairs of state directly, not simply as my envoy. I would know your mind in such matters," she said, casually accepting the letter back as I handed it to her.

I thought for a moment, considering my answer. "They were very obviously making a tremendous effort to show the stability of their nation after recent events," I said.

My mother gave me a perfunctory nod that radiated her disengagement at my answer. "Basic, but true," she said, "and did you perceive anything else of such keen insight?"

Mentally, I ran through the events of the visit again, sifting and evaluating every interaction to find the needle in the haystack that she was expecting me to see. Our arrival. The tours of the city and its environs. The trip up to the former capital of Preskia where the new duchess received us...,

And then I had it. I realized what Her Majesty was waiting for me to see and the shades of meaning she looked at me to notice. Withholding a feeling of triumph that I wished I didn't feel, I shrugged casually and said, "I saw nothing else unless you're speaking of the archbishop's obvious collusion in the assassination of the archduke."

The empress's head jerked slightly in my direction, a move so small and quickly controlled that only someone with years of experience with her would have noticed. Experience that I had. Inside, a silent cheer went up in my mind.

"Indeed. Well noted, daughter," she said, her tone as

steady as if I had just mentioned the weather. She continued, “Show your work.”

I straightened my back and turned more fully to her. To an onlooker, I thought, we might have looked like two noblewomen gossiping over tea. Instead, we were discussing the dark dealings of assassination and political power bids. I began, “The entirety of our visit was, as I said, very carefully orchestrated. It was rather like being at a festival or a gigantic theater show. I almost felt that we were visiting some manner of a vacation spot, ‘the happiest place in the world.’ That in and of itself would make me suspicious as to what was being hidden from us. But our visit to the widowed duchess – and more specifically to the King’s Church – revealed the seams at the edges of their presentation. The archbishop had nothing but veiled contempt for King Adam; it was plain to see.”

“Indeed,” sighed the empress, “I expect that even Adam himself will eventually notice, and he’s a very simple boy.”

I repressed the reflex to laugh as the Empress of Yorch casually insulted the ruler of her most loyal ally as if he were a poor waiter in a tavern. She continued looking at me, expectation on her face. It was apparent that I wasn’t finished to her mind.

“Notwithstanding that, Archbishop Bengalli’s contempt would only have been a footnote were it not for a few other observations. First, he is very closely attended by several of the church priests. While perhaps that should not be unusual, at least one of these 'priests' was unquestionably nothing of the kind. He wore riding boots and assuredly had a blade hidden beneath his robe," I reported. For a moment, I remembered how my friends had once secreted blades under monk's robes. I shook away the memory; now was not the time. "Add to that the archbishop's obvious intimacy with the duchess," I added.

My mother stood and paced around her chair, gliding with her hands clasped behind her back and her head slightly bowed. The move felt like she was a schoolteacher during an examination. She stopped behind me, and from the corner of my eye, I saw her tilt her head up as she spoke.

"Intimacy?" she asked.

I sat still, looking at my hands folded in my lap and keeping my back straight. If it were to be a test, then I would happily meet it.

"Perhaps not physical – or perhaps not physical yet, more to the point – but very definitely there is a connection between them. Neither left the other behind very far at any of the events we attended in the city. And the glances passing between them were quite telling. Thus, if I *were* to draw conclusions...," I trailed off, waiting for her leave.

"Do so," she said. She resumed moving and was now standing behind her chair and looking out at the *Fenris's* wake.

"It's my theory that the duchess and the archbishop colluded in the elimination of her husband. I expect they are involved with a group that supplied them the means to have him eliminated. Possibly simply to bring about her ascension to power, or perhaps to some greater end."

There was a pause as I finished, and I waited again. I wish I could say that I was immune to the evaluation that was to come. That I didn't need her approval anymore. But, of course, she was my mother.

"Well done, Julea," she said finally, "I am pleased. You are not nearly as dull as Adam, though that is a somewhat low bar." She moved over to my couch and patted my shoulder from behind in approval.

Unbidden joy and disappointment in myself warred in me as I said, "Thank you, mother."

She continued her circuit around the platform as she spoke, giving me background information that she had been privy to long before our visit. There had been, she explained, an alliance of forces within the nation of Gladia. One that was very much opposed to the progressive policies of the Olindons. One that sought a return to the old ways of isolationism. The archbishop was central to it, as was the leader of the local thieves guild. She finally returned to her chair and stood in front of it as she concluded.

"So, Julea, princess of the realm, what does Yorch do

with an ally in such a state?" she asked as she looked at me.

I sighed, thinking. The final test, I realized, was on me. I held my face still as if it were a mask. I knew well that I would be judged on my expression as much as on my answer. I decided on the course I would take and why, squared my shoulders to her, and began.

"Yorch does not abandon our allies. Their internal strife is their own business as long as it is not an active threat to us. King Adam's disingenuous invitation would be a cause for concern, as it could be seen as a lie, one meant to appease us after their tumult. As you said, though, Adam is— he is not that sort. What could be seen as dullness is also easily interpreted as authenticity. I see this as more likely. Therefore, Yorch waits and supports its ally as ever."

Empress Ardallah of Yorch sat down as I finished and leaned back in her chair. She was quiet for a long moment before she nodded. "So Yorch will do," she said.

I looked at her for a moment, considering. "You had already come to this conclusion, hadn't you?" I said.

"Of course, daughter. I have been doing this for a very long time. But it seemed a reasonable time for an evaluation of my heir," she said, a very placid smile on her lips. "Tea?" she asked, pulling at a tasseled cord on her chair. A bell rang somewhere in the distance.

"Thank you," I said, "I would love some."

Servants came and went, and we sat and sipped our

tea in formal silence. Somehow, the empress was able to consume the piping hot tea immediately and without sound. I did my best, but the slight slurping noise I made on my first few sips drew a disapproving glare, and I decided to wait for the tea to cool somewhat.

"We will be in Euticha soon, is that correct?" I asked. I was making conversation now, as we both were well and truly aware of our scheduled visit to the city.

"I have been told we will arrive in the harbor sometime after sundown. We will enter the docks with first light," the empress replied. Her tone was light but distant, an inflection I had heard many times during the various formalities of court. She managed to remain just above apparent boredom, but it was clear that her thoughts were elsewhere.

I pressed forward with little else to do, as one does not excuse oneself from the imperial presence, regardless of relationship. "Do we expect any particular problems there? I mean, Euticha is a free city, one not explicitly an ally," I said. I tested the tea, and it seemed unlikely to raise blisters in my mouth, so I took a sip.

Something about my statement had brought her full attention back. "Isn't it?" she said, "Euticha is a bit of a deviance; that much is true. Lord Westfall has managed to maintain a level of autonomy from the nearby dominions through sheer willpower and temerity. The goods and services that pass through his city provide him with much wealth and influence, and he wields them like a cloak. And like a sword, when he wishes. But the fact of it is that Euticha does not exist, save for the goodwill of Yorch and Gladia. Thus, I consider it an ally, in a practical way if not in a formal one." There was something behind her words that I couldn't identify. It was as if this particular arrangement was almost a personal issue.

"I've never met Lord Westfall," I said, prodding a little, "I don't recall him ever coming to court."

She shook her head breezily as she took a sip of her tea. "You have not, and he has not," she said, "but you may have briefly met his consultant two years ago. Master Malazander Pwent. He represented Euticha for the High Regent at the Assemblage."

I thought back. The Assemblage was a biennial conference sponsored by the empire. Representatives of the major kingdoms from up and down the coast of the Great Eastern Ocean would come to Yorch and negotiate treaties, air grievances, and otherwise seek civilized solutions to problems between kingdoms. In truth, it usually became a fortnight-long party punctuated by formal shouting matches. If nothing else, though, it allowed faces to be put to the names of the representatives of the other realms. Master Pwent had, come to think of it, left an impression, both in his appearance – he was a short, broad-shouldered man with enough hair to have been part beast – and in his manner, which was crude and arrogant. He also had made it his business to find me far more often than chance would have allowed.

My mother saw the look on my face as the memory of him came back to me. “Ah, yes. I see you recall him now,” she said.

I grimaced.

She continued, “I agree that his manners are wanting. Fortunately, it is likely the High Regent himself will entertain us during our visit. Perhaps it will be that will make the consultant less troubling to you.”

“If I can avoid him entirely, the visit will be a success,” I said. I swallowed the last of my tea in an effort to eliminate the distaste his memory brought.

“If you have finished your tea, I am sure you have preparations to make before we reach the city. You may go,” she said with a gentle nod. Whether there was more to say on the matter of Euticha or not, the audience was over. I set my cup down on the table and rose. I bowed deeply and backed away to the edge of the dais before turning and walking to the entrance. I tapped once, and the doors swung out and away, revealing Rohb standing at attention outside. I exited into the hallway, and he fell into step behind me.

“Nice visit?” he said under his breath as we moved out of the hearing of the chamber guards.

"Lovely as ever," I said, a tiny grin on my mouth as I looked at him out of the corner of my eye.

"Nice to see a warm family from time to time," he said, his sarcasm clear but well veiled.

I led him around to the stairs that would take us up to the second level, down the narrow hall there, and into the set of three rooms that formed my lodgings on the mighty ship. We entered into my more reasonably sized sitting room, where the necessary tables and chairs were arranged and fastened to allow me to engage in a formal audience with guests. I had never used them, of course, unless Rohb was to be counted as a guest. But, it was designed for that purpose, and who was I to question the shipwrights? To the left, toward the stern, was my bedchamber. Beyond that was a small room that served as a washroom. Rohb became immediately uncomfortable, both because the chamber was built for a normal-sized person, which he was not, and because we were now alone, and despite three years of service, he still felt awkward when we were alone. I stopped myself from thinking about Dana and how we had treasured the opportunities to speak privately. There was no use going down that path. Instead, I crossed to the outer wall and sat on the padded bench with a sigh. I had only had tea with her, but every muscle in my body felt like I had been chopping wood. I reached down and unfastened my boots.

"Tell me what you know of Euticha," I said through

the grunts of pulling off my footwear. There were, of course, maidservants I could call for this purpose, but somehow the act of taking off my own boots was important to me.

Rohb was still standing at the door, having not moved since we entered. My left foot now free, I looked up at him as I tossed the boot aside.

"Rohb, would you sit? Please?" I pleaded. We'd had the discussion before, and each time he would relax and be fine until the next time. I didn't feel like doing the entire dance just then, so I firmly pointed at a seat across from me and gave him a stern look. The giant looked at the bench and gingerly moved over and sat in it.

The tiny woman makes the giant sheepish, I thought, *the world is a strange place.*

I resumed working on my right boot. "So? Euticha?" I prompted.

Having a subject seemed to help him take the focus from his discomfort, and he began to talk in earnest. "Great town," he said, "I saw it first when I was just a lad, on my way up to join the army in Yorch. It was the biggest and fanciest place I'd ever seen. Made seeing the Imperial City a little less overwhelming, really. Sort of an appetizer to the main course if you take me."

"Really? More so than the Gladian cities we just left?" I thought of the capital in Seoda and the old city of Preskia in the south. They were very impressive in general, not like

Yorch was impressive, but undoubtedly cosmopolitan. I reached down and massaged my left ankle. It regularly ached a little after a long day. In my mind, I sent a silent curse to the shadow snakes of Aosta.

"Much," Rohb was saying, "Euticha gets paid for every shipment that passes through it. And every shipment, north or south, passes there. Result is like someone took part of Yorch and stuck it in the south. But it's not a tame place, princess. Looks are deceiving."

"How so?"

"Lots going on behind the civilization. Euticha is also the doorway for less above-board exchanges too. Don't go prodding in any dark alleys, is all I'm sayin'."

I leaned back and looked at him. Despite himself, he had relaxed and was leaning against the wall behind him.

"Well, we won't be there long, and I expect we'll be attended to by the authorities the whole time. So I doubt that will be an issue," I said. There *may* have been a hint of wistfulness in my voice.

"I got you anyway," he said with a shrug, "I ain't letting anything happen to you. Deal with your mother? No way."

I smiled ruefully.

"After which, I expect our friends would rain down on me too, they found out," he said, leaning his head back. "I'd catch it comin' and goin'. No thanks; easier to keep you safe."

"You're so warm and comforting, do you know that?" I said with a chuckle.

The *Fenris* anchored just beyond Euticha's harbor just after the sun had set. Our approach was such that the sun blinded us as it came down, and while I strove to see the city, I was forced to settle for the shadowed silhouette left by the twilight sky. Numerous pinpricks of light flared and spread in random patterns across the water, faintly hinting at what waited in the darkness. Finally, the night watchmen came onto the deck and took their stations as a clear indication that it was time that I retire. For the empress's sake, if not my own.

I rose at dawn after the abbreviated sleep of a summer night and began preparations. Her Imperial Majesty had made it clear on our initial approach to Gladia that the first impression made on leaving the *Fenris* would be the one most remembered by onlookers. The nobles may see us enough to adjust their expectations, but members of the populace might only ever see us once, and it was our duty to give them a proper showing. I couldn't help but remember Dana's comments on our arrival in Lochhaven years ago and how she only then realized that the people may see our visit as the most noteworthy thing they'd ever experienced. It was a duty. I pulled out a maroon dress and had managed to get it draped over myself when a knock came on my door. I sighed, annoyed that I hadn't started earlier to avoid this part of the process, and called out for the visitors I had expected – but didn't truly desire – to enter. A moment later, three young girls of no more than twenty came into the room. They bowed deeply, staying down until I reminded myself to tell them to rise. I avoided this as often as I could, but on this journey, it was expected, and I knew that they would be heartbroken if I shooed them away. Immediately on rising, they set about their work, beginning with securing the holds and ties on the dress. It hung loosely on me despite their efforts, but once the corset was fastened, I knew it wouldn't be an issue. The tallest girl began to fuss with my hair, and I sat down to make her work more accessible. Shortly, they had finished their labors, and I stood in front of the oval mirror in the corner and evaluated their work. The dress had sleeves that were fitted from my wrist to the middle of my upper arm. From there, they bloused open to the top of my shoulder. The low-cut neckline was decorated with gold and green scrollwork, which matched it well to the dark green corset I wore to complete the outfit. The gold and green trim wrapped the bottom of the skirting as well and served to disguise again the black boots I wore out of preference and defiance. I was relieved that I had the skirting already in place when the girls entered, as they would be most affected if my little show of rebellion were discovered. The tall girl – her name was Madeline, as I had managed to get out of her – took the front sections of my hair, rolled them around the sides of my head, and braided them together in the back. She turned to me now with a golden chain necklace and offered it to me.

"No, thank you, dear," I said, "I would prefer the gemstone. The one to the right of where you found that." She returned a moment later with another golden necklace, this one with a large and somewhat irregular green gem in the center. I nodded, and she fastened it around my neck.

"Thank you, ladies," I said with a tone of finality. The three attendants took the hint and quickly left, leaving me alone. Once I was sure they were gone, I went to a small drawer near the far end of the room and retrieved a short dagger, stepped my right leg up on the bench, and fitted it into the inside of the boot. Just then, the outer door swung open, and I spun my head to find Rohb standing in the doorway.

"Excuse me, captain," I said haughtily.

"I'm sorry, ma'am," he said, ducking his eyes as if he were walking in on me unclothed, "the maids said you were ready...," He trailed off as if realizing that he had not, in truth, caught me dressing, but had instead caught me in a compromising act of a different kind. I put my foot back on the ground and faced him.

"Would Your Imperial Highness care to explain herself?" he asked, his grin now showing a shock of white teeth.

“She would not,” I said. I could feel a little heat in my cheeks.

Rohb shrugged a massive shoulder and bowed his head. He cleared his throat, masking a chuckle, and waved his hand to escort me out.

“Dana would understand,” I muttered to him as I stepped past.

“Yeah, but she’d laugh too,” he muttered. I gently drove my elbow into his leather-armored chest playfully. We made our way down the stairs and into the small gathering area on the lower floor to wait. Enough time had passed for me to consider how awkward the Imperial guards looked standing at attention in the small room when finally the door behind us opened, and my mother entered with her entourage. Where the other Imperial officers and soldiers were dressed similarly to Rohb in a combination of gray and brown, this was not so of her honor guard. Instead, the six deadly warriors that comprised the Guardians of the Imperial Presence – a group most often referred to as ‘the Wolfpack’ –wore a version of the same uniform but in white and red instead. Shining silver long-swords hung at their sides, and helmets with silver faceplates hid their faces, leaving only their shadowed eyes visible. They veritably flowed into the room and took up equal positions around an open space where, dressed in her most glowing white and gold, Empress Ardallah of Yorch stepped a moment later. Rohb and I stood aside as they moved past, and the moment they were in the middle of the room, the guardsmen opened the doors to the deck, and the whole group moved forward. We fell into line immediately behind the last two Wolfpack members and proceeded out into the sunlit morning in the harbor of Euticha.

I have seen impressive sights in my relatively short life. As a member of the Imperial household, I have been afforded many opportunities to see things that most never do. The Great City of Yorch. The Imperial Throne. The Festival of the One in the Emperor's Church. A green fire that crystalizes the very ground below it. Blue and yellow crystals that raise the dead. To this list, I can add the harbor of Euticha comfortably. Around the *Fenris*, merchant ships without count – of every size and description – moved in to and away from docks that ran as far as the eye could see. Floating piers, bent at angles to allow greater access to more types of ship, broke up the harbor into sections, and in and out of these vessels of all kinds moved with scant inches between them, guided by the smaller craft that were managing all of the traffic. A tall hillock jutted up from the sea on a northeast prominence, on top of which sat a stout tower. From its top, mirrors sent flashes of reflected sunlight down to a similar tower on the other side of the harbor nearer the docks. Beyond all of this was the city itself, low functional buildings near the shore that gave way to structures that grew taller and grander as they moved away from the water, such that it looked as if the city itself were rising as it went inland. Furthest away to the southeast, a tall palace stood overlooking the entire conurbation. The whole of it was, in turn, surrounded by low hills off of which wisps of morning fog swirled and tumbled down over the walls of the city.

“Damn,” Rohb said, just loud enough for my ears, “I do not remember this.”

“You, sir, are terrible at reconnaissance,” I whispered.

“Well, ma’am, that’s because I can’t even spell that,” he grumbled.

Our entourage proceeded from the deck of the *Fenris* down a long, broad, and surprisingly stable ramp that was now affixed to the ship’s side. In less time than it takes to tell, we had walked from the flagship down the ramp and up the long dock until we reached the shore of Euticha proper and our reception. A solid wall of armed men stood in a semi-circular arc around a small stone-paved landing at the end of the dock. They were adorned in brushed steel armor and helms that completely obscured their faces, two rows deep. The men in front stood posed with their hands folded on the pommels of long, heavy-looking two-handed swords staked in the ground before them. The second row of similarly arrayed men held long halberds, the axe-like ends of each arranged like flags. From the center of the arc, those on the left were pointed left, and the opposite on the right. But it was, actually, in the middle of the formation that the focus lay. A huge lion of a man with perfectly coifed red hair and a trimmed red beard stepped forward from the crowd of soldiers. He wore a white uniform trimmed with a gray, metallic edging and had a large embroidered dragon signet in the same metallic thread on his chest. A matching white and gray half-cloak covered his left arm and rose in a high collar around his head. Beside him and slightly behind stood a much shorter, gray cloaked figure. It moved as if the man's pale shadow had taken on a life of its own but was still following behind its former master. The Wolfpack redistributed themselves to either side of the empress while I stepped up beside her on her right, leaving Rohb several feet behind us.

The shadowy gray figure stepped up and approached us, stopping some five to ten feet away. There was a pause, then with a practiced motion, the figure tossed back the cloak and removed the hood to reveal the hirsute and decidedly unwelcome visage of Malazander Pwent, Counselor to the High Regent of Euticha. He nodded to my mother in a practiced, if matter of fact, manner.

"Greetings to you, Empress Ardallah Niconnal bar Morrisia of Yorch," he said, his voice pitched to be heard both to the soldiers around us as well as the onlookers beyond. "I greet you in the name of His Lordship Anthony Westfall, the High Regent of the Free State of Euticha."

I felt an almost irresistible desire to shudder, followed by a nearly as overwhelming desire for a bath. For a moment, I imagined that I could smell the unseemly odor of the gray cloak he wore – the morning was already telling the story of the humidity of the coming day; how he wore the heavy cape and hood with all that hair in the heat, I couldn't imagine. I watched as his eyes darted back and forth from the Wolfpack to my mother and finally to rest on me. He grinned, a most unpleasant sight.

"And to you, Princess Julea. It is a personal pleasure to see you again," He said. He bowed his head again; only this time, it seemed different. If one can lasciviously bow, Malazander Pwent managed to do it.

"Master Pwent," my mother said then with a hint of neither pleasure nor displeasure in her voice, "We are pleased to visit our allies here in the south. Your customs are different from ours, and so we would ask, are we to speak always through you?" She made a show of looking up at the man in white behind Pwent, "or are we able to have true communion with His Lordship directly?"

Pwent took a breath to answer when the lion man behind him stepped forward, placing his left hand heavily on the counselor's shoulder. "Your Imperial Majesty," he said, Pwent disappearing behind him as he came closer to the empress. “I am very pleased you are here,” he finished as he drew up face to face. There was a pause, and then he bowed deeply to her. As he stood, the empress nodded her head to him in return. I shot a look to Pwent, his displeasure barely restrained in his twisted expression until he noticed my glare, and his face went blank.

“And this,” I turned just in time to see the High Regent approach me, “must of necessity be the Princess Julea. Your Imperial Highness, I am charmed.” He bowed to me as he had to the empress moments before. I curtsied, then stood straight.

“It is my pleasure, Lord Westfall,” I said.

He shook his head, amiably. “I’m sorry, Your Imperial Highness, but while that may be true, it pales in comparison to the joy in an old politician’s heart at the beauty of a young noblewoman’s presence.” He smiled, and I found myself surprised at how sincere he seemed to be. I am not accustomed to a ‘politician,’ old or otherwise, evidencing any sort of sincerity. The last time it happened, I was in the throne room of Castle Sterling some three years ago.

“Consider my home yours, Your Imperial Majesty,” Westfall said as he turned back to my mother. His voice was deep and rich and had a timbre that seemed to allow it to carry the length of the city dock with no rise in volume. He extended his left arm, and the empress laid her right hand on it. With this signal, the company of Eutichan soldiers moved into a parade guard formation around us while the Wolfpack stepped close to the empress and Westfall.

"Hunh," Rohb said, stepping up beside me again.

"Shhh," I hissed quietly. There were too many people too close to us for my bodyguard to begin waxing on disrespectfully, which was something I knew to be possible. Even likely. Rohb's reinstatement in the Imperial ranks three years before hadn't been easy despite his pivotal role in protecting me. He had left a reputation behind him when he resigned some years earlier – something having to do with assaulting a nobleman – that nearly sank the venture before we began. I had been forced to produce a letter from the empress to convince the military leaders to accept him back. But drawing attention to himself by, well, *expressing* himself was only going to bring scrutiny. I doubted my 'letter from the empress' would withstand much of that.

"Later," I whispered. Rohb winced a little but kept his peace.

The palace of the High Regent of Euticha was tremendous. I learned later that it contained some five hundred rooms, a thousand windows, several hundred chimneys, and dozens of staircases. I mention these statistics not because they are impressive; they are, unquestionably, though they are still shy of the Imperial Palace in Yorch. No, I mention them because they are of a scale that makes describing it in detail nearly impossible. Accept, then, that I am oversimplifying when I say that the edifice was immense. It consisted of a long central section and two perpendicular wings at each end, forming a squat 'H' shape if seen from above. We were ushered in through the lower floor and to the south side, nearer the ocean. From here, our hosts guided us up several of the 'dozens of staircases' mentioned above until we came out into a large ballroom on the uppermost floor. Inside, a quartet of musicians was playing. Behind them, a cluster of tall windows looked out over the city and toward the ocean. Near them, in the southwest corner of the room, a raised platform sat with three handsomely adorned plush chairs placed on it. The center of the room was taken up by a sizeable polished wood dance floor, to both sides of which were several tables enshrouded in white linen and surrounded by white wooden chairs. A small crowd of richly dressed patricians was milling about, and as we entered, the musicians paused while the blast of a metal horn sang out a crisp note announcing our arrival.

"Forgive me," I heard Lord Westfall say to my mother, "but so many of the noble houses wished to meet you that I thought this was the best way."

The empress smiled serenely and nodded before following him into the room and over to the southwest corner. A heavy silence hung in the air as they crossed the open floor. Once they had stepped onto the platform, they turned back to the room of expectant onlookers.

"Lords and Ladies," Westfall said, "I give to you Empress Ardallah Niconnal bar Morrisia of the mighty Empire of Yorch!"

Applause rose from the assembled crowd, and I thought that – for them – it was probably the most uproarious they had been in, well, ever.

"And, her lovely daughter, Princess Julea," he continued, gesturing toward me as he spoke over the waning applause, causing it to rise again.

"I'll be right over there," Rohb said quietly with a surreptitious nod of his head toward the side of the room. I nodded in response without looking at him and walked over to the platform, joining the High Regent and my mother. The applause died out, and we sat down on the chairs, displayed like prized meat in a market.

The festivities were blessedly less extensive than the pomp and circumstance initially indicated, and I heard Lord Westfall murmur to the empress that though he had been obligated to arrange the function, he had at least been able to put a definite endpoint in place. Thus, after only a few hours – that admittedly felt like many more as a steady troop of nobles came forward to meet the empress and me – he stood and, in a commanding voice, announced the end of the festivities.

"Our guests have had a long journey," he said by way

of explanation, "and they will have much further to go on their way to their home. Therefore, let us show them the hospitality of free people by giving them time to rest and recover." A smattering of applause rolled through the room. "Your Imperial Majesty," he said, turning to my mother, "would you like to address the assembled?"

The empress stood and stepped forward, somehow seeming to grow in stature as she did so. This was her element, I knew, and she seemed to radiate a calm and compelling authority.

"We are grateful to the people of this city for this cordial and honorable reception and your generous hospitality in general. The tales we have heard of you are certainly all true," she said.

Polite applause rippled again through the room. It seemed as though many of the guests were not entirely sure she was giving an unfettered compliment with that last statement. I wasn't sure either. I was sure, though, that the impression was precisely what she wished it to be.

"We are very pleased to be with you for the next two days. We hope both to see the wonders of your home here and to cement further the ties between us," she finished.

There was more polite applause as the empress and the High Regent gave one another a polite bow before they stepped from the platform, arm-in-arm once again. In concert with the Eutichan guards, the Wolfpack moved into position around us and directed us toward an exit on the south wall. Rohb was at my side once again as we exited into a plush corridor, the doors closing behind us when we were out. Our entourage stopped.

"This wing has been set aside for your use," the High Regent said, turning to my mother as they stepped apart, "I believe you will find the rooms on the western side here to have been prepared for you, while the rooms on the east should be more than acceptable for your daughter."

"That is most kind, Lord Westfall," the empress said, "We express our gratitude again to you."

"Perhaps, when you have rested and refreshed yourself, it would be beneficial for you and me to speak privately," he said. There was a caged look in his eyes, though he kept his manner light and cordial.

"Tomorrow may well present us that opportunity," she replied. I had studied her long enough to detect the note of satisfaction in her response. It was evident to me that this had been her plan all along. Likely, it was the real reason behind her carefully worded public statements at the reception. Now, as ever, she was playing the game of nations, and it was a game at which she was a master.

The High Regent of Euticha bowed his head to her. Then, after taking two steps backward, he turned and walked further down the corridor, disappearing into a distant hallway, no doubt to find another of the multitudinous stairways. The local guardsmen followed, leaving us alone with Rohb and the Wolfpack. Without a word, the Imperial guardians dispersed, leaving me, Rohb, and my mother alone in the hall. I had seen this in our stay in Gladia as well; her guards were going room by room through the quarters we would use, securing them and verifying that the 'hospitality' we were offered was trustworthy.

Empress Ardallah turned suddenly toward me. "You are staring, daughter. Am I somehow a novelty?" she said.

I shook my head slightly and said, "Certainly not. I am, however, curious as to your maneuvers with Lord Westfall."

"Posturing, dear," she said dismissively, "Yorch is making no motion to take this city as our own. But it never hurts to remind people of their relative position in the hierarchy. It makes negotiations on other matters..., more cordial."

"Are we in negotiations with Euticha?" I asked.

"We keep our options open, daughter," she smiled a somewhat wicked smile, "always." With that, the Imperial guard returned, their sweep having resulted in an evaluation that the rooms were acceptable. Her Imperial Majesty swept off then to the chambers set aside for her while Rohb and I followed a single Wolfpack officer down to the entry of the rooms I'd been assigned.

The main chamber of the suite I had been given was

done in a palette of golds and burgundies against a whitewashed plastered stone. Opposite the door, tall reinforced glass windows overlooked the city below. I noted that this meant that my mother's rooms would be looking out over the bay and felt a twinge of jealousy, though only that. She was, after all, the empress. Embroidered burgundy upholstery covered several gold-trimmed couches and chairs which sat on thick matching rugs. At the far end of the room were an array of three doors; two mounted in the far wall itself and one that led to an inset chamber, which I took to be a washroom.

"You have your own room," I said, nudging Rohb.

"I just need a couch," he said, uncomfortable again.

"You would need all the couches," I said, shaking my head. I walked across to the windows and worked the lever that allowed them to swing open on their gilded hinges. A warm breeze came in, though the ocean kept the air from being too uncomfortable. I looked out over the city from above now, the sunlight playing off the rooves below me. In the streets, the citizens went about their day. The excitement of our morning arrival was now fixed in the past for them. The city teemed with motion, and I thought of how it compared to home. Yorch too bustled with life, though there was a different quality to Euticha; a feeling of excitement or adventure that I couldn't quite elaborate on, but that had been tickling my thoughts since we had come onshore.

Rohb had wandered off to look into the other rooms, finally returning from the doorway to the right without his ever-present axe on his back.

"My room," he said, somewhat resignedly.

"Fine," I said, turning from the window and walking toward the other door, "then this one is mine. Do you think you could find out when our belongings will be brought up from the ship? I'm sure we'll have more duties by the time the evening comes."

Suddenly, there was a clattering noise behind me by the window I had just left. Rohb lurched forward and, with one strong arm, shoved me behind him while his other hand drew a dagger from his belt.

"It's probably a squirrel," I said, catching my balance after the shove, "would you settle down?"

"Not a squirrel," he said as his eyes locked on something lying on the floor. His tone was somber, and I stopped my attempts at banter. Cautiously, he moved forward, gesturing me to stay while keeping to the far side of the room. After a moment, he crouched, watching the windows until he finally looked down. There was a moment's hesitation, and then he stood up as if the floor had caught fire.

"God's teeth," he said.

"What is it?" I asked, stepping forward cautiously.

"I think it's the past," he said, giving me a look. As I

came closer, he stooped over and picked something up from the floor, holding it out to me as I approached.

In his hand, he held a black crossbow bolt wrapped in a sheet of paper. Its tip, instead of an arrowhead, was a white crystal.

CHAPTER FOUR

— KELLY —

J,

Etherian Gardens. Midnight.

It has been too long.

K

I like the night. For someone that has been known in alternate turns as 'Raven' and 'Blackcrow' – birds which both unexpectedly prefer the day – it could be considered a little bit peculiar. To be fair, though, the specific activities involved in each role had usually leaned toward the nocturnal. But the truth is that I just like the dark. Something is comforting to me about being active when everyone else seems at rest. So, when I say that the sun was long gone from the sky when I led my companions out into the growing shadows of the streets of Euticha, realize that I was far from dreading the oncoming dark; I welcomed it. When I mention, then, that my nerves were buzzing like a hive, it's apparent that it was something else that had me keyed up.

The city's northwestern section stretched up and away from the broad mouth of the Arcagawan river, where it emptied into the Great Ocean. As a result, it existed out of the spotlight of the commercial docks where so much international trade happened. While it was still affluent, it was less fashionable than the heart of the metropolis. Here, the local merchants – the ones that made their living providing services to the broader, international concerns – lived just below the threshold of notoriety. Which made it perfect, to be honest.

I sat in the deep black shadow of a walking bridge that ran over a small, man-made brook. The pathway of the water was carefully designed both to provide water and to beautify the Etherian Gardens. The crescent moon, so pale it would have been useless in any event, was rendered nearly invisible in the light of the torchlit path that led in both directions from the bridge through and around the bedarkened parkland. My friends and I had first arrived a little earlier, before sunset, while the celebrated park still buzzed with the late evening activity of the locals. It had been a simple matter then to disappear in the growing shadows as twilight came on, and before long, we were both alone and forgotten. As the wait stretched on, it became harder and harder to be patient. I sat closest to the darkness's edge, meaning that both Dana and Denis nudged me incessantly to peek out and see if Julea had, perhaps, come a little early. I would have complained, but really they were only providing me an excuse to do what I wanted to do anyway. It made little sense, I knew; getting away from the constant watch her life required at all would be hard enough, let alone slipping away early. But still, I would peek around each time and return with a sigh each time.

Finally, right around what I supposed was the midnight hour, I felt a jolt inside myself. Maybe I heard the tiny shuffling of footsteps from the far end of the bridge, or maybe it was just a coincidence, but I knew before I looked. She had come. Unprompted this time, I edged up and looked over the bridge's stone half-wall as I had been doing all evening. She would have been careful, and of course, would have taken precautions so as not to be followed, but I knew we needed to be sure. Euticha's independence meant it wasn't strictly under Yorch's jurisdiction. Still, it wouldn't be impossible to believe that some overzealous Imperial guardsman might have followed her just to try his luck at the 'Blackcrow.'

Peering over the top of the wall, I saw a single figure standing in the middle of the bridge, near one of the torches and facing the river. A dark-gray cloak flicked in the breeze and caught the torchlight like waves did starlight. I felt a rush of excitement that made me want to rush over to her, but hard-earned caution made me pause. Instead, I scanned up and down the path, my eyes finally finding a hulking shadow lurking in the overhang of a nearby tree at the far end. I watched, forcing myself to wait and see.

"Is it her?" Dana whispered so quietly that her voice was barely audible over the gentle burble of the river. I made a wait gesture with my hand where she could see it before I turned back to the scene. The cloaked figure looked around cautiously on the bridge and had just turned away from me as I looked out. The distant shadow moved, coming forward as if drawn, only to be waved back by a hand from the woman on the bridge. The shape slunk back, but not before I saw the outline of a mammoth axe on its back in the torchlight. The figure was Rohb, doing his duty and guarding his princess. As the recognition filled me, it overcame the caution that had only barely held me in check.

I hopped over the wall and strode across the bridge, resisting the powerful urge to run. I was three steps away when she spoke.

"You are late," she said.

I stopped midstride. "I...," I managed.

"Here we were forced to sneak out from under the nose of the Imperial guard; the least you could do was be on time," she continued, still not turning around.

I stood still, somewhere between confusion and overwhelming disillusionment.

She spun toward me suddenly, with a smile so bright that it outshone the torches. "And I care so little about that because you're finally here," she said in a single burst, and all of a sudden, she was across the few steps between us and had pulled me to her. I'm ashamed to admit that it took me even the second it did to see that she had been teasing me, but realize it I did, and I returned the embrace as relief washed over me.

"Kelly," she said. She looked up at me, and then we were kissing, and the entire world fell away. In my mind, I took a journey through a whole life that had never been – one of home and hearth and family together – and only when my imaginary self had died, old and satisfied, did my mind return to the present. We broke the kiss, but not the embrace.

"Missed you," was all I could get out, and I felt her head nodding against my chest. Then, slowly, very slowly, and with great reluctance, we stepped back, our hands slipping into one another as if to allow us to separate no further.

"A-hem," came an entirely unconvincing cough from a bit behind me, and I remembered that I was not alone, nor was I the only one she needed to see. I unwillingly released her hands and turned, revealing Dana and Denis, who had by now followed me onto the bridge. There was a second's pause; then, I watched as one of my two best friends and the woman I love veritably lurched forward into one another's arms. I stepped back discretely next to Denis, watching them with a feeling of warmth.

"A-hem," Denis said again, after a while. The two women whispered something to one another and then separated, turning to face him.

"You saved the best for last, right princess?" he said, a lopsided grin on his face and his arms outstretched.

"Obviously, dungeon rat," Julea said, stepping in and hugging him as well, "we all know you were always my favorite."

"Just wanted to remind everyone," he said as they stepped apart.

I looked down the bridge, noting Rohb was now out of the shadows and watching from a distance. I waved to him to come down, even as I reflexively scanned the shadows for strangers. I reached out and clutched his forearm with my hand as he returned the gesture. With his other hand, he clapped my shoulder, and I had a vivid memory of what it felt like to be hit by him in anger.

"Thank you," I said quietly.

He knit his brows. I nodded toward Julea, and he grinned.

"Turns out the most danger she gets in is when you people are around," he said. I smiled, but I'm sure my wince was evident. Kidding or not, that was a little too close to the truth. In my mind, I saw the imaginary life that had been so vivid during our kiss blow away like sand in a windstorm.

Whether intentionally or not, Rohb let me have the moment and turned to greet Denis and Dana. I caught Julea's eye, and for a moment, we spoke to one another without words.

"So, are we going to have a reunion in the middle of a bridge?" Denis said after a few minutes.

We all looked at him. "Not many options," I said, "unless you have another idea? You have another idea."

A wicked grin I had seen countless times crossed his face. "Come along," he said, "and don't lag. You get left; you have to find your own way home, okay?"

He took off down the path at a brisk pace, heading west through the gardens.

"Oh," Julea said, watching him as he rapidly disappeared into the dark, "he meant it." With that, we all fell in behind and matched his pace.

We passed out of the park's boundaries and into the meandering streets of northwest Euticha. The buildings here were old, and while in good repair, it was evident even in the dim torchlight that this whole section had been here much longer than the foremost part of the city to the southeast. The streets, too, indicated the age of the area, as they followed no plan except for whatever the original settlers required, which was now lost to history. Some of them widened and narrowed with no apparent reason; others doubled back on themselves so that they nearly formed a loop. A number were no better than alleys where no more than one or two people could walk abreast. The result was that none of us had any idea where we were going, or how we got there when we did, or how to get back. Except for Denis. He seemed very confident and surefooted as he strode, stopping only if he saw members of the city guard or any other people still active in the middle of the night. It was, for him, an unconscious habit that was incredibly valuable just then.

"Where are we going?" I asked after we had walked some ways. I had stayed by Julea, as much from wanting to be near her as anything. But even I was beginning to wonder about this little trek of his.

"Here," he said, stopping abruptly in front of what appeared to be the unadorned outside wall of a closed apothecary.

"Here?" I said, the others now coming up to us.

"Well, almost here," he said. He pointed to a cellar door off to one side. "It's actually there."

"The basement?" Rohb said.

"Yep," he replied. He walked over confidently and pulled open wooden covers of the cellar to reveal a well-kept stairwell that led down to a very solid-looking wooden door. He started down the stairs but stopped halfway and looked back at us. "Well? Come on," he said, then disappeared down the remainder of the steps.

"Some things don't change, do they?" the princess

said. There was a kind of jubilance in her voice as she spoke, and that, more than anything, made me smile. *At least she's enjoying it*, I thought, *even if he might be getting us into trouble*. Again. There was nothing for it, of course, as suddenly Julea was following him into the darkened stairwell. Dana looked at me, and I shrugged at her. Then, with Rohb at our backs, we followed our friends into the shadows.

Standing on the narrow landing at the bottom, Denis stood and rapped a very carefully timed pattern on the door. There was a pause, then a small panel near the left side – so small and shaded that it hadn't been visible before – lifted inward to reveal a shaft of warm torchlight. Denis whispered to the portal. Again, there was a pause, and the feeling of eyes on us became tangible. The portal snapped shut, and with the hidden grinding of stone and steel, the door swung slowly inward.

"Hey, captain," Denis said over his shoulder to Rohb, "could you swing those outer doors shut? Great." He turned and walked into the pale reflected light from the open doorway. Julea glanced at me, took my hand, and together we followed him into a narrow wooden hallway lit from the far end. A few yards later, we stepped into the light.

The room before us was large and square, with a polished black stone floor and a dark green ceiling from which numerous lanterns hung, filling the room with a golden glow. The walls were paneled in two colors of wood, the bottom part darker and trimmed with matching frames, while the upper half was lighter and adorned with random pieces of art, weapons, tools, and other objects at random. Opposite the door we entered from, a green and wooden bar filled half of the back wall, behind which countless glass bottles crowded together on wooden shelves. Around the room, without any sense of order, were sets of chairs clustered around round black iron tables with wood tabletops. At the numerous of these where people were sitting, a glass-enclosed candle burned in the center. In the middle of the left side, a black stone hearth filled the middle of the wall from floor to ceiling. No fire burned in it then, but a black leather-covered couch and two matching chairs hinted at quiet fireside conversations. Opposite these, a small raised platform was occupied by a woman minstrel on a stool plucking a mandolin. Her music mingled with the background sound of quiet conversation from the twenty or so occupants.

"Denis," said a voice to my left, and I turned to see a tiny man coming from the passage behind us. I realized that he must have been the person inside the small portal Denis had spoken through. His shaved head came just barely higher than my waist, but his voice was deep and rasped like a handsaw on steel.

"Maggie!" Denis said, turning to the man. He threw

his arms out in a welcome gesture.

"Don't call me that," the other replied with a sneer. I looked closer, sure that he was gargling on nails or something. "You got nerves, boy," he continued.

Denis dropped his arms but not his smile. "Look, Magnus, I know it hasn't always been great between us—," he started.

"Stabbed me," Magnus said, jabbing a thumb at his right shoulder.

My friend cocked his head and gave a wry look, "Did I, though? I mean, from a certain viewpoint, we were both at fault," he said.

Magnus took a step forward, his hand reaching toward the sword at his belt. I tensed, instinctively calculating distances and arcs if I had to draw my blade. Denis took a quick backward step and put his hands up in front of him as if to ward off the doorkeeper. I couldn't help noticing that the gesture also put his hands near the hilts of his twin daggers.

"Now, now," he said, "we called bygones on that."

"Enough," came a woman's voice from the far end of the room. I turned, noticing peripherally that Julea had taken a step back from me so as not to get in my way should there be action. Behind the bar, a huge grey-haired woman stood looking intently in our direction. At the sound, Magnus stopped and stepped back, his hand dropping from his sword's hilt. Then, with a bow of his head, he turned and disappeared past us and back into the entry hall. The woman was still glaring at us, or, more specifically, at Denis.

"Grab a table," Denis said with a casual grin, "I'll be right along." He turned and walked off toward the bar.

"At least it's not forest bandits," Dana muttered loud enough to send a giggle through Julea.

"I am not sure I know what you're talking about," I deadpanned. My mind flashed briefly on our banquet in the Aosta forest, and I grinned at them both. Julea squeezed my arm.

I looked around the room, taking in as much as I could of the wide variety of patrons. I walked toward the far side of the room with an idea to be close to the hearth. It was more of a preference of mine than a practical decision, especially on a warm night. On the other hand, the room benefited from being below ground, and the air was cool. We passed a table where two women sat working on a large pitcher of wine. They were both around the same age, maybe ten years beyond me, but there the similarities ended. The first sat with a kind of regal elegance, dressed in finery and sipping wine from her silver cup daintily. She eyed the group of us as we went past in the way of the high-born. Seated to her left, the other woman was crouched over her drink, a threadbare cloak on her shoulders and her head low. Just as we passed, the second woman reached out and took the hand of the first. I turned away, giving them their privacy, and looked around the room more, now clearly seeing that the variety I had initially noticed was outstripped by the pairings and groupings of people of unmatched station. The room was filled, actually, with what could only be called secret rendezvous.

Shortly, we found a table near the hearth, far enough from the minstrel to talk without competing with the music. We had a minute to settle when Denis returned, carrying a platter that held five mugs and a wooden board of bread and cheese. This he sat in the middle of the table before taking his seat opposite Julea and me.

"Here we are," he said with a contented sigh, "I think the wine's pretty good, but I've never had anything they serve at the big fancy palaces, so I'm sorry if it's not up to that standard."

Julea smiled at him as we all took one of the mugs. Denis made to take a sip but stopped when he noticed Rohb and I were watching Julea. He put his cup down and smiled at her. She took the tiniest sip of the wine, then gave us a nod. We nodded back and took a drink. I saw Dana wince almost imperceptibly.

Rohb, who had already broken a chunk of the bread off and taken a slice of the cheese, looked over at Denis. "So, what's this place, and how do they know you?" he said between swallows.

Denis, a piece of bread in his mouth too, spoke between bites. "Not my first time in this town, captain," he said, "and this place is..., well..., it's a place where you go when you aren't looking to be found. A neutral ground, if you take me."

"You've needed a neutral ground before, have you?" Julea said with a wink.

"Who doesn't, Your Highness-ness?" Denis said with a knowing grin.

Julea looked at Dana and me, and reality threatened our thoughts.

"Indeed," she said.

"Drink up!" Denis said, the two words dispelling the pallor in our minds. A riotous discussion began then, with each of us overtalking one another, telling stories of the previous three years. Julea told us about her ongoing training with her mother while we shared the sights and sounds of our travels. Eventually, the conversation waned somewhat, more from weariness than from a lack of content. The princess leaned in a bit during one long pause, casting a look from Dana on her left to me on her right.

"I, I just can't believe you're here. I'm so happy to see you. So you're both..., well?" she asked.

Dana and I looked at one another and silently decided that she would answer. "We're good, Jules. We have so many stories, and sure, there have been bumps in our road," at this, she shot me a glance, “but we are good.”

“Don’t worry, I keep an eye on ‘em,” Denis added.

Julea smiled at him, then turned to me. “I guess I’m asking about your..., er..., care?” She looked uncomfortably back and forth between us. “I mean, physically? It can’t always be easy to get the—, let’s call them supplies. The ones you need.”

“You mean the gems,” Dana said.

Julea shrugged uncomfortably. The subject was certainly not a new one to her, but it remained uncomfortable all the same. It made sense, I knew; the gems had changed her life almost as much as they had ours. Finally, after a hesitation, she said, “Yes. It’s been on my mind so many times. I know that you – that you both – need them to survive.”

I nodded, reinforcing the truth that she well knew – without an occasional treatment with the uncanny gemstones, neither Dana nor I would long evade the deaths we had each cheated years before.

“So how do you make sure you have them? I mean, how do you...?” she trailed off, waving her hand absently as if she wasn’t entirely sure what she was asking. I waited politely while she regrouped her thoughts. “The gemstones– they’re so incalculably rare. I know how much effort has been spent to find a supply of them. God’s teeth, I know better than anyone. How many can you have with you? Where do you get what you need? What happens to you when you can't find anymore?" she said, the questions tumbling out of her like a wave that had finally overwhelmed a seawall.

Dana looked at me. A pause followed, filled only by the sound of the mandolin music and the distant rumblings of conversations in the room. It had become, without intention, a telling moment. Here was another secret – one she and I both held – and she was watching me, waiting to see what I would do. I looked at the faces around the table as I thought about the conversation we'd had by the fire in Grechville. The commitment to honesty I had made. I thought about the danger of it all as well. Habit does not quickly retreat; oaths be damned. But ultimately, there was no real contest.

"We grow them," I said, keeping my voice quiet and holding Dana's gaze for a heartbeat before looking back to Julea. I put a piece of cheese in my mouth as if to punctuate the statement.

There was a long pause. Denis's mug made a 'clunk' sound on the table as his hand dropped.

"Damn," said Rohb.

"Wow," Denis said, "I really wasn't sure you were going to say it."

Dana looked at him. "*You* knew?" she said with her eyes wide.

He shrugged.

"Wait," Julea said, her mind catching up through the shock, "you *grow* them?"

"Yes," I said, "the blue and yellow crystals are grown; they form in a special mixture the hermits taught me to make. And I taught Dana."

Dana was looking at Denis. "How did you know?" she asked.

"I pay attention, Day. That's my whole trick," he said.

"But...," Julea said, looking intently at me now. I could see a million questions crowding around her mind, wrestling to see which would come out first. I decided it would be best to help.

"Only the Kelian emeralds are formed naturally," I said, "No one can say for sure how or where they first came from, but they are mined just like any stone. From studying them, though, the hermits that saved me learned to make – grow – similar stones. Less powerful, and with different properties, but very similar in makeup. The blue and yellow ones are examples. Their unique feature is that they bond with living things."

"And keep them – I mean us – alive," Dana said, finishing the wine in her mug.

I continued, "There are other colors; actually, almost any color you can think of; and they all have some exceptional quality. And, of course, the emeralds are unique. Natural, powerful, and unique."

Julea looked from me to Dana and back. I watched her as her mind went through all the implications of what we had said.

"That," she said finally, "might be one of the most terrifying things I can imagine."

Dana put her hand on the princess's arm. "It is. It's the doorway to everything Kelly's tried to keep secret all this time. Everything your mother doesn't accept."

I noticed Dana referred to Ardallah as 'your mother' rather than 'empress' or even 'Her Imperial Majesty.' It was significant, and it spoke to how upended her life had been since the day in the black ship when the gems brought her back from death. A moment passed, then while still looking down at the table, Julea rolled her arm over and slid it back toward her body until she could take Dana's hand in her own. She reached over with her other hand and took mine. "I understand," she said, "and as far as I can control, your secret dies with the five of us here."

Denis took a loud swallow and set his now empty mug down. He looked over at her and said, "That's great. But can we just say we're keeping it secret? No need to get so melodramatic, okay?"

The princess gave him a stern look but let it soften as he held her gaze with a sincerity that his lopsided grin only barely concealed.

"Great," he said with a relieved sigh, "I'm going to get

the next round." He grabbed the empty mugs and stalked off toward the bar.

We had four hours.

We stayed at that table into the night, and my princess scarcely let go of my hand the entire time. The stories continued, though perhaps more sequentially, and Rohb and Denis were now, possibly with the help of the wine that never seemed to stop coming, providing background commentary on the tales we told, smoothing out details except where there was laughter to be mined. Little by little, the room got quieter as the other occupants made their way out into the night. The minstrel stayed far longer than I expect she would have, save that Denis dropped a small cloth bag of coin on the stage the first time she looked like she meant to leave. But eventually, she did the calculation of how much time he had bought and decided that it was enough.

Four hours.

We stepped out of the dark stairwell and into the dark street by the apothecary. The torches were all out, save for the distant glow of the city's night guardsmen. We followed Denis through the winding roads back southward toward the city proper. Julea was walking with Dana now, their arms entwined and whispered secrets passing between them in the waning moments that remained to them. I felt a wistful smile on my face as I watched them through the shadows. Then, after navigating the labyrinthine streets for what felt like both forever and only a fleeting moment at the same time, we came out to a pathway that ran along the river and back toward the gardens. Here, half of the torches remained lit for the sake of the guard, their light glittering off the river's surface like stars above in the blackness. Abruptly we stopped. I looked around, instinctively alert, but there wasn't a threat to be seen. Instead, Rohb and Denis were now standing a few feet away. Dana, who had broken free from her friend, was walking over to them, leaving us behind. She looked over her shoulder at me with a gentle smile. I turned back to find Julea, now alone and facing me. An unbidden smile settled on my face, and I walked over to her.

"Princess," I said.

"Kelly," she said back, stepping in and putting her hands on my shoulders. She looked up at me, and even in the darkness, her green eyes seemed to glitter.

I jerked my head slightly toward our friends, now several feet away and affording us a private moment. "Did you do that?" I asked.

She smiled broadly, "Dear sir! What kind of lady do you think I am?"

I grinned.

"No, never mind," she said quickly, "I believe you already know." I felt her suppress a giggle. "But no, actually," she continued, looking back up at me, "I had nothing to do with that. It seems like our friends wished to give us some privacy."

"They are just the best," I said. I glanced over at the little group and then back to her. She was watching the three with a thoughtful expression on her face.

"They truly are," she said solemnly. The emotion suddenly fell over us like a blanket, and we turned and walked along the river walk, one arm still wrapped around one another, afraid to let go.

"Dana loves you two," she said after a silence, keeping the subject but shifting the focus. "she's quite very fond of the dungeon rat."

"Well, he grows on you," I said.

"Like moss?"

"No," I chuckled, "not like moss. I mean, he's..., he's not what you expect."

She squeezed me a little at that, chuckling. "But you knew, somehow," she said.

I shrugged. "Somehow, I guess. I can't fully explain it."

"Dana says that about you," Julea said.

I nodded, looking up toward my friends. "It's true. Sometimes you meet people, and it's like you're finding a piece of yourself. Or maybe a piece that just perfectly fits your piece. I don't know. That's as close as I can get to putting words to it," I said.

I looked back to see that she was looking down, an unreadable expression on her face. “Jules,” I said, “I don’t—,”

“It’s okay, Kelly,” she said. She looked up at me, her eyes bright. “I’m sorry. I’m not angry or sad about it; really, I’m not. There’s nothing better than that you three have found a...,” she paused a second, “a family together. I only want you to be happy. I just..., I just wish I could be part of it.” Her head dropped against my chest, and we slowed our pace.

“You are, Jules,” I said. I knew the words were hollow, but she needed to understand, and more words kept coming. “Dana sees you as a sister, stupid class distinctions be damned. Denis has mentioned a conversation he had with you on Edword’s ship a few times,” I said.

A sad smile grew on her face. “Ah, I remember. It was right after you explained that I couldn’t bring my best friend home after all,” she said.

“Well,” I continued, “all I know is that you are a constant in our lives, even while we’re apart. In some ways, you’re the axis of our little band.”

“Cold comfort, Blackcrow,” she said, her voice somewhat flat.

I nodded. “Point taken,” I said.

We walked in silence for a while. Julea pulled in tighter as we walked until finally, we stopped and fell into a full embrace. We stood like that for a long time. The memory of the kiss and the imaginary life from earlier flew back through my mind.

"You," I said, my voice thick with emotion that a gentle cough didn't seem to dispel, "need to find more reasons to come to neutral ground."

"Like Denis's underground pub?" she said with a sly grin.

"Like Euticha," I said, "at least not everyone is hunting me here."

She looked up at me then, her face full of emotion.

"I will," she said.

We tumbled into another kiss then, trying with all our might to brush away the truth of our lives and to believe, just for a moment, that it was possible.

We walked up to where our friends had been awaiting us further down the path and resumed walking together toward the Etherian Gardens, our arms still wrapped around one another. Julea reached out and took Dana's hand as we approached, and so we walked in a cluster toward the still dimly lit pathways of the garden, talking quietly among ourselves.

I can only say, concerning what happened next, that I know I should have been more careful, more alert. Caution and forethought are sort of the stock in trade of the life my companions and I lead, and letting my guard down is all but inexcusable. Right then, however, surrounded by my friends with the princess by my side, the garden could have been on fire, and I might not have noticed. To some degree or another, we were all distracted. And that, as it turns out, was to cost us dearly.

I only noticed the movement after the rustling sound from the shrubbery became so apparent that I looked around. A contingent of Eutichan soldiers, armed and armored and brandishing their weapons, swarmed out of the shadows and surrounded us. I turned and stepped out, placing Julea behind me and by Dana. My sword was half out of its sheath when a calm, clear voice spoke from directly in front of us.

"I would rather no one is hurt, good sir," the voice said, "and I assure you that if you draw that blade, there will be blood." A figure stepped forth from the crowd of soldiers, his own curved blade in a relaxed guard position before him.

"Back, devil," Rohb snarled, his hand on his axe. He and Denis had stepped to either side of the path in front of us. We now formed a kind of triangle with Dana behind us all and Julea and me in the middle.

"Captain," Julea said, her tone more a command than a request. I saw his stance shift to one less aggressive as if by reflex at her words. Denis's hands were on his chest, lightly resting on the wicked blades he kept there but not drawing them. I took the princess's direction and eased my sword back into its sheath.

The man with the curved blade seemed to relax slightly, and his sword drooped as he stood up straight. He was about my height and more heavily built if it was possible to guess his shape beneath the full suit of armor he wore. Over the silver steel, a banner hung from one shoulder across him and was cinched at his belt, white and bearing a four-pointed star on a circle in dark gray stitching that seemed to glitter in the torchlight. He had short-cropped light brown hair and a carefully groomed mustache and beard encircling his mouth. He bowed his head respectfully but never took his eyes from us.

"I am Captain Nicholas Andwen, Head of the Eutichan Guard, and you are bound by law," he said. There was no anger or malice in his voice, rather the cool dispassion of a professional at work.

"Captain—," I began, only to be cut short as Julea stepped in front of me.

"Good evening, captain. I am Princess Julea Niconnel of Yorch. Obviously, there has been some misunderstanding," she said, looking at him squarely. I noticed her subtly straighten as she spoke, pulling her shoulders back and her head up.

The captain looked back at her without levelly. "If we're to be accurate, ma'am, it would be 'good morning,' as the night has nearly passed us. And no, there's no mistake here. I have instructions to bring you back to the palace as well as to bind your companions, as I just said. I was also to be ready for resistance. Yet I believe," and here he turned his attention to me, "that we can proceed without unpleasantness, particularly to anyone who doesn't have the tools to protect themselves." The veiled threat was clear, and I wondered at it. Of all the things I might have expected Ardallah to do, putting her daughter in danger – even potentially – would never have occurred to me. The captain and I gazed at one another for a long moment, during which I heard Julea again.

"I am, as I am certain you know, a guest in your city," she said, pulling up a haughtiness that could only have come from her mother, "and I will see to it that this—, this fiasco you've visited on me, my guard, and our companions shall sit charged to your account."

Without looking, Andwen said, "I am sure you will make yourself known, ma'am. But what happens next is very much up to your associates here."

I felt the gazes of Denis and Rohb as they stole glances in my direction. The quiet 'scritch' of metal on metal came from Dana's location behind me, the familiar sound of her rapier against the upper lip of its sheath as she held it ready. We stood on a geyser, one ready to blow with only a word from me. I felt the buzzing on the back of my neck as my war nerves clicked into action. I took a breath, glanced at Julea by my side, and made a decision.

"Okay, captain," I said, lifting my hands in a gesture of surrender. "We'll accompany you back to the palace, where I'm sure we can sort this out like civilized people."

I could hear Denis in my head screaming something about that being as likely as one of us giving birth to the next First Abbot of the Church of the One. I pushed what very literally felt like his actual thoughts out of my mind and lifted off the baldric that held my sword, wound it around the blade and scabbard, and handed it to the soldier that had come over to take it. The same was done for the others, though the soldier assigned to carry Rohb's axe very much seemed like he got the worst of it. He hoisted the giant weapon onto his shoulder finally, where he bore the weight on his armored pauldron. The soldiers formed up around us, and we followed Andwen back south through the city, toward the palace and toward destiny.

We were marched through the darkened streets of Euticha, but not, as I expected, toward the castle. Instead, we followed the main roads toward the water and to the south end of the waterfront. There, we passed up a slight rise to an imposing stone building that stood aside from the waterfront, looking down on the docks. It consisted of a square of four towers, each three or four stories tall, interconnected by lower sections of only two floors. The approach took us up a flight of a dozen stone stairs into a central courtyard, then finally to the tower to the left side in the rear of the building – the tallest of the four. Even in the dim light, I could see the various paraphernalia that told me that the courtyard was commonly used for training and that the towers and buildings around us served to house much of the city guard during their shift. As we walked, Denis, who was to my right, had unmistakably noticed it as well, and his shadowed face glared at me with reproach. I couldn't say that I didn't deserve it, as many, many more soldiers now likely surrounded us than we had been, and our chances of an escape seemed to be shrinking by the moment. Once our escort ushered us into the tower, we climbed three flights of stairs, putting us on the uppermost floor of the structure when we finally came to our destination.

The stone chamber we came into was large, and I estimated that it was most of the entire space of the tower's floor. Above our heads, wooden arches crisscrossed a high plastered ceiling. They came down the walls to about a man's height from the floor, where they met heavy wooden paneling that encircled the room. Large, glass-enclosed torchlights were mounted on the wall every two or three panels, making the room bright enough that my eyes – after the long walk in the dark – took a moment to adjust. The floor was of the same grey stone as the building itself, though more well-polished. Several wooden benches were placed symmetrically around the room's perimeter, focusing attention on a small, dark wood platform at the far end opposite the door. The platform was vacant save for a single solidly-built wooden chair with a high back. Above this, large windows looked out toward the dark ocean outside. The guards walked with us until we stood before the high-backed chair, then they backed away toward the walls, leaving the five of us to stand alone.

"Our things are over there," Dana whispered, flicking her eyes to the left side wall of the room, and I turned my head nonchalantly around, noting the bundle that now sat on the floor near the corner. I looked back at her and nodded slightly.

Julea's eyes darted back and forth between us, then she whispered, "What are you two planning?"

Denis, just behind her, whispered back, "Nothing yet. We just like to know our options."

One of the wooden panels on the left wall opened, revealing it to be a hidden door. A moment later, accompanied by six soldiers in white and red, the Empress of Yorch entered the room. She wore her customary white and gold, of course, and despite it being deep in the middle of the night, she looked completely at ease and composed. It annoyed me intensely, as I was becoming keenly aware of the fact that none of us had slept in quite some time. Around her shoulders was draped a cape of deep scarlet trimmed with the same gold as her dress. She walked forward without haste and stepped up onto the platform, placed herself before the chair, and finally turned to us. Her alabaster skin had no hint of emotion – good or ill – as she looked at the five of us.

"That's the empress?" Denis muttered, receiving a subtle tap from Dana for his trouble. Julea and Dana bowed while Rohb dropped to one knee. I stood very still. Denis, who was unlikely to have acknowledged her anyway, folded his arms across his chest.

"Captain," the empress said to one of the six guards who were now equidistantly spaced around the platform, "escort our daughter back to her quarters."

The soldier at her right immediately turned and took a step toward us.

"Stop," Julea said. Her voice was clear, calm, and easily as commanding as her mother's had been. More from surprise than anything, the captain paused midstride. "Your Imperial Highness," my princess continued, her voice still steely and calm, "I will remain here. I do not know what matters you are seeking to address with these people, but they are my friends, and I will hear the proceedings."

The soldier stood very still, and part of me felt a little bad for him—a little.

The empress glared at Julea, who placidly returned the look. The stare went on for what felt like a long, uncomfortable time before finally, they turned away. I can't say for sure which one flinched first, but I know I was incredibly proud just then.

"Very well," Ardallah said, affecting a weary sigh as if she were conceding the point because it was beneath her. Then she continued, "It is just as well that you hear our judgment of these individuals. You should learn how to deal with such things." She took a step forward, straightening her back as she did so. Preparing for the performance.

"Rohb O'Laird, your service is no longer required by the throne. All Imperial status is henceforth rescinded. All rights to Imperial property or privileges are revoked. You will be left here in Euticha to find your way to wherever you choose."

I looked back at Rohb. He remained on his knee, looking up at her until she finished speaking. His face remained impassive, and then he did the one thing he could do. He stood up and folded his arms across his chest.

The empress turned just a tiny amount to her right, and in that single gesture, dismissed him from her attention. She looked at Dana. "Lady Dana Lunavale bar Donnara, you have chosen to cast your lot in with a known traitor to the throne. These acts are treason, and your life is forfeit."

Julea convulsed so violently that I thought she might leap straight onto the platform. "Mother!" she yelled.

Ardallah stood unmoving, though I saw her eyes dart

for an instant to her daughter. Suddenly I realized – this was part of her game. She wanted Julea to react, to feel emotion so that she could manipulate her. I wondered which of her goals was more significant – throwing a leash on Jules or having revenge on us. Well…, me.

"However," the empress said, "because of your long service and your deep connection to our household, we commute your sentence. You are banished from the empire and stripped of your lands and rank."

The last came like a physical blow, and I saw in my mind the silver medallion that Dana constantly wore, the one that represented her status as a Silver Spar. The honor and respect of the empire, all in a single bit of jewelry. It mattered to her. Ardallah was taking from her part of herself. But Dana stood— still and silent.

Ardallah looked away from her, dismissing her as well. Her eyes turned now to me. A humorless grin came onto her face.

"Blackcrow," she said, "We judge that you are to be executed."

Julea leaned into me, her hand suddenly on my arm.

"It is clear that our mercy in exiling you was in error," she continued, "your existence has infected our court with disloyalty and rebellion in every corner. Even our own daughter has defied us. This cannot be allowed to stand."

"Wait," Denis's voice came suddenly from behind me.

He walked around Dana and stopped in front of me, just to one side. He continued, “What in all the hells is going on right now?”

Ardallah looked at him, her eyes narrowing for a moment. Her eyebrows went up, and she said, “Ah. You must be the gutter trash that has—,”

“It’s ‘dungeon rat,’” Denis said, cutting her off for what may have been the first time in her adult life. He looked back and forth around the room. “And nobody has answered my question yet. What is this garbage? This crone goes off on everyone like she’s the return of the One, and everyone just lets it happen?” He turned to look at her.

I heard an audible gasp from Rohb at the word ‘crone,’ but I had no time to react. Denis was still talking.

“Hell’s bells. This man you call ‘Blackcrow’ saved your daughter’s life. And he did it because they love one another, not because of you, lady. These,” he swept his hands around in our general direction, “These are some of the best people I’ve ever known, and maybe the best anywhere. From what I can tell, nobody’s saying that about you until you threaten them. Where do you come off all up on your pedestal?”

Ardallah could not have been more outraged if he had physically struck her. She stared at him with her mouth agape, the biting tongue that usually came so quickly to her dormant. He glared steadily at her, his question hanging in the air.

"I am the empress of Yorch!" she spat out without any of her usual eloquence.

Denis rolled his head dismissively, "Oh, whoopie," he said, "that buys you nothing."

Before I could react – before anyone could react – he lunged forward. The soldier she had called captain a moment before belatedly threw himself in my friend's path to grab him. Denis's move was a feint, though, and the captain found only thin air as Denis pivoted on his back foot at the last moment and flowed around the man. In another step, he was on the platform, an arm's reach away from Ardallah.

"Who's above who now?" he said, a fierce growl in his voice. There was a look on the empress's face I had never seen. Fear. A personal kind of dread that it was very likely she had never experienced before.

"Den," I said, keeping my voice steady. It pulled both his and Ardallah's gaze to me. "Stand down. This isn't the way," I said calmly. He glared at me, his anger so high that I wasn't entirely sure he understood what I was saying. Two of the other guards, now shaken out of their shock, seized the opportunity and lurched forward. In seconds had him by both arms and were pulling him away from the platform. They retreated to the far side of the room.

"Empress," I said, words now coming to me that hadn't been there moments before, "as I understand the law, you have no authority to take me into custody in a free state."

I waved my hand around at the chamber as I continued, "I believe Euticha is just such a state."

Ardallah, who had recovered much of herself now, turned and faced me. "That was true hours ago, Blackcrow. It is no longer," she said, waving her hand toward the door from which she had come. Lord Anthony Westfall stepped out and bowed his head to her.

I felt my stomach wrench as Westfall moved to the side and watched the unfolding situation placidly. I stared at him, waiting for any hope that what seemed to be happening – that Euticha had become a political ally of Yorch and forsaken its neutral stance – was not the truth. I cast around, first to Dana, then Rohb, then Julea, and finally back to Ardallah. There I found a cold humorless smile that didn't touch her eyes.

"Wait," I heard my voice say, sounding in my ears as though it was coming over a vast chasm. I struggled to control my breathing, which suddenly felt labored. I felt eyes turn to me, and I was vaguely aware that Julea had stepped toward me. I held the empress's stare, every nerve in my body screaming to react. In our travels, my friends and I had faced death and worse on more than one occasion, but somehow this; facing the ruler that I had once served; wrenched me to my very core.

"If that is your decision, then there's no reason to punish Rohb and Lady Dana," I said finally, "as I will no longer be an 'infection' to you." In the back of my head, there was a voice screaming something that I couldn't quite make out through the cloud of emotion and stress. But somehow, I could feel that it was essential, and the voice grew louder and louder in my mind with each moment.

Ardallah made a casual brushing motion with her left hand. "You are in no position to bargain, Blackcrow."

"I am," Julea said suddenly, taking a step forward so that she was now directly beside me. She stared intently at the empress and spoke, her voice as steady and potent as I'd ever heard it. "I am the heir to the throne. But, more, I am your flesh and blood. *I* ask for clemency for all of these people. It is reason enough that they have saved my life in the past. But also because the simple truth is that they are my friends."

"Woo!" came a cheer from the far corner of the room as Denis expressed his thoughts.

Ardallah looked at her daughter with a veiled expression of frustration and disappointment. I looked at Julea, noticing as I did that the Eutichan soldiers were now grouped very close around the three of us still before the platform. It was clear that Denis's bravado had put them on alert. Nevertheless, the princess stood as calm and unwavering as I'd ever seen her as she and her mother stared one another down.

"Mercy has always been a weakness of ours," Ardallah

said finally, still looking at the princess. "Very well. We hereby restore the rank of both Dana Lunavale and Rohb O'Laird. Both will return with us to Yorch and receive new assignments under our master of the army." She turned back to me, a snarl of a grin on her lips, "But the sentence of death remains on the Blackcrow. He is too dangerous to live, regardless of your compassion, daughter."

Julea's hand was suddenly on my arm, and I saw her look over at Dana. My imminent death was bad – especially from my viewpoint – but Dana's return to the empire was a more significant issue. The secret of the gem lore was once again in jeopardy.

Whether it was the touch of her hand, her confident confrontation with her mother, or even Denis's shouted cheer, something quieted the riot of thoughts in my mind, and the loud voice in the back became suddenly clear.

"Guard," Ardallah was saying, "bind the Blackcrow and escort him to the *Fenris* where—,"

"How did you ally with Euticha so quickly?" I said, cutting her off. It was the second time in the brief meeting it had happened and no less of a shock to her than when Denis had done it. She glared at me, but I pressed on, the truth suddenly obvious. "It wasn't quick, though, was it? You didn't negotiate an allegiance with Euticha in an afternoon; you've been in contact with Lord Westfall before this, haven't you?"

Her glare was steady. I cast a fleeting glance over to where Westfall stood, his head low and eyes averted.

"This was a trap the whole time," I said, "and you used your daughter as bait to get to us, didn't you?" My nerves were coalescing into white-hot fury. A fury that lay like a lump in the middle of my chest. She stared back at me, not one muscle in her face changing.

"And you don't even deny it," I said coldly, the anger now a tangible thing growing inside me.

"Mother?" Julea said, her voice almost a plea as if she was looking for any reason that what I'd said wasn't the truth.

Ardallah looked at her, and for a moment, I wasn't sure what she would say. But she was Ardallah, and she was the empress, and I should have known better.

"Of course, I don't deny it," she said, looking at her daughter with the same cold eyes that had cowed nations, "I do all things for the sake of Yorch. And dealing with traitors is imperial business."

Julea opened her mouth, but no words came out. I wanted to take her in my arms and run, but I was clear-thinking enough to know that any move I made would be like throwing dry tinder on a fire, so I simply reached out and retook her hand.

We froze in a tableau, a moment lasting a lifetime as loyalties and family ties were pulled and shattered, as realities poured in and doused fantasies of patriotism and maternal love. I don't know how long it lasted, and in truth, it may have continued on longer except for the noise.

In the midst of this, we heard a sound. Denis probably noticed it first from his vantage point off to the side, but soon we all heard it. Steel on steel; it was the sound of metal being twisted and stretched to its limits and beyond, and finally a cold, echoing snap. The doors swung open, and a swarm of black and red-clad figures swept into the room, quickly outnumbering Westfall's men. The Eutichans, now alerted, spun and drew their blades while the so-called 'Wolfpack' jumped up onto the platform and formed a barricade around Ardallah. Dana moved over next to me, positioning herself in front of Julea while Rohb moved to the other side. For a moment, no one moved. Then, from the darkened hallway, a throaty laugh echoed into us, punctuated by a quiet clockwork whirring. A figure entered the room, stopping just inside the door.

"Splendid. You're all exactly where I placed you," said Willm Steinhargh as he surveyed the room.

"Steelclaw," Rohb muttered.

CHAPTER FIVE

— DENIS —

I don't think of myself as someone that gets rattled easily. I mean, there have been times, of course. Kelly, Dana, and I have been pretty close to our last play in the great game a few times, and that sort of thing would make anyone's blood rush a bit faster. As far as just being generally shaken without the imminent threat of death, though, that's not usually my nature. And yes, granted, my best friend had just been condemned to death, so that might have taken me a little off my feet, but it was what happened next as the door of the courtroom crashed open that really turned my blood to ice.

The two imperials that dragged me away from Her Awfulness had – we'll call it 'escorted' – me off to the far-left side of the room and back in the corner, such that I was opposite the hidden door where they had entered originally. Here, a good portion of the goings-on with my friends was hidden from me by the other imperials and the Eutichan guardsmen. Still, I heard clearly the sentence handed down on Kelly, Julea's challenge, and even saw Westfall's entrance deflate the legal defense that I could see Kelly had been leaning on. Then we heard the sound of metal twisting against itself before the doors burst open, a crowd of Kathasiri assassins rushed in, and with them, my ancient past returned to haunt me. Ghostly visions swam into sight, unlocked from the graveyard in the back of my mind like hungry revenants.

A small village. Chaos. Everywhere, the smell of blood and death. A child sits beside two still forms. Distant screams fill its ears, louder even than its own cries. It paws at the closest of the bodies, but there's no response. Then, suddenly, an arm covered in rough black cloth seizes it from somewhere above, and then all is blurred motion and unintelligible noise. The vision shifts.

A young boy stands in a field, a small knife in his hand. He's wearing only a modest cloth around his waist, and he has been shaved bald. Some distance away, a man shouts in a language that is still mysterious to him, and a panther appears from the depths of a wooden crate, thin and with the alert eyes of a predator. It is enormous, nearly as big as the boy, and it sees him immediately. It prowls forward, stalking the child that is fighting desperately to stand ready, to hold back the nervous shivering that even now is threatening to leave him defenseless. To make him run. The cat lunges, and they come together in a struggle that will leave only one of them alive. Blurry moments later, the boy stands, smeared with blood, only most of which is not his own.

Years drop by, and another scene resolves. The boy is now a man in all but name. He wears black robes bound by a single black sash, and he's crouching behind a dense, impenetrable curtain. The small knife has been replaced by a short dagger that he holds expertly in his off hand. In the room beyond, a man enters, and a vicious smile crosses the boy's face. He readies the blade in his hand and creeps out to fulfill his mission. No sound is heard. Glory is achieved.

Again, the scene shifts, and again, it is night. Now there are men around him. Hundreds of men, dressed in black with red sashes across their chests and around their waists, are watching him silently. In a grand ceremony, a figure in red robes and a black leather mask hands him a sword that is not a sword and a red sash of his own. There is chanting as he puts the red cloth around himself and pulls the folds of his black tunic up, hiding his face. Then, he and the crowd of assassins turn toward an obsidian statue of a cloaked woman holding a ragged blade, not unlike each of theirs.

"Kathas," they chant. And he chants too.

When I finally got back to myself, the band of assassins was flowing out from the door and around the perimeter of the room, moving more like a flood of black and red water than men. As was the rule, they were indistinguishable from one another, each wearing the folded black linen that disguised their faces and hid the leather underlayer that served as their armor. The *lintus sanguis*, or the blood wrap, wound once across each one's torso and once around their waist, jarringly crimson against the black uniform. There was no mistake; death had swept into the room, and I knew it better than anyone.

The two imperials at my side were suddenly thoroughly disinterested in me. They had moved the instant the invaders appeared – while I was still lost in the past – advancing with their blades already drawn. I couldn't say if they were heading to reach the empress or engage the newcomers, but it didn't matter. They got no further than two steps before tiny black darts – fired by the nearest assassins from handheld blowguns – embedded themselves between pieces of armor that were very poorly designed for dealing with such weapons. The imperials spasmed, dropping their swords and clutching at their steel-enshrouded faces. In a moment, they were on the ground, twitching senselessly before going ultimately still.

Instinctively, I made a gurgling sound, clutched at my throat, and fell to the floor, twitching as convincingly as I could manage. I couldn't see any way for the fast-moving attackers to be keeping track of who shot who, so I just hoped each would assume someone else had killed me. With one last convulsion, one that positioned me in a way that I could watch the room, I lay still. It was from there I watched as Willm Steinhargh strode in.

Kelly and I had talked on several occasions over the years about returning north of the Superior Mountains to find out the fate of the fake king we had faced together. Stories of the harassing of his shipping by the *Midnight Wind* had reached us, but then all news of the north, or 'Sargeaux' as it was now named, seemed to dry up. Even from Kelly's sources went quiet, though I'm sure it was through them that he had learned the blaggard's proper name and the name he'd given his kingdom. Seeing him now, though, I couldn't help but think that the years had been less than kind. Not in his kit, of course; he wore ornate dark-steel armor, polished and trimmed at every joint and edge with brass or copper. A gold-trimmed black cloak hung over his left side, and a black and gold crown topped his head. His face, however, was gaunt, and darkness encircled his sunken eyes, though they still opened just a little bit too far, giving him a froglike look. His beard, now long enough to reach the upper part of his breastplate, was shot through with gray streaks, matching those in the hair that hung loose and untamed around his face. It was his right arm, though, that really commanded attention. Of course, we had heard stories of it as it was the source of his *nom de guerre*. Seeing it in person was something else entirely. Starting in the middle of his upper right arm came a brass and steel mechanism vaguely in the shape of a thick human arm. Big metal joints stuck out where both the elbow and wrist should be, and at the end was a misshapen hand-shaped contraption. The entire thing was punctuated with small vents that belched little puffs of steam intermittently and glass-covered ports through which tiny gearing and cables could be seen. A large window in the middle of the 'forearm' gave off a yellowish-orange light that flickered like a candle in a breeze with every gesture he made.

"Steelclaw," I heard Rohb say after he announced himself. I held back the snort of laughter that caught me by surprise— such a stupid name.

"Empress Ardallah," Steinhargh said, ignoring the Talhas, "I am pleased to see you face to face finally."

"Stand back," one of the Eutichan soldiers said, brandishing his sword. *Brave*, I thought, *but also stupid. Brave and stupid.*

Steinhargh looked at him. The distance made it difficult to tell whether he was impressed or annoyed, but after a moment, he glanced back over his shoulder toward the door. "Master Pwent," he shouted. Through the doors came a short, squat man whose beard and hairline were only separated by the narrow gap where his beady eyes looked out. He strode confidently past the crowd of assassins to stand next to Steinhargh.

"Stand down," he said to the Eutichan guards. "This is my order. Put your weapons away."

I think I mentioned earlier something about my blood running cold. Well, as I watched the Eutichans – in confusion at first, but with more conviction as more of them complied – replace their blades into their sheaths and relax their guard, that same feeling came back again. To be fair, I wasn't convinced they would have been that helpful against the Kathasiri, but at least it might have slowed the assassins down to have a few more people to kill. Now, there was no friction left. I chanced a glance down to where my feet had landed after my theatrical 'death.' It turned out that my feet were very close to the spot where our equipment lay in a heap. Our weapons were further back in the mound, too far to reach, but my foot was laying on the strap of a brown leather satchel. Dana's crystal supply satchel.

I eased my eyes back up to the encounter in the middle of the room, hoping no one had noticed my tiny movement. The confrontation there had continued unabated; no one paid any attention to poor dead me.

"—your master!" Ardallah's voice was saying.

"Don't be foolish, empress," Steinhargh said, "Master Pwent—, excuse me, 'Lord' Pwent *is* their master now. I have assured him of our support, and in a few short hours, this will be his city, and he will rule it in my stead."

"You're a dreamer," I heard Julea say. There were too many bodies between me and the scene for me to see any of my friends, but Kelly and Dana's silence unnerved me. Knowing them as I did, I knew it wasn't impossible that they were trying to hatch some plan to fight their way out. They didn't know, like I did, that anything like that would be a death sentence, not just for them but for everyone in the room. Well, maybe with the possible exception of the empress. I suspected that she would survive because I was pretty sure I knew what Steinhargh was planning.

"Perhaps I am, little princess," he said, condescension dripping from his voice, "but a successful one, despite you and these creatures you decide to surround yourself with."

"'Very successful.' Hmm. Can we shake on it?" Kelly said, and I felt a wave of relief. If he was smarting off, he wasn't plotting. At least not yet.

"Ah, the Blackcrow," Steinhargh said. He intended his voice to be jovial, to match Kelly's cavalier manner, but he failed miserably as his hatred oozed from every syllable. "Yes, come. Shake my hand," he snarled. I saw the 'hand' above the crowd as he lifted the mechanical monstrosity that was his right arm into the air. A blast of white flame burst forth from the 'palm,' swirling into a ball that floated in the air just barely above the heads of everyone standing. The imperials, the Eutichans, and my friends ducked as the fire rained down on them, dissipating in a blast of heat just before it reached them. The Kathasiri watched them impassively yet ever alert. But they watched *them*, and not me. I hooked the loop of the bag with my toe and, while everyone ducked the fire, I jerked my foot. The pouch slid up and stopped at my waist, where I draped my arm over it.

"God's teeth," I heard Rohb mutter.

"What's the matter, Blackcrow? No handshake now? Upset that I have taken some of your secrets? Stolen the fire of the *gods* that you kept to yourself?" Steinhargh no longer made any effort to disguise his rage, and his voice was harsh and ragged to the point of madness.

Ardallah now spoke, a twinge of annoyance in her still steady, cold voice. "King Willm Steinhargh, I believe we can negotiate. We are willing to put this evening aside as a simple demonstration rather than the disrespect it appe—,"

"Negotiate?" Steinhargh said, his anger trained on the empress now, "What do you believe I've come here for? To seek an alliance with Yorch? To become another of the insufferable toadies that manifest at your 'Assemblage?' You think too much of yourself, Ardallah. I'm not here to ally with you. I am here for three reasons only. First, to cement Lord Pwent's rulership of this city. To that end, my war fleet has anchored itself just beyond the docks."

"Wait— what? How?" Kelly said. I was proud of his eloquence.

"I find soldiers very unlikely to attack a fleet on which

their fathers and brothers and sons are bound to the masts," Steinhargh said. A snarling smile split his lips as he continued, "I, however, have no such hesitation on attacking this city, should there be any resistance."

I managed to slip my hand inside Dana's bag while otherwise staying very still. I probed with my fingers, finding vials and tools and other random stuff all carefully secured and organized inside. Slowly I put my hand further in, where it fell on two glass globes. I resisted the urge to grin as I carefully pulled my hand out of the bag.

"Two," Steinhargh continued, "to kill the man who mutilated me after making him watch as I destroy everyone and everything he ever cared about." He swept his mechanical arm in an arc in front of him, obviously threatening Kelly and the rest.

"And three," he said. He pointed the arm now forward as his voice became a rasp, "As part of that suffering, to seize the ruler of Yorch and the heir and to take control of the empire myself."

And..., I was right. I congratulated myself; of course, that's what he intended. I mean, despite our making it significantly harder, it was evident that his plan *did* work in Sargeaux. All we had done was make it more difficult by sparking a civil war that he ultimately won. Why not try again with Yorch, especially since it looked like he had new tricks up his sleeve? I did not intend that to be a joke.

This last statement of his was met by a sort of instinctual reaction from the imperials. Where they had been completely still, they suddenly formed up tighter around where Ardallah was standing and dropped into a fighting stance. The Eutichans had moved since Pwent had told them to stand down, and now they stepped even further back, leaving an open line of sight between my friends and me. Kelly stood facing Steinhargh, his back to the empress and Julea immediately behind him. Dana was on his far side, where both she and Rohb remained near the princess.

"Don't be foolish, Ardallah," Steinhargh said as the soldiers moved, "it will be easier with you alive, but my plans don't require it. The only blood that needs to spill today is—,"

"Kel!" I cut him off with a sharp cry to my friend, finishing his sentence somewhat unfortunately. In one motion, I pushed myself to my feet and lobbed one of the glass globes in a high arc toward Kelly. The nearest of the Kathasiri spun, momentarily off-guard at my sudden motion. I only had split seconds, but we had to act together for the full effect. From the edge of my vision, I saw Kelly lurch forward, catching the globe in his right hand while with his left, he reached back for Julea's hand. He pivoted, and in the same motion, threw the glass at the opposite wall precisely as I did the same with a backhand throw against the wall near me. The glass spheres smashed simultaneously, and suddenly, the room exploded in bright yellow light as if the air itself had caught fire. More than the light, though, the air itself became opaque, and suddenly I was completely blind. Which would be bad, except that everyone else – soldier and assassin alike – was too.

Well, not the same as *everyone* else. I'm not stupid enough to throw something that's going to unleash the midday sun with my eyes open. So even though the inside of my eyelids glowed bright red like I was on a Gladian beach, I was blind, not blinded. That's a very important tactical difference right there. The room filled now with the howls of pain that came from the guards and the Kathasiri. That was itself also another kind of cover. I moved backward by memory toward where I knew the pile of our equipment was heaped and rummaged around until I felt my hands on the crossed straps that held my daggers. I was slipping it over my shoulders when a hand fell on my arm.

"Kid," Kelly said, a statement rather than a question.

"Yeah," I replied, grabbing his wrist and pulling it toward the pile of equipment. Once there, I could feel him rummaging around for his things.

"You have to get Jules out of here," he said quietly. There was still plenty of noise in the room, much of it now the sounds of clumsy stumbling about, but since we couldn't tell how close any of our enemies were, caution made sense. He continued, "Take her out that hidden door across the room and try to find Westfall. Our best chance is to get him on our side." I heard the familiar metallic ring of his blade coming out of its sheath.

"We'll hold here," Dana's voice said from somewhere just beyond his. I felt a woman's hand on my arm and realized Kelly had passed Julea over to me.

"You guys don't know who you're –," I started to say before Kelly cut in.

"No time, kid. Get her out of here and keep her safe," he said, his voice sharp and quick. For another half a second, I wanted to argue, to tell him that even together, we didn't stand much chance against a murder of Kathasiri, let alone separated. But he was right; we had no time, and I knew the princess was his priority, come whatever.

"We're gone," I said. I patted Julea's hand on my biceps as a signal, and then I got up and crept along the back wall, letting it lead us toward the other side of the room, the corner, and the hidden door.

"Denis...," Julea said with an unspoken protest already in the sound of her voice.

"Hush," I said, and she did. Already the red glow through my eyelids was dimmer, and it wouldn't be long before any chance of getting out unseen had passed. I'll say this for Julea; she's pretty agile for someone in her fancy clothes at what must by now be the beginning of the morning watch. We moved faster than I would have expected along the back wall, past the rear part of the platform Ardallah had been standing on, and over to the far corner. I felt along until the edges of the hidden door greeted my fingertips.

"Here," I said quietly. I pushed, and the panel gave slightly. I needed to know if we had been noticed, so I took the risk and opened my eyes a crack. The room's air was now a dimly glowing fog that seemed to be getting more transparent, moment by moment. Actually, I hadn't had any idea what the globes would do in an enclosed space like the courtroom. I'd seen Dana use one once to light up a cavern where some bandits had holed up, and all I saw from the outside of the cave was a bright yellow glow and wisps of heavy glowing fog. The effect in the room was much better than that. There was some movement in the haze, and then I heard the sound of metal on metal from the other side of the room. There was a crashing sound from somewhere in the middle where Steinhargh had been, and then a blast of white flame shot up into the air.

"Time to go," I said to Julea, shoving with everything I could muster against the wall. The panel folded inward as the sound of counterweights from somewhere nearby echoed with the grinding of stone on stone. We slipped through and closed it behind us. Once the door was closed, she opened her eyes and glanced around.

"We have to find Westfall," she said, repeating Kelly's earlier thoughts.

"Well, how far could he have gotten? Come on," I said.

I stepped around her, and we made our way down the narrow candlelit hallway. It was true; he couldn't have gotten far. The only question was how long it was before we'd be forced to guess the direction he had chosen. Fortune, or whatever, was on our side, though. Just before the hallway terminated at a stairwell leading down – and thereafter anywhere, I guess – we came on the potentially former High Regent of Euticha and three of his soldiers. Two stood between him and us, while the third remained beyond in the shadows.

"Lord Westfall," Julea called out. The soldiers turned, drawing their blades in the narrow passageway. Which was, of course, stupid. The walls were no more than four or five feet apart; exactly where did they think they were going to swing those things? I had my daggers instinctively in my hands and was taking a defensive position when the princess touched my shoulder and spoke again.

"Lord Westfall, we are not your enemies," she said, "but you do have enemies here. Malazander Pwent just announced his allegiance with the man upstairs who intends to imprison my mother and seize the throne of the empire. He has taken command of the soldiers in the courtroom and intends to take your position as well."

Westfall looked at her with a look of confusion and tempered horror. His jaw worked as if he were physically chewing the thoughts in his mind.

"Not a joke," I said with as much gravity as I could muster.

"Pwent is seizing command?" The voice came from the third soldier. He moved slightly into the light, and we saw it was Captain Andwen. I should note that he did not have his sword drawn.

"He is," Julea said, "and he intends to take the city and rule in the name of Willm Steinhargh, the man in the black armor."

"How is this even possible?" Westfall finally said, clearly struggling to get his grasp on what was happening.

"Look," I said, exasperated beyond what I can express, "Lord Westfall, you decided to climb into a cobra den and make a deal with Ardallah. The problem is, there are a *lot* of cobras in there with you."

Westfall's head drooped. "I intended no such alliance. But the empress—,"

"Time for that later," I said, cutting him off. Honestly, fancy folk just love their own voices. "Our friends are in serious trouble back there. Your soldiers would sure help."

Westfall seemed to jerk like he'd been slapped awake. He spun to Andwen. "Captain. Rally the soldiers. Bring every man here. Master Pwent is to be bound by law on my order." Andwen nodded without hesitation and disappeared down the stairs.

"Your Highness," he said, turning back to Julea, "My

deepest apologies."

"Later," I said, stepping back, "we need to get back and help my friends." I turned around and saw a look on the princess's face.

"*Our* friends," I corrected. She grinned faintly, and then the five of us were off, back up the passage toward the hidden door. We got almost half of the way back when all hell broke loose. The hallway itself began to pitch back and forth as if it had suddenly transformed into a rope bridge in a windstorm. I stumbled backward into Julea, who caught me with one arm and held me upright while she held the base of one of the wall sconces with her other hand to support herself. Westfall and the others stumbled backward into a pile as the floor and walls pitched and shifted beneath us. The stone and mortar made grinding sounds as it moved in ways that rock shouldn't. Ahead, a thunderous roar echoed down the hallway from the closed door, a deafening sound of thunder and glass and chaos. Julea looked over as I again got my feet under me.

"Was that...?" she asked, her face pale with shock. I looked back at her with no answer. I mean, it *sounded* like something our friends could have done, but then again, it also sounded cataclysmic, and that wasn't typically their style. The hallway had settled down enough that I ran forward, leaving Julea with Westfall and his men. I pulled on the inner handle of the door, ready to rush into the fight we had left behind.

The door wouldn't budge. I tried again, but it held fast. Julea caught up then, the Eutichans in tow, and the soldiers and the High Regent pulled together while I backed away and looked for a lock or a catch that I had missed before.

"The shifting must have put something in the way of the counterweight," Julea said, looking at me earnestly now, "we need to go the other way."

I looked at Westfall as he released the handle. He nodded his agreement with the princess. I turned and sprinted back down the hall, again leaving them behind me. Somehow, I knew that something wasn't right; I couldn't say what it was. I told myself that maybe it was just having seen the Kathasiri again, but I still felt like something was decidedly wrong, and I needed to get back to Kelly and Dana as quickly as I could. In moments, I was at the stairwell where Andwen had left, and I stopped. I looked around in the pale candlelight of the passage for the handle I knew had to be there. And then, there it was, a small knob just to the right of the stairs. I pulled it, and another door opened, leading to the small antechamber outside the courtroom and to four Kathasiri assassins waiting there.

Reflexes had me in motion before I truly knew what was happening. I threw myself forward into the room in a tumble that took me past the figure nearest to me and up to a second. I rose from my roll with my arms crossed, and both blades pointed out, pushing them up and through the assassin's hidden leather armor with all of the strength of my legs. I felt them bite home as they ground past the underlying armor. The former assassin slid to the floor, likely never knowing what had happened. The same was no longer the case for the one I had slipped past or his companions. Though none of them had noticed me or the secret passage I had come out of at first, my presence was certainly noticeable now as the limp form dropped off of my blades. The first assassin turned toward me, and after a fraction of a second, I saw his eyes – the only visible part of his face behind the black shroud – harden into a murderous stare.

"Apostate!" he shouted in a voice that sounded like rasping steel. He brandished his *novacul sanguis*, the ceremonial curved, dark-steel blade too short to be a sword, but too long to be a dagger, in his right hand and a small knife in his left as he took a defensive stance.

"Whatever," I said, facing him with my daggers in a matching pose. I was aware that the other two in the room were watching us, and I was hoping that they would keep doing so for a minute longer before they decided to rush over and assist their comrade in finishing me off. To that end, I went on the attack. I pivoted my left blade in my hand, reversing the grip as I stepped forward onto my right foot. As my weight shifted, I dropped down onto my left knee and began a spin in that direction. Both of my blades swept out, clawing at his thigh and waist. He lowered his short-sword from mid-guard to low, catching my front dagger and deflecting it away. His offhand knife came down from above toward my shoulder, but my spin carried me out of range, though not before the backside of my second dagger caught his wrist and sliced across it. He dropped his rear leg, pulling him out of my reach with a twist that was a mirror of my own. We came back to our feet facing one another. I was now, though, in a corner with nowhere to go.

"Traitor to Her might! You die now," snarled the other in the distinct accent of the southern isles. Tiny droplets of blood leaked from the hand that I had gashed, and though he still held the knife, I could see from the awkward angle that he had no strength to put behind it. But, more importantly, from where I stood now, I could see the other two, watching our duel from a few feet away. They were just intent enough in their observation that they could not have seen the Eutichan soldiers emerging from the hidden door behind them.

"Wait! What's that?" I said, making a show of looking behind them. Westfall and Julea now emerged from the door silently, he with his sword drawn and she with an unexpected dagger in her hand.

The Kathasiri were far too well-indoctrinated to fall for what they saw as a simple trick like that, of course. They had been carefully conditioned to explicitly *not* look. And so, they kept their eyes on me, waiting to administer the death blow should my immediate opponent fail. The Eutichans advanced unseen, and a heartbeat later, their weapons fell on the assassins from behind.

Their sudden cries of pain did an excellent job of distracting my dueling partner. He turned in time to see the four newcomers in the room and watch his companions fall. Turning away like that, though, is a bad idea when you're involved in a duel. He seemed to remember that fact suddenly and to me again, but just one second too late for his own good. I caught his sword arm at the elbow and threw my weight backward, sending him into a spin that drove him face-first into the stone wall behind me with a crunch. He crumpled, and I reversed my grip on my daggers to finish him off.

"Denis!" Julea called with a note of horror in her voice. I paused, looking down at the still form of the other.

"They'll keep coming back," I said in a voice just above a whisper. Talking to her felt like talking from a great distance. "They're like cockroaches; they'll keep coming back unless we exterminate them," I said from the past.

I felt her hand on my arm, and that was somehow enough to pull me back to myself. I looked at her.

"I...," I said.

"Later," she said, giving my arm a gentle squeeze. She

looked at the door to the court chamber. "Our friends," she said.

And that was enough. I looked at the door, noticing now for the first time a cloud of smoke and dust beyond, wisps of which had rolled several feet into the room where we were. I looked over at Westfall and his men and gave him a nod. Julea stepped aside, and together with the men of Euticha, I ran into the cloud.

I've heard people use the word 'catastrophe' when something bad happens. 'Oh, our cow died. It was a catastrophe,' they say. Or maybe they get held up by a bandit and lose their purse, and they say it was, 'A disaster. A real catastrophe.' I don't think those people have a proper scale for using the word. Sure, those are bad things, and I'm pretty sure that they *feel* like a disaster, but the actual scale is wrong. A volcano, say. Or an earthquake. I'd even say that one of the Triangle Blows could count if it hit enough ships or, gods forbid, landfall. That's a catastrophe. When I say that what I saw on the other side of the door was a catastrophe, know that I'm grouping it with that sort of thing.

I expected the room to be filled with smoke and dust when I came through at the door. But as it turned out, the place couldn't be said to be 'full' of anything anymore since most of the back half of the place was missing. The far wall behind the raised platform was almost completely gone. The whole bank of windows, a goodly section of the ceiling, and part of the roof simply weren't there anymore. Warm, damp breezes came off the sea and carried away the smoke and dust into the slowly lightening sky of morning. A vast pile of blackened stones – stones that had until recently been gainfully employed as a part of the tower wall – covered most of the floor opposite the door. There was no sign of the small platform at all. But the worst of it was the bodies scattered around the entire area. Kathasiri assassins and Eutichan soldiers lay twisted and unmoving all around. A pit formed in my stomach, and suddenly I started to scan the dust-covered forms carefully, looking for my friends.

"Rohb!" Julea called, rushing past me and toward the right side of the room where what looked like a small pile of rubble was moving slowly to reveal the big man. Rohb sat up, a stream of blood trickling down the left side of his face as he turned to Julea. She kneeled at his side as she pulled the gray cloak she wore off and dabbed gently at his head. He took the cloth, making a reassuring gesture with his other hand as he sat up straighter. Suddenly, the princess whirled around and looked at me. I saw in her eyes that the realization of what – and who – we *didn't* see was on her.

Westfall and his soldiers came in then, followed almost immediately by Andwen and another group of armed Eutichans.

"Pwent was seen on the docks, but the men lost him in the excitement of the flames," he reported to Westfall, who stood still, looking agape at the wreckage.

That was the last thing I distinctly heard for a while. I'm sure Westfall had the soldiers begin to assess the bodies in the room and do all the right things, but I only know about that from being told about it afterward. My mind decided that there was one and only one thing it needed to be focused on. I turned to the left and began to dig through the bodies and the rubble. Nearer the door, it wasn't hard; there it was mostly the bodies of assassins and soldiers, either unconscious or dead. Neither was of interest to me at that moment. I approached the mound of rubble, thinking for just a second that it seemed to be almost on top of where our equipment had lain, just a few short minutes ago. Back when we had been clever.

I dug. I had dropped my daggers somewhere in the room earlier – I couldn't remember doing it just then – so I dug with my bare hands. The stones were warm, and the black on them rubbed off like charcoal, so much so that my hands and arms were soon pitch black. Somehow seeing the black on my sleeves made my stomach turn, and I held back an unexpected desire to puke.

"Denis," Julea's voice stabbed through the weird filter on my thoughts. I turned, still holding a charred stone in my hand. She was as covered in dust and filth as I was, but now she was standing frozen. Her face was as white as..., well, as white as her mother's was, but hers had horror written all over it. I got up and went to her, following her gaze. There was an open pocket in the mound of stones that she had been digging in. A woman's arm wearing a familiar leather bracer protruded from the dirt and rubble inside, covered with gray dust. As still as death.

"Rohb! Westfall! Help me," I heard myself barking out orders like I was Kelly all of a sudden, but I didn't care. Carefully I started clearing stones from the top of the pile, digging down instead of sideways lest we do more harm than good. Rohb, his head still bleeding freely, was suddenly next to me, tossing stones off with abandon until we got to the bottom to reveal Dana, draped crosswise over the equally motionless form of Kelly. Julea dropped to her knees, reaching out with her hands to feel their faces.

"I think they're both breathing," she said, more than a little breathlessly herself. "It's hard to tell; it's so shallow."

"Bring two litters! And bring the surgeon," said Westfall in a commanding voice from somewhere close behind me. I crawled around the opposite side of the pile, and as gently as we could, Rohb and I lifted Dana out, followed by Kelly. Her legs seemed wrong, somehow bent at odd angles in places where they shouldn't be. But that wasn't the worst of it. Kelly lay face up; his left arm was twisted around so much that it looked more like an empty sleeve than anything. The left side of his head was shaped funny and covered in blood. Just so much blood. It was impossible to see where the blood was all coming from; there was so much. Julea crumpled to the ground next to him, gently stroking his face and weeping. I looked at Dana's head resting in my lap and then down at Kelly. Nausea rolled around in me. And anger. And fear.

CHAPTER SIX

– JULEA –

The memory came hard and clear in the dream as if it were no more than a season old:

I couldn't remember a bluer sky, and only the tiniest wisps of cloud in the far west marred it. The sunlight filled the world with intense brightness and warmth not yet diminished from summer, despite the late date on the calendar. The air, though, seemed more well-informed and so had a much more sensible coolness to it. A gentle breeze moved across the landscape somewhat randomly, jostling nearby leaves now tinged with the first hints of the extravaganza of colors that were yet to come. The entire scene lulled me into a feeling of relaxation I had rarely felt. I sighed, my eyes drooping closed.

"We are being naughty," I said with a sigh. A quiet laugh bubbled up from my companion that gently nudged my head where it lay on his stomach.

"You and I have very different definitions of 'naughty,' princess," he said. I propped myself up on one elbow to look up toward his face. He was lying perpendicular to me on the large blanket that we had spread. His eyes were closed, and he had bundled our two cloaks into a sort of pillow for his head. I glared at him, and in response, he opened one eye and looked down toward me. The look lasted for a long moment while we each suppressed smiles before I lay back down, my head again resting on his stomach. I felt him gently stroke my hair with his hand.

"Our definitions hardly matter. If my mother knew...," I said, the old familiar dread clouding my thoughts.

"I suspect that wouldn't be pleasant," he sighed, stopping me before the implied consequences became overwhelming, "so let's make it worth it in case that happens, okay? And..., maybe it never will." Again, I felt the gentle caress of his hand.

"Besides," he continued, "if Her Nibs *did* find out, I would simply explain that I was doing what you told me to. So, I'd be fine." He sighed peacefully.

"Too far," I said, giving him a soft poke in the stomach with my head. "You almost had me relaxed again."

"Oh, come now," he said, "are you telling me you're not relaxed?"

I sighed, letting my head loll to one side. "I am but a ball of nervous energy. You've truly upset me." I closed my eyes, nestling into him.

"I'm truly sorry, milady. Here, maybe one of these will help," my companion said, and a moment later, I felt the light press of a grape against my lips. I took it, biting it and letting its sweetness fill my mouth before I rolled a little onto my side so that I could look up to him again. He was popping a grape into his mouth even as he dropped the remaining bunch back into the basket with his other hand.

"What?" he said through the mouthful of grape.

I smiled. "Nothing. Just 'making it worth it,' as you say."

He smiled back, then let his head drop onto the bundle of cloaks again.

"Beautiful day. I kind of want to hold onto this one," he said.

I rolled back and looked at the perfectly blue sky again. "Me too," I said.

Dawn had come.

I don't honestly know how it happened. I remembered the rush to take Dana and Kelly from the rubble and out to the High Regent's surgeons in the antechamber. I remembered following them, Rohb and Denis beside me, out of the wreckage of the courtroom, through that chamber, and back down through the pandemonium in the barrack's keep where we had arrived a lifetime – yet still somehow only a few hours – before. After that, I don't know that I can say for sure what happened until I woke and found myself on a bench with the bright light of late summer pouring in through a window above me. I looked around nervously – gripped momentarily by my all too familiar anxiety of wakening – before I saw the giant form of Rohb seated not far away to my right. My distress eased, and I took in the room around me.

The bench on which I sat had a gentle curve that matched the shape of the stone wall behind it, where the high-set windows allowed in the late morning sunlight. Across from me, less than fifteen feet away, I was confident, sat a side table on the opposite wall. Displayed thereon were an array of pans, cups, and other more mysterious implements of the healing arts. In the space between that table and me, two small beds bore the figures of my friends, now thoroughly swathed in bandages, miscellaneous cloths, and blankets. Perched on a stool in the gap between them sat Denis, his elbows planted firmly on his knees as he rotated his head from watching one, then the other, then staring at the floor for a time before beginning the sequence again. I rose to my feet without speaking, eliciting a start from Rohb, who had not noticed my waking. If he had any reaction, Denis might have hesitated in his pattern an extra moment on Dana's bed as I stood. Then he continued his sequence. I walked over to the bedside and looked down in the same order, first at Dana, then across at Kelly. There was little to see, though; shapeless blankets covered both of them from the shoulders down, leaving only their faces exposed, if one could call the tiny bits that remained 'exposed.' Dana's head was bound in thick cloth bandages that formed a shape reminiscent of a mushroom cap. For a moment, I flashed on the tremendous amount of blood I had seen under her when we found them. I grimaced, imagining what might be under that shroud. On the other bed, the entire left side of Kelly's face was covered in similar bandaging, leaving only his mouth, nose, and right eye exposed. I felt myself staring, frozen as I desperately tried to see either of them move or breathe. Really, for any evidence that they were even alive.

"They're breathing," Denis said in a small, tired voice. He hadn't looked up but guessed my thoughts, nevertheless. "They are alive." His voice was dry and quiet, like a sponge that had been wrung out vigorously. His whole presence seemed somehow drained of the manic energy that usually characterized him. I tore my eyes away from my friends to look at him. He had not moved, his forearms still on his knees, but he had abandoned his active observations. Instead, his head just hung low, and his shoulders now seemed to be struggling under the weight. I considered that he had likely not slept in over a day, depending on the present time, and had experienced the same calamity I had. I walked around Dana's bed and rested my hand on his shoulder. Under the rough spun shirt, I felt the wiry muscles twitching with exhaustion.

"You need rest," I said.

"I need to be right where I am," he said, and the muscles in the shoulder went taught, though he did not pull away. Instead, his head came up, and he looked from Kelly to Dana again before he cast a glance back toward me. "Right where I am," he repeated.

I patted his shoulder gently – a gesture of understanding if not agreement – and moved past him to his right to sit partly on the edge of Kelly's bed. I looked at what I could see of the bandaged face, where purple and blue darkened the eye socket and hinting at what lay beyond under the bandages.

"The healers cleaned them up as best as they could," Denis said to the floor before his eyes. His serious demeanor was disconcerting; where he was ordinarily the definition of unworried whimsy, he was now intense and sober as he broodily watched over our friends. "They muttered quite a bit during the process but didn't say anything I understood. They left a bit ago; I keep expecting someone back so I can ask them what's going on."

I turned to Rohb, still standing by the bench where I had woken. I saw that he had a bandage wrapped around his head as well, though not nearly as extensively as either Dana or Kelly. He stood motionless with his massive arms folded across his chest. His eyes were vacant, though, and it was clear that his mind was far away from the little room.

"Captain?" I said, hoping to pull him back from

wherever he'd gone, and as if responding to a bell, his attention snapped back into the room. He dropped his arms and nodded to me.

"Ma'am," he said.

"Rohb," I said, changing the manner of address to be clear of a change of nature in the discussion, "what happened in that room? You were there."

"I was," he said, his head involuntarily shaking, "though I don't know as I know what happened."

"Try," Denis said, a little of his natural spark peeking through the clouds around him.

Rohb sat down on the bench with the air of someone asked to lift a great weight. He absently rubbed at the bandage in the place where whatever wound he had was and winced subtly. Finally, he leaned back and looked at us each in turn.

"First, you have to know I couldn't see at all for a good bit. I saw you jump up and shout to Kelly, but whatever you did, it happened so fast that I only barely got my eyes shut after the flash of light. I did better than most, I reckon, 'cause it sounded like bedlam broke loose around me. I remembered there being one of Steinhargh's men right near me, so I reached out and threw him in the general direction of the crowd.

"You threw him?" Denis asked, cocking his head.

"Yeah. I just reached out and got hold of someone

wrapped in cloth – I assumed it was one of the king's men since I didn't feel any armor like the Eutichan's had on – and threw whoever it was at the most noise. I must have hit someone 'cause I heard a lot of clattering and thrashing about. Anyway, I backed away toward where I reckoned the platform was, thinking I could get to you or the empress. I guess I misjudged where I was, and I tripped and fell over something on the floor. By the time I got up, I had got sorta turned around and didn't know which direction was which anymore. I crouched and listened, trying to get my bearings so I could find you, princess. But something hit me then and sent me sideways, which I think is how I got this," he gestured toward his head.

"Did you get up after that?" I asked.

"It took a minute, my bell got wrung pretty hard, but it was then that someone dropped something on my hand, and I realized it was the handle of my axe. I figured that meant that one, at least one of you all was still alive, and two, they could see well enough to match a weapon to its person. I guessed it was safe, so I took the risk and opened my eyes. The room was still really hazy and fuzzy, but I saw Dana and Kelly a few feet away fighting back-to-back. She was closest to me, so it must have been her that got my axe over to me."

I nodded. "Where was Steinhargh?"

Rohb shook his head in a pattern of uncertainty. "I couldn't tell at first. Truth is, I was still fuzzy from bein' hit.

So, I just got up and swung at the first shadow I could make out. I caught one of them across the chest, and he just sorta fell away into the mist, so I followed in that direction. That's when it got weirder."

"Weirder?" Denis asked.

"I could finally make out Steelclaw across the room from me, closer to the door. He lifted that arm of his and fired another blast of flame – same way he did earlier – but this time, it was bigger, and he pointed at the windows. The glass blew out, most of it went outside, but the air came in and started clearing the fog a lot faster. I could see the fella that I knocked over and was about to finish him off when something hit the tower from outside."

"From outside?" I said, "you're sure?"

He looked at me squarely. "No question, ma'am. I turned around and saw a blue light through the open windows just as they started to crumble. Whatever did that; it came from outside."

"So, it was a signal of some kind," Denis muttered.

"Come again?" Rohb said.

"The flame from Steinhargh's arm. Him blowing out the windows. He was sending a signal. He probably had his men stationed outside somewhere just in case he lost control of the situation."

"But what did he do?" I asked. "I mean, what can bring down a stone tower in a single moment?"

I looked at Rohb – whose answering shrug matched the thoughts in my head – and then at Denis. He was staring at Kelly.

"Steinhargh is using the gems. That's what you're thinking," I said.

His cheek twitched, though the rest of him remained stone still for a long moment. Finally, he stood up and faced me.

"I don't think there's any other answer," he said. "We know what they can do. Well, we know *some* of the things they can do. It's the only thing that makes sense."

An icy chill shot up my spine as the memories of all the years of Kelly's warnings, his cautions, his – *our* – sacrifices flooded through me. So, this was it then— the worst end he had ever dreaded.

"Hell's bells," Denis said, dropping back on the stool.

I looked over at Rohb. "Where was my mother?"

He shook his head. "Can't be sure. I got caught by some of the rubble, as you saw. I think I saw her with Steinhargh and his men near the door as the room came down."

"We have to have just missed them," Denis said. "Probably by seconds. They left the assassins that we fought to act as rearguards for them. He must have just gone through that room." His teeth were grinding as he spoke, as his frustration wrestled with exhaustion and came out the winner.

"You keep sayin' '*assassin*,'" Rohb said, interrupting. "Steelclaw's men in the black pajamas. You keep calling them that. Why?"

Denis turned toward me with a look that said he suddenly wished to be somewhere else. Somewhere especially where this was not being discussed. But I couldn't help him; I needed to know too. There was – and had always been – something about him that he avoided discussing. Somehow it fit into what happened, and that story needed to be told.

"You knew them," I said, my tone steady and empathetic.

He nodded. The exhaustion seemed to settle back on him.

"The one you fought called you 'Apostate,'" I said.

There was a long moment of silence where no one moved, and no one spoke. At length, I leaned over and again put my hand on Denis's shoulder. He took a deep breath, held it, then let it go very slowly before he spoke.

"They are the Kathasiri, the deadliest assassins in the world. For them, slaughter is a passion. Well, it's more than passion; it's ardor, it's zeal, it's devotion. It is their life and their religion. They worship Kathas, an old, you would say 'pagan,' goddess of death and change."

I glanced up at Rohb and back to Denis. "I have heard

that name, but I was told they were a myth. A story to frighten children."

"No," he said, "no myth. They're real. The stuff of nightmares made flesh. The bogeymen exist, and they're for sale."

"For sale?" I asked.

"Holy communion by assassination for hire. Through the deaths, they make offerings to their goddess. And then they get paid. Wins for everybody all around. Well, everybody left alive, I mean."

"Where did you run across them?" Rohb said.

Denis took another pause. And in that pause, I somehow knew what was coming, and it chilled me.

"The Kathasiri make their home on an island south of Gladia, between the Sea of Sorrow and the Great Ocean. People think that's where they're from, but it isn't, not really. That's just their home. They're *from* all over. See, every so often, the high priests go recruiting. By that, I mean that they randomly select a village somewhere, enter in the night, and kill everyone except the children. Some of the children – the ones they deem worth keeping. The rest get the blade along with every else, and the town gets erased from the map. Most of the time, and horrifyingly, it goes unnoticed. They make it look like wild animals, or sickness, or sometimes fire. But the children they keep are theirs now, raised as the next generation."

"So...," Rohb began, about to ask his question again.

"Your village," I said. I felt a twinge of pity, and I squeezed his shoulder gently.

"Just another one of many," Denis replied. I saw the bravado that he used as a shield swelling up from inside to reassert itself. This was raw for him, a revelation more candid than he liked or perhaps could tolerate. I could see that we would need to back away from the subject before too long. "I was raised as one of them, Rohb. And when I couldn't do it anymore, I left. But I'm considered 'marked' if you can imagine. They call me the "Apostate," 'the one who is out of his place.' And for my part, I steer as wide around them as I can."

At this, he reached up and gently touched my hand where it was on his shoulder. There was a pause, and then, just as gently, he picked my hand up and slid it away. I accepted the action and what it meant by folding my hands back onto my lap instead. I did not, however, get up or leave his side.

"Damn," Rohb said, slumping down on the bench as we fell into silent reflection.

So lost were the three of us, and so heavy with the thoughts of our friends were we, that we scarcely noticed the small figure in gray come into the room. Indeed, it wasn't until he cleared his throat in an apparent effort to get our attention that his presence registered enough for me to react.

I stood, my back instinctively straightening and my hands reflexively clasping one another before me as I considered the newcomer. He was, as I said, small – perhaps no more than up to my shoulder – and this was exaggerated somewhat by the considerable hunch to his shoulders. He wore a long heavy tunic of flat gray that fastened across his insignificant chest in the manner of an apron over matching gray pants. He let his gaze rove over the three of us, taking in the room with his ancient eyes. On seeing me stand, he moved over to place himself before me and bowed his head curtly.

“Princess Julea,” he said, and though his voice was raspy and thick, there was underneath it the shadow of one who was very alert and present.

“I am she,” I said with an answering nod.

He looked up, sparing a momentary glance to Denis and then to Rohb. He hesitated, and I fancied that I saw him inspecting the bandage on my bodyguard’s head even from across the room. Seemingly it satisfied him, as he then turned back and looked up at me. I could see his face, as it was now much closer than before and illuminated in the sunlight. It was wizened with the lines and ravages of many years. He was thin – gaunt, if I’m to be honest – and his cheekbones stood in sharp relief from his pale cheeks, while above them, furrowed thick white eyebrows separated his bald head from the unexpectedly alert green eyes that now met mine.

"I am Garanthet VosMullen, Chief Healer in service to the High Regent. Lord Westfall has commanded me to look after your companions. As much as I have been able, such have I done." He looked beyond me, first at Dana and then over at Kelly.

"I am forever grateful, Master Garanthet," I said, gratified that my courtly training was enough to restrain my roiling emotions. My stomach had remained knotted from the moment I had seen my two friends pulled from the rubble, and watching over them here had done nothing to calm me. I desperately wanted to scream and cry and curse and beg the One Himself to make things right. In truth, there was a version of me in my mind that stood alone in a vast open field doing all those things at that very moment – screaming and crying and cursing. But, on the outside? Outside I was the heir to the empire, and nothing ever had or ever would be able to pierce that armor.

VosMullen stepped past me, moving up the narrow aisle between the two patients where Denis and I had been talking. The former assassin stood quickly and moved to get out of the healer's way, though the furthest he could bring himself to go was the opposite side of Kelly's bed. The surgeon poked and prodded at Dana, his wizened hands resting here and there on her body through the bandages and blankets. Without a word, he turned and repeated the process on Kelly before he stepped away from both beds and stepped away, returning once more to his former location near the door. He pulled a white cloth from his pocket and began wiping it over his hands in a methodical and yet unconscious process. He turned and looked up at me, his ancient face unreadable.

"Your friends, somehow, live yet," he said, and though the words would have indicated this was favorable news, I saw that his tone and demeanor contradicted such a conclusion. "However, I believe it may be that before I finish speaking, neither you nor either of them will be altogether happy about that."

"How do you mean?" I asked, locked now in the role of noble while the woman inside me wailed.

The older man grunted. "I have served as a healer my whole life, which judging by the looks of you three may just be longer than your lives added together," he said, his voice dripping with distaste, "In that time, I have known death, seen death, touched death, and the means by which it's dealt intimately. You need to know this so that you understand what I say next. I tell you that I have no clue by what means it is that they are still alive. There is something at work here that I don't understand, and I am disquieted greatly by it."

We three held our peace. It was the least thing we could do for our friends.

"But whatever witchery is involved, it isn't enough,"

he said, sighing now. "The woman's spine is broken. Crushed, really, from her middle back to her hips. She'll never walk again, let alone anything else. In truth, she shouldn't even be breathing right now, even though she is. It won't last, though. Her breaths have gotten shallower since earlier this morning already. By tomorrow, maybe the day after, whatever the uncanny spell at work is will not be enough."

No one spoke. Garanthet took it as leave to continue. He patted his forehead with another of the small white cloths and looked over at Kelly.

"That one's just as bad. His left arm is all but gone there, where the rubble crushed it. I'd have taken what's left off already, but as it is, he'd never survive the process. Though, to be honest, it would only be hurrying the inevitable. Most seriously, his head's half crushed under that bandage, and there's nothing I can do for that."

The woman in my head had gone hoarse. I saw her curled up on a blanket in a sun-drenched field, weeping openly. In the outside world, the summer heat that filled the room seemed to vanish as I was swept by a cold that didn't exist, even as I stood and calmly nodded.

A quiet gurgle broke the silence as if it were a clap of thunder. I spun, following the sound to the head of Kelly's bed. Opposite me, Denis leaned in from his other side, resting his hand on Kelly's shoulder. Then, there was another sound, quieter but similar to the first.

"What is it?" I asked as I came to the head of the bed. Neither Rohb nor Garanthet moved, though I could feel their eyes on us.

"I think he's trying to say something," Denis said as he bent far over and put his ear so close to Kelly's mouth that it was all but touching. There was a long pause while he closed his eyes in concentration and waited. Then, Kelly made another sound, this time barely audible in the rest of the room. After another pause, Denis leaned back slightly and patted Kelly gently.

"Okay," he whispered, "I've got it." He stood up straight then, like a shock of lightning had just blazed through him. The signs of his earlier exhaustion and defeat seemed to evaporate into nothingness as he came around the bed and grabbed my shoulders, squaring me with him as he spoke.

"Princess, I need to talk to the High Regent. I need his fastest horses and his best carriage." There was a wildness in his eyes that should have spoken of desperation. It should have inspired calming words of acceptance and support; things that would help him accept what the surgeon had said were inevitable. But back in my mind, the weeping me in the field was slowly getting up. If it was madness that had seized him…, well, it had gripped me too.

I nodded; our eyes fixed on one another as I spoke. "I

can't believe that will be a problem. Why? What did you hear?"

Denis turned to Garanthet. Quickly, and despite the old surgeon's attempts at a protest, he instructed that Dana and Kelly be moved onto something portable that could be loaded and fastened into a carriage and that he should be prepared to travel as soon as possible. VosMullen, who was very definitely unaccustomed to being ordered about, looked at first as though he wanted to argue. But I watched the sheer intensity of Denis's instructions and the force of the personality behind them grind the healer's objections to so much dust before ever they were made. He slipped out of the room as Denis turned to Rohb next.

"Find our equipment; everything that was salvaged from the tower as well as what we have in our rooms. You won't have any trouble finding the inn; it's right across the street from that big fancy park where we met you. Meet us back here as quickly as you can."

Rohb nodded but then looked over at me. My head was swimming. Events were moving very fast indeed, and a reflex inside me forged by years of conditioning said that I should be the one in control of this. That I should have stopped Denis's manic instructions and told him no one was moving a finger until he told me exactly what was going on. But that's not what I did because, inside me, the woman in the field was smiling. She was on her feet, the sun was coming out of the clouds, and determination now filled her tear-stained face. I looked at Denis and asked the only question that suddenly seemed to matter.

"Where are we going?"

He turned to me, and his face split with his familiar grin as he spoke. "We're going to go save their lives. But to do that, we need to take them to Gretchville."

"Where? Why? What did Kelly say?"

"He said 'Eryth,'" Denis said triumphantly.

"What?" Rohb and I said together.

The black stallion's hooves thundered across the beach, kicking up sand and water as we raced along with the tide. I looked back long enough to see my companion on his steed, just a little behind and riding hard to catch up. To be fair, he was carrying the basket of food and the blanket that we had only shortly before used for our secret picnic, but a race is a race, and I was winning. I turned forward again and gave my horse a nudge of encouragement. I felt his muscles flex beneath me as he dropped his head, and we lunged forward, even faster than before. Unadulterated joy swelled as I clung to him and felt the wind and the sun and the spray of seawater on my face.

"Okay, we give!" came the shout from behind me as we reached an outcropping where the forest deeply into the beachfront and formed a small, sheltered cove. I tightened on the reigns, and the mighty beast slowed until we came to a stop just a few yards from the trees. A moment later, he guided his horse to a halt beside me.

"Exhilarating," I said, sure that my smile was in danger of splitting my face in two.

"For a princess of the blood, you're something of a wild child; you know that, right?" he asked. He guided his horse around such that the two animals were in opposite directions, whereas he and I were facing one another. Despite his protests, I could see joy dancing in the blue-gray eyes above his smile.

"Such I have heard before," I laughed as I leaned over and stroked the neck of my horse. "But it's the perfect day for a ride, and it is very good for the horses."

"For the horses. Right."

I looked back up at him. "It's a perfect day for a lot of things," I said. I could feel a touch of heat in my cheeks that told me there was some color to match. I thought to blame it on the ride, but there was also a hint of pink in his face. Gratified, I let it go.

"We should get back, though," he said, his smile slipping as his tone became more serious, "I know you have duties. We both do, though mine are perhaps a bit less significant."

I looked out at the water for a moment, taking in as much of the day as I could. Then, words came out from some inner place of raw longing—words without thought behind them.

"What if we don't go? What if we just picked a direction and rode and rode and never came back."

"Excuse me?" he gaped.

"Sure," I turned back, edging closer to him, "We just go. We could be out of the empire in no time. Then we could do what we want. No more 'duties,' no more 'obligations.' Just us and the wide world." The words were coming out too fast, and I'm sure they sounded as mad as..., well, as mad as they were.

He looked at me for a long time, so long that it was like he was looking through me. So long that I wondered what he was thinking. So long that I eventually believed I knew. Finally, he looked out toward the sea, took a breath, and exhaled it slowly.

"You paint beautiful pictures, Jules," he said, "but they're just pictures." He paused again. "Days like today are magical, but they don't last. Reality comes. And duty. And they can kill the magic if we don't remember that. But we'll always have today. A perfect day."

I looked at him, sad for the first and only time since that morning.

"We should get back. I know you have duties. We both do, though mine are perhaps a bit less significant," he repeated, his voice still steady but now colored with a restrained sadness. He guided his horse around until we faced the same way and took a step or two ahead before he stopped and waited for me.

It was the first time he had called me 'Jules.'

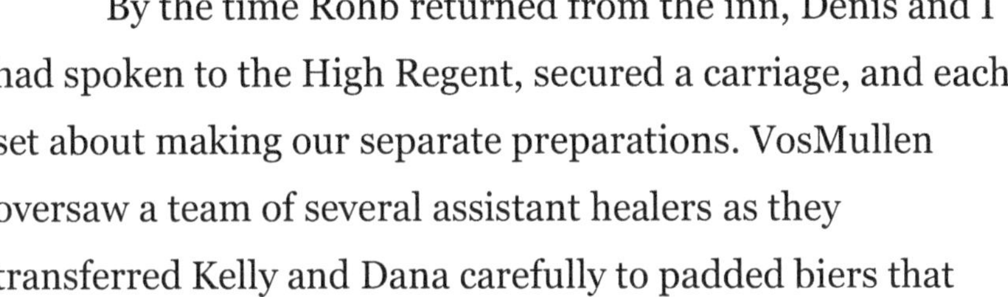

By the time Rohb returned from the inn, Denis and I had spoken to the High Regent, secured a carriage, and each set about making our separate preparations. VosMullen oversaw a team of several assistant healers as they transferred Kelly and Dana carefully to padded biers that would be suitable support for the journey. Once he was satisfied, he had them carried out to the courtyard and securely fastened into the carriage.

Lord Westfall had kindly given all of us use of his palace, which allowed us to clean up somewhat from the effects of the wreckage the night before, and I used the opportunity to change clothes into something more appropriate for traveling. I opted for brown britches and high boots, paired with a long blousy white top and an armored leather bodice. I strapped my sword on my hip and my dagger in my boot. I thought a moment before I retrieved the last piece of equipment I thought might come in handy. I took my leather choker from my personal belongings and fastened it around my neck, aligning its golden locket in the front. Inside the locket was the seal of the Imperial house, my identification as the heir in all imperially allied lands. I considered it in the mirror as I turned to leave, and I felt a quiet discontent awaken.

We all rendezvoused back at the barracks, where the healers were finishing loading Kelly and Dana's cots onto the carriage. I got quickly off the coach that bore me and Lord Westfall from the palace and immediately went around the back to where Denis and Rohb were working. The carriage itself was remarkable, with large, spoked wheels affixed to a long, wide frame made of what looked like steel. On this were mounted two compartments; one, slightly smaller and in the rear, was affixed directly to the steel structure and was used for cargo. Rohb grabbed the last chest and loaded it as I approached. The other section was the passenger chamber where Kelly, Dana, and everyone else would ride save for the driver. It was tall enough for a smallish person – me, for instance – to stand up in and had a slight curve at the corners. It sat on four flat metal panels that were indirectly affixed to the main steel base of the vehicle. At first, this arrangement seemed odd, for as I watched, the passenger chamber bobbed up and down slightly as the healers came and went. It then occurred to me that such motion must work in reverse when the carriage was rolling; the metal slats would absorb the irregularities in the road and smooth the ride for the occupants. I had never noticed that design before, though it seemed apparent that I must previously have ridden in a similar carriage with the empress.

You have duties. I heard in my mind a voice from the past. I shook my head to clear it.

Denis came up then, stepping back from where he had been watching the healers and stopping beside me. He had cleaned up too, now wearing his leather vest and daggers over an undyed fiber shirt and dark brown britches and boots. I wondered whether he would get any sleep or if that was even likely on this trip. It occurred to me then that I didn't even know how far Gretchville was from Euticha. As Rohb came up beside us, a wave of emotions swept through me, a mixture of worry for my friends and the unnamed discontent from earlier.

"Rohb," I said suddenly, the thought popping into my mind as if it were pushed there, "when did you see the empress last?"

Denis gave me a confused look as I turned to face my bodyguard. Rohb furrowed his brow, shifting the bandage on his head exaggeratedly.

"Clearly? Right before the room went bright. Had the Wolfpack by her," he said after some thought.

"And after the flash, when you could see again, you said you thought she was with Steinhargh and the Kathasiri?"

Rohb shrugged. "I saw her back. She was past Steelclaw from where I was – between him and the door. There were a bunch of those Kathasiri around her."

I sighed. My discontent was palpable now, like a splinter in my mind I couldn't stop touching. "He means to take over Yorch," I said, more to myself than for discussion.

"Steinhargh? Yeah, he said that," said Denis. There was a hint of frustration in his voice, and I could see how it was valid. He had our friends on his mind. We needed to be on the road as soon as possible for Kelly and Dana's sake. *Except...*,

"I'm the heir," I said, a part of the same ongoing internal monologue. *You have duties*, the insistent voice in my head repeated. I looked up at Rohb, then across at Denis, certainty crystalizing even as the words came out. "I can't go with you," I said, my voice sounding as if it was echoing from somewhere else.

"What?" Denis said. There was a barely restrained rage in that single word, a wave of anger from fear, anxiety, and sleeplessness. And what he would undoubtedly see as a betrayal.

"I have to get to Yorch and stop Steinhargh. It falls to me, both by duty and by necessity. I'm the only one that can align the houses if he plans to act as he did in the north." I felt my fingers unconsciously touch the locket on my throat.

"You..., you're going to Yorch?" Denis said, bewilderment and anger now all that was left. "What about Dana? What about Kelly? All of this was about you. They came here for you!"

"I have duties," I said, the cold evident even to myself. "Kelly would understand." Denis glared at me in silent fury.

"You can't," Rohb said, interjecting suddenly. I looked at him, and he pointed toward the docks. "They took the *Fenris*."

I blinked and felt a surge of frustration. Had I made the hardest decision only to have it nullified now? I spun to Lord Westfall.

"Lord Anthony," I said, "I require a ship to take me to Yorch with all haste."

The High Regent looked at me with a level of severity to which I was unaccustomed. "And I require a pony and a bag of gold," he answered, and the sarcasm stopped me cold. "Princess Julea, perhaps you have noticed that my city is in the midst of a crisis? My people come first. My needs. I have given you all that I'm able to, but I have nothing else."

I looked at him and slumped. He was right, of course; he had done much for us in the midst of what was for Euticha a nearly successful *coup d'état*. I felt myself wilt, even while I scanned from face to face, looking for any hope. And then, as if out of a dream, hope arrived in the sound of a deep, confident voice.

"Mebbe we can help, eh, Mr. Puppy?" the voice said loudly, coming from the main walk beyond and behind the carriage. I turned, even as a dozen Eutichan guards and everyone else did the same. Then, a moment later, two figures strode confidently into view, and my heart leapt.

"Maybe we can at that, Cap'n," said Lord Aeryk Escrios to Captain Edword Ribald as they casually walked up to the Eutichan guard, who had no idea what was going on. "They sure seem to be in need of some."

"Aeryk! Edword!" I blurted, the frustration and disappointment turning to joy. I ran over and pulled each of them into a tight embrace. Around us, the Eutichan guardsmen stood in a mixture of alertness and confusion. I looked back to Westfall, my arms still around Edword, and smiled. He bore the same lack of understanding on his face that his men displayed, but with a nod of reassurance from me, he signaled for them to stand down.

"Now, I didn't hear everything," Edword said, unceremoniously leaving his arm draped across my shoulder as we walked over to the others, "but if you need a ride, we can take an' give you one."

Aeryk gave a casual glance into the carriage, and his face went white. "Is that Dana and Kelly in there?" he said, his voice suddenly intense.

"It is," Denis said. "Steinhargh was here. This town is truly the place for reunions. They're dying, Aeryk. Unless I can get them the help they need, they'll die. To do that, I have to go now."

I turned to face the two sailors. "Steinhargh has also taken the empress prisoner. He's trying to take over the empire. I need to get back to Yorch."

The two pirates looked at one another, and I felt a silent conversation going on between them.

"Go," Edword said suddenly, turning to Denis, "take an' get the Blackcrow and the Silver Spar back on their feet."

"And we'll take you to Yorch," Aeryk said, nodding at me.

"Sorry," Rohb said, stepping forward and making the small circle seem even tighter with his proximity. "Look, *I* know you, and I trust you. But I am pretty sure that sending my princess off with a ship full of pirates is exactly the sort of thing I can't do." I shot him a look that he met sternly. It was a sternness that reminded me of Dana, and I felt a pain stab through my heart. There was no discussion on this one, I could see.

"Fine," Aeryk said, eliciting a look from Edword. "So, I'll go with Denis, and Rohb can accompany you to Yorch."

I thought for a moment Denis would object, but he remained silent. Then, for a moment, his mask slipped, and I saw the anxiety on his face. He didn't want to do this alone, which made my decision even more of a betrayal to him than I had thought. I winced inside.

There was another silent conversation between the pirates, then Edword turned to Rohb and me. "That work for you?" he asked.

Rohb glanced at me, then nodded.

“Then let’s get a move on,” Denis said, slightly too emphatically, “we need to go.”

There was a brief exchange while Rohb retrieved his supplies, and Aeryk took his bag of effects and put it into the carriage. Denis gave Rohb a nod and gripped his hand before turning toward the coach.

“Denis,” I said.

Without breaking stride or uttering a word, he climbed into the passenger compartment and out of view.

“Uh oh,” Aeryk whispered, following me as I stepped away from the carriage.

“He doesn’t understand,” I said, my voice small in my ears. “Kelly would.”

“Everyone has to make a path of their own, princess,” he said, “and as a result, one way or another, the piper has to be paid.” He smiled gently and hugged me. “Take good care. If the One is with us, we’ll see you soon,” he said.

“When did you get wise?” I said, a halfhearted grin finding its way onto my face. He smiled back and returned to the carriage, climbing up and onto the driver’s seat and taking the reins as he settled in. Within moments, they were around the bend and out of sight. I watched after them, feeling every emotion.

“*Wind* is in the harbor, princess,” Edword said, walking up and shaking me from my reverie. I turned to face him.

"How long before we can go?" I said, the chill of duty wrapping me and insulating me from the feelings that threatened to overwhelm me.

"Few hours if we push," he said. "Might be a little slower since my quartermaster has abandoned ship and all, but by nightfall for sure."

I nodded, gave one last glance down the now empty road, and turned away. Because I have duties.

CHAPTER SEVEN

– AERYK –

It strikes me as strange to say, but I was remarkably grateful to be driving the carriage. Not for the obvious reason – the desperate journey to save the lives of two of my best friends. That was an excellent objective, and I suppose it would have been foremost in my thoughts if I were a better person. But the honest truth was I hadn't gotten my land legs back since we got to port, so I was incredibly land-sick, and being in motion on the carriage was good for my nausea. The relief I felt was sufficient to occupy my thoughts to the extent that we were nearly outside the city before the reality of this adventure caught up with me.

I guided the carriage away from the High Regent's palace to the north and along a broad avenue into the surrounding area. It was a section of the city that reeked of the wealth of nobles. Just a short time earlier, my captain and I had come up from the docks to the south, through the working-class districts, before we arrived at the palace. Thus, it felt like the whole of the morning was somewhat like my life played backward as I'd started among the nobles and ended with the working class. Riding past the proud edifices of the upper-class of Euticha, I was awash with memories of my father – the Duke of Claire in the kingdom of Lochhaven to the west. I heard him clearly, muttering unfavorable comparisons between our castle home and those of his peerage under King Ronald. The level of splendor shown by your home, he had ingrained in my young mind, was as important to your value as a person was as your family, your clothes, your title, and most of all, the amount of coin you controlled. I wish to emphasize that the above list does not include any personal qualities such as honor, loyalty, love, kindness, or even basic decency. Over the last three years, I had come to very different conclusions regarding the measure of a man than the duke's, and I was the better for it. That clarity of purpose began with the man lying now on the verge of death just a few feet behind me.

All of this left me in an extended state of reverie for that part of the ride. Fortunately, I came back to the present just in time, as we reached the city's northern border and passed through the gates. Ahead of me, the road forked in three directions – south into the open fields, northeasterly along the city's outer wall, and almost directly north into dark forests and parts unknown. I knew the answer before I opened my mouth, but then again, it was always better to be sure. And who knows? Maybe this time, I'd be wrong.

"Where am I headed?" I called back toward the

carriage cabin. There was a long pause, some random thumping noises, and then Denis appeared from the small hatch on the front of the carriage's main body just behind the driver's perch. He came out deftly, closed the portal behind him, and dropped himself on the bench beside me.

"North," he said. Which was what I would have predicted. If there were a choice where one path seemed particularly obscure or threatening, that would be the one we were going to take. It was a given. I nodded in resignation, nudged the horses onto the northern road, and with a gentle flick of my wrists, set them on at a steady pace. Several moments passed by in silence, during which I used the classic excuse of a casual glance to evaluate the man beside me. He was noticeably bone-weary, a condition I could identify all too easily. I had many times seen sailors in the throes of exhaustion. Too often, either storm or battle pushed a man to his limits and beyond. In fact, I had seen it on the very journey that brought us to Euticha. Denis's state was every bit the match of that state, and I wondered how long it had been since he slept. His eyes stared straight ahead, and while I can't be sure, I never saw them blink. I began to feel a deep fear for my injured friends in the carriage. If even the freewheeling 'dungeon rat' was in a state like this, things had to be dire. Soon my need to know more of the situation outweighed my desire to give him his peace, and I broke the silence.

"Denis, what happened?"

"Steinhargh. Steinhargh happened," he said as he let go of a heavy sigh.

"What? How can that even be possible?"

"I don't know; I'm still working on that. What we do know is this – somehow, he knew the empress and Julea would be here in Euticha on their way back from the south. So at some point, he made a pact with Westfall's flunky – the hairy one, name of 'Pwent' – and with his help cornered us in the justice hall." He leaned back on the bench, rubbing his face with his hands as he spoke.

"The justice hall?" I asked. I was doing my best, sweeping together the bits and pieces of what he was telling me and trying to fill in the gaps his exhausted recitation was leaving out.

"Yeah," he chuckled wryly, "get this; Steinhargh wasn't the only one who was trying to stick it to us. The empress herself had made some 'arrangement' – and by 'arrangement,' I mean she strong-armed Westfall. She forced him to use his guard to arrest us when we met up with Julea despite being on supposedly 'independent' land. Which is how we got hauled into the justice hall and had a front-row seat while Kelly was condemned to death."

I frowned, still struggling to put together the story as best as I could. "You mean that the three of you came to Euticha for a chance to see the princess?"

Denis looked at me sidelong as if I were simple. I chose to let it pass. A piece of the jigsaw puzzle had fallen into place for me.

“Because Euticha is – at least it *was* – neutral ground,” I said in realization, “an independent unallied state. Kelly’s exile didn’t extend here. You’re saying that somehow, Ardallah set up a deal to take him despite that.”

Denis’s head nodded in time with the gentle swaying of the carriage.

“And then Steinhargh came too?”

The nodding continued.

I let that sink into my thoughts for a minute, despite the struggle for calm I was feeling. “So, what happened then?” I finally asked.

Denis slumped forward, his arms on his knees. “The funny bit is, it seems we were only a secondary target for ol’ Steelclaw. Or maybe we were first? The order doesn’t matter, I guess. His other intent was to take the empress and seize the throne of Yorch.”

“What?” I blurted, much more loudly than necessary.

“Yeah. So, this big confrontation was going on, and there were assassins everywhere and—,”

“Assassins? Wait, what about assassins?”

“Steinhargh contracted the Kathasiri. They’re acting as his foot soldiers. Now let me finish?”

I waited, despite the imminent need to tell him that I

wouldn't need to interrupt him if he'd just tell the story so that I could understand it. But then again, there was so very much story to tell; I didn't know if that would have been possible.

"Like I said," he continued, sagging a little more over his knees again, "we were in this crowd of people, all of whom wanted to kill one or more of us for a whole bunch of reasons. We managed to make a distraction, and I got the princess out of the room. Before I could get back, though, something..., happened. From what Rohb says, fire and thunder tore through the outer tower wall. In the chaos, Steinhargh, the empress, and the Kathasiri all vanished. And Kelly and Dana were buried under rubble. Just..., just all of the of rubble."

I swallowed. When we entered Euticha's harbor that morning, the lookout noticed a tower with a massive hole in the side, clearly visible from the bay. It had been smoking still. I dismissed it, maybe simply in the vain hope that it wasn't significant. I should have known better.

"'Fire and thunder?' That sounds eerily familiar – was it the emeralds?" I said, the answer already forming in my mind.

"It was gem work for sure," he muttered, resignation heavy in his voice. "But it came from outside; it wasn't us that did it. Somehow it was Steinhargh. Somehow he has gems and the knowledge to use them."

I lolled my head back and forth before I shot him a look. “Would you believe me if I said that I knew? I mean that I was all but certain that Steinhargh was up to something? We came to Euticha because we’d seen evidence of something that made Edword and me almost sure.”

Denis gave me a long, steady look as if he were reaching inside my head and scooping out the truth for himself. Then, abruptly, he dropped his gaze and sighed. “Sure. Why not?” he said.

“But how? How did he learn to use them? That’s still a secret, right?”

“I’ve been thinking about that all night,” Denis said, shrugging one shoulder. “I expect that he spent a lot of time trying to figure out how we got away three years ago. Ol’ Steelclaw knew the legend of the emeralds, but I bet he hadn’t ever seen them in action. Remember? He seemed more interested in them as a symbol than anything else. Then we used them to bully and blast our way out of his little fiefdom. Between that and Kelly’s hacking off his arm, I think that probably stayed with him.”

“Us,” I said, the resignation in his voice seeping into me too.

“Yeah,” Denis said, “I think we might have created a monster. But now, see, I don’t care. Dana and Kelly are dying. The healer back there is doing all he can to keep them going as long as possible, which he tells me won’t be long. So the only hope we have is in finding the monks or hermits or whatever you want to call them, the ones that saved Kelly years ago, and that they can perform a miracle."

"And we're just going to go find them?" I said, my hopes – thin to begin with – shrinking to a pinprick.

"Well, the truth is that I know exactly where to start looking," he said, and for the first time during that ride, a hint of his usual brash swagger returned. "We're going to Gretchville."

I rustled the reins as the horse's pace advanced to a trot. "Great," I said, "I have no idea where that is."

Denis was poor company after that conversation, his weariness leaving him unable to do anything but ride in silence. After another hour or so, I was finally able to convince him to go back inside. He ultimately agreed to at least keep watch on Kelly and Dana, if not precisely rest. I was left alone with my thoughts, which is both a good and bad thing. Mostly I spent the time cursing the thrice-damned Triangle Blow. Everything could have been different if it weren't for that.

This one'll come for us, Edword had said that night; the night after we fished Candice from the wreckage of the Eutichan fleet – the same night that we figured out Steelclaw had somehow cracked the secret of the emeralds. We had turned the *Wind* toward Euticha and set her to run full out when the captain's supernatural feel for the sea proved true once again. The Blow hit us within the hour, and after it began, chaos reigned. We fought the storm, but in the way of all things, we weren't but insects fighting the powers of the world. Some of the boys were scrubbed from the deck by horrendous winds. Winds that alternately blew sprays of water and blasts of ice so fierce they all but tore through our leathers. Edword had us turn bow first into the squall and lash everyone and everything down. Worst of all, at least for our pride, the *Wind's* miraculous engine, the power that made her leap through wave and sky, simply wouldn't work. She was as any other ship, tossed about and impotent. And as we fought the devil storm, time stopped having meaning, and the only concern was that of clinging to our lives.

Then, it was over. We had been beaten back to death's door but not pushed through it. Edword and I threw our backs into putting the ship back into order shoulder to shoulder with the rest of the crew. There was a brief ceremony for the lost – a woefully inadequate affair – and a promise of something more when we had an opportunity. But everyone knew that our priority was to get back to Euticha as quickly as we could, and though she was still hobbled and without her unearthly gifts, the *Wind* was as fast a ship as any ever built. And so, through storm and sea, we had arrived that morning; a day later than we should have and hours too late to help. Again I cursed the Triangle

Blows.

I decided to at least spell the horses at a roadside inn, so I stopped the carriage and flagged down a stable boy. For a coin, he ran off into the main building to get the owner while I stretched my legs and worked out the kinks from the ride. Thanks be to the One, the land-sickness seemed to have eased, and I felt more pleasure than distress as I walked a few paces on solid ground. There was a mechanical rattle from the carriage behind me, and I turned to look as the side door opened. A skeletal bald man revealed himself, blinking in the light. He stepped lightly to the ground and gently closed the door behind him as he cast his gaze from side to side, finally locking his bright green eyes on me. Without hesitation or pause, he stalked directly toward me until he stopped just a couple of feet away, facing me squarely.

"Pirate," he said, sounding more as if he were identifying me than addressing me.

"Healer," I said. He frowned, and I realized that I had misunderstood the game.

"I am Garanthet VosMullen, Chief Healer to the High Regent of Euticha. Why have we stopped?" I couldn't help noticing the confident air about him, a steadiness that seemed intrinsic. Considering that, from an objective viewpoint, he was an old man out in the wilderness confronting a pirate, he was either being impressively assertive or blindingly stupid.

"Master Healer," I said, switching to the courtly manners that had been my default for most of my life. I bowed with an appropriate flourish. "I am Aeryk, quartermaster of the ship *Midnight Wind*. It is also my privilege to be your driver to Gretchville. You should know that your patients are precious to me, and I am in your debt for your service."

VosMullen looked as if I had slapped him. If I never thank my childhood for anything else, the effect of noble protocol on that man just then would be the one thing. The little healer twitched, looking away from me for the first time, then back with a restored composure.

"That being true, quartermaster, then I really must stress that we must keep moving. My patients have very little time," he said.

I nodded, maintaining the protocol. "Indeed, and I would wish no waste of time. However, the horses have been moving at pace for a good part of the day, and they need to rest lest we lose them entirely. I guarantee we will be on the road again as quickly as I can manage."

He eyed me warily; my response was undoubtedly one he was disappointed to hear, yet one for which he had no rejoinder. Haltingly, he turned and began to walk back to the carriage.

"Master Healer," I called out. He stopped and turned halfway back to look in my direction. "My friends," I continued, dropping the rigidity of protocol, “how are they faring?”

VosMullen hesitated, looked me over one last time, then cast his eyes down. “They’re dying, son,” he said, “and there’s not one thing I can do but slow it down some.”

A moment of silence passed, then, with a quick step, he returned to the carriage and climbed in.

“Kraken’s blood,” I muttered.

A sudden thought came to me then, one that the man I had been in the past would never have even considered. That man, as it turned out, was not in residence any longer. I turned and went into the inn without a second’s hesitation. It took me a little time to find the proprietor, some time to explain to him what I wanted, and a very brief moment of negotiation before I turned and left him with a bag of coin on the table. Before I was even back to the carriage, the stable boy I had initially hailed was joined by two others, each guiding a horse from the barn that stood a short distance away behind the inn itself. The door on the carriage rattled again, and this time Denis emerged, dropping lightly to the ground and closing the door behind him. He watched as the stable hands detached our horses from the harness linkage and guided the two fresh ones into their former positions.

“What’s going on?” he said in a hush as if speaking too loudly might scatter both animals and humans.

“I made a deal,” I said, shrugging one shoulder as we

watched the work together. "We need to keep moving, and we can't spare the time for the horses to rest properly. So, I traded them for two of the innkeeper's own animals."

Denis's brow furrowed as he looked at the new horses. "They're kinda skinny," he said.

"Oh, don't get me wrong. It was a terrible trade," I said, again with a shrug of my shoulder, "I got two skinny plough horses, and he got two well-bred parade mounts and a bag of my money. But I didn't think that was the point."

I felt a pat on my shoulder, accompanied by the slap of a hand on leather. "Nice work, your lordship." I glanced back to see the lopsided grin I'd come to know. "Now it's your turn to ride," he said, giving a head tilt toward the carriage cabin. "I'm rested enough, and unlike you, I know where I'm headed. Keep an eye on the healer and our friends."

I thought to complain – to argue – but he made sense, and life at sea had taught me that you get rest whenever you can. So I nodded in agreement, clapped his shoulder in return, and moved off toward the carriage. I gave one last look toward Denis as he climbed up to the driver's bench and settled himself in before I opened the cabin door and crawled inside. I had barely closed the door behind me when the carriage started forward, and by the time I sat down, we were moving steadily again along the road.

Once I was inside, I took my first undistracted look

around the carriage's cabin. From outside, the slight curves at the corners had given me the impression that the interior would feel cramped, but it was quite the opposite in reality. If anything, it felt more spacious on the inside than it genuinely was. The walls were covered with a dense burgundy fabric over some kind of soft but firm padding. It was tacked in place at the corners and along the middle, and the whole design reminded me of a couch I remembered from my mother's sitting room. It smelled much fresher than I had expected as well, with only a hint of lilac and wood in the air. I glanced up and immediately understood how that was the case. The roof was formed from a series of parallel slats that were partially tilted up, allowing for daylight and fresh air to filter in. A geared track ran down the far side of the ceiling and terminated at a crank that, when turned, would open or close these as desired. A bench seat stretched across the entire width of the cabin at the front, padded similarly to the walls, and it was here I sat to review the rest of the interior.

Above me, the small hatch that Denis had used to join me on the driver's bench was fastened shut. As I looked toward the rear of the cabin, I saw that two more seats ran along either of the inner sides of the carriage, stretching from the doors to the far back wall. Dana and Kelly were laid there, one on each side, secured and padded by straps and blankets. Between them, VosMullen was seated on a small stool, busily dividing his ministrations between the two. A black satchel sat on the floor, and from it, he took out unidentifiable mechanisms made of brass and glass that he held against one of them and then the other. First, he would frown, produce a small vial of some form of liquid that was only partially visible in the reflected sunlight. Then, he would lean over, presumably dripping some of the mysterious solution into what was probably the obscured mouth of one of them, then re-administer the brass and glass device. The liquid, I deduced, was the source of the lilac scent, as there was a more potent whiff when he used it. He gave me a quick look and a brief nod as if to acknowledge my presence, then returned his attention to the patients.

I wish I could report that I watched over my friends and their physician carefully on that trip, but the fact was that, once I had settled in, my own exhaustion dragged me deep into sleep's depths, and I don't remember much of the next portion of the ride at all.

I woke in the dark, with flickering light coming in through the windows on the port side of the carriage and the harsh sound of shouting. The old, familiar jolt of awareness went through me as my hand instinctively went to the staff at my side. Night had fallen, that seemed certain, and the only light in the carriage came from what I took to be lit torches outside. I looked and saw that Kelly and Dana were still in place, though the healer was gone. I dropped into a crouch, hand on the door latch, and peered through the cloudy glass of the window. Four torches were spaced irregularly around a semicircle of open space outside the carriage door. There was a blackness beyond them that seemed to be moving, and I took it to be the shadowy forms of people milling about. In the middle of the open area, though, stood a crouched figure in a fighting stance. Denis.

"Oh, boy," I muttered. The muscles in my back bunched, as they always did, and I took a moment to loosen them consciously. I took one breath, gave a careful twist of the door latch, and threw myself out, landing in a crouch to Denis's left with my staff in a low guard.

"Nice of you to show up," he said without turning toward me. His left hand was steadily in front of him, one vicious dagger pointed out, while the other was held in his right in a reverse grip and out to his side.

"You could have knocked or shouted or something," I said. I had guessed correctly, the moving 'blackness' was a crowd of some fifteen or twenty people, all in long black cloaks, watching us warily. In the middle, slightly closer to us than the others, was a man about my height, cloaked in black as the others were but brandishing a curved golden sword toward Denis.

"So, are these those assassins you mentioned?" I said, watching the golden blade steadily.

"No," Denis said, "these toilet stains are just in our way." His left hand flexed on the handle of his blade.

"We'll be seeing your carriage, or you go no farther," the golden-bladed figure said in a clear, steady voice. His sword neither wavered nor dipped as he addressed us, and I wondered at just exactly who we were facing out here in what appeared to be complete wilderness.

"You'll let us go where we need to go, and we'll do it past you, or we'll do it over you. It really makes no difference to me," Denis snarled.

"Where's the healer?" I said, hoping against hope he wasn't a hostage.

"Here," said a small voice from behind me. I gave a glance over my shoulder, where I saw a thin hand waving out from underneath the carriage.

"Excellent," I muttered.

"You'll not pass," the figure said.

I saw my successive motions in my mind. First, I would drop low and outside, allowing Denis to move freely. Then I would come up with a side swing of my staff, hopefully hobbling the swordsman. That would let me get back to my feet and face the crowd to the left with Denis at my back and no enemies close enough to be an immediate threat. My back bunched again, and I started to throw myself forward when a woman's voice rang out from the middle of the crowd.

"Now stop this, all of you!" it said. The voice had a tone of scolding that somehow made me want to apologize for whatever I did. A figure came forward from the cluster of black, seemingly pushing the others out of its way. Or maybe they were stepping aside in deference? It was hard to tell in the dark. Besides, I had only stopped my forward movement at the last instant, and so I wound up stumbling forward, catching my balance with the help of my staff at the last moment. It was not my most exceptional maneuver. The figure stopped between the rest of the crowd and us, looked back and forth from one to the other of us, and finally moved over toward Denis, pulling back the dark hood and revealing the stately face of an older woman.

"Laddie, aren't you supposed to be in Euticha?" she said, cocking her head. The flickering torchlight revealed the spread of a grin across her face, and as it did, the tension in the air evaporated. Denis stood straight, slipping his blades back into their sheathes.

"I was," he said with a shake of his head, "but...," he trailed off.

The woman looked from him to the carriage, pausing only a moment as she noticed VosMullen climbing out from beneath. She looked back to Denis, the grin now replaced by a frozen look of concern. "Where are your companions? What happened?"

"Inside," Denis said, turning away from the woman

and striding back to the carriage side. "They're not good," he said as he pulled the door open.

She followed, moving with surprising speed and grace. Her black robes swirled as she moved to, and then inside, the carriage. There was a momentary pause as the rest of us waited for what would come next. I caught Denis's eye and gave him a questioning look that he ignored, turning back to the open cabin. Suddenly the woman swept back out of the hatch, gliding swiftly back to the assembled group of her companions and us.

"Finn!" she called as she walked. The swordsman that had moments before been facing off with Denis and me stepped forward, his golden blade disappearing inside his cloak. "Take the carriage back to the outpost. Do it now," she said in a voice that was very much accustomed to being obeyed. The figure, now removing his own hood and revealing a dark-haired man's face, nodded without a word and moved off toward the carriage. She then turned to Denis, who was still standing beside me. I stepped closer to them, hoping to clear up the growing confusion that was near to choking my thoughts.

"Tell me," she said, looking at Denis. Her voice was serious but calm. She wanted information without the distraction of emotion. All action, no hesitation. It was honestly impressive.

"A tower wall was made to fall on them," he said, and

I was surprised by the matter-of-factness she seemed to extract. He continued, "It's the work of an old enemy who found us in Euticha."

She glanced at me, but if she was at all interested in who I was, she gave no indication then, her eyes quickly flashing back to Denis. "Was it the work of the stones?"

"I think so," he said. Such casual mention of the gemstones felt surreal to me. Of course, I was accustomed to the unknown – I was a sailor on the *Midnight Wind*, after all – but Kelian emeralds and their like had always evoked such hushed tones that the open discussion felt uncomfortable.

The carriage had started to move off under the hand of the man she had called Finn, and I spared it a glance before turning back to her. "What about their supplies? Do you have them?" she asked. A rising tone of concern was now evident in her voice, doing nothing to calm my nerves.

Denis shook his head.

She looked at him very intensely. "Tell me you have the sword," she said.

Denis gave her a grave look, but there was a hint of puzzlement in his eyes.

Something like horror passed across her face, and, for the first time, I felt a shiver go through me. I couldn't say precisely why, but it seemed that whatever might scare her would be something about which you should worry. Just then, the angular form of VosMullen pushed his way between us. He spun around, sparing a moment's snarling displeasure for each of us before settling his eyes on Denis.

"What in the name of the One are you doing? Those people are going to die without my help! Where are they being taken? Who are these people? What is—"

"Shh. The adults are talking," Denis said, cutting him off. The healer's face turned red enough to be seen even in the dim light of the torches.

"I demand—," he started again.

"No, no," the woman said, both cutting him off and prompting him to turn toward her, "you aren't demanding anything, physician. We are now out of your purview. Your assistance was appreciated, but now I have to ask you to be quiet and not be a hindrance." She gave Denis one last look that could have either been one of acknowledgment or disapproval – or possibly both, actually – and turned back toward the rest of her associates.

"Who was that?" VosMullen said after a moment, his venom unabated. "I am the Chief Healer of Euticha. I will not be dismissed by some backwoods charlatan and her mindless lackeys."

"Garanthet, shut up," I said, surprising myself both by just how much he was annoying me and by remembering his first name. He looked at me in surprise, then stepped back. He was no less angry, but he seemed to have decided against pressing the issue. It may have been the realization that he was alone in the wilds with an outlaw, a pirate, and a crowd of shadowy figures he had just called 'mindless lackeys.' I can't be sure. Instead of pondering it, I looked over to Denis.

"These are the monks?" I asked him. He was watching the carriage as it moved into the woods.

"Close enough to them," he said, "And that is Eryth. She is the one that saved Kelly the first time. Exactly who we were looking for if you can believe it. If anyone can help them, it's her."

One black-cloaked figure remained standing a few feet away from us, holding one of the torches and waiting patiently. Meanwhile, the others either followed in the direction the carriage had gone or simply melted back into the woods. I felt transfixed, frozen in time; I knew we had to follow after our friends, but somehow it was all so much I couldn't bring myself to start. Denis remained still as well, and I felt a strange kinship. We were men of action, by choice or circumstance, and now our part in the story was to wait while others took the stage. Dormancy meant that we now had time to think, and that was a fearful and overwhelming thing.

Denis came back to awareness first and looked at me. We nodded to one another in a quiet acknowledgment of our feelings and turned toward the silent torchbearer. He took this as the cue to lead on, turning and walking off into the dark forest, neither waiting nor checking whether we were following.

I can't precisely describe the path we took. Partly that was due to the darkness, and partly it was because our guide was moving too fast for me to have the extra attention even to try to navigate. I'm pretty confident that on several occasions, our path went in a complete circle that should have intersected where we had previously walked but didn't. Coupled with the fact that we seemed to be going uphill and down again repeatedly, I was hopelessly lost. My only focus was the torchlight of our guide, some dozen feet ahead. How it was that he was moving with such surety, I really couldn't say.

"God's teeth, how are they getting the blasted carriage through this?" Denis's voice came from very close to my right, though I couldn't make him out in the dark.

"Where are we?" I said. I hadn't spoken up till then as I wasn't sure if we were trying to be stealthy or not. But if he was going to talk, I decided I should be able to too.

"Not far from Gretchville," he said, "though I can't say how close."

"We didn't get there?"

"No. We got found first." For a moment, the torch ahead seemed to flare up, and I was able to see his face. He was looking around, casting his eyes in every direction, seemingly at once. "Night fell a while ago. Speaking of that, you were really out, hunh?"

I shrugged and said, "It was a long trip to Euticha." I felt a twinge, thinking of the storm. "Then we hit the road almost the minute we saw you. I just had nothing left."

"I know the feeling," he said flatly. We fell silent, following our guide as he dropped down a slight incline and turned to the left. "Anyway," he continued when the path leveled back off a moment later, "I kept going, relying on that little lantern on the carriage to see the road and hoping we didn't attract any attention, animal or outlaw. Though come to think of it, a couple of bandits might have been a good place to put some of my anger."

"I hear that. When I woke up, that's what I thought happened," I said.

"Seemed reasonable," he said.

"Sure. So, what happened?"

"We were coming up to a steep ridge, like a big black wall ahead of us. The road turned at an angle to veer away from it, and I was turning to follow. That's when the lantern went poof."

"Poof," I repeated.

"Poof. Like the light just stopped," Denis said, sounding like he was talking to a child. "I reined in the horses when I realized we were surrounded. The torches appeared out of nowhere all at once, so at least I could make them out in the dark. I thought just to snap the reins and see where we landed."

I shook my head even though I knew he wouldn't be able to see it. "Probably wouldn't have gotten far. Besides, with Kelly and Dana...," I let the idea trail off.

"I know, I thought about that. It didn't matter, though. That horse's ass of a healer jumped out of the door and started ranting that we needed to go and that 'time was more important than ever.' Idiot."

"Are they okay?" I said, not even thinking that he wouldn't know I was referring to Kelly and Dana.

"No idea. By the time VosMullen hit the ground, he had noticed all the cloaked people and dove under the carriage."

"Oh, for the love of the One," I said in a huff.

"Exactly. So, I threw the brake on and jumped down. I figured I had to keep the little numbskull alive for Kelly and Dana's sake. So, I mouthed off to them to take their attention off him, and that's when you came out."

"Any idea where we're going?" I said.

Denis shook his head, and I suddenly realized that I could see it. I looked ahead and saw a gentle glow from beyond a low rise. Our guide had stopped on the crest and was waiting for us.

"Nope, but I think we're there," Denis said.

We took the few remaining steps to the top of the rise and looked down. The ridge we thought we were on was indeed a well-camouflaged wall that ran around a large camp area. 'Camp' isn't the right word, though, for what was before us was more of a small town than a camp. A network of minor roads crisscrossed the area in a winding, natural pattern, describing discreet sites with numerous low hills covered in grasses and plants. The hills were deceiving, though, as each had one side that was not a hill but rather a stone wall with one or more windows and a door. Poles with small wire cages at the top were perched at the intersections where the paths met, each no larger than a man's head. These held irregular lumps of something I couldn't identify but that was glowing with a gentle, warm light.

"Wow," Denis said after a soft whistle, "and I thought Gadai's tree fort was something."

I looked at our guide and noticed that he was holding more than the torch. There was a rope in his other hand that disappeared into the darkness above him. He nodded toward our feet, gesturing with the hand holding the torch. I looked where he indicated and saw a set of square stones jutting out of the wall, staggered and at decreasing height, forming a set of stairs that descended to the ground below. I stepped out, carefully following them down with Denis right behind me and our guide just behind. I turned and looked back as I got to the bottom to find that our companion had stopped about halfway down the steps. From where he stood, he had slowly released the rope, and in response, there was some unidentifiable motion at the top of the stairs. Finally, he released the cord entirely, and the movement ceased; the sky above was still again.

"Camouflage," I muttered, "Something that hides the inside from the outside that we couldn't even see up close."

"Creepy camouflage," Denis agreed, "I didn't see anything of this place until we were all but on top of it."

"I wonder how the carriage got in," I said, looking around somewhat furtively as our guide walked silently past us, heading just a little to one side of the 'town.' In the brighter light from the – I guess I'll call them 'lanterns' – I could get a better look at our guide. The figure was entirely disguised by the black cloak and hood, which obscured everything save for the hint of a hairless lower jaw when the light was just right. More layers of black clothing were the only visible detail under the outer layer. So, really, the only concretely identifiable thing I can say was that he – or she – was a little shorter than Denis or me. I did, though, get a better look at what I had initially taken to be the torch he carried, and I realized now that it was a smaller version of the lanterns in town. Which is to say, it was a stick about three feet long with a metal cage on its end. Inside the cage was an irregular lump of yellow crystal that had glowed with enough brightness that I hadn't realized it wasn't a flame. At some point since we'd entered, the crystal was extinguished, though, and was indistinguishable from a large piece of typical amber.

"The weird stuff," I mumbled to myself, remembering Edword's opinion of it all.

"That's why we came, I guess," Denis replied, though I hadn't addressed him. "I guess we kind of asked for it." He shrugged a shoulder dismissively. It was a very Denis thing to say, but it seemed somewhat forced, and I wondered just what was going through his mind as we passed the strange little hills with their doorways and the glowing crystal lanterns.

Time has a strange way of shifting how rapidly it passes, depending on the situation. It's an observation that comes up repeatedly in this tale, and this was no different. The carriage ride, which had taken hours, seemed now to have passed quickly, whereas the walk from the forest where we had met the strangers to our final destination at one of the larger hill-houses seemed interminable. Finally, we arrived in a small clearing that abutted a particularly long hill and its stone façade. The High Regent's carriage sat abandoned to the right of where we emerged, its side door hanging open. The horses were gone, and I wondered after them for a moment. They had been a terrible bargain, but they had performed admirably for us, and I hoped they were being cared for well. Several black-cloaked figures – I guessed the same ones that had met us initially – stood somewhat randomly around the clearing as if waiting for something. Two stood on either side of the door into the long hill, and both were working very hard at not responding to the tirade from Garanthet VosMullen, who stood before them animatedly waving his arms and making demands. I felt a shock of surprise go through me as I realized that I'd lost track of him before we'd begun the walk to the settlement and that I had no idea where he had gone. Notably, I hadn't missed him.

"Hey, Garanthet!" Denis called, jarring the little healer from his diatribe and causing him to whirl in our direction. On seeing us, he stormed across the open space with an enthusiasm that made me think he was excited to have another target to castigate.

"I demand," he began, and I knew it was going to be downhill for him from there on, "that they admit me to this charlatan's ward!" He kept walking until he was far too close to Denis. It seemed evident to me that the little man was uninformed as to just how dangerous my friend was.

"Master Healer," I said quickly, hoping to stem the tide before there was unpleasantness, "can you first tell us what is happening?"

VosMullen looked at me at first as if he didn't remember me at all, then stepped toward me as his words came out in a burst.

"'What is happening?' Is that what you asked me, quartermaster? I'll tell you. We were brought here in a manner that I cannot even explain. The carriage windows showed me only cold fire and dry water and light and darkness for the entire ride."

I blinked. "Cold fire" and "dry water" sounded strangely specific – and much too poetic – for VosMullen. I instead got the impression that he had been significantly affected by whatever it actually was. I also wondered that he had been gathered to the carriage at all.

"Then we came here, to this seemingly deserted rural settlement," he waved his arms around to indicate the other hills and the town in general, "where I haven't seen a soul save for the ones that have effectively kidnapped us!"

"Are you kid—," Denis started, but I touched his arm, and he abated.

"Then," the healer continued, and if he had noticed Denis's burgeoning interruption, he paid it no heed, "my patients were swept from my care by that forest witch and into the ward there, and I have been locked out!" He pointed toward the guards at the doorway where he had been standing when we arrived. I looked up, and just then, Eryth came out through the large, green door on the ward hill. She said something to one of the two guards, and he rushed off, then she came over toward us. Both Denis and I brushed heedlessly past VosMullen and met her halfway. She had a look on her face that I recognized in spite of never meeting her before that day.

"It's bad," I said. I have always been extraordinarily good at stating the obvious. It's good to have a skill.

"It is," she said gravely, "and if it were anyone else, they would be beyond all hope. As it is, they may still be."

Denis eyed her for a moment. "But...?" he said, extending the '*u*' sound.

She looked up, and despite the unabated seriousness of her tone, there was a momentary twinkle in her eye. "But they may *not* be. I will try," she said.

Denis exhaled a breath that he may have been holding since the night before. His whole posture seemed to loosen, and he nodded slowly.

"Don't be so positive, laddie," Eryth said, raising a hand and capturing both of our attention. "What I'm going to do has never been tried before in our history. In fact, neither of the things I will do has. There would seem to be a different answer for each of our young friends, though both processes are equally arcane. I don't know what the result will be, and I don't know exactly what we will recover even in success. The result may be one for which they do not thank us." Her eyes went unfocused and then dropped toward the ground. I felt a gnawing in my chest that seemed to make it hard to breathe. "It may be that we should let them rest," she finished a moment later, as if from far away.

"Well, the hell with that," Denis blurted, causing Eryth's face to snap up. He shot a tiny glance at me and then looked back and held her eyes. “We got them here. Now you do the stuff,” he said, with a certainty that was perhaps unrealistic. I am positive he didn’t care, though. “This story doesn’t end now. Not yet, not today. Maybe someday, but not today. Now you go in there and do whatever it is you need to, and you make it okay. We have a lot more to do, the three of us, and they are not going to ‘rest.’ They don’t get to quit. That’s not our thing.”

The tension in my chest seemed to pop like a soap bubble, and suddenly I felt a rush of excitement shoot through me. And maybe, irrational or not, hope.

Eryth looked at Denis for a long, intense moment. Then, a tiny curl of a grin curled her lips.

“You’re something else again, laddie,” she said quietly, “something else again.”

Across the clearing, one of the black-cloaked figures – presumably the guard she had sent away – came into view from behind the carriage with a small cart. It was about the size of a farmer’s wagon, six or so feet long and perhaps half that wide, with four large wheels supporting it. But instead of a flatbed where the produce would be displayed, it carried a cabinet full of doors and drawers of various sizes. These were all latched and locked closed in defense against the jostling of its motion over the roadway. Swirling, knotted patterns traced the frame, alternately etched and burned and painted into the wood. Eryth turned to the bearer and dispatched him back to the door of the ward hill-building with a wave. With careful steps, he entered the door and brought the cart inside. As he disappeared, she turned back to us.

"This will take time," she said, "and you three cannot stay here."

"Excuse me?" Denis said, barely restrained rage rising in his voice.

"Easy," she said, gently smiling at him, "I mean that this will take time. Days. And the recovery, if there is to be a recovery, will take even longer. You will need to find lodging."

Denis and I looked at one another, then around at the small hill buildings that surrounded us. Finally, I looked back at Eryth, my wordless question clear.

"I see. I see, but you don't," she said with a gentle shake of her head. "Understand, you are friends to us. We believe this. It is not an issue of trust; it is your safety—both here and when you leave. You have seen the danger the knowledge we bear brings. We can't – we *won't* – put you in that position.

Out of the corner of my eye, I saw Denis's hands unconsciously moving to his chest.

"Dear boy, don't embarrass my men," Eryth said, noticing his motion at the same time as I did. "They are unprepared to fight the Apostate, Denis, but they are many and have their own resources."

Denis froze, his mind rapidly processing what she said before coming to a decision. Finally, he let his hands drop.

"Lord Aeryk, Denis, trust me," she said, looking from one to the other of us. The fact that she knew me by name was only something that I would consciously consider unusual later; at that moment, it seemed completely natural. I nodded and looked at Denis. It took him longer, but ultimately he nodded as well.

She returned the nod with a gentle smile, then turned and started for the ward. "I will have Finn guide you out shortly, but I need him for the first part of this process, and so you may be here for some time yet. Gretchville is not far; I believe you can find lodging there. For now, rest. I will have some food brought for you as well," she said as she walked, giving the nod to another of the nearby cloaked figures. With a bow, he ran off. Or she. Whatever. Eryth reached the entrance to the ward and gave us a look back over her shoulder. "We will see, lads. We will see," she said, then she was gone, disappearing behind the closing door.

"This is intolerable!" VosMullen's voice burst into the quiet she'd left behind. He had been standing several feet behind us during our discussion with Eryth, but now he stormed up, radiating his annoyance and wounded pride. "I demand that you have them let me in there at once! I came here to care for my patients, and I don't have any idea what backwoods voodoo you are allowing that witch to perform!"

Denis's hands moved too fast for the eye to follow, the metallic sound of drawn steel reaching my ears long after the daggers were already out. He was suddenly inches away from the little man, his blades held in an '*X*' near the healer's throat.

"I," Denis said, his voice very controlled but his eyes boring into VosMullen's, "very much appreciate your help with my friends." He remained perfectly still, letting his words sink in. "But if you do not stop being a high-and-mighty pain in the arse, I guarantee that I will stop you. I am not in the mood," he finished. Time did its thing again, and the single moment stretched until it seemed very long. Mainly, I expect, for the healer. I had a fleeting thought as to whether VosMullen might need a new pair of pants.

"Okay," I said as casually as if they had been discussing the weather, "where is that food she mentioned then?" Life at sea, particularly among pirates, gives one a kind of mental insulation from the intensity of such situations.

Just as quickly as they had appeared, the twin blades vanished again into their sheathes. Denis took a step back and looked at me. "I'm with you there, your lordship. I could do with some food. Do you think these folks have any wine?"

What sounded like the roar of an avalanche rolled out of the ward hill suddenly. We turned toward it even as a vibration ran through the ground beneath our feet. Through the stone-framed windows, a greenish-yellow light appeared. Within a few moments, it went from a dim flicker to a brightness rivaling the noon sun. I squinted and then turned away, shielding my eyes with my hand. Denis had his hands in front of his eyes as well. VosMullen had, instead, dropped to the shaking ground, his head buried in his arms. After a moment, the light faded, leaving only a dull glow behind the windows.

"I take it back, Garanthet," Denis said, watching the receding light through his outstretched fingers, "you go ahead and go on in."

CHAPTER EIGHT

— JAYMES —

Winter had come early, and it came with all the things that make me hate it. There was snow, ice, cold winds, and then more cold winds. The worst part, though, was how it made my city feel. I have lived in Yorch all my life, and there isn't one little bit of it I'd trade. But the winter had closed it up, and it felt more like a graveyard than home. Even the Winter Wyl, the biggest party we had all year, may as well have been canceled; the cold was just too much for the bonfires and dancing to ward off. And now it was weeks later and still just as cold and dark, and there didn't seem to be an end in sight. And the life of my city felt all but completely drained away.

Of course, there was more to the story than that. We'd had cold winters before. I suppose that some of them had even been worse, really. But the weather was matched these days by a chill coming from the palace since the empress returned. And since the Battle in the Bay happened.

I felt the wind whip up again, hitting me from the right as I crossed the street. It came up from the ocean, swept across the docks, and then through the streets. My cloak was heavy wool, my winter one, but it didn't matter. The wind felt like it was biting into me like the wolf-fish of the harbor through fishing nets. It brushed my hood back like it wanted to attack my face better. I looked around quickly and tugged the hood back into place. As I did, I saw two of the city guard passing nearby, just beyond the closed front of Old Brawn's Corner Store. Thankfully, if they noticed me at all, they didn't turn. In my head, I bet myself that they were just as cold as I was, despite the heavy fur wraps they wore over their armor.

I hurried my steps, and soon enough, I was across the cobblestones and in the shelter of Maramon's Storehouse. Inside he kept all of the bits and bobs he used to fix merchant ships, which was his trade. I didn't care much. Shipbuilding just isn't that interesting. But the alley blocked the wind and was such a relief that I drew a deep breath. Which was a mistake, for sure. The cold air hit my lungs and sent me into a coughing fit. I leaned heavily on the ice-covered wall of the storehouse and struggled to clear my throat. It took several breaths through the thick wool of my hood before I was back to normal, and I sneaked a look back out onto the street as soon as I was. The guards hadn't returned. They were probably a fair distance away by now, which was a relief, though thinking that – feeling that – made me stop and shake my head. *Not being noticed by the city guard shouldn't have to be a thing a body is worried about, should it?* I thought. But then I remembered, much had changed since the end of summer. And it hadn't just been the weather.

It took a few more minutes of walking through a few alleys and quiet passages before I got to the steps leading up to the pub door. I could have got there more directly, but staying in the shadows was sort of second nature nowadays. I took one more look around as the snow fell on the quiet afternoon streets before I climbed the stairs and went inside the *Codslinger*. The outside door led to a small hallway that took me to my right, where another door – much fancier, with thick, etched glass panes from top to bottom – opened into the actual pub. The warmth of the hearth hit me first, and I said a quiet *thank you* to it before I turned to the rest of the room.

The *'Slinger* was three times as long as it was wide, with a bar all along the right side and a few small tables everywhere else. There was another room far in the rear, a private one, and a staircase that led upstairs to the owner's private home. A second hearth toward the back matched the friendly one that had greeted me as I came in the door, and between the two of them, even the nasty chill outside was pushed away.

I walked over and settled onto the stool at the corner of the bar top, shifting so that my cloak draped over my legs but my hands would be free. Finally, I flipped my hood back from my head and brushed my hands through my hair.

"Yer gettin' snow on my bar." I looked up at the voice and saw two very, very important sights. The first was the big earthen mug of beer now sitting in front of me. The second was the pretty bartender who'd put it there and who was now scowling at me in a weirdly friendly way. Niamh.

"It's kinda just water now," I said, brushing my hands against one another before I reached for the beer.

"I don't care," she grumbled, "there's no way I can know where that sandy mop you call hair has been. This is a clean place."

She leered at me a moment longer before her smile punched through, and she shook her head at me. Niamh was a friend; I didn't have so many of those all the time.

"It's cold outside," I said after a draught of the beer. The *'Slinger* wasn't an especially popular place, nor was it somewhere that visitors to the Great City would be looking to find. It was just a bar. No music, no special food that made people just 'have to go.' But the beer was homemade, the fires were warm, and my friend owned it. That made it a comfortable place in a town that was slowly becoming less and less so.

The sun had been bathing the harbor just a bit after midday, and despite the heat – and the resulting sweat – it seemed like the entire population of the city had turned out. Of course, that wasn't a surprise; the imperial family was coming home, and that was a time for a celebration. In fairness, we Yorchians used just about *any* reason to have a party, but this was a really good one, and even the stuffier citizens had caught the bug. The heralds had announced days ago when we could expect the *Fenris* to return, even if how they knew the time was always a mystery to me. I mean, it seemed like sea travel wasn't very good at keeping a schedule. But the celebration was planned, and the people came, and as it turned out, the predictions were weirdly accurate. Well, for the *time* of arrival, anyway. But I'm getting ahead of myself.

Word came down from the lighthouses that the watchmen had spotted a small fleet of ships coming from the south. I thought that was strange as The *Fenris* hadn't left with a large fleet. But then again, I thought, maybe the Gladians had come for a visit in return. That seemed possible. In any case, it wasn't long before word came that the *Fenris* was now visible among the other ships. All was well. And then it stopped being well just as quickly. As the vessels came into view from the shore, the band played, and the press of bodies pushed forward as everyone tried to catch a glimpse. Then, a single black ship swept in from the east so suddenly that it seemed to have just appeared from nowhere. A bright arc of fire spewed out of its side and into the sky.

Even from the shore, we could see as the fire rained down on the ships around the *Fenris* like a glowing hailstorm. Then the approaching fleet reacted; blue flames leapt from the sides of the boats closest to the attacker. Their weapons were different, though. Instead of arcing overhead, these surges of blue fire ran right along the surface of the water. Behind where I stood, the band – which had only now caught on that something wasn't right – stopped playing, and a few voices in the crowd gasped and screamed. I expected the attacking ship to burst into flames, but instead..., it bounced? That's the best word I have for it. It moved sideways from the way it had been sailing like it was a stone skipped across water. When it stopped, it seemed to lay almost flat on the water for a long time. Two ships from the flotilla around the *Fenris* broke away from its companions and headed toward the seemingly capsized attacking ship. The rest of the fleet – including the *Fenris* – continued in toward the docks.

For a few minutes, confusion held on to the crowd around me on the shore, but as the *Fenris* came close and lined up for docking, a weird kind of dizzy joy washed over everyone. The musicians started to play again, people pressed forward again, and for all that we had just seen, the crowd more or less went right back to where we started.

At first, I craned my neck to see what was going on out on the water. But the crowd and the noise and basically everything else wouldn't let me, and soon enough, I was watching the Wolfpack coming out onto the *Fenris's* deck from the cabins below with the rest of the citizenry. Despite myself, I was excited. I mean, I have as much reason to dislike Her Highness as anyone, but it still wasn't every day that the Empress of Yorch was this close to us. I thought to glance over at the raised platform that stood just a little north from me and a short bit away from the water. It was angled just so and in such a way that the Golden Palace would be behind it. The result was that the palace was staged behind the empress when she addressed the citizenry. That was the tradition, of course; whenever she or the princess came out in public for an event, they would give a short speech. In the empress's case, she would sometimes select a few people for an audience, which was a big deal. The royal court, ambassadors of state, and occasionally grave legal issues regularly came before the empress, and she would often make short work of whatever the problem was. A citizen granted an audience could discuss anything with her, and with just a stroke of her scribe's pen, she could change anything. It was a ticket to dreams. It was part of the reason people were so excited.

I looked back just in time to see her Imperial Highness, Ardallah Niconnal bar Morrisia of Yorch, Gloriana, Sola, Lunis, and Stelis, step out to the middle of the *Fenris's* deck. She wore a white gown decorated with tiny slivers of silver sprinkled across it. They caught the afternoon sunlight and flickered the way that the waves did in the early evening. Her long white hair was draped in a braid from the golden circlet of her crown down her right shoulder. I had to admit, like her or not, she pretty much was the picture of Imperial majesty. The crowd cheered as she turned to face them from the deck, but the cheer fell off in stages as a second figure came out from the ship's cabin. It was a man, armored in steel that was almost black and trimmed in gold. A long cloak – also black with gold trim – draped down his back and over his right side. Most unusually of all, a golden crown with black inlays sat on his head.

The stranger moved around behind the empress to her right side, paused, and offered his arm to her. There was a heartbeat of time where the entire crowd seemed stunned, too confused to know precisely what reaction was appropriate, and a silence that felt unholy fell over the pier. However, it passed as quickly as it came when as she threaded her arm through his. Together, they walked down the gangplank, off of the ship, and up the dock. The musicians, always clever about such things, started to play the imperial march, which served to cue the crowd. The cheers ratcheted back up to their original volume. Once again, and for the second time in just a few minutes, it seemed like things were back to normal. Unfortunately, it was also the second time they were not.

"Are ye in there?"

I shook my head and looked up at Niamh. She had her eyebrows scrunched together; her head cocked to one side.

"What?" I said.

"Ye kinda went away for a bit; I was talkin' to ye about things," she said. She resumed wiping the bar top to my right, looking at it harder than needed.

"Sorry," I muttered into my mug, "lost in thought."

"Try not ta do that whilst I'm sayin' somethin' important, eh?" she said, flipping the towel over her shoulder as she came back and leaned closer to me. "Some things it's best not to have to say twice, Jay. There are eyes everywhere. Even here."

I nodded my defeat and put the mug back down on the counter. I let my eyes wander down the length of the room. There were only a few other people around, though I couldn't tell as to any occupants in the private room in the back. It didn't matter; if she'd been telling me something that made her get so stern that her accent cleared up, it was a big deal, and I should have been listening more than thinking.

I nudged the empty mug toward her, taking care that my cloak didn't drop off my shoulders and reveal anything untoward to the people that may or may not have been listening. She looked at it.

"Sky and sea, boyo. Did ye even taste it?" she said with a smirk.

It took me a second. “Oh,” I said finally, “yeah, it was great.”

She shook her head and wandered away, coming back a short bit later with another full mug. “Try not to inhale this one, eh?”

I smiled. I’ve been told that my smile is ‘lopsided’ and that it makes me look more cocky than happy. Niamh knows me well enough, though, so I wasn’t concerned. I drank the beer. “What’s the story?” I asked, keeping my eyes down and my voice low.

Niamh had stayed at the inside corner of the bar when she gave me my drink, so I knew she still wanted to talk. Now, she squatted down and looked for all onlookers like she was fussing with something under the bar. Some bartender business. Definitely not having a private conversation with the big cloaked guy.

“Rumor has it that there was a ruckus on the western border,” she said in a voice that reached me and only me. “Border station was attacked, the way I hear it. Came in the middle of the night they did, and gone before an alarm went up. The soldiers who weren’t on duty didn’t know anything ‘til first light.”

“How many bodies?” I said. Border attacks were pretty rare, but not like ‘unicorn’ rare; they did happen from time to time. I wondered why she was telling me about this one.

"None," she said, looking in my eyes for the first time.

I looked at her directly then, just to be sure what I was thinking was what she was trying to get me to think. Her eyes told me I was.

I shook my head. She stood up and started wiping the – by now very clean – section of the bar again. "But it could be," she said.

"I can't see it," I said. "It's just more of the same."

"The same...?"

"The noise. The distraction. Steinhargh's smokescreen."

"Oh, that 'same.'"

The empress and the stranger walked calmly up from the docks. They remained sure and graceful as they, together, climbed the steps onto the empress's platform. With a nod, she released his arm and stepped forward to the railing at the front where she would address the city. She stood very still, letting her people see her before she spoke. As designed, the Golden Palace now framed her for everyone below, and even though I was a little to one side, the effect was still noticeable. Several cheers of "The Empress and the One!" went up from the crowd before she made a gesture for quiet. Stillness rippled out like a wave, the chant dying away until only the sound of the waves on the pier could be heard.

"Yorchians," she began, "our most noble people. We

return to you today with great joy in our hearts. Our empire is a beacon of civilization, and being again within the warm boundaries of our home is nearly enough to salve the evils of this journey past. For with our joy comes great tragedy as well."

At her mention of 'evils,' a dull murmur rustled through the crowd. By the time she said tragedy, there was actual fear on the faces of the people. The empress paused until everyone was settled.

"Know this; this journey was long, and while there were joys to be had, the perils and the cost were high. Our ally and friend, the nation of Gladia, is a land of tumult. The Archduke's death is but a symptom of a disease that rots them from within their very houses. An association of villains who call themselves the Fellowship of Gladia are attempting to overthrow their king. It was this vile group behind not simply the assassination of Archduke VanDunklen, but also an uprising of thieves in the land, and sadly, even assaults made on our imperial person."

The murmur of the crowd swelled again, and this time she had to raise her hand to restore the quiet.

"Their ultimate failure is only due to the assistance of the man you see here. People of Yorch, I give you King Willm Steinhargh of Sargeaux." The empress took a step back, and the stranger stepped forward to address the crowd.

I say again, *the empress took a step back, and the*

stranger stepped forward to address the crowd. The quiet she had called for went from one of obedience to one of shock.

"Good people of Yorch," King Willm's voice boomed out into the creepy quiet like a foghorn in the mist. "Your empress is both kind and generous. We only did what we thought was right when we became aware of the plots against her and her daughter. My fleet arrived in the port of Euticha at a most fortuitous time. We only did what we could to assure that the underhanded plots of this 'Fellowship' – these terrorists – were unsuccessful in their attempts to unseat Her Imperial Majesty. And thus we did, despite the collusion of the High Regent of Euticha himself!"

A low murmur again ran through the people around me, but I didn't really hear much. I was trying to make sense of what he was saying. *Euticha was in league with some rebels in Gladia? Did I have that right?* I shook my head; for all that could be said about it, Euticha wasn't an enemy of Yorch..., was it? Then, from somewhere in the crowd, a question rose above the general rumble of discussion. A question that both yanked me out of my thoughts and quieted the muttering of the audience.

"Where's the princess?"

I looked up, and I could see that King Willm had heard the question too. Despite the apparent bulk of his armor, his shoulders seemed to slump, and he looked back toward Empress Ardallah. She dropped her eyes at that, and he slowly turned to face the crowd again, shrugging like he was resetting himself.

"Unfortunately," he said, then paused. He took a breath, then started again. "Unfortunately, your brave princess, the Lady Julea, was a casualty of this vile cabal, and to my unending shame, I was unable to protect her." He paused, leaning heavily with his left hand on the railing as if under a great weight.

The crowd reacted like a single being; the gasp that escaped them was so loud I wondered if it might take all the air away. Princess Julea was the face of the throne for most of us; many of those older than me had watched her grow from a tomboy child into the graceful woman that she was. Had been. Where her mother was the unreachably high, Julea had come out to the people, spoken to them personally, and even had a drink in the taverns on occasion. She was beloved. She was a real person to them. She was the future.

And now this stranger was standing by her mother and telling us she was gone. It was more than a lot of the crowd could take. It was more than I could take, for sure. Somewhere far away from where my thoughts had gone, I heard King Willm trying to reassure us all that he and his fleet were going to remain on guard to protect the empress. That Her Imperial Majesty had graciously offered rooms in the palace for him. That they would stay as long as they were needed.

I know he said all those things, but I don't remember them except in clouds. What I do remember was that that was the last genuinely bright day in my city.

"Ye're doin' it again," Niamh said.

I looked at the empty mug, then up to her green eyes that seemed to be both angry at me and entertained at the same time. I couldn't decide if she was talking about my getting lost in another memory or my draining another beer.

"Don't matter what you think anyhow," she said, setting another mug in front of me.

"Then why tell me?" I asked. I was a little gruff, but not too much. She was, after all, handing me another beer. I took a drink.

"Because whether ye think it matters or not, *she* does," Niamh said. She had been moving some of the glasses and other whatnot behind the bar while I drank. It was just busy work to keep her nearby but not conspicuous. But at this, she stopped and looked very obviously in my eyes.

"Sky and sea," I blew out a breath. She stood still, just watching me. I shook my head. "She needs to let it go," I said. I drank again.

Niamh fidgeted with the empty glass in her hand like it was helping her think.

"Long wait for a ship that isn't coming," I muttered. I

lifted the mug, but it suddenly seemed like it had gotten heavier, and I saw that Niamh had put her hand on the other side of it and was holding it down. I looked up and met a look from her that I can only describe as "steely."

"Look, Jay, I think ye're right. But you and me've had a long time to adjust to disappointment. She ain't."

I jerked the mug away from her hand, and she let me. "Good time for her to learn, then," I said.

Niamh looked down at the bar for a long time before she looked back up at me. When she spoke, it was somewhere between counseling and consoling. "Ye may be right about that too. But if ye are – if 'we' are – then wouldn't that make our support more important?"

I finished the mug but kept my eyes on it.

"Isn't that what we swore when the Raven took us on?" she said.

Damn her eyes.

"What's she want?" I said to my empty mug.

"She wants to meet. I expect she'll be askin' for news. Either news ye've got, or news ye can find."

"Fine," I said, though it wasn't. "Set it up."

She stood up straight and played at folding her cleaning rag. "Glad ye come to yer senses," she said through a fresh grin, "'Cause we have just about an hour to get there, an' we need to get Muiris on the way."

It took a moment – maybe it was the beer – for me to

realize what had just happened. "You already told her that we'd come," I said.

She shrugged. "It was a fair guess."

It was bad enough to have to go through with it, but not having any time to get myself ready for it was so much worse.

"Shyte," I said.

In the days after the empress's return, the national mourning set in for the princess. All businesses were closed, the docks were shut down except for the most high-value cargoes, and the Imperial guard wore black half-cloaks over their standard uniforms. The palace was still, and even the Imperial Gardens – funnily enough, the place where the princess had most loved to be – was closed to the public. Flowers and other tributes were left at the gates but never taken in or cleaned up. By the third day, the piles of gifts were wilted and sad, as sad as the city around them.

I spent a lot of that time with a beer in my hand. Well, beer in me in general, I guess. I'd dealt with a lot of things in my life in Yorch, and especially in my behind-the-scenes life, but the princess's future place as empress was the bright spot in a sea of disappointments. With that future lost, I mostly didn't care anymore. I realized later that I should have paid more attention.

It was little things at first. The guard was doubled at

the palace for security. Businesses needed a new license to open when the mourning period was over. A lot more of the city guard started walking the street, regularly stopping people to ask "a couple of questions." It was all in the name of safety, of course, so most people let it go, and more than a few said that they felt the empire was safer with the new normal. No one ever seemed to ask where the new guardsmen were coming from, either. I didn't. And so, fall went on, and changes kept coming, and no one cared.

Then on Harvest Eve Night, after drinking much too much rye, I stumbled out of the *'Slinger* and fell onto a giant Talhas man in the street. I bounced off him and tumbled into a small, cloaked woman whose hood slipped back and revealed the face of Princess Julea Niconnal.

"Hey," I slurred, "ain't you suppos' to be dead?"

"But it's stupid," Muiris said over the cold wind. He walked along a step behind Niamh and me, and despite all his whining, he kept pace with us.

"Yep," I said. It was easier for me to talk since the wind was coming from in front of us and carried my voice back. "I think so too. We're still going."

Niamh ignored us, her head down in the wind, and her heavy beige cloak pulled around her. You wouldn't think it to look at her – she was slight, unremarkably tall, and had long chestnut brown hair that she did very little with unless it was to braid it to keep it out of her way – but she was one of the hardiest people I knew. Hidden under her boxy, unflattering work clothes, she had that odd, wiry strength that you don't expect. For example, there was no way to tell if she felt the cold as much I did that night or not.

Muiris, on the other hand, was the first to let you know how he was feeling. He trailed along behind us, his carefully arranged black cloak wrapped around him and a red, thickly knit scarf around his face. He was a 'Safety Administrator,' a city job that kept him paid and clothed and fat and happy. I hated it.

We reached the docks just after the sun had set, and the snow that had been falling steadily all day had turned into a real honest storm. Luckily, we could have found our way where we were going if we were blindfolded.

The old storage building's side door opened with a creak that was quickly muffled by the snow. Inside, we made our way through the stacks of boxes and things until we reached a big, oil-stained crate in the far corner. Niamh, who stayed a step ahead of me the whole way, pulled hard on one of the planks at the end. It looked for all the world like it was holding the crate together, but instead, with her effort, the whole end panel swung open on hidden hinges. Inside, a stairwell descended into the ground and into darkness. Without hesitating, Niamh disappeared down the steps. I let Muiris go ahead of me, gave one last look around, then pulled the crate door closed behind me as I too went down into the inky blackness. Thinking on it after the fact, I should probably have stayed there a few minutes more.

A hidden latch made a soft click as the door closed, shutting out the outer world. It was dark and almost immediately stuffy, but that only lasted for a moment before a shaft of light glowed from the deepest part of the stairwell. By it, I saw Niamh putting aside a wooden panel she had taken from a now well-lit opening. The light, which was probably actually very dim but seemed like the daylight against the black, flickered as Niamh stooped and went through. Muiris followed, and I went last again. It wasn't easy; the little hole wasn't made for people my size, and I also had to drag the panel back into place behind me. I was rumpled and annoyed but had gotten inside, and I turned to follow the others and immediately planted my face into a giant cobweb.

"Gah," I said, clawing at my eyes and mouth and spitting by reflex. I'm sure that the first brush of my hand got rid of the web, but I kept wiping at my eyes just to be sure. For what felt like the thousandth time, I mumbled that this little hideaway was not made for normal-sized people.

"Nicely done, Sir Jaymes," said a woman's voice off to my right. I wiped my face one last time and opened my eyes to see Princess Julea sitting at a small side table, watching me with some amusement.

"Your Majesty," I said, bowing my head and dropping to one knee.

"Stop," she said. I looked up to see her gesturing for me to stand, a more sober expression coming to her face. "I think we can agree that the formalities can be pushed aside, given our present circumstances." I turned to see that Niamh and Muiris were kneeling as well, a couple of feet away and unmoving. I waited for a second, unsure, but finally, I stood up.

"I'm not sure 'Sir' is appropriate, then, ma'am," I said.

The princess wobbled her head at me, then said, "I see your point. Let's agree to a protocol, shall we? You will be 'Jaymes,' and I will be 'Julea.' How does that sound?"

"I'm going to have a problem with that, ma'am," I said.

She looked at me, gave a quick look across to my friends, then back. "Fine," she said as if she were giving up, "Is 'princess' acceptable?"

"Yes, ma'am," I said, paused, then corrected, "er..., yes, princess."

"Oh, for the sake of the One," said the dark-skinned Talhas standing just behind her. He was called Rohb O'Laird, I knew, though I hadn't personally met him yet, and he had been the princess's personal guard for three years. There was some curiosity about what had happened to her previous guard, but I didn't much care. I was, though, really curious how he'd managed to get into this secret room. He was huge, even to me.

"Would you all please sit?" said the princess.

I walked over and sat at the closest chair at the table, followed a moment later by both Niamh and Muiris. They seemed a little uncomfortable – maybe starstruck. I thought that was funny for Niamh, especially since she, in particular, had been so casual about it when we spoke at the bar. Muiris was quiet, and I wondered if it was because, very directly speaking, the princess was his boss.

"Jaymes," she said. Her voice was clear, like a temple bell, and yet oddly familiar. It was like she was a friend I'd known forever but had never seen. "How are you keeping? I know the patrols are getting more intense."

"I'm doing, princess," I said, not entirely sure what I meant. "I mean, Yorch is a very different place. It isn't entirely easy for men like me to slip about these days. But so far, so good."

She nodded, and I guess she was satisfied with the answer.

"You know, it would be a lot easier if you'd just show yourself," Muiris said. This prompted everyone in the room to look at him; Niamh, Rohb, me, and even Princess Julea.

He looked back and forth between us unruffled. If he'd been starstruck before, he wasn't anymore. He was back to his usual, contrary self. He continued, "No offense, princess, but the city fell apart because they were told you were dead. You're not. So, it seems like everything would be fine if you'd just pop up and say hello."

She eyed him for a moment, taking his measure. Then, as if by reflex, she glanced back over her left shoulder and raised her hand. I looked up, only then noticing that somehow her bodyguard had produced a giant ax from somewhere and was holding it in a very unfriendly way. At the motion of her hand, Rohb's body shifted, and the ax head lowered to the floor slowly. His eyes, however, stayed on Muiris.

"There's more going on than you might know, Administrator," Princess Julea said, turning back to him. If what he said bothered her, it was impossible to tell. She stood and paced as much as the tiny space allowed. The room was not much bigger than ten feet square, if it was that, with a packed earth floor and unfinished stone walls. It was in every way a simple hole in the ground, and the only things that made it a room were the small table and chairs and the lantern that hung in the corner. Seeing the princess there, glorious despite the commoner's clothes she wore, was hard to fit in my head.

"The man with my mother, King Willm, as you know him, is not at all what he has presented to you. The western land he rules – Sargeaux – he rules from subterfuge, fraud, and bloodshed. It was there my companions and I were imprisoned briefly three years ago. I escaped with the assistance of...," she paused. It almost looked like her voice caught, but I couldn't tell. She continued a moment later, "of some dear friends. But Steinhargh remained, and he has plotted against us all these three years."

"Ma'am, er, princess," Niamh said, halting at first but finding her voice as she went on, "what you're saying fits what we know. I think we've suspected as much these months. But you've been with us for some time – since Harvest Eve – why are you explaining this only now?"

The princess turned and looked at her squarely. "There are two reasons. Partly, I was waiting for— Well, I was hoping there was help on the way, though that doesn't seem to be the case, and waiting is not helping matters. But the primary reason is that I needed to be sure I could trust you. Yorch is full of vultures these days, and my presence here could start a firestorm that could tear the city apart in a very literal way."

Muiris lolled his head.

"Administrator, I promise you, when I say the city itself could be in danger, you will trust that I am not speaking from hyperbole. I have seen what this man is capable of." There was a bite of steel in her voice that was, let's say, unexpected from someone of royal blood. You usually don't hear someone say "hyperbole" in a way that makes you think they're considering beating you if you don't listen.

Muiris, showing abnormal wisdom, nodded and kept silent.

The princess was quiet for a minute. “It is funny, you know,” she said finally, looking away from us as if looking into a distance that wasn’t there, “There was a time I wouldn’t have tried to reach out to you at all. ‘Trusting’ isn’t a lesson that’s taught in the halls of the palace, typically. Especially not those not of noble blood. That journey three years ago is where I learned that sometimes even a prisoner in a dungeon is worthy of trust.”

That didn’t sound very sensible to me, and out of the corner of my eye, I could see that Niamh and Muiris didn’t think so either. None of us said so, of course.

Princess Julea seemed to snap back to herself in a flash, standing straight and looking over at us again. “The story they told at the dock was a very carefully worded lie. Scarcely a word of it was true. Whatever happened in Gladia had nothing to do with us or with the events of our journey home. Steinhargh found a way to get to the empress and me in Euticha and nearly overthrew Lord Westfall in the process. I expect that he intended to keep me imprisoned and use me to control my mother. I was spirited away, let us say, while he was distracted. But, it would appear that he has found some other way to maintain control.”

“The guard would stand by you,” Muiris said, steady

in his idea. He wasn't so much attempting a challenge this time, though. Instead, I could see him trying to pull together all of the parts of the story. It was his way to poke at the seams of things. "That would be enough to chase him out into the open, right?" he asked.

The princess shook her head. "Steinhargh has access to power that you've not seen. If, and I'm not certain my presence would be enough to do it, but if we drove him from the palace while his fleet remained in the harbor, it is within his ability to raze half the city before our navy figures out who its actual friends and enemies are."

A flicker of memory popped to life in my mind. It must have shown on my face because the princess looked hard at me for a moment. I caught her eye, and she gave the slightest nod.

So that was it, I thought. *The thing he was worried about finally happened*. I'd have thought some more, but Muiris was talking again.

"So, what did you call us here for?" he asked. "I mean, I don't know what we can do."

She sat down in her chair again. Slumped, really. Maybe I had been a little awed when I came into the room too. Being in the presence of the heir to the empire and such can do that. Now that I could see a little clearer, though, what I saw was exhaustion and sadness. Outside of her bodyguard, she hadn't had anyone she felt safe with for months, at least. She had just said as much. Her world was all manner of backward. On top of that, something was eating at her. I had a feeling that it had to do with the 'friends' she'd mentioned. It's a strange feeling to pity a princess.

"There are two reasons I called you here," she began, sitting straight again, "first, there are rumors of attacks in the southwest. I need to know more about them, preferably soon."

"Why?" I said. It felt weird to ask; she was just supposed to give commands, and we were supposed to do what she said. But everything was cockeyed, and if what I said was disrespectful, neither she nor the giant behind her reacted.

"The Assemblage is in spring. Steinhargh will be looking to secure his power before then, which means he will need to move very quickly and very dramatically. Those attacks are either of two things. Option one, they're part of his plot to grab more power."

"Tell the people, 'I'll defend ye while yer empress is still grieving,'" Niamh said, her accent coming back as she got more comfortable.

"Yes, that is certainly one possible plot," Julea said, smiling at her. "The other possibility is that the attacks are coming from outside, and that may be better news. The High Regent of Euticha knows the truth of what happened, and it may be that he's trying to send some kind of message of support. It is also possible he is attempting to find out if I'm even still alive."

"He doesn't know?" I asked.

"He knows we were alive when we left, but then, our ship fell in the Battle of the Bay. I'm sure news of that has reached him by now," she said.

"Y' were on the black ship?" Niamh said with a start.

"We were," Rohb said, speaking up for the first time. "We sailed here on the *Midnight Wind* under Captain Edward Ribald."

"The pirate?" I spat.

"Yes, the pirate," the princess said with a sad smile, "A pirate that has helped save my life twice. A pirate that put Captain O'Laird and me on a small boat and cut us away just before he was hit amidships with an uncanny fire that capsized his pride and joy."

"In other words, a friend," Rohb said as if that said it all. It actually did.

"We'll see what we can find out," I said. Niamh and Muiris nodded, and we stood to leave. Muiris stopped, though, and turned once more to the princess, meeting her eyes.

"What was the other reason?" he said.

"The other...?"

"You said there were two reasons you called us in and

told us all this finally. One was to get our help. Okay. But what was the other?"

Princess Julea looked at him for a long time, then over at Niamh and me in turn before she spoke. "A dear friend told me about you three a very long time ago. He said if I ever needed anything, I only had to find you. I never had need. If I'm to be honest, I probably wouldn't have tried, in years past, regardless of need. But here we are. And truthfully? Talking with you..., it..., well, I just feel like it brings him closer."

My jaw worked soundlessly as I tried to find some words to say that wouldn't crush me under memory. Niamh, bless her, filled the quiet.

"Do... do ye think he might *be* closer at some point?" Her voice was hopeful, and it was clear she had the same thought pressing on her that I did.

The princess looked down at her hands as she permitted a slight slump in her posture. "For true, Lady Niamh, I might have hoped so. But after all these weeks, I believe he might be beyond us all now. Maybe beyond this world as well."

My ears filled with that quiet that comes when you've just been struck. It wasn't just a lack of sound; it was a lack of anything— just nothingness. No one moved; no one spoke. The reality of her words sank in like water in dry sand. Which all very much contributed to how what came next happened.

I don't remember the next few minutes real well. We were just standing there, thinking about what she said when there was a crash from the entryway and the room exploded into motion. From the door, men in the armor and colors of the city guard rushed into the tiny space. I remember that I started backing away, not that there was anywhere to go, and then that the ceiling above me split open with a loud crack. Rubble and splinters fell as more men kept coming in through the door. I saw a flash from across the room of lantern light reflecting off of Captain Rohb's ax in midswing. All the while, there was the steady chant of the guard's captain calling for his men to "go, go, go."

At least, that's what I've put together. At the time, it was lights and noise and confusion. Hands groped down from above, clutching at my shoulders and my cloak. In a way, that's likely what saved me. I don't like being grabbed, even in jest, and it causes me to react without thinking. Those reflexes came in very handy just then because what I did next I did by reflex. With one hand, I tugged at the clasps that held my cloak, freeing me from the grasp of one attacker. With the other, I grabbed at the remaining arms, still pawing at my shoulder, catching one in my grip. I pulled down and forward, and the figure of a guardsman tumbled down from above and into the room. I pushed off of his crumpled form and, with that for a boost, climbed past the broken edges of the hideout's ruined ceiling. I rolled on the ground to distance myself from the hole and stood, now back in the storehouse we'd entered earlier and several feet from the false crate. Two more of the guards stood a few feet to my right next to a stored anchor, while a third – still holding my cloak from moments before – faced me from the opposite side of the hole I'd just climbed out. He glared at me in frustration, but my hands were already in motion. I swept my hands across my vest and the sides of my legs, pulling out several of the small knives that were sheathed there and throwing them briskly. The first caught the nearest guard in the seam of his armor where his pauldron and breastplate didn't quite meet. He stumbled backward, clutching at the wound even as his armor shifted and locked the blade in place. My second throw hit the guard across the hole from me squarely in the faceplate of his helmet. He dropped to the ground like a sack of vegetables. I can't say what exactly I hit, but the result was what I wanted, so it didn't matter to me. The remaining guard managed to turn at the last second, and my final knife glanced off of his helmet. With a snarl, he charged toward me.

"Shyte," I breathed.

The little throwing knives worked well for many things, especially for being easy to carry around a city without attracting attention. But a charging man covered in metal plate armor isn't one of them. I turned and ran toward the darker part of the warehouse. I could hear the clunking of his feet behind me and much too close. The guards had brought lanterns, and they'd placed them around the hole they'd hacked over the hideout, and these gave some light to the rest of the building interior, though it quickly dimmed with distance. After a couple of steps into denser shadows, I cut to the right, behind a pile of stored somethings, and into total darkness. I would say what the 'somethings' were, but it was dark, and I didn't care. It smelled like wood, and it gave me cover, and that was enough for me. I stopped and held my breath. My heart seemed very loud in my ears, but I didn't have time to think about it a lot, as my pursuer came into view almost immediately. He was still moving at a good speed – slowing down is more challenging when you're covered in steel – and was looking toward the remaining light rather than toward me. The shadows did their job for me, and I jumped onto him without warning, his eyes going wide in surprise. I landed on him high and tucked my legs so that my total weight was on his back. Together with his own bulk, it was too much for him to bear, and he toppled forward. I landed atop him and, with both hands, pulled his helmet loose and smashed it down on his exposed head. I have to thank the One that he hadn't fastened the chin strap. He went limp and quiet. I lay atop him very still, listening behind me for any sign there were more of them about, but all was quiet. It took me a minute to realize that it didn't make sense; there had to be others. If nothing else, I should have heard noises from the ones in the hideaway. I grabbed the sword my metal pillow had dropped when he fell and moved to the edge of the shadows, peering around the corner of a crate to get a look back without drawing any attention. As it turns out, I didn't need the caution. There were no more of the guard in the area. I could also see that the little lanterns were being overdone by a bright glow coming up from the hole they surrounded. An orange and yellow, flickery glow.

Fire.

My friends.

The princess.

I was in motion before I knew it, running back toward the hole and the fire. I couldn't even get close to the edge; the smoke and heat were already too much to approach. I stopped, then tried to edge closer, thinking of my friends. All around me, I could see now, the warehouse itself was half-full of thick brown smoke, and more seemed to be coming every moment. I looked around, but between the smoke and the tears that it was now bringing to my eyes, I couldn't see another soul, not the guards, not my friends, not anyone. I turned to head toward the entrance we'd used, but in three steps, I was in the wall of smoke and completely blind. All I succeeded in doing was finding my cloak where it had been dropped. I threw it around my shoulders and backed away from the smoke. Back the way I'd run just moments before. There was, I knew, another exit in the far corner of the building. It was the only way out, which meant that anyone looking for me would be waiting there. But since it was the only other way out, my options seemed few.

The smoke was filling the building faster now, and I was sure that it couldn't only be coming from the hideout. They had to have set the entire warehouse on fire. On the upside, there was now more firelight to see by; I got to the other exit without an issue. I paused. Whatever had happened had left me alone. Niamh and Muiris, the princess and her bodyguard, were all gone – missing or, the One forbid, consumed in the fire. I had no way to know. I let a shiver pass through me that wasn't related to the temperature.

The only way out is usually through, Talon. So, get on with getting through. The voice in my head was as clear as it had been when it was said years before. It gave me more of a shiver than usual after the conversation with the princess, but that only made it more motivating.

The *'Slinger*, I thought. *That's where they'll be. Any of them, if they can.* I just needed to get through the door, get through whatever was beyond it, and get back there. I waved the stolen sword in my hand, testing its weight. Whatever was on the other side of the door, I was going through it. I threw the latch and heaved the heavy oak door open with one motion.

Outside, six bodies lay scattered about, snow starting to collect on the steel armor of their still forms. Around these, four figures stood waiting, flanking the door but scanning in every direction up and down the street cautiously. I brought the sword up to guard position as the figure to my left turned and faced me, two vicious daggers in hand. He tensed as he saw my stolen weapon.

"Wait," came a man's voice from one of the other three. I looked over to a lean figure in a black coat. He turned toward me and paused. A black cloak hung over his left side, fastened beneath a leather pauldron, and his face was hidden under a black hood. "He's one of ours," he continued. The man with the two daggers lowered them though he remained tensely alert.

"You know him?" A woman's voice, this time. She was near me, opposite the one with the daggers. She was also cloaked and hooded, though the wool had been bleached bone-white making her seem part of the snow that was still falling thickly. A rapier blade flashed in the pale light.

"Of course, he does," said the fourth one, several feet away. He spun a quarterstaff expertly if casually as he spoke. "This happens to me every time I travel with him. You two know that," he continued, letting his staff rest on his shoulder, even as he craned his neck for a look further down the street, past the corner of the building toward the far end.

Then he turned back, his voice becoming serious. "Kelly, we should move," he said.

"Who are you people?" I said. There were so many things I wanted to know just then, but that it seemed a good place to start.

The figure in black stepped forward, pulling the hood back and revealing his face in the dim light.

"Good to see you too, Jaymes," he said with a smile that blew years away like fall leaves. "So tell me, where can we get out of this weather?"

CHAPTER NINE

— DANA —

The snow fell thick and heavy, spun in circles by gusts of wind through the city streets as we moved away from the docks and back to the city proper. Kelly's friend, the one he had called Jaymes, led the way, several feet in front of us and moving purposefully. He was tall and thickly built, with a shaggy mop of curly hair the color of sand. He hadn't spoken since we'd found him at the warehouse, and the look on his face on seeing Kelly was hard to read. Just ahead of me, Kelly and Aeryk followed close behind him while Denis and I kept tabs on the rear, a surety that the city guard – if they were that – were not following us. The blowing snow was a problem, though, as we could only see a short distance, but then again, it also wiped away our footsteps so quickly that, on the whole, I suppose it was more helpful than harmful.

"*Codslinger*?" I heard Denis mutter to me through the wind.

"I've no idea," I replied, "the pubs around here all seem fish-based."

For a moment, he was quiet, pausing to survey the

cross streets for any movement. I stopped with him, peering into whatever distance I could. Nothing moved, save the wind and the snow.

"Terrible name for a pub," he said into the silence as he began to move again after the others.

I shrugged, "It doesn't scream fancy, does it?"

He nestled further into his dark green cloak, fending off the cold for a moment before he responded. "Or appetizing," he said finally. "Sounds more like dock work. Or maybe a sport for the arrogant."

We kept on pace for a few more minutes before we came up short behind the others. Gas-fed lanterns lit the street, giving off their dim glow through the snow and casting a faint golden haze on everything. Now, some distance ahead of us, a much brighter light flickered into view, cast from some source further down the cross street and out of sight; a light bright enough that it seemed as if a hundred lanterns were just around the corner.

"No," Jaymes muttered quietly before breaking into a run, his hood falling back and his cloak billowing out.

"Wait," Kelly said, but to no avail, as Jaymes disappeared around the corner. We followed, quickly but more cautiously. Denis craned his neck, looking in both directions down the street behind us to make doubly sure we were alone – that there wasn't some trap about to snap closed on us. But, a few steps later, we came out onto the cross street where we finally could see the massive fire.

Ahead was a single building completely engulfed in flames, and even from where we were yet yards away, the heat was intense. Licking tounges of fire twisted and whipped around the structure, driven by the wind into vivid spirals that left whispy ghosts in my sight. The funnel-like shape of the blaze was probably the only thing that saved the other buildings nearby. Still, it gave the whole conflagration an almost columnar appearance, like a gigantic torch in the night that evaporated high above into the blizzard. Ahead of us by a couple of paces as he had been the whole way, Jaymes stood perfectly still in the orange glow, staring at the blaze.

"Jaymes," Kelly said, reaching over to his shoulder after a moment, "we have to go." But the other man remained still as if the fire had drained all the life out of him.

"So that settles it," Denis mumbled at my side. I looked at him from the shelter of my cloak's hood. He turned to look behind us again. "I was betting myself whether we'd freeze to death or get pinched by the guard first. What with the enormous fire, I'm pretty sure it'll be the guard."

"Your imagination is uncomfortable," Aeryk said from off to one side. But I noted that he didn't disagree.

I shook my head in a vague gesture of disapproval, but inside me, I could hear an unbidden voice loudly agreeing with him. It should be no surprise that the voice sounded very much like Denis's. But that didn't change the facts; even if we had avoided pursuit, this fire would bring the city services. That would not go well for us. I looked back at the slowly crumbling building.

"Kelly—," I said through the wind.

"Shake it off, Talon," Kelly said in a commanding tone. At that, Jaymes turned away from the fire, awareness seemingly driven back into him from some unseen source. He looked at us, then at Kelly directly. "We need a safe house," Kelly continued, his voice his normal tone again, though no less severe.

"Follow me. It's a ways, but it's reachable," Jaymes said over the howl of wind and fire. He cast an unreadable look at Kelly, pulled up his hood, and stalked off into an alley across the road. Kelly waved us on, and we followed, in only a few moments past the fire. We wound through the twisting alleys of the backstreets of Yorch and finally beyond them as we passed outside the city.

The wind seemed to lessen quite a bit with every step we took from the capital, which made sense. The farther we headed west, first through the streets, then beyond the wall, the farther we got from the waterfront and the piercing winds off of the sea. By the time we reached the edge of the forest, which was a goodly distance later, the wind was all but gone. The snowfall continued unabated, but even that became less of a problem after we reached the canopy of the trees. I could describe that walk as a pleasant one had it not been for the icy cold, the pace, and the fact that we were always vigilant for evidence of pursuit. Even so, I was very close to enjoying it. Winter had always been my favorite season going back to childhood. I imagine it began the winter after the barn fire that scarred me so severely. I remember the winter air and readily available ice as comforting to me as I healed from the burns on my back. It seemed so long ago now, but the fact was, it was not physically far from where we walked. My family home had been not far west of the capital, and I imagined that we were heading more toward it than we were away from it. But, of course, my parents had sold the farm many years ago, and I hadn't returned since I received my commission. It chose then to reappear in my memory in sharp detail, and as we walked through the dense frozen woods on no path I could discern, my inner eye saw the sights and sounds of childhood again.

"Coin for your thoughts," Kelly said, jarring me back to the present.

"You would be shortchanged," I said.

"My coin, I'll decide," he replied.

I shrugged, which was an almost imperceptible gesture beneath my heavy cloak. "I haven't been back here in a while. Yorch in general, obviously. But also *here*, here. I grew up not far from these woods."

"Really?" he said, looking around as if he might see

the place. "I suppose I should have thought of that. I mean, I knew you grew up near the city, and there are a lot of homesteads throughout this area. I guess we never talked specifics."

"There wasn't much point. It wasn't like we were coming here any time soon," I said, "what with the whole *exile* and *possible end of the world* hanging over our heads."

He was quiet for a moment, and I thought that I might have cut too close to his sensitivities. Alienation from the empire had defined our lives for years – his much longer than mine. It was a painful subject and one about which I knew he carried unnecessary guilt. I was about to say something when he coughed out a quiet laugh.

"That would probably do it," he said. I could almost hear the wry smile in his voice, and it gave me some relief. We walked in silence.

"Do you trust this man?" I asked, changing the subject with a nod toward Jaymes. I whispered, but the woods were so quiet that my voice boomed in my ears. I looked forward to see if the tall man had reacted, but he continued to walk on our invisible path without indication.

"I always have," Kelly said, "I knew him years ago when I was Jules's personal guard and then after I was appointed Raven. He was one of a group of...," he trailed off as if thinking before he finally continued, "assistants? Informants? Agents? I don't know what the right word is.

Back then, they were barely more than kids, of course, but they were a tremendous help. They could hear things I couldn't, go places I couldn't. And sometimes even act when I wasn't able. And in return, I did what I could for them. Found them training, coin, lodging – whatever I could provide that made sense."

I thought about it for a moment. Not the *what* of his description, really; I accepted that readily. It was *why* I accepted it so readily that took a moment. Then I realized that drawing people to himself was what Kelly did. It was his way. I looked over at him.

"What's 'talon'?" I said.

"A nickname. It was Jaymes that used it originally. If I was the Raven, then...,"

"Then he – or they – were 'talons,'" I finished, nodding.

He shrugged, the black cloak jostling slightly on his shoulder.

"That's adorable," Denis's voice said from behind us.

I turned, finding him and Aeryk much closer behind us than I had realized. Kelly's hood shifted as he shook his head.

"It *is* really quiet out here," Aeryk said, "so it's not as though we had to strain to hear." I could hear the repressed chuckle in his voice.

"It is very quiet out here," Jaymes said suddenly from

up ahead. The sound stopped us, and we looked up at him in what seemed a single motion. He had stopped, his right hand resting on a small birch tree beside him. He looked back over his shoulder as he spoke in a low tone. “And you’ll remember that I’ve always had excellent hearing, Raven. Maybe the chat should wait for the cabin?”

The pause that followed carried a strain in it that made me wonder. Before it went on too long, though, Kelly broke the silence.

“Fair point. How much further?”

Jaymes turned away. “Far enough to be safe. Not so far as to die on the way.” He trudged off through the snow.

“Who shoved the bee in his drawers?” Denis said, enunciating as always what we all thought.

“That,” Kelly sighed, “was probably me.”

The moon was high when we reached a small, semi-frozen creek. We followed the river’s path uphill for a while, finally arriving at a level, tree-enclosed, stretch of ground on which sat a large cabin. It was roughly yet solidly built of logs and pitch with a wide porch that looked down onto the stream. Jaymes moved across the small clearing and stopped at a non-distinct treestump. He kneeled and seemed to feel around the roots for a moment, then stood and strode over to the cabin and unlocked the door, disappearing through the opening. Quick, questioning glances passed between the four of us, but with few options, we turned and followed him inside.

In the few moments between opening the door and our entrance, Jaymes had lit a candle which, as our eyes had adjusted to the starlit snow outside, seemed nearly as bright as the burning pub had earlier that evening. It flickered as we entered – stabilizing a moment after Denis closed the door – and allowed us to see the room. It looked as though it consumed half of the size of the building's floor plan. The door we'd entered was centered on the outer wall. It stood directly across from a mammoth stone fireplace set in the interior wall on the opposite side of the room. Heavy wooden furniture was scattered about the space, with lanterns, plates, and other sundry. Immediately around the hearth, two chairs bookended a long, stout bench with a high wooden back. They were all three covered with a variety of blankets and pillows in a casual array. The dark opening of a door that led to the remainder of the cabin interior was to hearth's right. Twin tapestries hung on the walls that formed the sides of the room, embroidered with hunting scenes. They were old, faded even in the dim light, but somehow perfectly fitting. Several rugs were scattered randomly on the mortared stone floor, with an unusual one covered in thick brown fur immediately before the fireplace.

"I like it," Aeryk said appreciatively.

"I like not being in the snow anymore," Denis said, "but you're right, I've been in worse."

Kelly chuffed, “Well, yeah. Where did we meet you ag—,” his voice was cut off by a dull thud as Jaymes’s fist crashed into the side of his head. Kelly sprawled across the floor as if a horse had kicked him.

“You son of a b—” The sound of steel blades sliding from scabbards cut off Jaymes’s words as both Denis and I drew out our weapons in a flash of reflex.

“Wait,” Kelly grunted, his words muffled at first by the floor as he slowly rose. It was enough that we didn’t drop the newcomer where he stood, but neither of us dropped our blades, either. Instead, we remained at the ready as we watched our friend stand slowly back up.

There was a long, silent moment as Kelly stood and faced Jaymes, his face hidden still inside the shadows of his hood. Something silently passed between them, something that excluded the rest of us. The tension in the room built but then washed away like a wave on the shore.

“I’ll go get some wood for the fire,” Jaymes said, breaking the gaze that had held the two transfixed. He turned and left the room, heading back outside and closing the heavy oak door behind him.

Denis, unsurprisingly, broke the silence. “So, does *anyone* in this town like you?” he said, casually slipping the twin daggers back into their sheaths.

A sound came from Kelly’s hood that could have been a cough or a laugh. “I’m starting to wonder, kid. I’m beginning to think that the princess herself might be the only one."

Aeryk spun his staff out of the guard position he'd been holding it in and set it against the long bench by the fireplace. He looked around the room for a moment, then stole up the glowing candle and began to walk the perimeter, using it to light the various other candles around the room. Finished, he then turned his attention to the door frame to the right of the fireplace.

"I'm going to get the lay of the land. If anyone else gets punched, shout," he muttered. Then he disappeared into the shadow of the door, the candle smearing the moving shadows on the wall as he passed through. I brushed back my hood and moved over toward Kelly, half-standing, half-leaning against the high back of the bench. His head sagged, and though I still couldn't see his face under the black hood, it was easy to see feelings roiling inside my friend.

"Kidding aside..," Denis began, still standing near the door.

"Do you do that?" Kelly said, jumping into the short pause.

Denis shrugged, a strangely severe look playing across his face for an instant. "If I have to," he said, then continued as if nothing had happened, "anyway, what is the deal? I mean, what'd you do to that guy?"

"I left," Kelly said without emotion. "To be fair, he and

the others got what the princess didn't – an explanation. I told them about the situation and why I had to go. I explained why I wouldn't tell the empress the secrets I know. It was all very logical."

"Which doesn't make it easier sometimes," I added.

Kelly blew out a sigh. "No," he said, "not really. The thing is, Jaymes wanted to come with me. Be a squire or something like that."

"To which you said no," I said, "because, of course, you did."

"And you of all people would understand that," Kelly said. I thought about the memories from earlier in the evening, my thoughts of home and family. All of the things that had been denied me. And all because of the dangers of what I knew and what I had become. And I understood why he wouldn't let someone take on this life of alienation if they didn't have to. I nodded.

"Well, he's certainly gotten over it," Denis said, slumping onto the arm of one of the nearby chairs.

"Obviously," Kelly said. Just then, the door pushed open, and Jaymes came in backward, pulling a small wooden cart laden with short logs. With a flip of his grip that looked far easier than it must have been considering the load, he dumped the wood onto an open patch of the floor, where it formed a relatively neat mound. He remained silent as he took the cart back outside, returned, and went about the business of starting a fire. To his credit and in very short order, the hearth filled with the orange light of licking flames, and its warmth began to fill the room. I removed my cloak and draped it over the chair where Denis still perched. He had sluffed his cloak off moments before and thereby claimed the chair as our 'closet.' Kelly hadn't moved, save to turn around to watch the fire. He was sufficiently lost in thought that he had all but become a statue. Jaymes backed away from the hearth as the fire reached the point where it sustained itself and then turned away from it and came back around the long bench to us. Kelly stirred, turning to face him as he came closer.

I saw the motion the instant the distance between them closed. Jaymes's right hand struck out once again, a lightning-fast cross body strike aimed once again at Kelly's head. This time, however, Kelly's hand moved as well, and somewhat faster. He caught the incoming blow on his left bracer while it was still inches from impact. The bigger man had put a lot into the strike, but my friend's arm remained unmoved.

"You get one, boy," Kelly said, his voice coming out as if he were discussing the weather. "You've had it. It's time to move on." A heartbeat, then both men dropped their arms.

"Now? You come back now?" Jaymes snarled.

"Now," Kelly said as he reached up and pulled back his hood, "I had to."

Jaymes's eyes widened, and he froze in place, staring at my friend. Kelly's hair had grown out over the months of our recovery, and he had it swept back and to the side in a somewhat shaggy mop. But it wasn't the hair that had taken Jaymes by surprise. The left side of Kelly's face from his cheekbone back was covered in an increasingly dense pattern of black lines. They looked like ink marks that an artist might use to designate shadow, and they grew thicker until, where it met the hairline itself, it was effectively solid black. The hatching pattern continued around the socket of his left eye and reached the bridge of his nose, the effect being like some kind of costume makeup. His eye itself looked as it always had – though maybe a paler shade of blue-gray than before. It caught the light from the fire differently, now, twinkling a little like—

Well, like a gemstone, I suppose.

"It was a bit of a rough ride getting here," Kelly said, filling the silence left by Jaymes's bewilderment. He smiled, the same smile as ever. "And actually?" he continued, "a lot is going on just now. Maybe we should focus on getting the princess away from the madman who's trying to take over the empire."

"What...?" Jaymes stammered out. His hand twitched as if he wanted to reach out to the peculiar black markings but thought better of it.

"Scars. Sort of," Kelly said, shrugging a little.

"Might be we should start at the beginning," Denis said. He stretched and walked over to the little seating area formed around the fireplace.

"We should. If you're in?" Kelly said. He was looking at Jaymes while the question hung persistently in the air. For the second time, something passed silently between the two men. This time, it was something much gentler. If I had to put a word to it, I might have called it forgiveness.

We followed Denis's lead and moved into the firelight proper. Kelly took off the half cloak that covered his left side, then removed the long black coat and pauldron he had been wearing til now, setting them on our 'closet chair' as he passed. Jaymes, I could see, continued to watch him as he did all this. He gave the black glove on Kelly's left hand a considered look but said nothing. We settled in then, our weapons removed, though near at hand, and we settled into the seating around the warm fire. Jaymes removed a set of belts that held a ridiculous number of throwing knives and draped it over the back of the long bench as he sat on one end, nearest the chair where Kelly had already seated himself. I took a spot on the other end, my rapier on the floor by my feet.

"God's teeth!" Jaymes said suddenly, and I looked up to see him looking at me. Despite myself, I felt my cheeks color. I wasn't offended; it was easy to guess what was the meaning behind the curse. It's simply that I am never going to be comfortable being the subject of attention.

“It’s similar,” I said, holding my composure by speaking as calmly as I could. I swept my hand up toward my face, gesturing toward what I knew had drawn the attention. In a similar manner to Kelly, my skin was crisscrossed with a gossamer-like pattern of fine white lines. Depending on how I was clothed, they were most visible along my hairline, down my neck and throat, and across my shoulders. My hips and torso were nearly pure white in some areas, but those were explicitly not visible in public.

The markings on both Kelly and I had been much more pronounced immediately after Eryth and her people’s treatments. When I regained consciousness and saw myself in one of their remarkably vivid mirrors, the white pattern was thicker and reached down nearly to my eyebrows, and most of the left side of Kelly’s face was solid black. We had each been healed in different ways, they explained to us. Neither process was at all related to the treatments that had saved us previously. Eryth looked drawn and tired when she looked in on us, and I wasn’t sure whether that was from worry or from some personal exertion that I didn’t know. I suspect now that it was both. The gemstone ‘scarring,’ which is how I’ve come to think of it, faded over the first few weeks. It had stabilized for a while now, the marks changing very little for some time. I recalled the fine lines on my back after my first healing, which had never varied. I expected that these new tracks would be the same. Eryth said that she expected them to be only part of the side effects. I didn't particularly care for considering what that might mean.

Aeryk returned then, bearing a large wooden plank laden with cheeses and salted meats. He looked around for a moment, then cracked a small smile. "Always a priority to grab something to keep yourself going when the opportunity arises," he said far more brightly than was warranted. "I hope whoever had these stores set aside won't miss them too much," he continued, placing the makeshift platter on the floor somewhat centrally. We each reached down to take some of the provisions.

"There was wine, too," Jaymes said, "I have a small cask in the back."

Aeryk popped back up and disappeared again into the other room without a word.

"*You* have," Denis repeated. "So, this lodge is yours?"

"Humble, but comfortable," Jaymes said. I felt a discomfort roll off of him as if he were defensive of the simple place. Or perhaps it was that he felt exposed. I wondered how many people, let alone strangers, had been here.

"I find it very much so," I said through what I hoped was a warm smile. I am not a fan of expressing emotion on purpose, and I often felt obliged to force it. He nodded, and the discomfort seemed to fade. More accurately, *that* part of his discomfort faded.

Aeryk returned with cups and wine, and we quieted for a short while as we ate. Then, without introduction or fanfare, Kelly took us back in time and related the story of how we had come to face the threat of Willm Steinhargh of Sargeaux. It was odd, hearing him tell our story in such great detail. Denis would occasionally toss in more information or another point of view, but for the most part, Kelly told the story as if he were telling the tale of a well-trodden legend. Thinking of the people we had been back then, hearing again the actions we had taken back in a time that was both just a few years and also a lifetime ago, I quietly smiled at my friend. For all the things Kelly can do well, few give him such absolute joy as when he tells a story. Of course, he would never admit that, but I knew. I had called him a warrior-poet once, a comment that he brushed off, saying that he didn't like poetry. Which was, I surmised, based on the big dumb grin he didn't think I saw, a lie, which was an example of one of the things that he *didn't* do well.

Jaymes stood and stoked the fire as Kelly finished, adding some wood and mostly just fussing with the flames. He stared into the heart of it as Kelly concluded.

"And so we came here. I expected that the princess would seek you out if she survived the destruction of the *Midnight Wind*," he said. I saw Aeryk twitch at the mention of the *Wind*, and I felt for him. We didn't know what had happened at sea that day, and there was no way we could until we spoke to Rohb or Jules. Kelly told it as a fact, but I know Aeryk held fast that Edword had had something left in his bag of tricks.

"She did," Jaymes said to the fire. "She sought us out because you told her we'd help. I didn't believe it at first, but she said just that just tonight."

Kelly nodded with a slight sag. There was relief there, and I felt it too. If she was still alive earlier tonight, there was still a chance.

"What I don't understand is this. Why hunt down the princess and not just kill her outright? That gives him a seat in the palace and no potential heir to the throne to bother him, which is exactly what he had *before* he took her. So why keep her alive at all?" Jaymes said, turning to scan our faces.

"Leverage," Denis said in a flat, mechanical tone. Jaymes looked at him. "You don't think enough like a shark, Talon. Sure, up to today, he had a seat in the palace and Ardallah under his thumb. But only barely. Ardallah is a predator herself. If she can find a way to sidestep the Kathasiri assassins walking her halls and the other mercenaries, she will have old Steelclaw for lunch. Plus, there's the unknown of the princess; he may have been sure he had killed her but was he *sure*," Denis put the second "sure" in air quotes.

Jaymes's brow furrowed as he considered. "So take

the princess and keep her captive. Threaten her life if the empress steps out of line," he said.

Denis touched his temple and nodded. "All the reins firmly in his hands. Er—, hand. Whatever," he said, relaxing back on the bench and biting off a bit of the salted meat in his hand.

Aeryk stood and paced in the small space to my right, between me and the hearth. He sipped his wine, then paced some more. Finally, he said, "Look, I know marching off and doing the impossible is the sort of thing we're supposed to be good at. But even if we are all completely correct about all that, we're still lung-full."

"'Lung-full?'" I said.

"Lung-full," he repeated, "drowned. Dead in the water. Without a chance. We're talking about getting a prisoner out of the dungeon of Yorch. You two," he cast a look at me and then at Kelly, "especially should know that's not possible. Not without an army, and maybe not even then. On top of that, the place is currently crawling with hired, blood-thirsty assassins."

There was a long pause because there had to be. The thing was, the pirate Lord of Claire wasn't wrong. Yorch wasn't some rural castle keep in the north. This wasn't Sterling, where we'd all but walked out just by being clever. This was Yorch, the beacon of civilization in the known world. This was the most powerful empire in the known world. The best-trained army in the known world. And, yes, the most inaccessible dungeon in the whole world.

We sat in silence, Aeryk's words hanging in the air. Jaymes and Aeryk shared a single expression of defeat, loss, and failure. The dark cloud that swirled around them felt like a presence in the room that pulled at me, whispering, *It's no use. You've already lost*. But as the cloud threatened me, I looked over at Kelly and Denis. They were facing one another, their eyes darting as if reading books that only they could see. I felt the dark cloud recede as I realized what I was watching. My friends were planning. In the face of impossible odds, the worst we'd yet faced, the two of them had started looking for a solution without a hint of despair. Because, of course, they did. It was all they *ever* did. The point was, we *had* to try. We had to succeed. Not just for ourselves, not even for Jules. For the very survival of that beacon of civilization. To quit meant to leave Yorch in the hands of Steinhargh, and that was unconscionable.

It was at that moment of intensity that there came a gentle rapping from the door— five gentle taps. By the fifth one, every weapon in the room came to hand as we faced the door in a flurry of motion. Gazes shot around the room, from one to the other of us, finally settling on Jaymes. He stood, eying the door with three razor-sharp knives protruding from his grip. A heartbeat passed, and the gentle tapping sound came again, faint but with an understated urgency.

Jaymes looked back to Kelly standing just behind him, flashes of firelight reflecting off the steel longsword in his hand. He gave a slight nod, and the big man smoothly crossed the room to the door. He put his hand on the catch, reinforcing the latched position rather than moving to open it. It squeaked slightly at the increased weight – a seemingly deafening sound in the silence that had fallen on us. I felt the heft of my rapier shift as I moved to balance it in the third position, ready to strike or defend depending on what came next.

"Sir Jaymes." A whispered woman's voice came, muffled but not extinguished by the thick wood door and with it, something tickled at the back of my memory. I saw Kelly shift all but imperceptibly and knew that he had felt it too. Jaymes, in contrast, moved swiftly. The blades he had been holding slipped away like the tools of a stage magician as he pulled the latch free. With a pull, he opened the door just enough to admit a single, snow-powdered figure in a black fur-trimmed cloak. As Jaymes resecured the door, the figure pulled off the furred hood, thick ringlets of dark hair spilling out around the unmistakable face of the Imperial Scribe of Yorch.

"Larissa?" I heard myself say, far louder than I meant to.

Larissa Coffey turned to me, and her dark brown eyes doubled in size. "Lady Dana?" she gasped. Seemingly oblivious to the weaponry on display, Larissa crossed the room in seconds and grabbed me by my shoulders as if to assure herself I was not an illusion. She looked me up and down, her eyes only passingly distracted by the white lines around my face, then swept me up into a tight hug. The Scribe was one of the few women that were a match for me in size and possibly the only one I could imagine grabbing me in an embrace without my invitation – aside from Jules, perhaps. I felt my breath all but go out from me as she did, and though in other circumstances might have resisted, I couldn't help but feel a familiar comfort. After a short moment that felt much longer, she released me from the hug though her hands remained on my arms as surety that I was real.

"I don't believe it," she said quietly, again looking me up and down. I put my free hand – the other was still awkwardly holding my blade – on her shoulder in return and smiled.

"I think," Kelly said from the other side of the room, "that's the general feeling at the moment, Lady Larissa." She spun around as if she'd heard hungry wolves approaching, and her eyes settled on him in a flash. I watched as a chaotic storm of emotions washed away her happiness at seeing me as recognition hit her.

"Blackcrow," she nearly spat.

Kelly said nothing. He blew out a breath and tossed

his sword on a nearby table with a note of irritation.

"Nope," I heard Denis mutter from my left, "not one single person in this country likes him."

Hints of red discolored Larissa's chocolate skin as I watched her anger build. "This is all your doing, isn't it?" she said. She looked around the room for the first time and seemed to take in the rest of us. Then, she shot a look back at me, one that carried doubt and, if not fear, then a hint of betrayal. A voice inside me chided *An exiled traitor, a former assassin, a pirate, and an outlaw. What would you expect her to think?* Gently, I touched her arm, though she was turning back to Kelly.

"Riss," I said quietly, adding a beseeching tone to my voice, "please listen. It isn't what you think." Her head jerked at my use of the nickname; the one Julea had used on more than one occasion when she had seemed so very serious to us. Of course, she hated it, but it seemed to accomplish what I intended; it reminded her of my connection to the princess. Our princess. Then I watched her as she consciously relaxed her tensed muscles, just a fraction, and gave Kelly a nod.

"Lady Larissa," he began again. He seemed to be swallowing whatever irritation she had brought up in him reasonably well. Considering she was the one that had enacted his exile, and from his point of view, done so with a hint of joyful triumph, I had to give him credit for that. He took a breath and raised his hands. "I have abided the exile, and as soon as this is over, I will continue to do so," he said. He paused, then continued with an intensity he rarely used, "But the blaggard who now walks by the empress side is a threat to the throne and the Imperial family personally, if not the state as a whole. And for that, I will not sit aside."

She seemed to twitch when he mentioned the Imperial family, and I remembered that she believed the princess was dead, lost at sea. She and Kelly glared at one another for a long time while the rest of us watched. Then, finally, she turned to me, an unspoken question on her face. I nodded.

"I know how you feel, my lady," I said, "I thought the same thing once. But he's in the right; he always was. And whether you believe that or not, whether you approve or not, you know his feelings for Julea."

She looked over at Jaymes, and it occurred to me that she had come to see him specifically, not knowing about any of the rest of us. There was a connection there. His opinion would matter, and for a moment, all I could think about was his still unaddressed feelings toward Kelly. He looked at her seriously and nodded. The Scribe squared her shoulders and looked back at Kelly. "Very well, Blackcrow. You have many speaking for you, and these are unique circumstances."

"Great," Kelly said, wryness worming its way into his voice, "that's just all kinds of magnanimous of you."

I'd have kicked him had I been closer, but Larissa

ignored the sourness of his tone and turned to Jaymes. "Sir Jaymes, something is happening. A large group of the stranger's mercenaries, as well as a few of those dark shadowy hirelings, were very active earlier tonight. They left the palace at an odd hour, and when they returned, they went down into the dungeons. Something had happened."

We passed a look around before Jaymes replied. "The princess, her bodyguard, and two of my companions – along with me – were attacked earlier," he reported evenly, "We imagine that the princess at least was put into the prison for leverage against Her Imperial Majesty."

Larissa's eyes widened. "The princess is alive?" she said with a gasp.

"She was earlier this evening," Kelly said as he took a step forward and spoke to the quiet tension in the room. "She was taken by a group of men wearing Imperial livery. I'm going to guess they were in company with the dark and shadowy sort you just mentioned."

Larissa looked at him, for the first time lacking the antagonism that had been on her face up to then. "That, that…," she sputtered, struggling against the words that were coming to her.

Kelly raised a hand and nodded his understanding. She exhaled a gust of unspent venom.

"As it happens," Aeryk said, "we were just discussing what we could do about that."

The Scribe turned to him, and it seemed to settle her into herself. As if somehow seeing a stranger was enough to remind her of her station and its associated decorum. She nodded thoughtfully and calmly, though the concern of moments before remained across her face.

"The problem is that *we* don't have any way to get to her in the palace dungeons," Kelly said. He put a little extra weight on the word *we*, and instantly I knew what he was thinking. One look at Larissa's face told me that she had not missed the hint.

"Unfortunately, the palace is about equally full of loyal soldiers, and this interloper's hired thugs," she said.

"Not bad odds," Denis muttered.

"And you are?" Larissa said, whirling on him with enough force that her cloak swung wide around her.

"A friend of the princess," Denis said. He grinned mirthlessly and leaned back on a table, crossing his arms. "One of a few in this room. Every one of which is willing to take that bet."

Larissa regarded him for a moment, then said, "Even if that were true, that's not the extent of the problem. The thugs are only one faction of his followers. There are those shadowy creatures. He has—,"

"A crowd of assassins in black with him as well," Denis said, "yeah, yeah. We know."

She looked at him again. He smiled at her and

shrugged.

Kelly stepped over to Larissa and waited for her to face him. “Can you get the four of us into the palace?”

“Five,” Jaymes said.

Kelly turned, and the two men locked gazes for a moment. Jaymes nodded. Kelly turned back to the Scribe.

“The five of us,” he corrected.

“It won’t matter,” she protested.

“That’s not what I asked,” Kelly said.

She looked around the room, and I could not have imagined her having a more strained look if she found herself in a madhouse where the lunatics had taken control. But, perhaps, I realized when I thought about what we were planning, that was an accurate description anyway.

A long moment later, she turned back to Kelly and bowed her head in a nod. “Dawn tomorrow,” she said, “I will make arrangements at the Scupper Gate on the north by the river. Do not be late.”

She and Kelly looked at one another for a moment. She had known him, I knew, years before. Better than I had back then. He had been Julea’s personal bodyguard as I had, and for longer. As such, the Scribe knew him as she had known me. The bitterness in her – her contempt for the ‘Blackcrow’ – was partly personal; I could see it. But for one brief moment, there was a spark from those old memories, and concern played across her face. A concern not just for

Julea but for the man she had known.

"Thank you," Kelly said, almost inaudibly.

Just as swiftly as the moment had come, it passed. Larissa's face cleared, and she turned toward the door.

"The blood be on your account, Blackcrow. Yours and the rest of these fools who follow you," she said, "Sir Jaymes, a word?"

Jaymes stepped forward, and the two stepped outside together, leaving the rest of us inside in silence, the fire crackling the only sound.

Kelly stared at the door, a dark look on his face. I stepped over and put my hand on his shoulder. It was hard to say what he was thinking or what feelings seeing Larissa again had stirred within him, so I simply stood there and let him brood. Jaymes returned after a moment and, after resecuring the door, looked at Kelly expectantly.

"You heard the Imperial Scribe," he said, banishing the dark look and turning to each of us in turn. He took a breath and smiled wryly. I let my hand drop away as he continued. "Best get some rest; we've got to go get ourselves killed in the morning," he said.

"Oh good," Aeryk said, "I was worried I wouldn't have any plans for tomorrow." I gave him a glance of approval. The heir to Castle Claire had changed over his pirate career, and I had to admit that I liked those changes.

"There are a couple of rooms for sleeping upstairs and

other supplies and such in the back rooms," Jaymes said, waving toward the interior door that Aeryk had used earlier. "The room to the left of the stairs is mine; the other two have beds and such. They're not much, but they'll beat sleeping in the snow."

"I'll take the bench down here," Kelly said, strolling back to the bench by the fire, "you three fight it out for the rooms."

"Fight nothing. I'll bunk with you, pirate," Denis said. He walked off toward the door that led to the stairs. "Neither of us is fighting her for a room."

"Rightest thing you've ever said, dungeon rat," Aeryk said, falling in behind him.

Kelly flashed me a smile as I followed them a moment later, Jaymes close behind.

"We stand to get in a great deal of trouble for doing this," I said.

Julea smiled at me over a sidelong glance as we entered the pub door. "Well, to be specific, *you* stand to get in some trouble. It's unlikely that I would get more than a stern talking to and a disapproving look," she said.

"That consoles me very little," I told her, following her through the heavy oak doorframe and into the main room of the dockside pub. The place was bustling with people, and I could feel my anxiety level rise even further. As if it needed help. As the princess's guard, any situation that introduced a degree of uncertainty brought – by definition – tension with it. Going into a public house, in the waterfront district, among the people…, well, that was a wholly new level. We shuffled our way through the crowd until we found a small alcove. Of course, there were no seats available; the room was all but a solid mass of humanity, and there was a body on every flat surface that was even close to seating height. But the corner we found, an intersection of the stone sidewall and a massive oaken divider partition with a small shelf, was as good a place as any to settle and better than many.

Julea placed herself in the corner, leaning on one arm and surveying the room. She – well, we – wore long cloaks of light cotton material, dyed a medium tan color. I was sure the color was intended to disguise road dust that would accumulate quickly on a more typical wearer. Under these, we each wore unexceptional, somewhat itchy, bone-white blouses and dark britches. And no finery. I consoled myself that, unless I had cause to pull out my blade, there was nothing that would indicate that we were anything other than travelers that had found our way to a packed room for music and drink, which awakened a different thought.

"Drink," I said, both as a question and a statement. The princess nodded, nonchalantly tapping her foot to the music that washed over us from the band playing across the room. It sounded like a sea shanty, bawdy, and over tempo. I shuddered to think what we might hear as the night wore on. *Best to get on with the drinking, then,* I thought. It took a little effort, but I managed to wind my way across the floor and wedge myself into a small opening at the corner of the bar. I flailed my hands and, in time, received the barmaid's attention. She was only a bit older than I, and I could see from the look in her eyes that there was weathering on her soul. She took my order and filled it quickly, wasting no time on flirtation when she could see there would be no profit in it. I was grateful, aware the entire time that I'd left the princess of the realm alone in a dockside pub. I laid the coins on the bar top – including a decent tip – and was rewarded with a raised eyebrow and a smile.

I returned to our corner, but as I did, I came up short. For a moment, I thought maybe I had come to the wrong section of the wall, as instead of Julea, I found two stout men laughing and jostling one another. I looked around, taking a moment to wonder what the punishment might be for mislaying the heir to the empire. Then, reassured that I was in the right place, I stepped forward and found that, in the corner where I had left her, Julea remained, now sipping on a mug of ale and listening as the first of the two men animatedly told a story. I considered the two drinks in my hands and decided that having one extra ale was not a tragedy. I moved to regain my place by the princess, but as I did, the storyteller gestured, narrowly missing the mugs in my hands. Thankfully, I was able to adjust without losing the ale, but nonetheless, the near accident had brought a pause to the story and all attention to me. I glanced from one man to the other before moving forward to my original position on Jules's left. The second man, who was now opposite me on the princess's other side, looked me up and down with a disquieting intensity. My standard process was to forestall such looks with a lofty but practical flash of my Imperial uniform. However, as I did not have such just then, I settled for a stern look of disinterest. Which only brought a smile to the men's faces, as well as to my royal friend.

"'Ello," said the storyteller as this was going on, "nice to see another fine lady 'ere in our homely pub." He grinned, and I was struck by the fact that several of his teeth were the color of tar.

"Dana," Jules said, a strangely unconcerned smile on her ale-dampened lips, "This is Cappy and Dale," she gestured first to the man with the peculiar dental color and then to the other, who had still not taken the hint about staring at me. She continued, "They're merchants. Cappy has a ship and takes cargo fares from here to Euticha. That is where you said you were from, right, Cappy?"

"Aye," Cappy said, his proud smile punctuated with checkerboard teeth, "Native o' Yorch, though. Born an' raised, ma'am. Happy t' be 'ome for a spell."

"And Dale runs a warehouse just a bit from here, near

the docks. They were just telling me about a pirate sighting they experienced this past spring," Jules said behind a swallow of ale. I quickly joined her, and Cappy began his tale where he had left off, supplemented in a practiced rhythm by Dale's running commentary. They had told this tale before, and their delivery was well-rehearsed. Julea's laughter, which seemed out of place in the rough-and-tumble pub, filled the air, and I gave her a look. Her duties didn't let her laugh much, and since the exile of my predecessor, she didn't even seem very inclined. But here, away from the palace, amid the music and the people, that sadness seemed far away. She caught my look from the corner of her eye as she took another swallow and smiled at me, meaningfully, as if reading my mind. I smiled back, and then we turned our attention back to Cappy and Dale and whatever their next story was.

Darkness enveloped the pub then, darkness so thick it felt physically able to choke me. Cappy reached out with arms that were no longer a man's but rather wheezing clockwork mechanisms that glowed with a sickly greenish light. I stepped forward to place myself between the thing and Julea, but my shoulders and arms were pulled back by what felt like heavy ropes. I looked down to see black, glistening tentacles pulling me away from my friend toward Dale, who was no longer a man. His eyes had drawn back inside of his head behind skin that had transformed into something black and leathery. His mouth was open in an impossibly large maw lined with teeth. I looked to Jules, now ensnared in the malevolent grasp of the mechanized arms. Cappy had changed too. His face, a twisted perversion of a man's, was bathed in the greenish light from the mechanisms and covered in a stinking sweat. I tried to call for help, to call out to Jules, to do anything. But a black tentacle tightened around my throat, and I lost my breath.

"It's over," hissed a voice that sounded like Steinhargh's from the creature that had once been Cappy, "I win."

The tentacle around my throat tightened—

I awoke with a gasp and felt cold night air fill my lungs without resistance. Without thought, my hands clutched the handle of my sword where it lay beside the bed as I looked around the room frantically. It took a moment – more than that, if I'm to be honest – to realize I was still in the small bedroom in Jaymes's cabin. Safe. I willed my muscles to relax, but only to limited success. My hand would not release the handle of the rapier, and my heart continued its thrumming. Eventually, I sat up, swinging my legs off the bed and planting my feet on the wooden floor. There was a warmth there, diffused through the flooring from the nearby chimney stones. Cool air hit what I now realized was a sheen of sweat on my skin, and the dream receded in my mind. I was grateful to the chill for that, but before long, I stood and put my cloak around me. It was only then that I found myself able to return my blade to its place beside the bed.

Okay, no more sleep for a while, I thought. I eased the door open and stepped into the short hallway leading to the stairs. I didn't have a destination in mind other than possibly getting a drink of water from the stores below, but at the sound of my friend's voices, I knew exactly where I meant to go. As I approached, their conversation, which was at first just low, muffled tones in my ears, gradually resolved into speech.

"I don't like it, kid," Kelly was saying.

"Well, that doesn't really matter, Kel," Denis replied, "I think it's exactly the kind of thing that could work. But, also, it's my decision."

"What's your decision?" I said as I came through the door. Kelly and Denis were sitting furthest from the doorway, on the bench and the table, respectively, and they turned to me as I entered. A veiled look passed Kelly's face as he nodded to me, and whether it was because of their discussion or because he detected something in me, he pushed it aside.

"Our dungeon rat here wants to deal with the Kathasiri for us," he said, looking back at Denis. I looked over at him.

"Okay, he makes that sound much more heroic than I

mean it to," Denis said, "I just think that I might have a way to distract the Kathasiri if we need to."

"By challenging their high priest," Kelly said, never taking his eyes off him. I nodded thoughtfully, dropping on the other end of the bench.

"That's idiotic," I said, imbuing my voice with all of the sounds of dismissal I could. I rubbed at my temples in disapproval.

"You too, eh?" Denis stood and brushed his hair back with both hands. He paced in a small patch next to the chair as he spoke, looking at me directly. "First, that's not what I said. Okay, let me explain it again. He's a stubborn bird, but you might be more sensible. I'm not suggesting that this is our first plan, all right? Maybe not even in the top half of our list of plans. But let's do some numbers. Just to make it easy, let's say there are a hundred fighters in the palace, including Yorchians, mercenaries, and Kathasiri. And let's say they're evenly distributed between the three, okay? Worst case. So, if I can distract the Kathasiri – take them out of the picture – then you only have real Yorchians and Steinhargh's mercenaries left. And if the true Yorchians see the princess, they flip sides. All I'm saying is that it's the best way to even the field if we get our backs against the wall."

I looked at Kelly. He was leaning forward and rubbing his eyes with the palms of his hands. "Ask him how," he said without looking up.

I looked back at Denis. He lolled his head back on his shoulders before looking at me again. “Okay, I’m going to oversimplify some, but here it is. The Kathasiri are governed by a council of priests. When I left, they passed judgment on me – branded me, excommunicated me, all that. The normal process would have been to serve justice by giving me the right to challenge. There would have been a trial, and I would have defended myself in combat. But I left. No trial. No combat. No *judgment*. Technically, they still owe me that. Taking me back for the trial is their holy duty, and it would overrule the right of contract.”

I blinked. I looked at Kelly, who was watching me expectantly. I blinked again and looked back at him.

“No,” I said.

Denis looked back and forth between us. There was a long moment of quiet where the fire – still well-tended and bright – crackled alone. Finally, he rolled his eyes at us.

“Listen, mom and dad, I’m not taking it off our list of options. It’s there if we need it,” he said. Another pause. He sighed and said, “But fine. Last resort only.”

Kelly stood up and reached his hand out. For a moment, nothing happened, then Denis reached over, and they grabbed one another’s forearms. A wordless exchange went between them, one that somehow made me proud they were my friends. Then the moment passed, the handshake released, and Kelly dropped back down onto the bench.

"Well, good night to you both. Got to get some sleep before the festivities tomorrow," Denis said in a voice thick with resolve. He picked up a small metal cup off the mantle and disappeared through the door without another word.

"Idiot," Kelly muttered. He flopped back against the backrest and let his head lean onto the top, his eyes closed.

"Only as idiotic as his friends. It's a fair play," I offered, leaning back and cuddling deeper into my cloak, which was now warmed by the fire.

Kelly's head rolled my way, and his eyes opened slightly to look at me. "You too?" he asked.

I shrugged, shifting on the bench so that I was facing him, my legs pulled up under the cloak as if it were a blanket. "He's not doing anything you wouldn't – or I wouldn't – if we had the means. Seriously, right now, answer this. If you could save Jules – and the throne, we can't forget that – if you could do that and all you had to do was risk your own life, what would you do?"

He looked at me. I could see he wanted to say something, but he obviously didn't like what it was, and so he stayed frustrated and quiet.

"Exactly," I said with a note of triumph. "And you need to think of something else, too."

He groaned. "What?" he said, rolling his face away and closing his eyes again.

I spoke, my next words coming in a steady, insistent

cadence. "Denis doesn't care a whit about the throne of Yorch. He's Jules's friend, sure, but think about it. He's spent, what? A few hours with her? He's not like us; he hasn't known her for years and years."

I let the words sink in before I continued. "He's not doing this – not offering his freedom and maybe his life – for Jules. Certainly not for Yorch."

Kelly's head rolled over again, his eyes open now and looking at me intently. I leaned over and put my hand on his arm.

"He's doing it for us," I said finally. Kelly stared at me for several heartbeats, then looked up with unfocused eyes. I leaned back, removing my hand. "I agree with you. There's got to be a better way than him sacrificing himself that way. But don't call him an idiot for offering it for someone you and I care about."

The word hung in the air for a time while the fire crackled. Eventually, one of the logs shifted, prompting Kelly to go over and prod it with a poker until it was stable once again. He watched the flames for a bit before he came and sat back down. He pulled at one of the blankets and draped it over his shoulders before settling back in the corner.

"You should be sleeping," he said, "I think we have to be up in something like five minutes." He grinned as he gave me a look.

"Sleep's not my friend tonight," I said. I turned toward

the fire.

“Nightmare,” he said. It wasn’t a question. He had read it on my face earlier. I said nothing as I watched the flames. I could feel him nod, though I didn’t look. The dream seemed further away, somehow, having been here with him and Denis. The panic I’d woke with was just a memory now, but a memory that made me dread sleeping again.

As if in answer to my thoughts, Kelly handed me a blanket. I took it, then looked up as he moved one of the chairs in front of the end of the bench, settled back into his spot, put his feet up on the chair, and draped his blanket over himself. He looked at the rest of the bench, the remaining length of which was open, then at me, and then leaned back and closed his eyes.

I set aside my cloak, wrapping the blanket he’d given me around myself, and stretched out along the open bench, resting my head on the pile of pillows at the end. I closed my eyes. And I slept.

CHAPTER TEN
— KELLY —

Dawn was near to breaking when we returned to the city's northern border, the first glow of the sun just peeking over the horizon. The sky had grown clear after the passing of the blizzard the night before, and a few stars remained stubbornly visible in the growing light. Mornings are beginnings, and that seems like the right place to start, as this one signaled the beginning of the end of our tale.

Of the many public and hidden entrances to the palace, the Scupper's Gate is particularly obscure. It stood carved in the castle's foundation stone on the northwest side, where it served as access for the tradesmen that brought provisions for the Imperial household and its countless members. The Golden Palace of the Empire sits in the northernmost part of Yorch, elevated on solid bedrock such that it can be seen at all times from nearly anywhere in the sprawl that was the Imperial capital. A large river branch, narrow but deep, ran in a meandering path from the western highlands to empty into the great Carmac River, which wrapped around Yorch to the west and south. This particular tributary wound around the palace's stone foundations the same way the main body of the Carmac did the city proper, forming a natural moat. The water was still high as we arrived, indicating just how wet the autumn had been. An autumn that I had effectively skipped altogether while Dana and I lain in the house of healing.

We arrived at the gate just before dawn, leaving Jaymes's cabin behind during the witching hours when the world was still dark. And frigid. However, it remained cold now as the sun crept closer to the eastern horizon, so maybe the dead of night had only seemed worse. I had imagined that we'd be walking back to the city in the same manner that we left, but as we made to travel, Jaymes led us to a small farm not far from his home. There, he revealed a tall wagon to which he lashed two stout horses. We climbed into the back for the trip, and I wondered whether we had just stolen a cart or if perhaps Jaymes had some arrangement with the homeowners. I will confess, though, that within moments of having that thought, it occurred to me that I didn't care. We needed to get to Yorch, and this was far better and faster than walking.

Two imperial guards stood before the heavy, steel-reinforced oak doors of the Scupper's Gate aside large stone pits where warm fires blazed. After hours on the cold dark road, their light was warm and welcoming, but the guardsmen were anything but that. Instead, they stepped forward and poised their polearms such that they crossed, blocking access to the last few feet before the gate. Jaymes drew us up to a stop while we were yet several feet away, and we climbed off the wagon. The thick snows from the night before formed deep piles and drifts, despite being light, as snow is wont to be in intense cold. Some poor imperial servant had cleared the roadway, though, and thus we stood on relatively dry ground. Jaymes reached back on the cart, behind the driver's bench, and retrieved a package – about three feet long and irregularly wrapped in a heavy canvas. He rested it on his right shoulder, gripping the bottom in his hand, then joined the rest of us as we before approaching the gate and its guardians. A hint of recognition flickered in me, and I tilted my head.

"Yes," he said, a familiar lop-sided grin briefly appearing on his face, "this is what you think it is."

I nodded, returning the grin. "Well, all right then," I said.

We turned, and I stepped to the front, Denis and Dana falling in on my right and left and Aeryk and Jaymes right behind. The guard on my left stepped forward as we approached, rotating his spear down and placing the axe-like point between us. I stopped, lifting both of my hands in a gesture of peace. Precisely then, the gate slid open, and a figure in a luxurious black cloak stepped out, quickly crossing the few feet to the soldiers. Neither guard turned to the newcomer, and very quickly, the figure stepped next to the nearest guardsman and whispered to him too quietly for us to hear. His head jerked, turning swiftly toward the voice. Then, just as quickly, he stepped back to the fire pit and his original stance. Another whispered message to the second guard rendered precisely the same result. The cloaked figure turned and went back to the open gate, stopping just outside and extending an ornately gloved hand in a gesture that indicated we should follow. Cautiously, I stepped forward, observing the two men as I did. I needn't have bothered. Both of them stood as still as statues; the only motion was the fur of their heavy cloaks twitching in the breeze. Unimpeded, we walked past them and through the gate.

"Carry on, then," Denis said as he passed, giving both men an unrequited nod. He shrugged as I gave him a look.

Inside, we found ourselves in a wide tunnel that had been expertly carved out of the surrounding rock. It felt warmer. Not warm by any means, but without the steady press of the wind, it was better, at least. The corridor we were in was wide, fifteen feet or so, and lit by a series of small gas lanterns mounted on the walls. A system of copper pipes extended down the passage, mounted on the stone at just above head height. This framework formed both the fuel supply and the support for the evenly spaced lanterns. The result was that the cavern was brighter inside than the pre-dawn sky outside, and it took a moment for my vision to adjust. I blinked while Larissa finished latching the door and pulled off the hood of her black cloak.

"I did my part, Blackcrow," she said, a nebulous look on her face.

"You did," I said, nodding, "I appreciate it."

She looked at me for a long moment, and I could see the conflict in her still. After all, she'd spent her life serving the throne, and there I stood in all my exiled glory, inside the Golden Palace, no less. And she'd helped me get there. She had clearly learned to hate me in the years since I'd been removed from the empire, whether intentionally or by default. But, help us she had, and I had to admire that.

"Mercenaries have replaced every one of the guards in the dungeon," she said, moving deftly on from my thanks without acknowledging it. "King Willm suggested that our Yorchian soldiers were more elite and could be better used elsewhere. Moreover, the dungeons were of late nearly empty, so he felt his hirelings would be sufficient." She paused in thought before she haltingly continued, "Her Imperial Majesty— agreed." There was more to be said there – more that she wanted to say, I'd have gambled – but she stopped. Those were confidences she was not going to share in the presence of the Blackcrow.

"A dungeon full of sell-swords means no one sees the princess," Aeryk said.

"Keeps her being alive a secret," added Jaymes, "and

keeps his place at the empress's side secure."

"And, of course, no witnesses to whatever happens," Dana intoned.

Larissa gave her a look that did nothing more than underscore how ominous that observation was. She turned back to me. "There is a shift change at sunrise. There will be a brief window where there will only be a few on duty while the full garrisons are in transition. That's going to be your best chance to get to the princess," she said.

I nodded. "We better get moving then. Where will you be?"

"Formal audiences in the chamber begin shortly after dawn. I have to be there," she said. She walked over to Jaymes and put her hand on his arm. He looked at her, and they stood like that for a moment longer than simple friendship would have warranted. Then she turned and began to move down the passageway. Abruptly she stopped, turned around, and grabbed Dana in a tight hug. She whispered something to her, then let go and turned to me. I returned the look as evenly as possible, denying both the good and bad of our history together. But something softened in her eyes, and she reached over and took my hand wordlessly. A moment passed; she squeezed my hand tightly in both of hers, then let it go and hurried off, down the hallway, then into a side passage and out of sight.

"That was awkward. I felt like I was intruding being

here, Kel," Aeryk said into the heavy silence that fell.

"Maybe a little," I said, slowly pushing memories of the past that the Scribe stirred up back into the lockbox in my mind where they lived. Then, with a shake of my head, I turned to my friends. "All right then. The dungeon is opposite where we are, across where the river flows under this part of the palace. We can get across in the access passage that passes over the water just a little ways ahead. In the old days, it would be all but empty at this time of the morning, so I think we'll be fine until we get to the entrance to the dungeon pits themselves."

"Pits?" Denis asked.

"Pits," I repeated.

"Going to need some more description," he said.

I knelt and started swiping my finger along the ground as I talked. The floor was dusty but not thick enough to leave an overly visible line, so I relied on imagination to fill in the blanks.

"The dungeon itself is built into five pits that are carved into the bedrock of the castle itself. Each pit is six-sided, about thirty feet across, and is over two hundred feet deep," I explained. I gestured with my hands to indicate the basic dimensions based on the half-visible sketch, then I continued, "On each of the six faces is a cell, which is a twelve-by-twelve square about eight feet high. They're staggered, so they descend from the top cell right under the pit's top and continue down in a spiral to the deepest and darkest."

"That seems awful fancy for a prison," Jaymes said.

"It's actually brilliant," Denis added, "and also terrifying." He was staring at the space in front of me where I had been describing the arrangement. "No one is next to you, so there's no wall to get through. And if I were designing it," he looked at me and wiggled his finger up and down, "the access is only by a platform that guards raise and lower as needed. No escape route."

"Exactly that," I said, remembering again that he prided himself on his dungeon expertise. "Waste gets thrown down into the pit, so the only contact with the prisoners is lowering food or retrieving them."

"Light?" Jaymes asked.

"Gas-fed lanterns on the pit walls, spaced out of reach of the cells. The piping is recessed, so it can't be used to climb out easily."

"The greatest dungeon in the world," Dana said. "And the only one we need to break into."

"Today," Denis said, tossing her a shrug. "You never know. Tomorrow might mean a whole different dungeon we need to break into."

"Stop saying break into," Aeryk said, "it's discomforting."

"We don't know which pit they are likely to be in," I

said, dragging us back on topic, "and the shift change isn't going to last long enough for a lot of exploration. This is going to be about getting lucky. The good news is that we know the dungeons are fairly empty."

"Except for the hired killers that are either there or on the way there," Aeryk said.

"Oh, come on," I said, straightening up, "we were expecting that anyway."

Aeryk looked from me to Den and Dana and back. He shrugged. "Well, yeah. That's true enough."

Jaymes flipped the canvas package off of his shoulder and unwrapped it, tossing the cloth aside. An intricately etched silver warhammer with a long leather-wrapped handle reflected the lantern light like a mirror as if it were glowing from an inner light.

"Malatak," I said.

Jaymes swung the hammer back and forth and once in a full circle before looking over at me. "I kept it," he said, his voice low and severe, "I couldn't bring myself to use it, but I'd never get rid of it." He lifted it to his face, inspecting the inscriptions on its head. Then he gave me a look and held it out toward me. I placed my hand on the inscribed head and waited.

"Where gods fear, I follow," he said.

"Where gods fear, I lead," I said. He nodded, and for reasons I can't explain, a weight seemed to leave me that I hadn't known I was carrying.

"Well, that was very nice," Denis said into the sober moment, "but I think we have a date with a princess?"

I looked at him, a chuckle bubbling at the back of my throat. "I think you're right. Let's go."

The underbelly of the Golden Palace had changed little in the years I'd been gone, and the service passages I remembered had not become any more populous, much to my relief. We moved quickly and quietly through the hallways, relying on either my or Dana's recollections. Even though it was still cold, we left our heavy cloaks just inside the Scupper's Gate, preferring a lighter load to the comfort of their warmth. Amazingly, we reached the access hallway to the dungeon level without incident. Of course, that was all but the last thing that happened like that.

"There are five armed guards in there," Denis whispered as he came back into the shadows with us in a crouch.

"Five?" Aeryk said, "I guess that's not too bad."

"No, no," Denis said, glancing back down the hallway leading to the dungeon entrance, "I mean five just in that first room. No idea what's beyond that."

Aeryk gave him a look that seemed deflated even in the darkness. We hunched in a small storage alcove aside the central passage leading from the dungeons to a heavy set of oak doors. Beyond those was the public courtyard of the castle where prisoners, criminals, and occasionally rebellious Imperial Ravens were brought to be bound for trial or, afterward, publicly sentenced. As such, the vast stone hallway and its gentle downward slope were very familiar to me. Denis had slipped out to survey the entrance of the dungeon proper and had now returned.

I absently brushed my hand through my hair and blew out a quiet breath. “Well,” I said, “one of three things is true. Number one – we’ve missed the opportunity Larissa told us about, and all five of the pits now have five fresh guards stationed around them. Two – we came at exactly the right time, and those five are all that there are. Or, three – we came at exactly the wrong time, and there are now two sets of guards at the pits, the ones coming off duty and the ones going on.”

“The worst possible option,” Dana said, “is the most likely, given our history.”

Denis looked down the hallway for all of this, but I noticed his fingers twitching in what looked like random patterns, first one, then another extending and then bending, without order, and different from one hand to the other. Suddenly he stopped, his hands relaxed, and he turned back to the group.

“I say we’re right on time, and those five are the night shift. They look like they’ve been on duty for a while. No way to know about the other pits or how far away their relief is. I do know that waiting won't help. We go now, and we get out quick," he said suddenly and with complete confidence.

"Wha—?" Jaymes said, looking back and forth from one to another of us, confused. Dana smiled at him while Aeryk repositioned in preparation to move.

I patted his shoulder and gave him a grin. "Time to go," I said, drawing my sword as punctuation. I thought for a second how different it felt than my ebony blade I was so used to, the center of balance being just a touch further up its length so that it felt slightly awkward in my grip. It was one of many changes thrust on me in the preceding months. It may have been the least of them, but it brought the others back to my attention despite my efforts to push them aside. Involuntarily, I flexed the fingers of my strange new left hand. Like most of my body's left side, it felt both familiar and odd at the same time. Everywhere that the black marks – or the scars, as Dana referred the patterns on her own flesh – had replaced my skin, I felt less intensely. There was still a sense of touch, but everything I felt, I felt as if I was feeling it through thin leather that wasn't actually there. Dana said that her experience was very much the opposite and that since her recovery, she was sure she could feel every individual piece of her hair as it touched her forehead.

I used the phrase 'covering the skin' there, but that's completely wrong. The black marks *were* my skin now. And my veins. And my muscles. And many of the bones beneath, or so it was explained to me. The black *stuff* – and the white material that had been infused in Dana – was some product of the gems and Eryth's concoctions. But I couldn't look at it as something external anymore. It was part of me, pain-free and healthy. Stronger, too. I had no idea how strong, for sure; we'd had to leave before I'd been able to test them. There were other side effects, Eryth had warned us. *I've no way to know what we've done, and you're on your own if you go*, her words echoed in my mind. But Julea needed us, and that was that. My left hand flexed again, gloves creaking over the black flesh, while I rebalanced the wrongly weighted sword in my other hand. I turned to the passage with my friends beside me to launch once more into the fight. The buzzing of nerves came back to the base of my neck like an old friend. I gratefully noted that the feeling was as vivid as it ever had been, black flesh be hanged. And then we were in motion.

The first prison pit guard chamber was a large, circular room around the first prisoner pit's mouth. The opening took up most of what would have been floor, though, so it would be better described as a walkway around eight feet wide encircling the six-sided chasm. A slightly wider area immediately inside the entrance created a small space for the guards to use while on duty. There, three small tables and accompanying chairs sat in an orderly row at an angle.

Their positioning allowed a view of the pit, the entrance, and the passage to the next chamber without effort. Each chamber in the dungeon led to the following one in the same layout, spiraling inward to the final, most secure one in the center. As we entered, we saw a man seated at each of the tables, each wearing the armor and livery of an Imperial guard. Two of the three were leaning back in their chairs with their feet up, while the third lay sprawled forward and looked asleep. The remaining two of the five Denis had reported to us leaned against the nearby wall; their heads drooped forward inattentively.

These aren't Yorchians, that's for sure, I thought. *Imperial officers would have strung them up or kicked them out for slacking off like that.* With a stab of disappointment, I realized that I now agreed with the officers, which caused me a bit of an existential crisis. Fortunately, it only lasted a fraction of a second as the prickling in my neck streaked down my arms, and as it always did, time slowed down. The nearest of the mercenaries was also the first to respond, shoving himself off the wall where he leaned and drawing his longsword in a single motion as we raced into the room. I spun off toward him while my four friends continued toward the others. My opponent squared himself at my approach, his blade up in a ready position, and his weight spread evenly. He was a professional, as was evident by his practiced bearing, and not just a low-rent sell-sword who fancied himself a warrior. His eyes locked on me, obviously waiting for whatever tell I might have that would hint at my next move. For a fraction of a second, his eyes darted to one side before snapping back to me. Had he not been so entirely flawless in his engagement up to then, I might have missed it. I flashed a look to where he had and saw what it was that he just could not resist checking.

"Kid! Alarm cord!" I barked, pointing with my off-hand toward the far wall. With that, I focused on my target. I crossed the distance left between us in a full sprint. I didn't slow down at all, not even a fraction. My opponent's eyes stayed mostly steady but flashed in instinctual alarm as I raced toward him. To give credit where it's due – he held his position a good long while, all things considered. Longer than many might have with a surprise lunatic in black running at them full out. At the last second, he shifted his sword to attack. Whether he meant to stab at my chest or ward me off with a side strike, I don't know, and it didn't matter. Once his blade had moved to the side, I dropped onto my left leg mid-run. I went down to the ground with the total of the momentum I'd gathered, the resistance of the floor on my shin sending me into a tight spin. I whirled, bringing my blade around in a sweeping slash that came far too fast to be blocked with his weapon, which was now far out of position. My rotation stopped as I passed him, leaving me up on my right knee. My sword had bitten hard through the gap in his armor just above his thigh, releasing the tendons that held him upright. He collapsed, a grunt of agony his only sound. I stood, facing him, but he stayed on the ground, rocking slightly and clutching at the wound in his hip. I stood over him, holding my blade in striking distance of his face, and checked in on my friends.

Dana stood opposite me, the second of the formerly standing mercenaries lying at her feet, motionless. To her right, Aeryk pressed his staff across the throat of a third, whose struggles to escape were growing weaker by the moment. Denis was beyond them, trading slashes with a fourth of the mercenaries and dodging back and forth while thrusting tentatively with one of his daggers. Jaymes stood before the final guard, the sleeper, who was carefully using his little table to keep distance between himself and the big man. I didn't know how long it had gone on, but I had turned in time to see it end. Jaymes's shoulder flexed, and the warhammer in his hand swung up vertically from his side. Malatak hit the table's top squarely from the underside, and the thick oak panels exploded in a shower of splinters as the remains fell away, leaving nothing between the mercenary and the warrior. There was another flicker of motion, and the second strike of the hammer lifted the guard off the ground, tossing him across the room. He landed a handful of feet from where I stood, shattered pieces of his longsword clattering to the floor like metallic snowflakes around him.

Ah. Malatak, I thought.

There was a sudden scream that quickly faded into an echo before dying off. I turned and saw Denis standing alone at the edge of the pit. He looked around at the rest of us.

"Slipped," he said with a glance into the pit and a shrug.

"Took you long enough," I said, keeping one eye on the guard on the floor. He appeared to be losing consciousness.

"Well," the dungeon rat said, spinning his single dagger with a flourish, "I would have been faster if I wasn't doing your job." He jutted his chin toward the wall that I'd pointed at moments before. Draped against it and nearly hidden in shadow was a black cord that disappeared into a hole in the ceiling stone. The rope was now, though, pinned to the stone wall by Denis's other dagger.

"Hey, would you rather they'd have pulled it? We didn't need more of these guys," I said.

"Doesn't the big guy have a bunch of knives he could throw?" Denis said, shoving one of the tables over to the wall and climbing on it. "I mean, I am very fond of these daggers. I don't want to keep throwing them into stone walls." He wiggled the blade back and forth until it came loose from the joint in the stone where it was lodged. He took a moment to cut the cord off before climbing down.

"I didn't even see that," Jaymes said, watching him

with a look of respect.

“Another reason why I yelled for him instead of you,” I said with a shrug, “I just didn’t know he was going to winge on about it.”

“‘Winge,’” Dana said with a snort.

“I’m not winge-ing,” Denis muttered. He gave the dagger’s blade a brief inspection before sheathing it and climbing down.

“Um, the princess?” Aeryk said, his eyebrows raised.

“Right,” Denis said, jumping on the opportunity to change the subject, “Mr. Puppy over here is right. Aren’t we here for a princess?”

“Hey,” Aeryk said, shooting him a look.

I raised my hands. “Good point, good point. Okay, we need to find in which pit she and the others might be. Jaymes, you come with Denis and me. We’ll go and check out the other dungeon pits. If we run across more of this lot, we’ll sing out,” I turned to Dana and continued, “Day, can you and Mr. Puppy over there watch the entrance?”

“Hey,” Aeryk said again, looking at me.

“Are we sure everyone isn’t right here?” Jaymes said, looking over the edge into the darkness of the chasm.

“Pretty sure,” I said, “the lanterns are off.”

“You think Steinhargh cares about the lights?” He continued to look over the edge warily.

I nodded. “Doubtful. But the guards still have to feed

any prisoners, which is much more difficult to do in the dark. And dangerous. So, no light, no prisoners."

"At least, not live ones," Denis offered.

"Just get going," Dana said, ignoring the comment. She returned to the entrance where we'd come in and did a quick check of the outside hall before she settled next to the opening.

"Might be that we should put these in a cell, too," Jaymes said. He moved over to a panel mounted in a niche on the nearby wall, pulling it open to reveal a large wheel mounted on a spindle. It was large enough that it was apparent that it was intended for two men to operate, though Jaymes had little trouble moving it. Above our heads, a wooden platform groaned as it moved down slightly from the shadows that had been hiding it. Jaymes turned back to us.

"Or, you know...," Denis said, glancing at the dark pit and letting his voice trail off.

"No, kid, we're not just shoving them in," I sighed.

He shrugged. "I'm only saying that the one that fell in a minute ago isn't a problem anymore."

Jaymes looked at him curiously.

"He fell," Denis said with a shrug, "Honest. Just fell."

"Come on, you two," I said, starting for the other doorway. I looked back at Dana, who returned the look with concern.

"We'll get her back," I said.

She nodded.

We went quickly through the following three chambers, hastened by the fact that they were entirely deserted. If I'd had any uncommitted attention at the time, I suppose I might have wondered why the majority of the prison was empty, though, in hindsight, it's easy to guess. If Steinhargh intended to bring – and keep – the princess down here, he wouldn't want to have any witnesses until she was safely and finally secured somewhere out of the sight or hearing of anyone that wasn't in his employ. Which meant that there couldn't be any other prisoners until he was done with her, whatever that meant. As for the former prisoner's fate, well, that was a mystery and one that was far from my thoughts. We reached the entrance to the fifth and final pit but stopped short. The sound of quiet grunting and the telltale scuff of boots on stone echoed quietly from the room ahead. I held up my left hand, gesturing for Denis and Jaymes to flank me as we all settled into defensive stances. The lantern light of the final dungeon chamber flickered as something we couldn't yet see moved between it and the far wall. Suddenly, three figures emerged from the room and stopped in the doorway; a giant Talhas warrior flanked by two more normal-sized figures glared at us. Everyone froze for a moment.

"Jaymes!" the woman said, and as she did, their faces stepped out of my memory. Niamh Coillte and Muiris Baltha stood on either side of Captain Rohb O'Laird with looks of shock and relief on their faces. Rohb was in sore straits, I could see, as his face was swollen and he was favoring his right leg. Niamh and Muiris had been helping him walk, but he was able to stand on his own. That became very clear a moment later when Niamh finally looked over and recognized me.

"Raven?" she croaked, dropping the big man's arm from her shoulder and approaching me.

"Niamh," I said, suddenly feeling the weight of history like a heavy blanket. She looked in my eyes, scanned over my face quickly – possibly noting the black scars – then settled her gaze on my eyes again.

And then she slapped me full-on in the face. It's worth noting that the vague numbness of the black scars is occasionally a blessing. I rolled with it and slowly turned back as the stinging eased where she'd hit my more traditional skin. But just as suddenly, she was in my arms, holding me as if I were the only thing keeping her from drowning and burying her face in my neck. I put my arms around her and held her without a word.

"Okay, one person likes him," Denis muttered after a quiet moment, "and even she slapped him first."

"Hush," Jaymes said, and I could see him watching us with just the faintest crease of a grin on his mouth.

"Great timing," Muiris said. He was more cautious

about Rohb's stability, making sure the big man was comfortably standing solo before taking a step over to me and offering his hand. I gripped his forearm with my right hand, despite Niamh still being wrapped around me.

"Y're an arse," she whispered just loudly enough to hear.

"I don't think that counts as news," I said.

"Gods, I've missed ye," she said in a whisper. I couldn't answer that, not without choking up, so I just nodded against her head. She seemed satisfied with that, and a moment later, she let me go and stepped back.

I looked at her and Muiris with a moment of wistfulness. I hadn't ever expected to be here again, at least not while Ardallah sat on the throne, and so I hadn't planned what I would say to them when I saw them. And I suppose that if I had, it wouldn't have mattered, as this was unlikely to be the way I'd planned it. But they were alive, healthy, and still capable enough to get out of a dungeon cell without help. And it was that thought that suddenly pulled another into sharp relief.

"Where's Princess Julea?" I said. I found myself glancing around behind them as if she might be waiting. Which was stupid, but it was involuntary. Foolish hope, it appears, is involuntary.

"They came for her," Muiris said, stepping back to where Rohb could lean on him again, "a little bit ago. I'm not sure how long, but not very."

"Men in uniforms, and a bunch o' the ones in black," Niamh said, "I'm fair sure there wasn't a one of them that was from here. 'You're expected,' they said, 'for an audience with the emperor.'"

I shot a look over at Denis, and a palpable wave of frustration passed between us.

"I tried to convince 'em that she was otherwise engaged," Rohb said, punctuated with a wet cough. I looked at him, and he waved a hand as if to wave me off.

"They didn't take that well," Muiris said.

"I covered for you, though," Rohb said through a glower.

"Maybe next time we discuss the plan beforehand," Muiris said. He lifted his hand to display a small brass key. He'd filched the cell door key from the guard as Rohb occupied him. It offered no clue how they'd climbed up to the platform, but that was a tale for another time. He continued, "It's possible you wouldn't have needed to take quite so much of the attention as you did?"

Rohb nodded weakly in reluctant agreement.

"What now?" Jaymes said, giving a glance toward the exit.

"Back to the others," I said. My voice sounded very far away in my ears as the failure of our plan muted everything else. We'd done it – the impossible. We had made our way into the dungeon of Yorch. We'd gotten in; by guile and the beautiful whims of coincidence, we had gotten in. And it didn't matter. Julea was gone, taken just before we'd arrived.

I could feel all of their eyes on me as we walked back past the deserted prison pits to rejoin Aeryk and Dana. The dungeon's silence felt heavier now, our footfalls echoing off the empty chambers but sounding somehow more muted than before when we were trying to be quiet. No prisoners because the princess had been there, but now she wasn't. She was elsewhere, soon to be standing in the grand chamber of the tower of Yorch before the same throne where I received my judgment. Ardallah appeared in my mind's eye, condemning me, exiling me, naming me Blackcrow. The vision merged with an image of Julea tumbling to the floor of Steinhargh's throne room in Sargeaux. Throne rooms, I decided, were viler places than dungeons.

We rejoined Aeryk and Dana in the first chamber much more quickly than we'd left them. They were alone, the fallen guards likely locked in a cell, and they were watching the main entrance from either side.

"No sign of patrols or others since you left," the pirate said, addressing us without turning from the door.

"No sign of any kind, in truth," Dana added, "which is very peculiar." She turned to us as we entered, and I watched her as her eyes searched the group. She hesitated on seeing Rohb, then finally settled on me.

“They took her earlier today,” I said, “just before we got here, it seems.”

We held one another’s gaze for a moment, sharing the frustration and disappointment without words.

“She’ll be before the throne by now,” Niamh said, resignation pushing to make itself heard in her voice despite herself.

“Be a bit,” Rohb grunted. He’d nudged himself loose of Muiris and Niamh’s assistance and was now several feet behind us and using one of the remaining tables for support.

“What’s that mean?” Jaymes said. He’d been giving Rohb sidelong looks since we’d found the others. I wondered if it were simply the novelty of not being the largest person in the room.

“Nobody goes from dungeon to the Throne direct,” he said.

“This is true,” Dana said. Her voice was weary, disappointment coating it like frost on an autumn morning. “No one enters the Golden Chamber without being appropriately prepared. Especially not someone of royal blood. They’ll have taken her to be properly bathed and clothed first.”

I felt my shoulders slump. Julea would be surrounded by guards and servants continuously from the moment they retrieved her until she was in the royal chamber. Again, my mind whisked me back to the day of my exile. Adorned in finery as if I were attending a royal ball, I'd been marched through the cathedral-like throne room to the foot of the dais. Outside the grand windows, I could see the sky and the bay. The sun caught the etchings in the glass and flickered in tiny rainbows all around the throne itself until Ardallah appeared, and the light lit her traditional white and gold dress.

I stopped. The phrase '*Ardallah appeared*' ran through my mind again. She *appeared*. Tiny thought breadcrumbs led me along in my mind.

"The throne," I heard a muttered version of my voice say from very far away.

"Yes," Muiris said as if speaking to a child or a lunatic, "they've taken the princess to the throne room to meet with Steinhargh. Are you okay there?"

I looked at him, realized what he said just as the breadcrumbs finally bore fruit, and cocked my head. "No, wise-ass, the throne itself. That's the solution."

"Okay, as you would say, 'show your work,'" Dana said, stepping up closer to my side.

"The throne room is all but sacred here. Like we just said, no one, let alone the princess, will be brought there directly without being 'prepared.' The same thing is true about Ardallah, even more so. The empress is far too lofty to enter or leave the room the same way everyone else does," I said, walking back through my previous thoughts carefully, making sure that I hadn't missed anything.

"Okay," Aeryk said, elongating the 'a' to hint at the need for more information.

"She enters and leaves through a private entrance. One that only she can access. Well, okay, it might be that the princess had access. I'm sure she knows it exists in any case. But it's all part of the theater. The empress enters and leaves completely unseen. And it's in the throne itself."

Dana's brow furrowed. "You think we're going to be able to get in through a secret door in the throne?"

I felt a grin begin on my face. "I do. Think about it. It's a secret passage only the empress, possibly her heir, and possibly her closest confidants would know exists. And what am I saying— Ardallah doesn't have any confidants. Anyway, maybe Steinhargh has access to it by now – I can't be sure – but I know one thing, either way, there won't be any guards there. No sell-swords and no assassins. It's the kind of secret Ardallah would keep as ."

"But how do we find it?" Niamh said.

"Okay, it's just possible that one other person might know how to get to it," I said. I folded my arms, fully aware of just how arrogant it made me looked.

"The Imperial Raven," Muiris said. He laughed despite himself.

"Okay," Jaymes said, somewhat less amused, "let's say that we can get through this secret passage. So what? We're going to wind up in a room full of this madman's hired blades and assassins. There's no way we're walking away from that."

"Grumpy," Aeryk said, "I'm usually the killjoy."

"Has to be considered," I said, "however grumpy he may seem. But here's the key. We know that ol' Steelclaw uses his mercenaries and the Kathasiri to do the dirty work. From what Larissa told us, a good number of the real Yorchian army isn't even aware of what's going on. So, I say we make them aware. Jaymes, take Muiris, Niamh, and Rohb. You're all citizens in good standing. Get to the palace barracks and find the captain of the watch."

"Gobhneh," Rohb said, "little guy, made out of gristle."

"Sure," I said. The name meant nothing to me, but then again, I'd been gone a while. If that meant something to them, fine. I continued, "I don't care if you have to set this Gobhneh on fire, get him and as much of the active, real army as you can to the throne room as quickly as their feet will take them."

"Do we know which barracks has the sell-swords and which has the soldiers?" Niamh asked.

Rohb said, "I've got an idea. Palace guard quarters are separate from regular issue army. Figure we start where Gobhneh's quarters are. Assuming the regs aren't as infiltrated as the guard, that's the way. One thing's sure; we'll find out fast enough."

"Just come as quick as possible. Dana, Aeryk, Denis, and I will get ourselves into the throne room and stall as long as we can. Our goal is to get the soldiers there for support before we get gutted by mercenaries and assassins," I said.

"Uh, Kel?" Dana said suddenly.

"Yeah?"

"Where's Denis?"

I looked around. "Oh. Oh, damn."

CHAPTER ELEVEN
– DENIS –

The mind can be a strange place when you're otherwise occupied. Memories tend to get dug up and then float to the surface. You know, like sewage.

I spun sideways as the red-edged black blade swung over my head, taking a bit of one curl of my blonde hair with it. The spin took me into a roll and carried me just shy of the near side of a slightly bent sapling – a sapling that grew at the very edge of a sheer cliff above which I was fighting. I ended the roll upright with only a moment to plant my feet before I had to throw myself to the side again, narrowly dodging the stab of the shorter, second blade that sliced through the air where my shoulder had just been. I landed flat on my chest, though, without the benefit of momentum, and instinctively started to scramble to get my limbs under me – anything to get back in motion. I felt a weight drop down onto my lower back too quickly, and I knew I was out of time. An unseen hand grabbed my hair, pulling my head and chest up off the ground while the pressure on my spine pushed my stomach and hips down, arching my back painfully. My muscles screamed their protest as the agony built through me, then the press of steel on my throat pushed everything else away. I dropped my blades from my hands in submission.

"You're dead," whispered a harsh voice. The razor-sharp blade at my throat slid, parting my skin. Then it abruptly stopped, the grip on my hair released, and the weight on my back vanished. I flopped to the ground and grabbed at my throat, a trickle of fresh blood spilling onto my fingers as I rolled over to find Tybor standing over me, casually wiping his short sword's bloody edge with his thumb.

"You're still sloppy, slug," he snarled, inspecting his blade closely, "and you don't think ahead. If you weren't of the Blood, I'd have given your flesh to Kathas just now."

I rose slowly, stopped when I had gotten to my knees, and bowed my head low. I waited like that, as was the custom.

"Oh, stand up," he said, his voice dripping with disdain, "you're not worth the time. The new scar on your throat will serve as your training for today." I heard the sound of his knives sliding back into their sheaths beneath his black sleeves. I lifted my head, turning to find my own discarded blades as I did so. Sudden pain struck me blind as Tybor kicked me squarely in the left temple, sending me sprawling to the ground again. He let out a puff of laughter and turned away as I waited for my vision to clear and the pain to subside. As I came back to myself, I scrambled around, retrieving my blades before finally standing up. I awkwardly slipped the weapons into their hidden sheaths and looked up.

Tybor stood leaning back on the small tree where I'd been moments before, his arms folded and his gaze on the ground. He was taller than me, though that was mostly due to his age. A lot could change in five years, and I'd not yet finished my sixteenth. My body hadn't finally settled on my height. His black hair, long on one side and shaved on the other, hung down the right side of his face, which kept me from seeing his expression.

"I lasted longer, guru," I said. I felt the need to defend my performance, though it was a fool's errand. I knew there was no point.

The older boy snorted. "Lasting longer is only postponing death if you do not triumph, slug. You cannot offer the sacrament to Kathas if you're the one that's leaking it." He nudged himself off the tree so that he was standing before me directly and glared at me. Blood still oozed from my throat where I had received the lesson's "training," mud from the jungle floor was caked on – and in some places in – the black and red training uniform I wore, my hair was matted and soaked with my sweat in the damp jungle heat, and I could feel the beginnings of a dark bruise above my left eye. I made every effort to stand as straight as he did, though, and struggled to control my breath.

"You're pathetic, slug," Tybor said. He stepped closer, close enough to fill my field of view before he continued, "You are unworthy to be Blooded. You're just the son of some dung-heel farmer that the Brethren dragged back here like so much trail filth. I am a child of the Blood. Being saddled with your miserable carcass as my pupil is my only dishonor. And one day, it will be my pleasure to cleanse the Blood of your presence."

Some alien, unexpected feeling welled up within me, and I raised my eyes to meet his. A riot of new, intense emotions rolled around inside my chest as I held his gaze just a little bit longer than a slug should look at his guru. I watched as something passed behind his eyes in that moment – something that could, of course, absolutely not be fear – before his face hardened. I returned my eyes to the ground then, and as the moment passed, I dropped to my knees, my head low.

"Of course, guru." My words came out passive and without emotion. I couldn't see with my head down, of course, but I swore I heard a very particular sound. Among the whispery quiet of the jungle, there came the sound of a blade sliding free from its sheath. I waited, not breathing. Perhaps I would meet Kathas sooner rather than later. But nothing happened. And there was no other sound save those of the humid air in the wilds around me. Finally, when it seemed to me that I'd waited long enough, I looked up and found myself alone. I stood, walked over to the cliff's edge, looked out over the canopy of life that covered the Assassin's Isle, and thought. I thought for a long time, so long that night was falling before I turned and headed back down the mountainside to the great temple of Markash. I thought about many things that day. Some things which I'd never conceived of in my short life in the Brotherhood of the Blood. Not that any of it came to very much that particular day. Most of it didn't come to much for quite a few years yet. But there were seeds planted that day while I looked at the jungle, and they did grow.

I don't make a habit of exaggeration. It almost never does any good for any of the parties involved. Either it turns into flattery – which is just manipulation, and if you're going to manipulate someone, you should just own it and lie outright – or it's bragging, which no one believes anyhow even if it's true. Worst, exaggeration always clouds the facts, and it is really critical to have those clear in your mind. So, when I describe the palace of Yorch as "enormous," I genuinely mean it. By any definition that matters, it's just a smaller, more enclosed city that is entirely inside of Yorch. A small city that was currently filled with mercenaries that would try to kill me on sight, actual Yorchian soldiers who would try to kill me on sight, and a group of sacred assassins that, yeah, would try to kill me on sight.

And also, it was this last group that I was actively trying to find. Sneaking away from my capable, intelligent, hyper-aware, and not entirely normal best friends had been the easy part.

As far as my assets went, I had a pretty good idea of where they would want to be. And also, I had been one of them for most of my life. So, keeping to the shadows, I headed toward what I thought would be the most likely base they would use inside the palace. Its heart. And by that, I mean the kitchens.

I was out and away from the dungeons with no fuss at all. The minute my friends started talking about the fact that Julea wouldn't be taken directly to the throne room, that there would be a period of preparation time, I knew Kelly was going to come up with some way to get to her. From there, it was a short step for me to see that we were firmly in the arena of what he'd dismissed the previous night as my plan of "last resort." And yes, I didn't feel like discussing it in committee, so I just slipped off while Kelly painstakingly explained it to the rest of the crew. I first aimed to get some distance between myself and the others to guard against any misguided efforts to stop me. After that, I did my best to navigate toward the center of the palace. All that had required was to continue down the entrance tunnel we had used until a crossing passage took me in the right direction. Or at least what I thought was the right direction.

Eventually, I made my way into a well-worn but vacant hallway, well-lit by the gas lanterns that we had seen used everywhere. The floor showed evidence of a lot of use, despite it currently being unoccupied as far as I could see. It's not smart to trust things like that, especially when a crowd of assassins is lurking about the place. They tend to be sneaky bastards. I kept to the shadows, moving from dark patch to dark patch, and watched both ahead of me and behind me at the same time. In the course of this, I stepped behind a support pillar and peered down the hall. Several dozen feet farther along, a shadow moved in a way that was, well, wrong. All of the shadows in the tunnels moved slightly, of course. Gentle wafts of air blowing on the little gas flames caused a constant, if only slight, flickering. Drafts like that, though, do not cause a shadow to move steadily over several feet. I froze, held my breath, and watched from behind the column. I could see that actually, two shadows were moving together, and rather obviously now that I'd noticed them. They drew closer, and it became easier to make out details. There were two figures, both cloaked in black, though as I watched, a slight hint of red would occasionally show as they moved. My opportunity was presenting itself much sooner than I'd expected. I gently placed my hands on the hilts of my daggers, waited until only a couple of feet separated us, then stepped into the light.

“Apostate!” hissed the figure to my right as recognition overreached surprise. My sudden appearance had taken them off-guard, but they recovered quickly. We all now stood in the better-lit center of the passage, giving us a good view of one another. The one who had spoken was already flipping his cloak back to reach for his weapons before the other held up a hand to stop him. Of course, seeing that let me know which of them was in charge. The first figure stopped, his hands still crossed in his sleeves near his blades, but he held back as his leader spoke.

“You dare?” his deep, rich voice echoed in the silent hall.

“I dare,” I said, my hands still on my dagger’s hilts. “I call for *Na’Sa’Grosh*.” (It’s worth mentioning here that I’m translating the speech from the *tegha rekh*, the language of the Kathasiri. It means ‘dark words,’ and it’s only taught to the members of the Blood, so some translation is necessary. But some things – like *Na’Sa’Grosh* – don’t translate well, so I’m not going to bother. If I had to try, it might come out something like ‘the right of the blood for the blood’ or something equally awkward.)

“You are the Apostate!” the second said, his voice a louder rasp now. “You have no right to call for the ritual,” he spat.

I took a breath. This was the challenge that would be my first hurdle. If I couldn't get past it, then the best hope I would have would be to make a run for it.

Exile from the cult of Kathas – the Brotherhood of the Blood – was a very ritualized affair. Anyone who violated the holy writ of the Blooded – or someone that just wanted to leave – had to appear before a High Priest. Each 'hive' of assassins, which included every one of the Brethren assigned to a specific contract, bowed before their appointed High Priest. The one in that position served as field captain, contract administrator, and all-around boss. If he or she – the Kathasiri were evenly split between men and women – ruled that the situation required it, a potential exile would return to the temple of Markash for a trial by mortal combat. Except for some old stories that no one could really verify, in every case, the *Na'Sa'Grosh* ended with the defector being offered to Kathas – and by that, I mean they bled to death on the temple floor.

My solution was just to disappear, and that's just what I did. No fuss, no mess. As long as I stayed away from the Blooded, I had been free to live my life. Going back to them, however, meant the trial.

"That is a decision for the High Priest," I said. I bit the words off just enough to sound dismissive of him. "Has the Law of the Blood been set aside for the rule of a slug?" I put my gaze back to the leader, who still stood with his hand raised. He considered me with his eyes narrowed over the black of his scarf. I was pushing for the rule of law and trying to sound like the ultimate rule, despite being the one that had wholly dodged it for years. The fact that doing that was irritating the junior assassin was just a bonus.

"You have not faced the trial?" he said after a moment.

"I have not. I stand outside, but without the sanctity of the ritual," I said. Which was a fact, and as I said, that's always a good thing to have on your side. I had left without going through the process that would have severed me from the Blood. And which would have probably killed me, which sounded back then like a solid reason to skip the whole fiasco. "I am a full brother by Right of the Passage. I am owed the trial, and until there is judgment, I am Blooded."

My plan up to then had been to make the argument directly to the High Priest here in Yorch. He'd be the one in charge of this massive hive now working for Steinhargh, so he'd have the authority to deal with me. But I had to get there, and these two were my best chance. Plus, this was as good a place as any to test the argument.

And then, in a move that was not unexpected, the junior assassin charged at me. He brushed past the still upraised hand of his senior with only the slight ring of his blades sliding free to announce it. I'd been watching him sidelong, mostly because he seemed jumpy, so I wasn't entirely off my guard, thankfully. I stepped forward, shortening the distance between us and changing the range at which he'd been aiming. The arc of his swing brought the longer of his two blades down behind me, through space I no longer occupied. I caught his right elbow on my left shoulder and pivoted, putting his body between me and his opposite arm, which was coming across in a follow-up strike. I caught his wrist, wrenched it at an angle, and spun him aside with his own momentum. He tumbled into the nearby stone column with a thump and the sound of something tearing. I glanced back at his companion and saw he had remained motionless, silently watching us. My daggers were now in my hands as I squared off with the attacker. He was still facing the wall, and only as he slowly turned around did I see that his shorter knife was no longer in his hand but was protruding at a downward angle from his chest. He looked down at the wound and then up at me as his eyes went sightless, and he fell to the ground.

I have killed before. A lot, actually. The fact is, I couldn't even begin to guess how many times I've taken a life; I was a Kathasiri assassin, after all. But the fact was that I hadn't taken a life since I'd left the Brethren. In particular, I hadn't killed since I'd been with Dana and Kelly; I'd actively avoided it. And sure, someone could argue that I hadn't killed anyone in that hallway – that it had been an accident. But at that moment? Those things didn't matter. I felt nausea well up in my stomach, and if I had eaten breakfast, I'd surely have returned it. I watched the cooling corpse of what had just been a living person slide to the ground like a bag of wet garbage, and it was as if I was in an awful dream that had just taken a turn for the worse.

You don't have time for this, my voice said in my head. *Kelly and Dana need you.*

I turned back to the remaining assassin, who was now looking directly at me. Whatever deliberation he'd previously been engaged in appeared to be over. If he was paying any attention at all to the lifeless body lying on the floor, it was impossible to tell.

"You will see the High Priest. Sacred blood now spilled has paid for the right, no matter what your past. Follow," he said and turned back down the hallway without another word or glance toward me.

I sheathed my daggers and fell in step behind him, struggling to get my mind back on what I was doing and not on the dead man we left in a heap behind us.

It took no time at all to reach the hive. I had been right in thinking that the assassins would want to be by the kitchens, but as we got closer and I looked over the numerous tables and cabinets that now occupied the hallways, I realized where it was we were going. It would be a location near the kitchen that would feel most 'homey' to the

Blooded. We went to the butchery.

The assassin leading me stopped at a set of double doors and held a hand up. He had been silent as we walked, which made sense. Likely, he was still of two minds about whether I was indeed still 'Of the Blood' or if I was 'The Apostate,' and he wasn't going to risk his own holy status with the Bloody Mother unnecessarily. He turned to the doors and pulled, the metal-bound wood swinging outward effortlessly. He strode through the opening while I stood in the shadow of the door, watching and awaiting the summons.

The room inside was huge and made of well-cut stone, gray and stark, and lit with the standard gas-fed lanterns that seemed to be everywhere. It seemed strange that the place was no brighter than the halls had been, though the reason was quickly apparent. Something like half of the lanterns remained unlit, shrouding the corners of the area in darkness while allowing the room's center to be somewhat better illuminated. The shadows, I surmised, contained the bedding for the upper tier of the assassins – the High Priest and his inner circle. The remainder of the Kathasiri would be secreted throughout the palace, infesting the place like vermin. A raised platform took up a section of the floor off to the right. It was partially in the lighted area and partially hidden in shadow such that an even semicircle was visible. Three chairs sat evenly spaced in this illuminated area, ready for the High Priest and his seconds when needed.

All of that was noteworthy, but I nearly missed all of it because when the doors swung open, the smell that hit me was practically a physical blow. A combination of old blood and offal and rot all swirled up my nostrils as I took an innocent breath as if they were competing to see what could make me vomit faster. I held it together, despite the horrible reek. Horrible, but familiar. Memories of the temple of Markash rose in my mind; the red flames lighting black stone, the hot, humid jungle air, and the smell not unlike this one. The smell of death. The scent of my childhood.

Some people get cakes when they're children.

Abruptly, there was a flurry of motion in the room. Numerous black-garbed figures melted out of the shadows and clustered around the one that had been my guide. In spite of that, the room remained eerily quiet. The whole lot of them 'spoke' with the silent hand signals that formed a second language to the Blooded. I couldn't see well enough to translate, but it was clear that my arrival had inspired a lot of discussion. Then, just as quickly as it had started, the 'conversation' ended, and the majority of the assassins vanished back into the shadows. Three forms now occupied the chairs on the platform, though. As soon as the other shadows fell still, the central figure stood up. The High Priest took a single step forward, folded his arms, and placed his hands together close to the lower part of his chest with the tips of his fingers and his thumbs touching and forming a triangle. My guide, now standing alone in the middle of the room, turned toward the door and gestured to me. I walked in, the stench clawing at both my nose and my memory with every step. Behind me, as I reached the center of the room, I heard the door latch closed. I turned to the High Priest.

"The Apostate," said my guide with a flourish. Then he stepped back and away from me and disappeared into the shadows with the others.

I spoke up first, "That has not yet been wholly established. Begging your pardon." I placed my hands in front of my chest in a mirror of his.

"Denis." The voice that came from the High Priest was deep and sounded like the grinding of stone. It also tugged at one as yet unpulled memory from the back of my mind.

"Tybor?" I asked, reigning in – mostly successfully – my surprise. An audible hiss escaped the priest to his right as I spoke the name, but the High Priest only reached up and pulled back the black cowl from over his face and mouth. He said nothing as he revealed to the room his unveiled face—the face of my old tutor.

"Of course," he said, the same cold grin on his mouth that I remembered from childhood, "Kathas is wise, and she repays blood with blood. How obvious that she would have me be the one to pass judgment on you." He sneered through the last bit, though it couldn't hide the deep satisfaction in the tone. He looked much the same as he had all the years before, snake-eyed and viscerally alert. His sharp features were still highlighted by the long, jet-black hair he kept draped over his left eye in contrast to the shaved right side. His gaze seemed to pull in the lantern light and reflect it with a scarlet tint, and his teeth may as well have been fangs as he smiled mirthlessly.

"That," I said as calmly as if I were discussing the weather, "is not your place, High Priest." I kept my eyes locked on his – looking away would mark me as prey – but I stayed calm and kept my tone deferential. Here was where my actual walk into the lion's mouth began, and one misstep would end with me adding to the smell of blood in this room, and not in a good way. "I am a Son of the Blood," I continued, picking every word carefully, "I am owed the rites before I am truly outcast."

"You abdicated that right when you ran!" Tybor said, quiet but ferocious. "You abdicated that right when you betrayed Kathas!"

The figures on the platform moved their hands. Whatever else I'd accomplished, I'd gotten the priests' attention well enough that they were talking. Tybor lifted his hand to still them, and a moment later, his hands were again in front of his chest, and the other two were silent – in both senses. I kept my eyes on Tybor.

"That is certainly one way of looking at it," I said,

"though there are others. However, it could be said that my presence here – voluntarily before you, of all people – would argue that it is one of those other interpretations that is more like the truth."

"You did not know that I was assigned priesthood of this hive," Tybor said.

"You don't know that," I bluffed.

"Oh, but I do," he almost hissed, "You gave yourself away when you said my name."

"Apparently, we will need to agree to disagree," I said, bowing my head without moving my eyes from him. Momentum was my friend at this point, so I continued, "Obviously, Kathas' infinite wisdom is clear for us. It is the very purpose of *Na'Sa'Grosh* – to clarify that which is unclear among the Blooded. Isn't that the case, High Priest?"

The priest to Tybor's right stood up. It was enough of a surprise that I looked over at him. A moment later, the other stood as well. Tybor turned and looked from one to the other. Silent hand signals began to pass back and forth between them. Behind me, though I hadn't turned to look, I could feel the presence of the others. Some of the Brethren had stepped out of the shadows and were close enough to me now that they could reach me if I moved. It was a sensible move, really. They were making sure I didn't do anything dishonorable while the deliberations were going on. Very concerned about honor, these child thieves and murderers.

The discussion on the platform went on for what felt like a century. Of course, one area where time can trick you is when you're in danger of being bled like cattle. In actual time, as would be easy to see later, it was only minutes. Finally, Tybor stepped back from the other two and turned around toward me.

"You have not had the trial," Tybor said. His voice, while still a deep growl, was strained.

I shook my head.

"You are then consigned for such at the great temple of Markash, where you will face the *Na'Sa'Grosh*. But, until this takes place, you are bound here to us," he paused, obviously forcing the words out, "your brothers in the Blood."

The figures on the stage – including a reluctant Tybor – clapped their hands once. In answer, the shadows around the room answered back with a perfectly synchronized single clap from each assassin in the darkness. And just like that, at least until they killed me in the temple, I was again Blooded.

All of which was the easy part of my plan, to be honest. This next part would be where things got dodgy.

From the shadows to my left, one of the Blooded stepped into the light. He was carrying a folded pile of black cloth and leather that was wrapped in a red sash. On top of the bundle was the *novacul sanguis* blade and its companion dagger, both black and red and deadly. He – or, in fairness, she; it really was impossible to tell – stopped next to me and held the bundle out.

"High Priest," I said without reaching for the uniform, "I call to speak."

Tybor turned to look at me as a cloud of angry confusion etched into his features. By law, any of the brethren could speak directly to the hive master – the High Priest – with those words. They were, of course, usually reserved for only the direst of situations. Say, for example, some low-ranking, newly Blooded slug had come across a bit of secret information that was vital for the hive to know. Such surprises had endangered contracts in the past. With the right of speech, they could immediately have a hearing at the highest level. It was a system meant to sidestep the loss of time that bureaucracy introduced. And, yes, if the council decided that the information was irrelevant or that the right of speech was used too casually, it would be the last thing that slug ever spoke, except maybe to Kathas herself. As such, it was not the sort of thing a freshly reinstated brother who was still on thin, thin ice would invoke just moments after his reinstatement.

"Speak your truth," he said. The words sounded slightly choked, but he got them out. Based on my history with him, the fact that he'd gone this long without screaming or kicking an innocent puppy was a superhuman feat. I toyed with the idea that maybe he'd grown in the last few years.

Well, I toyed with that idea until I looked into his eyes and saw the barely restrained contempt. *Nope*, I thought, *same nasty bastard.*

"Some ways above where we are now, the contractor of this hive plots to steal the throne of this land," I started. Truthfully, I hadn't exactly planned how to get from that statement to where I wanted to go, but I wasn't exactly in a position to sit and hatch a strategy.

"This is known," grumbled Tybor, "it does not concern us." I swear I heard relief in the growl of his voice as if he had been expecting that what I would say would be some kind of sneak attack. He just needed a little more patience.

"He seeks to kill those who currently sit on the throne. But those deaths will not be part of the sacrament – that blood will not be given to us, and therefore not to Kathas. Thus, our agreement is wanting."

Tybor sneered, "Willm Steinhargh has led us to bounteous sacraments. And in addition, he has paid us well in coin. The contract is balanced."

And in a flash, I saw my way forward. But, it was going to be costly. So, I took a breath, steadied myself, and spoke.

"You are mistaken, High Priest. Coin may line someone's pockets, but our holy contract remains flawed. For this, I came here. Not only has he denied us the blood that is our gift to the goddess, many of the lives he's taken –

ones that should have been given to Her – he's taken with his uncanny machines. It is a sacrilege and a stain on our honor before the Bloody Mother. This crime is so glaring that even I – the one hastily and unjustly called 'Apostate' – have returned to correct it. Perhaps your vision is clouded by some personal arrangement? I can't say. But, if you, of all people, do not see the sin here, then you are not fit to govern. Kathas calls for a new High Priest." I felt my weight shift reflexively, and my knees unlocked, even as I remained outwardly still with my eyes never leaving Tybor. Time slowed as I felt the tension rise, and the room's silence fell like a blanket as my words echoed off the walls. Hisses began to radiate from the shadows around me as the Blooded reacted to my testimony. It seems that challenging the High Priest of a giant hive just minutes after walking in the door – letting alone my pending trial – was not something for which silent gestures were good enough.

Tybor stepped forward, the restraints on his rage beginning to fray. "You dare!" he barked, his voice a thunderclap among the whispers in the room.

"I do," I said. And before I finished the second word, my blades were in the air.

Kelly and I had a discussion one time about just how short combat really is. Or more to the point, the way people that have never been in a fight seemed so often confused by it. They hear stories of heroes clashing with villains and the flashing of steel back and forth and think that is the way of things. He said that fights between true warriors, the ones that have had training and have seen real battle, are over much quicker than the stories would have you believe. People are much more fragile, and weapons properly used are much deadlier than the stories would tell. It's how the tales keep the audience interested. In general, though, he said, a real fight is often over in a few strokes. I believe him; the truth is that every time I'd ever seen him or Dana fighting – and the fact is that they're the exact kind of warrior he was talking about – it was over pretty quickly. As for me, it's a bit different. I hadn't trained as a warrior or a soldier. I was raised as one of the Blood. Our gurus taught us to be assassins. We didn't study to fight, just to kill.

Tybor was never going to consider my challenge as a real one, and I knew that. Comes to it, I had no idea what the contract said; I was bluffing from memory and reputation. And I wasn't trying to goad him into a grand duel; we Kathasiri don't do grand duels. My only goal was to put doubt into the thoughts of every other person in the room. That accomplished, what came next was a foregone conclusion, and I followed through on it. My daggers flew true, hitting him exactly where his hidden armor was either weakest or missing before he even had a chance to hear my words. My off-hand blade sank into the joint of his right thigh and hip, while its companion sank deeply into the soft flesh of his throat. He fell, his eyes rolling back as he did. Before he'd hit the ground, I seized the two red and black knives from the bundle still being offered to me and hopped up on the platform, standing over Tybor's body and facing the center of the room. Several figures from the shadows had come out into the light, blades in their hands and closing toward me slowly. I crossed the sacred weapons and held them in front of my chest while I spoke into the silent hostility on display.

"I am Denis Goldarian of the Blood. I claim succession by right of inheritance and sacrament. Tybor al Crolish was my tutor, and I have given him to the Blood Mother."

For however long this lasted – see my earlier comments about time getting fuzzy at moments like this – I am reasonably sure that my heart was not beating. I am positive that I was not breathing. It's not unreasonable, as, between the ranks of black and red garbed assassins in the room and the two silent ones literally on the platform with me, there was a lot of ill will on display. I kept my awareness on the closest ones, but the lighted area in front of me was slowly becoming more and more crowded.

"I take the mantle that was his," I said, "for the sake of our honor before the Blood Mother. Is there a challenge to that act?"

It was getting hard to speak – I'm not kidding about the breathing thing – and no one else was making any noise, which made the whole scene surreal as silence descended. Then I heard a sound from my left, a kind of gentle, wooden thump. I risked a glance over my shoulder. The priest had dropped to his knees; his blades crossed over his chest identically to the way I held mine. I turned back to the room and saw the other assassins dropping into the same stance, one after the other. I looked finally to my right and saw that the other priest there had pulled off the face scarf that had hidden her, revealing a woman's face framed in short, red hair.

"We accept you, High Priest," she said with a nod. "By our laws, you have the right of succession from your guru. Until Kathas decides your fate in the *Na'Sa'Grosh*, it is you we will follow."

And that's the story of how I adopted my very own little hive of sacred murderers.

My heart started beating at some point, and it seemed to want to make up for the lost time, so it went completely wild when it did. My breath caught up with me, too, filling my lungs with glorious, if disgusting scented, air. That was good, as it brought me immediately back to the moment and why I was there at all. I dropped the black and red blades in favor of pulling my own out of the corpse of my childhood tormentor, still lying at my feet. Then I stood straight and looked at the room.

"I spoke truth to Tybor. The maniac who contracted us does not show Kathas due honor. He uses the Blooded as though we were no more than the hired sell-swords that flank him. Consider the destruction in Euticha months ago! Did the death and destruction there honor the Blood Mother? How many of our brethren have given themselves to Kathas because of him, yet how much has he returned?" I was, of course, making a lot of this up as I went. I had no idea how many, if any, Kathasiri died in the blast in Euticha. It was a fair bet, though. And one thing I banked on was that to the brethren, mass death and destruction was a loss of life that did not honor their goddess, and that was something with which I could work.

The assembled assassins stood silently, listening to me, and that was all I needed. As long as no one called my bluff, I could build up a case for their loyalty. That would only require using Kathas's name a few times and promising them blood to give her. Once I shored up my newly minted authority, they would follow my commands off of a cliff.

"Gather the Brethren across the palace," I said, taking the one last leap of 'faith' I needed to take, "we go to the throne room to break the oathbreaker."

As one, the shadows in the room bowed their heads, stood, and swept out through the doors that suddenly seemed to open of their own accord. I looked down at Tybor's still form, where its blood pooled under it. The blood sacrament that was the center of Kathasiri worship dripped off the platform's edge and onto the stone floor, where it dribbled into the drain. I'd killed again. Twice in the span of a few minutes. This time felt different, though. Tybor died as he'd lived – brutally and selfishly. The odd thought struck me that he would have thought of this as a good death. He would think that because he was cruel, heartless, and selfish. Because he was a Kathasiri. And because he was an idiot.

I looked up and found myself alone. The entire hive had slipped away with no more than the sound of a butterfly's wing. And, I now realized, I had no one to follow to the throne room, wherever that was.

"Hell's bells," I muttered. I swept up the bundle of robes and ran to find my pet assassins.

CHAPTER TWELVE

— JULEA —

I have lived my life in and around the Grand Throne of Yorch since I was a child. As a little girl, I'd hidden and played among the small trees and greenery that lined the vast marble floor. I'd run wild and free on those same floors other times when the room was not occupied. There had been, truth be told, more than one occasion when I was ushered out unceremoniously by one of the palace staff or, one particularly auspicious time, by the captain of the Wolfpack himself. I'd seen the closest heart to mine exiled as I stood by in this room. I had been made an ambassador in an assignment that, in the end, brought him back to me here as well. Yet, nothing in all of that history prepared me for this day, the day I was ushered onto the dais before the Golden Throne to face Willm Steinhargh.

"You are a remarkably resilient woman, Princess Julea," he said, looking down from the higher platform where he stood, lit from behind by the not yet risen sun. Immediately behind him, I noted, stood my mother, her face placid and unreadable. His voice was as deep as it had ever been, though it seemed harsher – if that were possible – as if it were coming from a throat that was torn and ragged.

"Not exceptionally," I said, my tone flat, "but challenging me does require a little more imagination than what I've seen on display these last few months." I folded my hands in front of me, and despite the grip on my shoulders of two mercenaries – for despite their Imperial armor, it was clear that's what they were – I stood straight and looked at him directly.

"Charming," Steinhargh snarled. He came down several of the higher steps toward me, stopping at half the distance before he continued, "But that was never an issue. What *is* an issue is what I am to do with you now?"

I arched an eyebrow, aware rather abruptly of two things. First, the eyebrow movement was something that I'd watched my mother do countless times, and second, my mother was not arching her eyebrow. Nor was she speaking. She stood quietly on the upper platform where she'd been when I entered and remained still and motionless. A vague disquiet filled my mind with a persistent question; *what is going on here?*

Steinhargh continued, oblivious to the motions of anyone's eyebrows. "You see, I've built a substantially unassailable position here based on your death at the hands of those rogues in the harbor."

"Those rogues, as you call—," I started, but the

blaggard raised his hand – his flesh hand – and the men holding me tightened their grips. That message received, I quieted again.

“The people were simply crushed, you know,” he said, a sort of sickly false emotion permeating each word as he paced a little to one side. He stopped suddenly and looked at me. “Oh, but I suppose you do! You were tramping about with the low-born and your filthy Talhas brute all this time. Yes, I’m sure the populace would just love to hear that.”

“Do you seriously believe that the people would support you over me because of your slander?” I cocked my head the way you do when you’re talking to a child or someone with a mental dysfunction, “The people will eat you and your hirelings alive with a snap of our fingers.”

“*Our*?” Steinhargh started, then looked at me with mock confusion. He turned his head, casting a flicker of a glance at the empress, then back to me with feigned realization. “Ah. You’re thinking of your mother. Perfectly understandable. Wrong, but understandable.” He turned toward her more fully at that, nodding his head respectfully. “Your Imperial Majesty, it appears that your daughter does not fully comprehend the situation. I would be happy to continue, but perhaps you would like to help the poor deluded girl.”

And then Empress Ardallah Niconnal bar Morrisia, Gloriana, Sola, Lunis, and Stelis reached through me and pulled out my heart.

"King Willm is quite correct, Julea," she said, "You are, in the eyes of the population, either dead or a liar. But, as you are obviously standing here, the former is not true, so it will of needs be the latter. And neither the throne nor the people would support a liar in the royal house."

"Mother!" I felt my stomach convulse as if it had received a physical blow as the word erupted from my mouth, followed by the only other sound I could make. "Why?"

"As with all things, daughter," she said, tilting her head gently to one side as she looked at me, "for the good of the Empire. Willm brings us riches that we cannot simply ignore." Her eyes moved deliberately to Steinhargh, who brushed his half-cloak aside to reveal his mechanical arm, glowing eerily from within with a sickly yellow light.

"The gems?" I said, dropping any pretense of calm; my voice came out in unfiltered anger, "This is all about access to the power of the gems?"

Ardallah stepped forward to the edge of the upper dais. "But of course it is, child," she said, looking more directly down on me, "Everything is. The Assemblage is imminent. Gladia has of late experienced an assassination in one of their noble houses. Yorch must be able to show our strength in the face of the unsettled times around us. Our union with King Willm assures that."

I looked back at Steinhargh. He stood with his natural arm folded across his chest and resting on the top of the mechanical. I glared at him and the horrid metal thing and wished that my stare could somehow stab him through his repulsive smile. And then I saw it. There, hanging from his belt, was the hilt of Kelly's black sword. I felt suddenly limp as if all six months of working in the shadows – hiding, plotting, finding allies, all of it – had come back to exact their toll on me in a single moment. The image of Dana and Kelly, lying on their deathbeds half a year ago, seemingly with one last hope. The feeling of guilt that I had abandoned them to come here instead. The fight to survive when the *Midnight Wind* was attacked. All of it. Everything I had drained out of me, and I nearly collapsed. If it hadn't been for the tiny stubborn streak in me, one that wouldn't give this vile creature the satisfaction of it, I might have. But instead, I felt myself break inside, and my head dropped.

"Oh, good. You've realized the true nature of things," Willm said. My eyes had closed, but I heard the distinct sounds of his footsteps going back up onto the higher platform. There was a nudge from my guards, and I opened my eyes in time to see that he was beckoning us forward, and I walked carefully up the steps, the mercenaries' hands firmly on my shoulders. Shortly, we reached the top, where Steinhargh and Ardallah stood just a couple feet from me.

Steinhargh sighed, then spoke as if he were

deliberating over a court decision, "My options – and really the only options for the good of the Empire – are as follows. Option one is that I simply have you quietly stowed away in the deepest part of the dungeons, where you will live a quiet and exceptionally brutal life. Of course, I would have to scar you up somewhat so that you would never be recognized, but such is the cost of kindness, and I am most willing to pay."

"Kindness?" I said with a rueful choke.

"Oh yes, kindness," he said. He paced a bit, and I had a fleeting memory of him the first time we'd met years before, in a confrontation not wholly unlike this one. Steinhargh continued, "Simply killing you would be far simpler; 'kindness' is all that prompts me to make room for two other options. That was the first; would you be interested in the second?"

I looked at Ardallah, and she returned the look steadily. And this was her ultimate truth—the Empire came before all, even me. The education I'd had, the 'rules' I'd been taught to follow all led unrelentingly to this. My stomach roiled at it. I had to confront the truth—that a monster had raised me—and it sickened me. I looked at Steinhargh, the sickness giving me a kind of newfound strength.

"And that is?"

"You will be my wife," he said as if he were describing lukewarm water, "and together, we three will rule Yorch and defend it with all the power available to us." The mechanical fingers of his right 'hand' flexed as he spoke.

My disgust must have flashed across my face because he furrowed his brow for a moment. But just as I thought he might erupt in anger, he instead coughed out a humorless laugh.

"I realize this binding would simply be for show, girl. You despise me, and I find you willful and common, particularly for such a pedigreed woman. But you are not without your," he looked me up and down dramatically, "charms, as I've noted in the past, and while this business would be unnecessary, our union would serve to cement me even more solidly here. It would also allow you to return to public life with the sanction of both Her Imperial Majesty and me, the Savior of the Empire."

I felt myself freeze in place, the enormity of his affront chilling me to the core. Outwardly though, I gave one brief glance toward Ardallah and assessed her cold acceptance of his statement before returning my glare to him. He was smiling, the smile of a predator with its prey cornered and helpless.

"Now, now, princess," he said through a cloud of condescension, "you don't need to delay. I've seen to all the necessary details. The Archbishop of the One is on his way, and I've even provided ample witnesses." He gestured toward the room behind me, inviting me to turn. I looked, and my breath caught. Sometime during our discussion, a crowd had come into the chamber without my notice. Now, from the edge of the throne platform back to the distant entrance, the entire room was crowded with men in Yorchian uniforms. Many were easily identifiable as mercenaries like the ones that were flanking me. But others, I could see now, weren't. There were many native Yorchian soldiers in the crowd, throwing their lot in with what they no doubt saw as the new order. Scattered randomly among these were figures in black and red – the bloodthirsty Kathasiri. But the most stunning betrayal was also the one nearest the throne, where the six members of the Wolfpack stood attentively. Treachery, it seemed, was now everywhere, and why not? The empress had effectively approved it all. Every eye in the crowd watched us on the dais.

"You do see now, don't you?" Steinhargh's voice said from somewhere both close by and yet somehow distant, "This game is over. You have but one real option left to you."

Once more, I looked over at the empress. Her hands were folded in front of her the same way I so often folded my own. Her features were soft, almost peaceful, and in that expression, the truth of it all was driven home again. The Empire was her daystar – her one and only priority. It always had been. My very existence was only to ensure the future of the power of Yorch. My birth – my life – was meant to fulfill a role in the great, overarching Imperial story.

"To hell with you," I said, my face like granite as I glared at the woman I'd called mother. My voice came out calmly but with the power of a thunderclap. It was as if my shattered heart had whirled itself into a private Triangle Blow of hatred and disgust that now flowed out of me. "To hell with you both," I continued, turning the storm of hatred onto Steinhargh.

The so-called Savior of the Empire jerked back just a little. Or maybe I just saw it that way because I wanted so badly for it to be true. A heartbeat passed, and then he sighed, his control – spurred on by his utter certainty of triumph – settling back over him.

"A pity," he said, "such a waste."

There was a solid 'thump' sound, and I felt myself flinch, instinct telling me that it was some new, unseen assault. But Steinhargh jumped as well and whirled to face the throne seat – the source of the sound. By now, the sun had fully ascended over the horizon, and it bathed the room in early morning light so intense that it was necessary to squint. But even through that, what we saw made my jaw drop. A figure in black sat perched on the arm of the throne itself, one leg draped onto the floor and his other foot firmly on the seat. Next to him, a tall woman stood with the blade of a silver rapier gently resting on her shoulder, while on the opposite side of the throne, a leather-clad man leaned casually on a partly gilded quarterstaff. I blinked, my mind struggling to resolve the impossible sight in front of me with what I had believed until that moment was the truth.

The figure in black clapped his hands, the clapping of the leather a dull sound that echoed around the vast chamber. “Wow,” said the familiar voice, “I have to say, Steelclaw, you bring the phrase *delusions of grandeur* to a whole new level. What’s next? Are you planning on making yourself the High Holy Father of the church?”

At the sound of the voice, the clouds of morning lifted from my mind. “Kelly!” I shouted, the word bursting from me with a mixture of horror and hope.

“Your Highness, you keep terrible company,” he said. He hadn’t moved – his eyes remained locked on Steinhargh – but a tiny grin curled the corner of his mouth. The side of his face that had been bandaged when I saw him last was whole but changed. His flesh now faded to a blackness that was as dark as his armor. Dana, too, standing there beside him, seemed different, but the exact details were lost to me in a mixture of sunlight and emotion.

“You? You’re alive?” Steinhargh spat. He raised his mechanical arm, pointing it at the throne, and I felt the blood freeze in my veins. Out of the corner of my eye, I saw Ardallah flinch, and it occurred to me that she had a stronger reaction to the idea of the throne being damaged than she had to the threat of her daughter being executed just moments before.

Kelly raised his hand very quickly and waved a finger. "Ah-ah. You might want to think twice about that," he said and raised his other hand above his head. He held a stone, about the size of a man's fist, high enough for everyone in the chamber to see. It was colorless and as transparent as a finely wrought window. Where it caught the sunlight behind him, the light twinkled through it, scattering beams of every color in random directions. One bright blue beam reflected down on his face, illuminating a full-blown smile.

The sound of motion came from behind me, and with a glance, I saw that the Wolfpack had moved. They and several of the closest soldiers had started part-way up the steps of the throne platform.

"You might want to think twice about what they do, too," Kelly said quickly, gesturing toward the men behind us, "you don't realize what this is, but let's just say I've decided that 'scorching the land' is now on the table."

Steinhargh raised his hand, and the soldiers stopped where they were and waited. The usurper king glared at Kelly, who had by now stood and squared off with him directly.

"You dare toy with me?" he snarled.

Kelly shrugged. "I might have, once. Before. Things like swiping your stuff from your bed chamber all those years ago and running off with your pet pirate were all tremendous fun. But then you dropped a building on my friend and me, and you're standing there threatening to kill the woman I love. So, yeah. I'm past playing games, which is why I brought this. Of course, you don't know what this is, do you?" He held out the strange stone, which had the interesting effect of making everyone else reflexively move back just a little.

Steinhargh was silent, but the muscle around his eye quivered slightly. Whether it was rage or uncertainty, I couldn't discern.

"Let me help you," Kelly said, matching Steinhargh's condescension from earlier note for note. "It's cute that you think you know gem lore. You wave them around like you've found just the best toys to play with. But let me give you a lesson from the adult class. This is morden stone. It reacts with man-made gemstones. Say, for example, that one there in your arm-thing? It could react in a very, very dramatic fashion. You remember those weapon riggings on your ships, right? The ones that you used to destroy the tower in Euticha? Those are a candle in the noon sun compared to what this can do. And all it needs is a little confab with your little stone there. Shall we test?"

I felt the air take on a strangeness, like the eeriness of the quiet before a thunderstorm, as the two men faced one another. Slowly and deliberately, Steinhargh drew the black blade from his hip, letting it settle down at his side. Aeryk – for now, I could see the third figure for who he was – swung his staff into a defensive stance, and Dana's rapier twitched from resting on her shoulder down and forward into a middle guard position. Kelly, however, stood stock still, a half-formed grin back on his face as he – with practiced casualness – flipped the stone onto the back of his hand and then back into his palm.

"You lie," Steinhargh growled, with much less certainty than he intended, "there is no such thing."

Kelly narrowed his eyes, the grin fading to a humorless solemnity. "And you're a fool. And we can test both at the same time. Feel like a gamble?" he said, somehow managing a quiet tone that still echoed off the walls of the giant room.

He had barely finished speaking when suddenly and with a deceptive economy of motion, the usurper king slipped to the right, dipped behind Ardallah, and placed the blade at her throat. The guards beside me clamped down on my shoulders, expecting me to react. I will report that I made no such motion. However, I can't say whether that is something I'm proud of or not.

Ardallah's eyes went wide, and she made to pull away, but Steinhargh had latched onto her upper arm with his mechanical claw in the same motion as he'd swung the sword around, and she had nowhere to go. The blade bit slightly into her throat as she tested the grip, releasing a trickle of Imperial blood that dripped slowly down onto her snow-white dress.

Kelly started, obviously taken off guard. He passed the crystal stone to his left hand and drew his longsword in a single motion, ending in a defensive stance.

"You are a pitiful fool, Blackcrow," Steinhargh said, his voice a growl from over the empress's shoulder. I looked quickly around, only to find the crowd of traitors, assassins, and mercenaries in the room transfixed by the confrontation in front of us all and unable or unwilling to interfere. I turned back as the usurper continued. "Oh yes, we've discussed you, peasant. Such a pathetic story, it is. The son of a minor house who worked so, so hard to be a good little soldier. Years of collecting scraps of praise from your goddess-like empress, only to be exiled for your trouble. And look at you now. Still unable to stomach a threat to her life. You are weak, and you are beaten. So put your toy away or watch your empress fall."

Despite myself, I felt my stomach clench at the words. I looked to Kelly, who remained frozen in place. But then, his eyes shot to me, only for a heartbeat, and there I saw his truth. Steinhargh wasn't wrong about his past. Whatever he'd learned from the empress about Kelly over the last few months was accurate. But the glance told me the most crucial part of that sentence. The word *was*. Perhaps Kelly had been that. Ardallah knew how to read people well, as it made manipulation so much easier. So, indeed, that may have been the truth once. But he wasn't that now. He'd become a different man than she remembered. And in her error, I felt hope flicker.

And as if on cue, a noise broke the tense silence as the immense throne room doors burst open. All eyes went to the chamber entrance, where a mass of Imperial guardsmen began to crowd through. Steinhargh's crowd fell back in confusion, and soon the end of the room was filled with a new group of armed men in Imperial livery. These, though, had wrapped white scarves around their necks, and they flooded in as one. At the front strode Captain Gobhneh Stormshank, captain of the watch. He was flanked by Rohb, Jaymes, Niamh, and Muiris.

"What in the nine pits of the damned is all this?" Stormshank bellowed, his Talhas accent booming off the walls of the room.

"Thank the One," I heard Aeryk mutter to himself. And then I saw it. Kelly had been stalling, trusting that his friends would come. Counting on them, the same way he'd told me to. And true to form, they'd come.

A roar of rage erupted from Steinhargh. He released Ardallah, shoved her to the ground, and looked rapidly around the room with an unfettered fury. He glared at Kelly, and his face split into the wild, bloodthirsty, bestial smile that signaled the loss of whatever reason he had. With one savage thrust, the beast spun and drove the black sword through the kneeling form of the empress of Yorch. Her body collapsed to the ground in a heap as he wrenched the blade free.

Time simply stopped. I looked at the crumpled body on the floor. I looked at the pristine white dress, now spread on the marble, as it was slowly subsumed by the crimson pool spreading from beneath her. Empress Ardallah Niconnal bar Morrisia was larger than life, larger than any single person could ever – should ever – be. Her strength granted her a majesty far beyond her title, and no one left her presence without feeling like they had been in the company of grand nobility. Her entire life – every single decision – had been in service of that calling. She lived like a descended goddess but faced death like the mortal she ultimately was. The mortal we all ultimately are. My mother died in silence, surrounded by people but totally alone.

Then there came the rush of noise as time moved forward again; a clattering of armor and weapons, the discordant shouts of men rushing in to meet one another in battle, my heartbeat suddenly loud and thrumming in my ears. I was vaguely aware that the first voice I'd heard had been that of Steinhargh, unleashing his minions on the defenders of the realm. My realm, I realized suddenly. My chaperones released my shoulders and rushed into the melee, their mercenary instincts so hungry for a fight that they quickly disregarded their assignment to watch me. I moved as fast as I could in my elegant but completely non-battle-ready dress to get away from the front of the dais. Slipping past the dead body of the empress, I wedged myself into an angular nook in the wall not far from the throne. The bright sunlight left this particular cavity in a heavy shadow, and I nestled down into a very unladylike crouch. Only then did I look up to see Steinhargh and Kelly facing off just a few feet away.

"How's that feel?" Kelly said, his anger choked through clenched teeth. His question confused me until I noticed Steinhargh was wobbling unsteadily, swaying as if he had suddenly become drunk. I watched, trying to make sense of it as the conflict rolled on around us.

The self-described 'savior of the Empire' made a noise that was meant to be threatening. What came out instead was a weak gurgle. He swayed again, waving the black blade in front of him weakly in an effort to keep Kelly at a distance.

"I bet not great," Kelly answered his own question, stepping forward in a feint that caused Steinhargh to weave to one side. "You really need to stop playing with things you don't understand."

"Shut up, filth," Steinhargh managed, some of his noxious hatred steeling him in his apparent weakness.

Kelly weaved and feinted forward again, causing another drunken stumble from his opponent. "That sword's not steel. I'm sure you know that. But you don't know what it is, and you don't know why it's not something to trifle with," he made another sidestep, swinging his sword and letting it ring harmlessly off the black blade as Steinhargh slapped at it away with herculean effort.

"It's drinking you dry, Steelclaw. That's what it does when it's used to take a life."

Steinhargh looked down at the sword in his hand, then back up, the animal hatred on his face now veiled in confusion.

"You killed with it. You woke it up. Now it's draining you," Kelly said through a vicious smile, "and it's very, very hungry when it wakes up."

The usurper of Yorch looked at the blade again and then threw it across the throne platform as if it had turned into a venomous snake. He looked up at Kelly, his face shifting almost instantly back to the wild hatred of moments before. He roared a shout of primal anger as he pointed his mechanical arm in the air and a belch of unearthly orange flame blasted from the end, lancing over Kelly and into the mammoth windows overlooking the bay. The massive panes of glass shattered, sending tiny shards into the swirl of air that now blew in from the bay. The flames' roar combined with the shattering of the glass and the whipping of the wind into a cacophony. For a brief moment, the sounds of the battle were washed away in the discord.

I shrank back and away from the shower of glass

fragments that drafted back into the room. Despite the danger of the falling shards, I looked out to see if Kelly was okay. He had thrown himself to the ground by to the throne and lay on his side as the falling glass slivers scattered around him. He saw me, then waved his hand in a 'get back' gesture. I shook my head and shrugged; there was no 'back' to 'get' to in the crevice I occupied.

"Blackcrow!" Steinhargh shouted. He stood still where he had been, surrounded by the glass and yet untouched by them, his uncanny flame blast having afforded some kind of unnatural protection. The morning wind now blew in through the open windows, filling the room with both the smell of the sea and the biting cold. He drew a short blade from some hidden sheath in his mechanical arm and turned toward Kelly.

"Nice tantrum," Kelly said as he rose from the floor by the throne, "what do you do when you can't get your porridge?"

Steinhargh snarled, "Lying bastard! Your 'morden stone' did nothing!"

Kelly held out the crystal still in his hand. "You mean this? Sure it did."

Steinhargh looked around, uncertain. The battle in the room continued, slowed only for those nearest the throne, but continuing unabated in the remainder of the room. On the lower platform by the throne, I could see our friends holding their ground, facing off against the traitorous Wolfpack. I turned back in time to watch as Kelly casually tossed the crystal stone out through the open windows into the bay.

"It kept you busy until my friends got here, you cowardly son of a whore," he said, a wolfish grin on his face.

They rushed at one another, Steinhargh blocking Kelly's sword with his mechanized arm while striking back with the short blade in his opposite hand. There was no skill, no trained system of swordsmanship, in Steinhargh's attacks. Instead, it was a primal rage and an animal hatred that drove him. Kelly may as well have been fighting an actual wild beast. But that same rage made him formidable, and the fight was frighteningly well matched.

"I would never have thought this would go the distance," said a quiet voice from right next to my left ear. I started and would likely have fallen out of my hiding place had a firm hand not grabbed me and pulled me back. I turned to see Denis's face greeting me with a devilish grin.

"Sorry about your mom," he continued, "but who'd have thought, eh?"

I didn't exactly know how to answer that, so I turned back to the clash before the throne. As I did, I leaned back into the rogue without thinking about it. Somehow his presence felt steadying – the physical proof that Kelly and Dana were there.

"I also think we're about done here," Denis said, and I noticed that the sounds from the rest of the room seemed to be quieting. I looked out, and indeed the battle seemed to be slowing. But there was something else as well. Or, more accurately, there was something more. The number of Kathasiri in the room had multiplied, and they, along with Gobhneh's men, had begun to overwhelm the mercenaries and traitors. The room was quieting as the combat ceased.

Kelly had noticed, too, as he dived around one of Steinhargh's slashes and came up facing the room, his back to the open window. He shifted his weight and held his sword in front of him in low guard. Steinhargh moved over by the throne, facing him and snarling.

"You've lost, O 'savior of the Empire,'" Kelly said with a note of finality. He jutted his chin to indicate the quieting of the combat in the hall. That motion somehow penetrated the fog of savagery, and Steinhargh turned and surveyed the chamber. Dana and Aeryk stood on the steps between the two levels of the throne dais, while Rohb, Jaymes, Muiris, and Niamh were spaced around them. Beyond, the victorious Imperial guard and the silent Kathasiri stood over Steinhargh's remaining supporters, all of whom were either beaten or surrendering. He turned back to Kelly, wild fear creeping in over his anger. He looked out at the bay.

"It's funny," Kelly said, glancing back over his shoulder to the sea where Steinhargh was looking, "but I just don't see any of your ships out there either. Hunh. You'd think the Imperial navy might have gotten some new orders or something." He turned back to Steinhargh, the wolfish grin again on his face.

There was a moment where no one moved. No one even seemed to breathe. Then a sound came from King Willm Steinhargh that was not human. It was beyond human —beyond animal. It was the sound of pure fury. No reason remained, and no beast could match the uncontrolled emotion. It was utter horror.

And then he lifted his mechanical arm and pointed it at Kelly.

CHAPTER THIRTEEN

— AERYK —

The emotion in the room changed like the snap of a carriage whip. For one brief moment, my friends and I were triumphant. As the others and I stepped up onto the throne platform to join Kelly, Julea, and Dana, it felt like we'd once again beaten the odds. That wasn't always the way of things, I knew. In my time at sea, I'd seen the fickleness of life. I'd come through mostly unscathed, but I knew better than most that no victory is to be trusted to until all the cards have been played. Maybe it was that lesson, nagging at the back of my thoughts even as we stood victorious, that freed me to act when the turn came. Steinhargh stood, defeated. His supporters had either been beaten or had switched their allegiance in the hope of mercy. If a bard were telling the story, this would have been where he'd have stopped. Perhaps with a flourish at the end about sunsets and celebrations. But this wasn't the tale of a bard.

In that moment of defeat, the usurper king raised his weapon at my friend, who had nowhere to run. The audacity of the act froze everyone in the room; the crowd of warriors and assassins around us was abruptly motionless and silent. For my part, I saw the mechanical contraption leveled at Kelly, and reflex took over. The staff in my hand whirled in my grip almost of its own accord, and I threw it with the power of muscles trained by the sea and pulled taught in panic. It left my hand as if driven by the very heart within me.

But not every heroic act begets a miracle. My balance was off, and as I threw, my foot shifted on the powdered glass shards that were what remained of the bay windows. Thus, my staff went wide. It was no more than a degree of arc, but that was enough. Instead of finding its target, it slammed into the corner of the high gold-sheathed back of the throne with a resounding metallic thud and spun harmlessly away. My heart pounded in resonance with the impact even as I felt it shrink inside of my chest, terrified and anxious.

But Steinhargh was seized by some self-defensive reflex. His body involuntarily jerked at the sound of the impact, and his head snapped to the noise. Hope burst in me for the tiniest fraction of an instant. Despite the failed throw, perhaps I'd provided enough of a distraction for Kelly to find some cover and cheat fate one more time. But that was not to be either. Some unholy focus, fueled by inhuman rage, snapped into place, and Steinhargh whirled back, realigning his vile weapon at Kelly again. I felt my breath catch.

But suddenly, a white blur burst from the shadows on the far side of the throne's upper platform. Princess Julea rushed out from the complete invisibility that her hiding place had supplied up to then, seized Steinhargh's metallic arm at its joint, and pulled at it with extraordinary strength – a strength driven more by her heart than by her muscles. The usurper of Yorch began a bellow of protest that was shortly lost in the blast of preternatural flame that gushed forth from the weapon into the air. The explosion went upwards toward the ceiling instead of at Kelly and slammed into the immense skylight above the chamber's center, where the light of the chill blue winter morning glowed. For the second time in a brief span, the sound of shattering glass split our ears as the force blew the giant skylight up and out into the morning sky. Then, seconds later, a rain of razor-sharp shards began in a grander, much more ruinous version of the display behind the throne moments ago. The crowd of assassins, mercenaries, and soldiers scrambled to find cover from the shower of deadly shards. Well, those who were able to, at any rate. Some were fallen from the battle, of course. There was little protection from the vicious deluge for even those who remained standing in the center of the audience chamber, where there was no shelter. The shards came heedless.

Thankfully, there was room for me to move. I threw myself forward onto the upper platform, curling into a roll as I did, hoping to shield as much of myself as possible with the leather of my armor. The throne platform's position at the far end of the room did put much of it out of the direct path of the falling skylight glass, but it was already heavily dusted with the shards from the earlier destruction of the windows. I landed on one side of the throne, mostly clear of the glass downpour behind me. Despite that, I still felt the sensation of multiple impacts on my back as if someone had thrown a handful of small stones at me, and I quietly praised the resilience of heavy leather. My right arm and leg, sadly, did not have the full benefit of that protection, and what felt like the stings of a wasp swarm on my limbs told me that I hadn't gotten away completely unscathed. I would find out later, when time allowed us to assess the damage, that the 'stings' I was personally getting were far from the worst of it. Back in the center of the chamber, larger pieces of glass rained down with edges sharper than any blade. These impaled many. In other cases, they slid past the arms, legs, heads, and torsos of those trapped below silently and painlessly. Painless in the moment, but all the more terrible for it, as the wounds left behind were deep and bled wildly. And, in many cases, fatally. At that moment, though, no future worry overrode my fear for my friends. Hastily, and probably much before it was genuinely prudent, I looked up.

Once, while sailing on the *Wind*, I met an old woman in a foreign bazaar. She had a small booth near the entrance of the transient pop-up market of curiosities and sundries that set up in a field near the dock. She greeted me with a crooked smile in a language that I neither understood nor even recognized and then handed me a sample of her art. It was a glass bottle – mostly round though slightly flat on the bottom – filled with water and sealed with a wax-covered cork at the top. Inside, on the flattened portion, was the small carved tableau of a wedding. One small figure of a man and one of a woman stood on a tiny model of a hill facing one another. A third figure, painted as a cleric from the Church, stood between them with his arms out. The wonder of it was that in the water were tiny flecks of something that reflected light randomly. The more the bottle was moved, the more the specks swirled and shimmered in the water. It was magical. I didn't keep it – I don't think she meant for me to – but I remember it as clearly as when I first saw it. And there on the dais of the throne of Yorch, I saw a dark reflection of that bottle. But this time, it wasn't magic that I saw; it was horror.

Time seemed once again to stop. Tiny fragments of shattered glass, no more than dust, floated in the air and glimmered in the morning sun as the flecks had in that bottle. Across the platform, Steinhargh and Julea stood frozen like figures on an illusory hill. But unlike the tiny figure in my memory, the princess had both of her hands above her head, holding fast to Steinhargh's vile mechanical arm, keeping it up in the air where she'd forced it to save Kelly. But instead of triumph, her face was frozen in a rictus of shock. I could see Steinhargh's left hand, clenched in a fist and pressed against her stomach just below her ribs. For an instant, I thought he'd punched her and thus her shocked look. But then, through the shimmering air, I saw blood. Her blood; oozing out from behind his fist. And then I saw that his fist held the hilt of a blade.

And then, time chose to move forward again. I scrambled to get to my feet, though my right arm and leg sent shocks of pain up my side where the glass had cut into me. I slid back down. I tried again, shoving myself up with my left hand instead as I looked wildly around for a weapon, any weapon. I heard a woman's voice – Dana, I realized – scream from somewhere in the distance, "No!" and I looked back over just in time to see a second blur launch itself from the hidden recess where Julea had been. This shape was black with flashes of red on it, and it moved with the speed of something that wasn't human. It slammed full force into Steinhargh's midsection, driving him backward and thus away from the princess. The usurper king doubled over with the impact as he stumbled away but began to recover almost immediately, his armor having taken most of the force of the blow. The moment the two were separated, Julea started to collapse, only to be caught, gently but deftly, by the black figure. It eased down to the ground with her, pulling back its black hood as it did to reveal Denis's face. The freshly installed leader of the Kathasiri leaned the new empress of Yorch against his leg and glared up at Steinhargh, murder in his eyes. But the villain had straightened by then and cast his feral eyes on the two of them, his fury renewed.

Move! I cursed silently at my right side. A wave of pain went through my leg and arm, but somehow in spite of it, I managed to get up on a knee.

Steinhargh howled in bloodthirsty rage as he brought his wicked mechanism to bear once again, pointing it now at Denis and Julea. She looked up at him and met his bestial visage with a glare of hatred and disgust on her face. I cursed through the pain again, but even as close as I was – the nearest of all of us at that moment – I knew I would never be able to reach him before he let loose the unnatural fire again. A savage, ghastly smile split Steinhargh's face as he readied himself. But he'd made the same mistake I had. I *wasn't* the nearest person to him on that platform; there was one other even closer than me. In his rage and in my loathing, we'd both forgotten about Kelly.

My friend appeared suddenly in my sight as if he had

simply apparated behind Steinhargh from nowhere. He drove his arm both under and around Steinhargh's weapon, a single motion that trapped it and held it from finding its target. Kelly threw his weight into a roll on his back leg, letting momentum pull both himself and his enemy into a backward tumble that left them in a heap several feet away. Glass from the pulverized windows crunched as both men stood again. But Kelly got his balance first and lunged forward, grabbing Steinhargh's natural arm by the wrist with his right hand while pressing his left into the metallic seams of the deadly weapon. They wrestled, edging closer to the window's ledge, each straining for the upper hand. And as they struggled back and forth, time dilated in the room, stretching everything.

Even then, despite the tension and emotion of the moment, something about the match didn't seem right. Whatever else was the case, Kelly was a warrior. I'd seen him dispatch trained soldiers twice his size with what appeared to be little or no effort, yet here he was, wrestling with a man whose only advantage had been his weapon. That background thought, however, was suddenly brushed aside as a high-pitched sound penetrated my awareness. I didn't know when it started, but it became impossible to ignore. And it seemed to come from the spectacle of the two men. More specifically, it seemed to be coming from Steinhargh's weapon.

"No!" he suddenly barked, his eyes locking on the arm with a genuine panic that was finally enough to push out the bestial rage.

"I *told* you," Kelly said, his voice full of fury and loud enough to be heard over the piercing whistle, "you shouldn't play with things you don't understand!" The shriek seemed to be everywhere by then, filling the room and sounding out of the windows over the bay. I winced as the sound had become physically painful, but I couldn't look away. Kelly's left hand was entirely inside the weapon now, and the yellow light inside had become as bright as the sun beyond.

"And now you'll pay for all of it!" Kelly said, and then the light became a terrible flash that washed all sight away. The light became a physical thing, no longer coming from the arm, but instead, it was everywhere. I looked down and closed my eyes tightly, afraid of being blinded, and that's when a force like a hurricane wind washed over me. Had I been standing, it would easily have knocked me back down. At the same instant, the sound stopped. In fact, all sounds ceased, and the world went silent. It was as if, in a blast of force and light, we'd all been struck deaf and blind. It was ethereal. It was terrifying. And then, the eerie wind stopped.

I opened my eyes again, much sooner than was wise. The residual light from whatever had happened seared at them anew, and my world resolved itself only into vague shadows. I looked toward where the windows should have been and briefly saw two blurry forms. Then, a moment later, they disappeared.

No! I heard my voice scream in my head even as my lungs and voice were swallowed by the silence. Somehow, I knew what was happening, and I had to do something. The pain in my limbs burned anew, but the fear of what I believed – what I knew – I had just seen pushed me forward. I scrambled blindly ahead, judging distance by memory and hope. When I chanced to open my eyes again, I found I had reached the edge of the open window above the bay. On one piece of the ruined window framing, a single hand clutched the edge, its fingers quivering as the broken frame bent more and more. I threw myself onto the ground and grabbed at the hand just as the piece of framework gave way. I slid forward so far that my head and chest slipped outside, leaving the top half of my body dangling somewhat precariously over the edge. There, hundreds of feet below, the bay water crashed onto the rocky shore. In my grip, though, I held Kelly's right arm as he dangled beneath me. The bent remnants of Steinhargh's weapon hung from his other hand at his side. His head drooped, and he stared down at the rocks and the sea below.

"Kel," I said. Sound, it seemed, had returned at some

point, though my voice sounded foreign to me. I could hear the sea below and the wind whipping around past me. It was reassuring, being able to both see and hear again. Though, it did not make the position we were in any less terrifying, unfortunately. Kelly didn't react, and I wasn't confident that I'd spoken loudly enough for him to hear.

"Kel," I repeated, louder. He looked up at me, and I felt my heart crack. Tears fell in long streaks down his cheeks as he blinked them away. His arm slipped in my grip, and it was then I realized that he wasn't even trying to hold on to me in return. I tightened my grip as best as I could, the effort of which renewed the stabbing pains up and down my right arm.

"It's over," I heard him say, almost too weakly to be heard over the wind and waves. I realized he wasn't just talking about Steinhargh and felt another pulse of pain in my heart again. I struggled to find something to say.

"You can't let her be alone," I heard my words, though now my voice sounded strange in a different way. It came out thick and unsteady, despite my efforts. "Not now," I finished.

My friend looked at me through his tears as if I'd slapped him. He blinked his eyes clear again, then looked back down to the sea below. A beat passed. Abruptly, the arm I held so tightly twitched, and I felt his grip clamp onto my forearm. He released the twisted remains of Steinhargh's weapon, and it tumbled down to disappear in the foam on the sea. He took a moment and wiped his face, then reached up and gripped my hands with his other arm as well. He looked me in the eyes, his familiar steadiness slipping back into place, and gave me a terse nod. I returned it in understanding.

A moment later, we were lying back on the throne platform. Kelly gave me another look that said more with just his eyes than either of us would have been able to express with words. Then we stood and went over to where the others were, where Julea lay.

Kelly dropped to the ground next to the princess. Denis looked over as he did, and then together, with swift but tender motion, they moved her just enough so that she lay against Kelly. She whimpered in discomfort at the jostling and looked up, only then finding Kelly's face. Her body sank against his, and she let out a little breath that ended in a wet cough. He brushed an errant strand of her hair gently away from her face while a tear traced its way down his cheek.

"That was uncalled for," he said quietly. The customary bravado was still there—though tempered now by the grim reality. It was their language; how could it not be?

"I think you may just have a point," Julea said weakly. Her breath was shallow, coming in gasps. Then another wet cough racked her. It passed, and as she calmed again, she closed her eyes as he petted her hair gently.

Dana dropped suddenly to the ground by her side, her eyes so full of tears I wondered that she could see. She took Julea's hand in her own and pressed it to her chest.

"Jules...," she said, her tears falling faster, choking out her voice.

Julea said nothing, but her hand weakly closed on Dana's as a tiny smile creased her face.

Denis crouched to Kelly's right, not moving far from his side since he'd transferred Julea to him. He put his hand on Kelly's shoulder, and the two friends shared a look. Again, an invisible, silent communication took place. Then Kelly looked away from him suddenly, a stab of emotion ripping his eyes from his friend and back to the woman he loved. Denis moved back, just enough that he was not invading their space, but not so far that he wasn't there for them.

"Princess," Kelly said quietly, looking down at her.

"My love."

Kelly took a breath, steadying himself, then petted her head again. "I wish...," he said, then started over, "Do you still remember the perfect day?"

Julea's eyes flicked open, and she looked up at him. Something passed between them just then, something to which the rest of us weren't privy. It wasn't verbal; it can't even be attributed to the look alone. I've never believed that a soul could talk to a soul like that, but that's the only way I can describe what happened at that moment.

"I do," she said in a whisper, "I remember it all the time." Her eyes closed, and I got the immediate feeling she saw something we couldn't.

"If we could...," he said, choked, then continued, "... do you wish we'd chosen differently?"

With incredible effort, Julea looked once more at him and nodded. "I do," she said. Then, her head relaxed again, and her eyes closed.

"No more duties, Jules," Kelly said in a whisper, "nothing but the magic."

And then, surrounded by the ones that loved her most, Empress Julea Niconnal bar Ardallah was gone.

CHAPTER FOURTEEN

— JAYMES —

The massive doors of the palace throne room stood wedged open as I came up the steps from the courtyard. I stopped for a moment and looked back out over my city from what I thought of as one of the best places to see it. The winter weather had broken on that morning two long weeks ago, and while the sun had been mostly hidden since then, the warm air had arrived, marking a clear-cut change of season. The heavy snows that had blanketed everything back then were almost entirely melted now, and the city looked like it had been freshly scrubbed clean despite the low, heavy clouds. But, of course, the cleaning wasn't limited to the weather. And the clouds that had settled in Yorch weren't just the ones in the skies.

The palace battle we'd fought a fortnight ago was now known as 'the Insurrection' among the citizenry. Word of the events had spread quickly. Actually, the story had reached the length and breadth of the city before sunset of that same day. The empress had been murdered. Murdered by the so-called 'Savior of the Empire," the man that had, in reality, been a vile foreign tyrant. The city and palace guard had been leavened with traitors and mercenaries he'd put into place to seize control of the throne. More, Princess Julea had not died six months ago as was announced but had been alive all that time. Alive, until the blaggard had killed her moments after he'd killed her mother. Yorch remained free from his control only because the exiled traitor – the Blackcrow – and his companions had risen against the villain. Grief had pierced the hearts of the people – the heart of the city itself – that day and had not let go. And with grief, fear. Fear of what was to come. I heaved a sigh and turned to the open doors. '*What's to come,'* I thought gravely, *is what brought me here.*

There was a time when entering into the Grand Chamber sent a shiver through me. I hadn't been to the palace many times when I was younger, and it never failed to inspire a shiver of reverence in me. It felt a bit like going into the worship hall in the Temple of the One, somehow sacred. Now, though, as I walked through the entrance and crossed the length of the main hall, still flanked by the enormous black columns of marble and the planters of fresh greenery, my reverence was instead a sadness; the glory now was replaced by memories of carnage. Flashes of blood and death swam into my view as I walked. The polished marble floors had been scrubbed clean, but everywhere I put my eyes, I saw the phantom stains of the battle. I looked up instead, just so that I was looking somewhere else, and saw a maze of scaffolding stretched under the partially repaired skylight. The hellish rain of glass flickered in my memory, and the still unhealed wounds on my body ached. The scaffold was abandoned at the moment. I imagined that the artisans who were doing the repair work were taking a break from the fevered work they'd been doing. Their absence left the work area feeling eerie and abandoned. Then again, everything had an otherness to me since that day. I shook myself from my thoughts and continued, stepping carefully past the footings of the scaffolding and approaching the throne dais itself. Lady Larissa Coffey, her back to the room and therefore to me, stood to the throne's right on the upper level. *That's where the princess died,* I thought without meaning to. At the thought, the memory of her loss came back to poke me. I shook it off as much as I could and cleared my throat loudly. I was sure that Lady Larissa had heard my footsteps on the marble, and I was expected, but it never hurts to be polite.

"Sir Jaymes," she said without turning around. I waited for a more straightforward invitation, but it didn't come, so I continued up the lower stairs with some uncertainty. I paused on the lower platform just in case that was as far as she wanted me to go. But Larissa didn't turn or react at all. I accepted that as permission, so I climbed the second set of stairs, stopping just as I reached the top.

"Ma'am," I said and started to drop down to my knee. This wasn't a trivial thing, as my leg had taken a direct hit from one of the bigger of the falling glass shards, and I'd been walking with an obvious limp since then. But – bless her – it was then that she finally turned toward me and gave me a brisk shake of her head.

"Don't you dare," she said. It sounded exactly like a command, though she did favor me with a slight smile, which softened it. And even if it had been a command, it was one I was grateful to follow.

"Sorry," I said, straightening, "I don't really know the protocol anymore."

She shrugged. "I don't think we have one yet, so let's not worry about it." Her smile wavered a little as she spoke but then came back again after a moment, along with a slight crinkle at the corner of one eye. She waved her hand toward where she had been looking when I came in. "I'm not sure about these," she said as she turned back in that direction, "The new pattern seems almost too much."

I followed her gesture and only then noticed that the windows behind the throne had been repaired. But, more than that, they had been redesigned. Now, instead of the large, superbly clear glass panes that had overlooked the bay below, there was an intricate, starburst pattern made up of both clear glass and golden tinted panels. They glowed gently with the muddy light from the clouds outside, but I imagined that, when they were lit by the morning sun, they would reflect the light in a way that made the throne itself appear to be glowing. I admit I don't have an eye for art, but even so, I was staggered by the craft involved. I did, though, notice that the new pattern also did an excellent job of disguising a new metal framework that now reinforced the window. Pretty and practical.

"Wow," I said.

"You don't think it's too much?" Larissa asked, giving me a sidelong look.

"I think it's amazing," I said, still taking it all in.

"See, I think it's a lot for an empty chair," she said.

I looked back at her to see her eyeing the throne thoughtfully.

"Empty?" I said, tilting my head, "I thought—"

She shook her head, and I stopped. "Stewards don't sit on the throne, of course. We may not have a lot of protocol for the current situation, but we do know that much," she said.

I must have looked confused because she continued, "There will be a formal seat for the Steward installed on the lower platform." She gestured toward the level that was down the stairs behind me.

I glanced back politely, then returned my attention to her. She kept her eyes on the throne though I don't think she actually saw it as much as it was just where her eyes stopped as her thoughts raced on. She continued, "We held off the business of it all during the funerals and the days of mourning, but time does march on. The workmen say that they'll be installing the chair before the skylight is done. Possibly even today." She looked again at the windows as if calling herself back to the present.

I'm very bad at talking around an uncomfortable topic. I prefer to just talk about it instead. So, I said the obvious thing. "I hope it's comfortable." Then I added, "for your sake."

Larissa turned fully toward me for the first time. She hesitated at first, as if deciding how to respond, but then sighed as exhaustion mixed with unease took over her expression. "If it is," she said, "I think it will be the only part of this responsibility that will be."

"I can't think of anyone better suited to it than you," I offered. I first heard the rumor that she had been selected to become Stewardess of the Empire just a few short hours after the funerals for Ardallah and Julea had ended. I hear a lot, actually. I know people that serve inside most of the noble houses of Yorch. They mostly worked as servants, and they passed on to me what they heard, which included quite a bit. The nobles seemed to agree on one thing. The coming Assemblage demanded that there be a clear leader in Yorch. Anything less than that would serve only to weaken the alliances that kept the peace. To that end, there was no time for the process – 'process' is the polite word used for politicking and backbiting in noble circles – of replacing the Imperial family. There was no credible heir in Ardallah's line, and only a very few members of the Niconnal family remained. That meant that anyone's claim to the throne was murky. And murky would lead to either a long debate or a short coup. What was needed, it was decided, was an administrator to take control while more investigation as to lineages could be done. The ancient role of Steward would be restored. And there was only one person that held enough respect among the nobility to take that job.

"I can," she said very quietly. She seemed to disappear into thought for a moment, and I found myself wondering just what it was that she was thinking. Then, abruptly, she shook her head. "Besides, you only say that because it isn't you," Larissa shot back with a snort of laughter.

I felt myself give her a half-grin but managed to keep my tone sober as I said, "I say that because I believe it."

Her eyes caught mine and held them for a moment.

She seemed to be testing my sincerity from the viewpoint of someone that often saw its opposite. Then, her expression softened in something like relief. I had apparently passed the test. She looked away toward the throne for a moment, took a breath, and then began pacing a little with her hands now clasped in front of her in a very 'Imperial' way.

"You may regret that sentiment, sir knight," she said, more formally than before. She reached the throne, paused, and turned back toward me. "I have an assignment for you," she said.

"Ma'am?" I asked, picking up the cue to put my manners back on.

"You know the situation with the guard here in the palace, correct?"

"I think so," I said, "I know that quite a few soldiers from the standing army have been moved into the city guard to replace the ones that defected to Steinhargh. And, I also know that the traitors that survived are currently in the dungeons along with their mercenary friends."

She nodded. "That is all true, if not the complete picture. What you don't know is just how many traitors were involved. Let me say at least that the number is much higher than we have admitted. Much higher. It appears this usurper tapped into a deeper well of dissatisfaction with Her Imperial Majesty than anyone knew existed. The result is that we've needed to reassign a larger number from the rank-and-file than we've admitted. That depleted the local garrisons to a dangerous degree. We are actively recruiting to replace those men. We need to have a full company in our ranks before the visitors to the Assemblage arrive."

"Makes sense," I said without thinking. Larissa gave me a look, and I was reminded that she was now the Stewardess of the Empire. I nodded in apology.

"Thank you for your approval," she said with a touch of mockery in her voice that I knew was not severe. I grinned at the gentle correction as she continued, "I am also keenly aware of the need to replace the Imperial Guard itself, the unit known commonly as the 'Wolfpack.' It is a high priority that those representing the throne have reliable protection. It is both necessary and deserved. And yes, I have a personal investment in this." She smiled.

"That seems sensible too," I said, translating the smile as permission to respond this time.

"In the past, the Guard protected the Imperial family, and each member was given an individual bodyguard. Two of your companions served the princess for a time in that role, as you know."

I nodded, a sharp sense of loss passing over me at the mention of the princess and my friends.

"I intend to redesign the entire arrangement. I'm

doing this both for practical and political reasons, Jaymes. I need to do something that shows that I have actively taken the mantle of authority, but not something that would upend a decision of the empress or the princess. You see, inaction would make me appear weak, where too emphatic an action could weaken my support in the houses." She paced again, and I waited. Political strategy wasn't my area, which led me to wonder just what in all this discussion was.

"So, what are you going to do? And why tell me?" I asked. Waiting was another thing I wasn't good at doing.

She stopped pacing and turned back to me. "I am issuing a decree that will create The Imperial Wolfpack – a new order of knights and warriors, who will be specifically tasked with the protection of the throne and its representatives by all means required."

I felt my eyes narrow. "'By all means required?'" I asked.

She nodded. "Physical protection, obviously. Information gathering, as needed. And any other duties that would serve to secure Yorch's government from all outside threats. Threats such as a usurper in 'champions' clothing." She spat the word 'champions' as if she had tasted something foul. She looked very sternly into my eyes and continued, "Manpower is a great struggle for us, as I said, but I require a trustworthy and loyal person to lead this order. And that person is you."

"I'm sorry?" I heard myself say over the whooshing sound that suddenly filled my ears.

"Sir Jaymes Barnangur of Yorch, I offer you the role of Captain of the Imperial Wolfpack and Chief Protector of the Throne," she said. The world went silent as she finished, and my eyes had a moment of tunnel vision. This sensation only took an hour to pass, or at least that's how it felt to me. Since Larissa hadn't moved by the time I could see again, I concluded only a couple of heartbeats had truly passed.

"I...," I started, then took a long, steadying breath. Then, a moment later, I dropped gently down onto one knee, notwithstanding the aches that caused, and bowed my head. "I accept, Stewardess," I said.

There was a moment where nothing happened. Then I felt her hand on my shoulder, and I took that as the signal I should stand up. She had taken a few steps away as I did, giving me more time to collect myself.

"Your first assignment, Captain," she said, smiling at my new title, "is to collect your company. I expect you have a few names already in mind?"

My thoughts swirled, the faces of my companions swimming in and out of view. I shook my head to clear it, which, by the way, never works, and then looked at Larissa.

"I have some ideas," I managed. The new Stewardess

folded her arms, and I couldn't help but be impressed how easily the new authority sat on her, despite what she said. We were, I saw, going to have a discussion, possibly even a negotiation. I was not being given free rein.

"I think first I need to consider my companions from the day of the Insurrection, and I'm going to guess there might be resistance to some of them; that maybe we won't agree on some?" I asked. She nodded, and I did too. At least I knew where I stood. "So let me start with two names that I think won't be a problem. Rohb O'Laird and Gobhneh Stormshank."

She nodded and said, "Correct. Both of these are already commissioned in Imperial service, and they are excellent choices. We will need to find someone to relieve Captain Stormshank of his palace responsibilities, but despite our manpower problems, we still have his lieutenant, and he is a capable man. Done. Go on."

"Muiris Baltha," I said, "I think you might know him as a servant in city administration." Muiris quite liked his comfortable life. A month ago, I'd have bet that he would never be interested in being in active service beyond his current post. And yet, he'd stood by us in the worst of circumstances. So it was worth an offer at the least.

"I have seen his name. As it happens, I know very little of him, but that also means that I have no cause for objection."

"Niamh Coillte. She was the owner of the tavern that was burned down when we were being hunted by Steinhargh," I offered. "She's fed me information for the sake of the crown for a long time, and as you saw, she's capable with a blade as well," I said, a little more confident now after three solid suggestions. The look on Larissa's face told me that my streak had ended at three, though.

"As she is no longer in Yorch, I am afraid she will not be available. Whether I would have found her acceptable or not," she said with a shake of her head. I felt my eyebrows rise in surprise. "The destruction of her alehouse in service to the throne troubled me when I heard of it," Larissa explained, "I sought to find a way to offset her loss. It was the least we could do for her service. Thus, I instructed that she be compensated from the imperial treasury. But, unfortunately, my messengers reported that she was gone, according to those that had worked for her."

I thought back. I hadn't seen Niamh face to face since we stood not far from where I was now and watched Julea die. I remembered seeing her in the crowd at the funeral, but I hadn't spoken to her. Honestly, amid the ceremony and the masses in attendance that day, I hadn't seen any of my friends. A pain stabbed through me as I realized yet another loss. It took an act of will, but I focused. There were other names, but none I felt confident to say. Each was known as either a pirate, an assassin, or a traitor. Well, except for one.

"Lady Dana," I said, my voice flat with repressed emotion.

Larissa smiled warmly, if not a little wistfully. "I'm sorry," she said, "I simply can't give you the new Imperial Scribe."

I blinked.

Larissa laughed gently. Her laugh echoed around the chamber, and I realized it was the first time I'd heard her laugh that morning. It may have been her first laugh in a long while. When her laughter slowed, she said, "I spoke to her briefly before the funerals last week. I wanted to remind her that her status in Yorch was safe. She stayed away to *avoid* being made an exile, and thus she was free to come home with no repercussions. I told her that her secrets, whatever they were, were her own. No one left was pursuing them as the empress had been. I told her that I'd seen too much devastation," and here she gestured to the ongoing repairs, "to want anything to do with them." I looked down to shut out the memories, only to find a tiny piece of glass sticking to my pants where I'd kneeled. I flicked it off. *Catastrophes don't pass without leaving wreckage behind,* I thought.

Larissa waited for me to straighten again, then

continued, “She chose to stay in Yorch; she planned to retire to her family’s lands. I said that I understood completely the need to retire from battle. But I told her that I needed her here, with me, if she would accept the role. She did.”

“Just like that?” I asked, cocking my head.

Larissa grinned, though there was more behind it than was apparent. “More or less,” she said.

I thought for a moment, then smiled. “Has anyone ever said ‘no’ to you?”

Larissa waved a hand absently and said, “Not permanently.” She shrugged a shoulder and, with that, returned to the main subject. “Is there anyone else you wish to recommend specifically, or should we fill out the company with members of the guard?” she asked.

I thought for a moment. Something tickled at the back of my thoughts, but I pushed whatever it was aside. “I think that’s the end of my list. Perhaps Gobhneh can recommend some of his men?” I said, folding my arms with finality.

“Excellent idea, Captain,” she said, smiling again. She nodded, not so much dismissing me as indicating I could go if I wanted.

I nodded and turned to leave. As I did, the ‘something’ tickling my thoughts turned into a boot kicking at the door – breaking through and then running out of my mouth. I wheeled to face the Stewardess of the Empire and words burst forth. “Why not pardon Kelly? Why leave him as an exile? So much of what happened that day was because he chose to fight for the throne. He deserved more. He deserves more. This is one time you should deny the empress’s will; noble houses be damned,” I said, the words a rush.

The words hung in the air as if a black fog had blown in, obscuring everything else. I looked at Larissa’s face and found the expression there both intense and unreadable. For a moment, I thought I’d done myself in. *Well, that was the shortest assignment in the palace ever, Jaymes. Those dungeon cells better be comfortable,* I thought absently.

And then her face melted into the gentle smile from earlier. When she spoke, her voice was quiet and a little sad. “I offered,” she said.

I stared at her, frozen. I’m pretty sure my mouth dropped open.

She continued, “I went to see him after the services. I had to clear the air between us. I apologized for how I’d treated him and judged him all these years. I told him that if I could..., You understand, I didn’t know if I would be approved as Stewardess or not at that point. But I said that I would support rescinding his exile and clearing his name. But do you know what he said? I can’t forget it. I remember it word for word. He said, ‘You don’t understand, ‘Riss. I no longer have anything to come back to.’”

"But," I said, words coming out of my mouth without my permission, "what about his family? His lands?"

Larissa shook her head slowly. "Ardallah had me expunge all of the records when she branded him as the Blackcrow. His family's name was wiped away. The lands became public property, and his house was divided among the other nobles. There was no one to protest; he's the last of his line." She paused and smiled sadly again. "And we both know that wasn't what he meant anyway. There was only one thing that would have made him stay here," she finished.

I stood in silence, with what seemed like the enormous injustice of it all clinging to me like heavy moss on the north face of a tree. "And after that, he left," I said quietly.

"With the pirates," she said, unable to keep her distaste for Aeryk and his company entirely out of her voice.

We stood very still for a very long time. At some point, and I didn't know when it was, Larissa had taken my hand.

"Jaymes," she said, "I can't explain all of it, though there is more that could be told. I, more than anyone, know the feeling that this is not what you'd have wanted. Even that it isn't right. But we each live our own lives, and in the end, we have to make our own choices."

"He said something like that to me when he was exiled," I muttered, "and I only just got over that." I blew out a sigh.

We remained still while my feelings adjusted to the new normal of life, yet again. I looked at her and received another smile before she released my hand and moved away. From somewhere that felt far away, I heard the sounds of the artisans returning to continue their work on the skylight. *They'll be installing the Steward's Seat soon,* I thought. *Or Stewardess, I guess.* I looked over at Larissa, now a few feet away. She stood with her arms folded, looking intently at the new golden windows that framed the throne.

"Are you sure it isn't too much?" she asked.

CHAPTER FIFTEEN

— KELLY —

A confused gull glided in a wide circle just to the *Wind's* port as he had been all morning. I knew he had because I'd watched him for most of that time. We were a goodly distance from the shore by then, and as far as I knew, there weren't any places nearby where a gull might be comfortable, so why he chose to follow us out over the deep didn't make a lot of sense to me. I pondered on him a bit. Of course, I'm well aware that the world doesn't run on sense, so let the lad have his fun, I decided. I leaned back against the aft railing, filling my chest with the warm and briny sea air. If someone had told me that just two weeks before, back when I was knee-deep in one of the heaviest snowstorms I can remember, that in just a short time, these warm winds would not just herald a coming spring but also hint at the summer to follow, I'd have laughed them out of the room. Change can come quickly, of course. That was true, not just for the weather. Someone could have said other things to me two weeks before that I would not have believed either. Things change.

I heard an unfamiliar creak from the starboard side of the crow's nest, which had been my preferred location since we'd left the Great City. The small platform circled the *Midnight Wind's* mainmast over a hundred feet up from the deck, and it made its fair share of creaks and groans with the motion of the ship. Over time, I'd become accustomed enough to them that I no longer really noticed. But this particular squeak was a new one. It was unfamiliar, and I recognized that it meant I was soon to be no longer alone. Sure enough, several moments later, I saw a short figure, clad in the billowing white shirt and brown linen britches common among the crew, climb over the railing at the corner of my vision. There was a pause, then suddenly the figure was on my lap, and I was enfolded in an embrace. I returned it, then drew back to look into the dancing green eyes of Julea Niconnal. She said nothing, except for what her bright smile told me, then she pressed in, and we kissed, and my heart burst open in my chest.

I don't know how long that lasted, but eventually, she broke away and slid over to lean against the railing to my left, her legs still draped over my own. Somehow, the blue of the sky intensified above, and I couldn't stop the stupid smile on my face.

"You shouldn't be up here," I said with as much mock sternness as I could gather, which I admit wasn't much. I looked her over. The sailor's clothes didn't fit her exactly –

she was more than a bit slighter than the average pirate – but they'd been tied and affixed to make up for it. The livery had never looked better, in my opinion. Her hair was pulled back in a long braid that she currently had draped over her right shoulder, where it reached down onto her chest. I felt my eyes involuntarily pull down to where her wound was but stopped them and looked back at her face, which was much more pleasant business.

"Neither should you, technically," she said, a touch of the old authority coloring her tone despite her still beaming smile.

"Tosh," I said, "I'm in the crow's nest. Where else would be more appropriate? Also, I didn't just nearly die."

"I should think you've done that quite enough," she said through a barely repressed giggle.

"Seems like that's becoming a habit for a few of us," I replied, much more grimly than intended.

"As long as it's only *nearly*," she said, dismissing my somber tone with a slight roll of her eyes, "then we're fine."

"Jules," I said, looking at her with an intensity that came from the still too vivid memory, "I almost lost you."

Her smile dimmed briefly, and she nodded and looked away. She turned her gaze out to the sea, the reality of what had happened washing over her. But when she turned back to me, her smile had returned.

"But you didn't," she said, her eyes twinkling.

The bustle of activity in the moments after Steinhargh died was overwhelming. Several of the guard – the loyal ones under Gobhneh's command – came forward and took positions around us. Meanwhile, Gobhneh himself, along with Rohb and the remainder of our allies, began managing the carnage and the enemies' surrender. Without a word, I carefully picked up Julea's limp form and moved quickly over to the throne with Denis, Dana, and Aeryk around me.

"Kid, I don't believe this," I said under my breath, my voice still heavy with the emotion from just moments before.

Denis threw a quick look back over his shoulder and then looked at me. His face was serious and lacking the customary cavalier grin. "Don't thank me yet. I don't even know what I did," he muttered.

Aeryk and Dana, walking just ahead of us, stopped and looked at one another as if they'd heard a thunderclap. Then, both looked back at us with wide eyes.

"Less staring, more moving," Denis said.

"Did you—" Dana started, and I gave her a look. She blinked and then looked over at Denis.

"Really need to be moving," he said again. He glared at Aeryk and then at the back of the throne. The pirate took the hint and quickly opened the hidden panel that led to the secret stairs through which we'd entered. He went in, followed in short order by Denis, me, and finally Dana, who shut the door behind us. The stairwell and its connecting corridor were narrow, and carrying Julea was awkward, but we managed our way quickly through and out into a small, well-appointed sitting room. The space was meant to be a storage room off the principal, central corridor that ran from wing to wing in the palace. It joined the private dwellings of the Imperial family with the public areas, and this little room was walked past by castle staff countless times a day. And unbeknownst to all of them, this tiny, unassuming space had been the empress's personal study – her private meditation room and the secret portal to the throne. Once inside, I moved to a small couch against the wall to my right and gently placed Julea on it.

"What did you do?" Dana finally got out. I looked back at her and shook my head, and she looked at Denis.

"What did *you* do?" she repeated, her inflection harsher.

Denis shrugged, the black Kathasiri robes rustling with the motion. "What I could," he said.

Julea's limp form suddenly convulsed, a gagging sound burbling up from her throat. I dropped down next to her and started pawing at the latches that held her corset on. In a flash, Denis was at my side, Dana and Aeryk flanking us. I pulled the corset open to find the white dress beneath soaked with crimson. Just below her ribs and slightly left of center, the wound glowed with a sickly greenish-yellow light.

I looked up at Denis.

"The blue-yellow sticks," he said, returning my look with haunted eyes, "I took one a long time ago."

"You what?" Dana blurted.

He gave her a quick look, then brought his eyes back to me. "Look, it was years ago. I saw what it did for Dana, and I figured it was a good thing to have around if I ever needed it," he said. There was a strange, even earnest, intensity on his face. His eyes fell down to the sickly glow as Julea's form convulsed again. "When Steelclaw stabbed her, and then I caught her, I knew. I know what a mortal wound looks like; I've seen my share. You all saw it; there wasn't a question. So then, when you and he were wrestling, I pulled out the dagger and put the crystals in."

"That's not how it works!" Dana veritably screamed at Denis, grabbing him and pulling him up from beside me. He pushed her back.

"I did what I could!" He shouted as they locked eyes.

I looked at Julea. She was spasming, tiny shivers wracking her arms and legs randomly. Gently, I reached over her body to help keep her in place on the couch.

"Did you know about this?" Dana said, wheeling on me suddenly.

"I only showed him the empty stick in my hand when he came over from the window," Denis said, intercepting her ire on my behalf, "after I'd already used it."

Dana looked at him again. “Do you understand the risk you’re taking? She could live but never be out of pain for the rest of her life. She could die right now in agony. She could—”

“Enough,” I barked, cutting her off, “I need a hand here. Can we find some sheets? Anything we can use to help restrain her and cushion the tremors.” Within moments, we’d put some pillows and wadded up cloth in place around the shivering form of Julea, shaping a kind of padded nest that would hopefully cushion her as she writhed. Reluctantly, I moved back, knowing that I, too, would be a danger to her if I held her too tightly. I couldn’t make myself back too far away, though. At length, I realized that Dana had come up to stand next to me. She put her hand on my shoulder and rested her head beside it.

“Sorry,” she said.

“I know,” I replied, “I know.”

“I don’t want false hope,” she said quietly.

I looked over at her, noting that Denis was just beyond. “I will take any hope at the moment,” I said. The quiet moment began to pull the curtain back on the exhaustion I was feeling. Yet, raw terror remained to hold me up, the terror of what was happening to my princess.

Denis looked over and gave a slight nod.

“Do you... do you think...?” Dana started twice, ultimately trailing off. She was watching the twitching form on the couch intently.

I stayed silent. At that moment, I had no answer. There was no way what Denis had done should work. As I understood it, the crystals required careful guidance, and without it, they were unpredictable; unstable. My whole body felt like it might give out at any moment, but it wouldn't fall. My black left hand filled my vision as I reached up to rub my eyes. I mused how, just minutes ago, my own crystal-infused hand had caused the complete destruction of Steinhargh's weapon just by my willing it. And then the solution hit me like a bolt of lightning.

"Dana, it's you," I said without context. I spun to face her.

She straightened and looked at me in shock. "What?"

"You. You can fix it. What Eryth did to you – it's like the opposite of me. Black and white, get it?"

She shook her head, "No."

Panic, excitement, and the flash of inspiration were all compressing themselves into my mind, making it almost impossible to get the words out.

"Go to her," I said, "and put your hands on the wound. Tight. Don't let go; just keep pressing."

She stared at me blankly.

"You're a pattern," I said. Everything seemed so slow; explaining felt like it was taking forever. "What the crystals are doing – did – for you; they'll realign and do it for her. It's got to work. Go!"

There was what felt like a hundred-year pause as Dana took the tiny scraps of information I'd offered and stitched it into sense in her mind. Then she all but leaped forward and dropped to Julea's side. With a tug, she tore the blood-soaked cloth at the wound site into a palm-sized hole. Carefully, she put her hand in and pressed it over the still weeping wound in her friend. The room seemed to 'thrum' with energy, as if the bolt of lightning I'd felt in my mind had become real and was about to explode from the walls. Denis and Aeryk looked over at me in turn before affixing their eyes on Dana and Julea.

Then, very anticlimactically, it was over. Julea's body bent with one last spasm and then went limp as her head seemed to drop deeper into the pillow beneath it. Silence fell in the room, more complete than ever, as I don't think any of us were breathing. And then one of us did.

Julea took a sudden, deep breath in, and then it came out in a peaceful sigh. She made a gentle moan and slept.

"No, I didn't. I didn't lose you, did I?" I smiled back at her as the memory of that day receded. She reached over and took my hand as if she'd been with me my thoughts.

Another of the unfamiliar creaks came from the far side of the crow's nest just then, similar to the one Jules had made when she came up. Shortly, a tall figure hauled himself up over the starboard railing. He was clad similarly to me, black pants and a loose shirt of bone-colored broadcloth held in at the waist by a wide belt. Additionally, though, he wore a long brown coat adorned with brass buttons that served more as decorations than they did as closures. He gripped the mast with his left hand as he settled both feet on the platform and adjusted to the exaggerated motion in the nest.

"Easier if you sit," I said without turning to him, "Every rock and roll of the ship is ten times more intense up here."

Aeryk eased down, first to his knee, before finally sitting completely and leaning against the railing opposite us. "Can you please tell me why in the hell we're up here, then?" he muttered.

"I was just explaining to my guest," I said, twitching my head at Julea, "it's called the 'crow's nest.' I would think the reason I'm up here would be obvious. As for you, maybe not so clear."

"The actual lookout won't come up while you're up here. He says he's heard stories," he grumbled.

I chuffed, then replied, "I know how to see, and I know how to yell. I think I'm qualified enough to be here. You can tell him that he can take some time off."

"Hardly the point," Aeryk said through a sigh.

"Oh, no worries," Julea said brightly, "I'll keep him on task."

Aeryk shook his head at her gruffly, though a smile was settling in on his face. He looked out over the sea.

"Good wind," Aeryk said after a moment, just to say something.

"Going the right direction," I said. Julea snickered. We let another moment pass, reveling in his discomfort, before letting him off the hook. "How's Edword?" I asked.

He shrugged. "Considering the state he's in, I'd say he's doing great," he said.

"'The state he's in,'" I repeated, a hint of salt in my voice.

Aeryk caught the tone and coughed a chuckle. "Okay, poor choice of words," he said, "I don't know what to say otherwise, though. I mean, the leg's gone from the knee down. He's got the peg on, but I don't know if that means he's 'recovering' at all."

Edword had stayed on the deck six months before when the *Wind* brought Julea and Rohb to Yorch to pursue Steinhargh. He'd stayed there when they were attacked, doing what he could to make sure the princess and her guard got away safely. But, unfortunately, the *Wind* took the uncanny gem-powered blasts from the enemy ships and nearly wound up on the bottom of the harbor while Edword paid the price of escape with his right leg. The pirate had healed quite a bit in the months since, and though Aeryk was calling his replacement leg a 'peg,' the contraption Edword wore reminded me no little bit of Steinhargh's vile 'arm.'

"Hardly a 'peg,'" I muttered aloud.

"Fair true," Aeryk said severely with a nod.

I glanced over to him, noting the brown coat again. "He give you any indication of whether he's ready to resume command?" I asked.

Aeryk shook his head. "Not to me. I'd think I'd be first to know."

"So it's still 'Captain Puppy?'" I said.

Julea giggled, just as she did each time his nickname came up.

"*Acting* captain," he said with a chuckle of his own, "acting Captain Puppy."

"I think it's perfect," she said.

"The coat doesn't fit right," he said, looking down and tugging on it seemingly at random.

I gave it a moment, then said, "It will, in time."

"I can't see how," Aeryk said, a tiny flicker of his old insecurity coming through, "I don't even know how the ship survived that attack. It should be a home for fish right now. What kind of captain doesn't know how his ship works?"

"An acting one," I said, smiling broadly, "and one that has the opportunity to learn."

The *Wind* had taken the attacks all along her port side that day, and she'd keeled over from the force. An average ship – a ship that hadn't been gifted by her designer like the

Midnight Wind had been – would have capsized and sunk. She did not, somehow. Instead, she'd rallied and held fast at the waterline. Within moments, she began moving away from the bay with more speed than her attackers could muster to catch her – despite being lain over on her starboard. Nearly all the crew managed to stay with her, and none had been lost. Some clung to the outside of the hull, and some were inside the partially submerged cargo area. According to them, the *Wind* "righted herself" without any assistance from them. She acted as if she were alive, did her best to save them, and looked to them for fixing after it was over. At least, that was how it was to hear them tell it. Aeryk was fond of pointing out that 'sailors tell stories,' and while I don't deny it, I couldn't help but wonder once again about the nature of this ship.

We were quiet for a moment, and I looked over to check on my gull friend. He was still there, floating on a rising bit of warm air so expertly that he wasn't even flapping his wings. He appeared just to hover there, falling neither ahead nor behind us.

"What do you think is really going to happen back there?" Aeryk said. I looked and saw that he was looking behind us, more or less in the direction we'd come. We were, of course, far enough from land that there was nothing actually to see, but the implication was clear. Julea followed our gaze, and her smile dimmed as she thought for a moment.

"If she can avoid the political – and potentially actual – attacks that will come her way, Larissa may be the best thing to happen to the empire in a very long time," she said. For the first time that morning, she sounded a bit like her old self when on Imperial business, severe and intense.

"That's a pretty big 'if,'" Aeryk said.

She turned back and looked at him directly. "It is. Yorch's nobility was held in check by the sheer force of my mother's will. Larissa is formidable, don't get me wrong, but she doesn't have the bloodline. Stewards aren't kings. Or empresses. She'll need to dance on a knife's edge to get the nobility on her side. It will take time," she said.

"You think she's in real danger?" Aeryk pressed.

I chimed in. "Well, she says that she's rebuilding the Wolfpack with Jaymes as the head. He's no politician, but that won't be the job anyway. What he is, is loyal. I almost pity someone that would test him." I couldn't repress the tiny curl of a grin of pride on my mouth.

Aeryk let his gaze pass from me to Jules and back. "You think she's got more to worry about politically," he said.

"She does. If she can keep the greater dragons of the court more concerned with one another than with her, she'll do okay," Julea said, "I don't see that as an easy path, though." I leaned my head back on the rail while her hand found mine again.

“She’s got some solid support,” Aeryk said with words that carried more than their share of meaning.

And with that, I fell into memory again.

The small dining room was so nearly unchanged from what it had been eight years before that it almost made me dizzy when I entered. Each detail, the dark oak wainscoting trimmed with small carved wolf’s heads, the golden foil that papered the rest of the walls, the whitewashed ceiling behind the oak framing, and the dark azure woven rug that covered the floor were all exactly as I remembered. Even the long, mahogany table that filled the room from the entrance at one end to the hearth at the other was exactly as my memory presented it. And every bit of it was spotless; it was as if no time had passed at all. But, of course, nostalgia wasn’t why I’d come.

At the far end of the table, next to the hearth where once I’d regularly sipped tea and traded stories with the palace staff, stood Dana. She had her hair up in a courtly style, and a gray velvet cloak was draped around her shoulders. She looked up from a sheaf of papers in her hand as I entered, rolling them gently as she did. She watched me calmly down the length of the room.

“How is she?” she said finally.

I hitched my hip on the edge of the table and sighed. “Recovering,” I said wearily, “I don’t think the stones worked as effectively as they would normally have."

"Well, they weren't administered very well," she grumbled.

"I'm not going to argue with success," I said with a shrug. We were dancing around the thing we both needed to and didn't want to discuss. I looked down at my hands, just to give my eyes somewhere neutral to look.

"She's still leaving, isn't she?" Dana said, grabbing the proverbial elephant in the room by its trunk.

I kept my eyes down as I said, "Yeah. She's coming with me when I go."

There was a gentle 'thump' from the end of the table. I looked and saw that she had planted her hand firmly on the tabletop, the papers she held now crumpled beneath. I stood and faced her.

"The funerals are proceeding," I said, turning fully into the storm of the subject now, "both of them. Julea intends to let the empire believe she died that day."

Dana didn't move or react, which wasn't a surprise as I hadn't said anything she didn't know. It did seem necessary to say it, though.

"Outside of Larissa and us, the rest of the world will believe the Niconnal line ended. It's looking like Larissa will be tapped to perform the duties of Steward. Or, rather Stewardess. I'm not sure if the title changes like that or not; it seems like it should," I said, mostly just to fill the uncomfortable silence.

She remained still, and then slowly and with unspoken gravity, she nodded her head. "She's never wanted the throne. The obligation. The pressure Ardallah put on her."

I stayed silent then. We both knew the truth of what she said, but she needed to talk it through. This was her acceptance to work out, and I would only be in the way.

She straightened and squared herself to me, the length of the table aligned now between us. "I'm staying in Yorch, Kelly. I already told Jules and the others, and now I'm telling you. This city is my home, it always has been, and I finally get to be here again."

I felt a swirl of emotions, something that was becoming my natural state; I was starting to think. I looked at her steadily.

"I don't know if you can understand," she continued. She was very obviously not moving from the spot where she stood, keeping the length of the table between us. "I just want to come home. I always have. I have family, a sister – did you even know that? That I have a sister? — that I haven't been able to see in three years."

"I didn't—," I sputtered. *Did I know that?* I thought. *And if I didn't, why not?*

She cocked her head as she said, "You're thinking about it, aren't you? You didn't know. I didn't mention it because it was just one more painful part of staying away. And you didn't ask. Isn't that interesting? But here's the thing, I was never exiled; I can come back. And I have a home and a life to come back to."

I saw as the words left her mouth that she wanted to pull them back. The thing is, regret or no, she knew what she was saying. And the fact is that she was right, and I couldn't argue it. She had family, a home, everything waiting for her here. It made as much sense as Julea's desire to leave if I let myself think about it – each of them was looking to find the life they wanted. She by staying, Julea by leaving.

"Jules?" I asked. It wasn't a complete sentence, but Dana understood my intent and answered me anyway.

"Like I said, I talked to her," she said, blinking away a tear that dampened her eye, "I explained how I felt. I tried to convince her to stay, but…," she trailed off.

"She can't," I said, finishing the thought. "If she stays, she's the empress. If you go, you lose your family. The evil or the deep blue sea."

"And if I stay, my best friends have to go," she said. Her voice caught a little, but she reined in the emotion.

I nodded. "I understand. I'm sure Jules did too. And you're right, you need to do what's best for you. Hard choices are not always wrong," I said. One common trait sadness and anger share is exhaustion. You have it when anger leaves, and you have it when sadness stays. I sagged with a new weariness. "If nothing else, the One knows, Larissa needs you. You deserve a life wherever you want one," I said.

Dana looked down, and a single teardrop fell, landing on the table runner in front of her. I blew out a breath and turned to leave.

"Larissa...," Dana said, just barely loud enough for me to hear. I stopped and looked back. It took a moment, but she looked up at me before she spoke again. "She... she told me she offered you a pardon — a release from exile. You could have stayed. Both of you together. She said you said no?" she asked. I could see tears on her cheeks very clearly now.

"I did."

"She said you told her you didn't have anything here to come home to."

I nodded. She was looking at me. She knew there was more, but she needed me to say it.

"The Yorch I once served is gone, Day. If I stayed, Julea would either stay and live a life she doesn't want, or she'd try to leave alone, and I will not let that happen."

"She would never leave you."

I smiled a little at that. "True or not, I know I won't leave her. Not ever again."

She looked at me intently while the light of understanding passed between us.

"Take care of yourself, Kelly," she said finally.

“You too,” I said. I turned and left the room, closing both the door and a chapter of my life as I did.

“I said, she’s got some solid support, right?” Aeryk repeated.

I looked over at him, the memory receding. “Yes. That she does,” I said, “I couldn’t imagine better.”

The sail on the foremast billowed suddenly to the east as a call of “Ho!” echoed from below. The three of us leaned in various directions to see the deck, where several of the crew were re-rigging the sail to better catch the shifting west wind. On the starboard rail, the figure of a young woman stood, a line strung around her right side and wrapped on her left arm. She wore a similar sailor’s garb to Julea – the same broadcloth shirt, belt, and boots, though her pants were tan – and she had her long brown hair pulled back in two thick braids behind her head. She was leaning hard away from the deck, suspended over the ocean, as she held the sail in position while the crew fastened it in place.

“A natural sailor, that one,” Aeryk said, looking back at me.

“You’re welcome,” I said, “although she was a natural pub-keeper too.”

“You wouldn’t think those skills would overlap, would you?” Julea said as she watched the action below.

I looked back down as Niamh swung herself back onto

the deck. I turned to Aeryk and said, "Niamh can do whatever she puts her mind to, captain. You'd be well-served to remember I told you that."

"Why'd she leave the city? You said she could have rebuilt?"

I shrugged one shoulder. "So I was told. Then she asked where you were headed and if she could come aboard."

"She keeps her own counsel, does she?" Aeryk asked.

"Always has," I said. I saw Niamh jump back onto the deck as the sail was made fast. The *Wind* pitched as the reset sails billowed, and the nest swung hard across from starboard to port. Aeryk blinked his eyes deliberately and took a breath.

"If you're going to puke, Captain Puppy, best not to do it where the men'll see," I said. I glanced across, strangely relieved to see the gull had adjusted his course and was still alongside the ship. I looked at Julea to see if the shift had unsettled her, but the broad smile and wild look in her eyes told me I needn't have bothered.

"If you're suggesting I leave you two alone, you best remember just who's in charge around here," Aeryk said, the sass strengthening him against his momentary nausea, "I'll stay up here all the way to Gladia if I want."

"We're going to Euticha," I said, looking at him for confirmation.

"Right," he said, maybe reading something in my look

that settled the subtle sparring, "the stopover in Euticha is on the way to Gladia."

I sighed and leaned back again.

"Kelly?"

"Yeah?"

"Why Euticha again?"

I glanced over to find him looking at me with his brow furrowed. I shook my head dismissively. "I need to get my horse," I said, "I left him in Euticha that time I almost died, remember?"

"Poor Locksley!" Julea burst out. "Honestly, the way you treat him, it's a wonder he stays with you."

Aeryk looked at me very intently. "You're aware that was over six months ago," he said.

"Which is why I need to go get him," I explained, shifting my tone and slowing down as if I were talking to a child.

If he thought to say more on the subject, he changed his mind. The fact is that he'd seen Locksley do any number of un-horse-like things in our adventures together, and waiting for me somewhere for six months would be pretty far down that list.

"I know having a horse aboard will be a little inconvenient, but we'll only be on as long as it takes to get to Seoda," I reassured him.

"If your horse waits for you for six months in the wilds

and still comes when you call for him, I'm pretty sure he won't be too much of a problem on the ship. For the sake of the One, he's likely a better sailor than these dogs," Aeryk scoffed with a glance down toward the deck. After a moment, he scratched his head and looked at me. "Say, what's in Seoda?" he asked.

"Gladians," I said by reflex, "specifically Seodans."

Aeryk glared at me.

"Incorrigible," Julea muttered.

I shook my head and said, more relevantly, "Nothing specific. But it's a big town that's not far from Inis Kath, and I have business there."

"Business?"

"Business," I said as memories came for me again.

The lone call of a single trumpet still rang in my ears, or possibly my heart, as I made my way back down the tower stairs. Larissa had been very clear that I should stay with Julea during the funeral and had secured a small balcony that overlooked the main square for us. It would not do, she said, for the deceased empress née princess to be seen at her own services. As for me, while she said that it was for security, I am reasonably convinced that it was more that she wanted me out of public view as well. Or, probably, much of the army. It was always possible that some had not gotten the message about my not being the enemy right now. It was the wrong time for confused unpleasantness. The palace gates stood un-customarily wide open, and from our vantage point, we could watch the crowd that filled the inner ward and spilled out onto the avenues beyond, down into the heart of the city. There was no possible way the people out there could have heard or seen the proceedings, but they still came. Julea pressed close to me and held my hand. She was still quite weak, and I could feel her weight against me as she used me for support. But she wouldn't sit. She said she needed to see the people. Despite the dampness and the chill that still clung to the air, they came. They came, and they wept, and then they headed home. I looked at her at the close of the services, tears rolling down her cheeks.

"I'm okay," she said, "I really am. This is for the best. It's all very touching, though, isn't it?"

When it was all over, I led her back down from the tower and back inside. The hallways had been cleared for the services, so there was no one to see her. Despite that, as a precaution, she wore a thick robe and kept the hood over her face. She held my arm, and I guided her cautiously back to the sequestered bedchamber where she'd been recovering. Standing at the doorway, two tall figures in identical black and red stood waiting. My hand went by instinct to the blade at my side, but before I drew it, I stopped. The silent figures – Kathasiri assassins though they were – weren't a danger. Not this time. No, their purpose was different, I knew, and likely they were not happy about it. I felt a humorless grin wrestle its way onto my face.

"He could have just sent a note," I said. Neither of the figures reacted; their dark eyes watched me without blinking. If they recognized – or were even interested in – Julea's identity, they made no indication.

I helped her into the room and to the couch that she indicated. She pulled me down to her and kissed my cheek.

"Be careful," she said.

"Don't worry," I said and winked, "I know a guy."

She gently slapped my shoulder and then leaned back on the couch. I stayed a moment to make sure she didn't need anything before I turned and left, closing the door behind me. I faced the two grim figures still standing to either side of the door.

"Fine," I said with a slow exhalation, "I'm game. Take me to him."

The silent assassins turned and moved down the hallway ahead of me without checking to see if I was following. I did, though, sure of the absolute distaste they had for the task of fetching me and aware that they would be happier if I got lost on my own. The word *happier* stuck in my mind, and I had a moment to muse on just what it was that would make an assassin happy. In any event, it didn't appear that they weren't actively trying to lose me, which made them at least good at following instructions.

Our path took us through several twists and turns and through as many hidden servant passages as it did public ones. Finally, some short distance from the kitchens, we came to the door of one of the large rooms used for dry storage. My guides stopped and took up silent positions on either side of a set of wide doors. From there, they stared at me, all traces of expression completely hidden behind their masks. Masks that were both physical as well as metaphorical.

"This must be the place," I muttered. Neither of the two moved. I waited a moment before I shrugged and said, "I really enjoyed our time together. I'll miss you two."

No response. I realized that my usually reliable well of irreverence seemed to be dry, so I shrugged again, brushed past them, and went through the heavy wooden door.

The room inside was dimmer than the hallway. Only about half of the wall-mounted gas lights encircling the ample space were lit. However, there was some little daylight visible from high-set ventilation windows on the right-side wall. Around the room's perimeter were stacks of crates and barrels, but the central area was empty except for a low, wooden platform slightly to one side. Three chairs, evenly spaced, sat on top of it, and in the center one sat Denis, his foot cocked up on the seat, and his arm draped on his knee. His eyes shot over to me as I entered, just for a flash, and then went back to looking at the open space in front of the platform.

Taking the hint, I walked calmly to where he indicated, which allowed me to casually look around into the shadowy fringes of the room. There, darkly clad figures lurked, moving about in the shadows. When I reached the center of the room, I stopped at the spot Denis's eyes had silently indicated and faced the Master of the Kathasiri.

"So, yeah," he said. He shifted, putting both feet on the ground and dropping his elbows onto his knees.

"Nice, um, audience chamber," I said. The urge to draw my sword tugged at the muscles of my right arm mercilessly. I tightened my right hand into a fist to hold it back.

"You should have seen the old place. Smelled like offal. The first instruction I gave them was to get us into another room," he said, then paused in thought. "Well," he continued a moment later, "I suppose that was actually the second instruction."

I nodded, a humorless chuckle escaping my mouth.

"She okay?" he said.

I looked at him. I was again keenly aware of the crowd of unholy assassins that lurked in the shadows around us. I didn't know how much we were being watched, but I had no desire to have this conversation in front of anyone, let alone the Kathasiri. But Denis's new status was going to make a genuinely private conversation unlikely. He watched me struggle. I knew he would understand if the response was bravado. But.

"Yes," I said, my tone flat and painfully honest.

He nodded. I glanced around the room again, the unspoken concern silently growing in my thoughts.

"Don't worry. They don't know, and they don't care," Denis said, noticing my discomfort.

I eyed him directly, "We can trust that?"

"It's not part of the contract, so it's unimportant," he said, hitching one shoulder in a dismissive shrug. I nodded, unconvinced.

"They were at the door," I said with a hint of nervousness.

"Someone's door. Someone *not part of the contract*," Denis said with particular emphasis. We locked eyes for a moment, and it snapped into place in my mind. Julea was part of the defunct contract, and therefore irrelevant. I nodded. It wasn't *relief* exactly, but my concern did ease.

"Also, we're leaving soon," he said, leaning back in his chair, "I declared the contract over with Steinhargh's death and the absence of other offerings. Custom dictated that we had to wait a bit so that we were sure about his being dead. Without a body, you know, we had to be sure. But we're on solid ground to leave now." He had let his voice get slightly louder, and though he didn't look around the room, I could see that he was making a formal statement to any of them that might have been listening.

"When?" I asked.

"With the tide," Denis said, his volume returning to the discreet tone that kept our discussion mostly between us. He sounded wistful, and that felt odd coming from him so directly. "As it happens, that will be around sunset, which is just thrilling to this lot. They love the dark," he snorted the last without genuine humor.

I suppressed a grin that pressed at my mouth. Then a wave of intensity crashed through me. Denis was leaving. Leaving to go to the Island of Assassins to face a trial. Because of me. Because of us.

"Den—," I said, my voice catching.

"So," he interrupted, leaning back again and hiking his foot back up onto the chair, "that means we'll be back on Inis Kath within the month. The *Na'Sa'Grosh* will be on the new moon after that. I figure that will almost be another month."

I nodded. I didn't know what else to do.

"Listen, Kelly," Denis said, his voice quiet and very serious suddenly, "I don't regret what I did. *I* wanted to. You didn't talk me into it. I know you think you're the axis of the world and that everything that happens is your fault...,"

He paused just long enough that the words hit home.

"... But you aren't. And it isn't. This decision was mine. I'm convinced it was worth it, so I'm taking the consequences. That's all there is to it."

He was looking at me with an intensity that belied the casual way he was draped in his chair and waited. In time, I nodded and looked down.

"I'm going to the temple just as I agreed. And I'm going to the trial. And if it doesn't go my way...," he paused. I closed my eyes for a moment, took a breath, and looked up at him. He was leaning over as far as he could, putting his face just inches from mine.

"Then you better have gotten your ass there in time to get me out of this," he said in a snarling whisper just loud enough for me to hear.

I felt a grin curl the corner of my mouth as the intensity evaporated.

"Don't you smile," he said with a tiny shake of his head, "I'm serious. You better have a plan and get me out of this."

I heard a shuffle in the shadows, a reminder of the assassins all around us. I didn't care.

"Even if I have to burn it all down, kid. Even if I have to burn it all down."

"Denis," Julea said, shaking me back to the present.

"Yeah," I said, "I owe him. Besides, I don't like assassins. Especially not those."

The ship pitched in the waves; the motion amplified

again. We fell silent for a moment. To the port, the gull continued to pace us, never too far or too close.

"What then?" Aeryk asked into the quiet.

I looked over at Julea. She had turned her head into the wind and was looking off toward the horizon. Tiny wisps of hair that had sneaked out of the braid flipped back and forth in the breeze.

"We'll figure something out," I said, as much to Aeryk as to myself.

He stared at me.

"That's my best answer right now," I said, chuckling. "I actually think we only have even odds that I won't die trying to save Denis's neck, so let's not spend too much time on the long term."

Julea made a playful gasping noise and punched my shoulder. "You best not! I will be outraged," she said.

"Well, if we all die saving the dungeon rat, we'll make sure we leave a note that you were outraged, ma'am," Aeryk said with a wink.

"We?" I asked. I looked at him.

He stood then, carefully stepping out over the railing of the crow's nest and onto the rigging. He took the first two steps down toward the deck, stopped, and leaned on the rail while giving me the kind of glare a parent gives to an idiot child.

"Kelly, you aren't going to Inis Kath alone. Neither

your lady there nor I am going to let that happen, and you can't stop it. Get that through your head. You've never really been as alone as you think," he said. We looked at one another for a moment. Then he looked over at Julea and winked. I opened my mouth to speak, but he started climbing down and out of sight.

"Chow is at sunset. Be good if you'd let my crew have the nest back by then," he called back up as he went. Then we were alone.

I slid over and rested my back against the port rail, draping my arm over Julea, who pressed in next to me. We sat like that for a long time, listening to the sound of the sea and the wind.

"You are going to need a new nickname for me," she said suddenly, looking up into my eyes.

"Pardon?"

"A nickname. You can't keep calling me 'princess' anymore. It's inaccurate," she said.

I chuckled. "Accuracy is important," I said, then thought a moment. "You're probably going to need a new name entirely. You can't very well go around introducing yourself as 'Julea Niconnel,' can you?"

"Hunh," she said, her brow furrowing, "I hadn't thought of that."

"Pick something you like," I said.

"'Starlight,'" she said, waving her hand in front of us

with a flourish.

"Oh, please."

We laughed together for a while, while Julea tried on names like "Rainbow," "Sunrise," and several others, each more ridiculous than the last.

"Wait, wait," I said, finally reigning in my laughter, "I just thought of something. You don't need a new *first* name. You just need a surname. That would be enough."

"'Julea Starlight,'" she said, spawning a new gust of giggling.

"Okay, okay. Maybe we just pick something that goes well with "Kelly" and "Julea," I said.

She stopped laughing and looked directly into my eyes.

"I mean," I said, my voice very serious, "shouldn't our last name work for both of us?"

"Are you...?" Julea started.

"I'm asking you to be my wife," I said. I shook my head and muttered, "Poorly. I'm asking you to be my wife poorly."

She grabbed my face and kissed me, pressing her whole weight on me all at once. The embrace continued until, finally, we broke apart.

"That was yes, right?" I said, breathless but smiling.

"Of course it was," she said.

"Oh, good. I wasn't sure."

"Shut up and kiss me, Blackcrow."

Over her shoulder, the white gull turned into a wide circle. It swung all the way around us, glowing all the while in the bright sun.

Glossary

King Adam Olindon

AHD-am oh-LIN-don

King of the southern kingdom of Gladia and long-time ally of the Empire of Yorch.

Conseiller Alfre Monague

kon-sil-AIR al-FRAY mon-a-GUE

The Selectman of the town of Gretchville.

Lord Anthony Westfall

AN-tho-nee WEST-fall

The High Regent of the free city of Euticha.

Arcagawan

ar-KAG-uh-wan

The massive river which runs from the mountain range in the west down to empty into the Great Ocean. The city of Euticha sits at its mouth.

The Assemblage

as-EM-blaj

The bi-annual gathering of all accorded allies of the Empire of Yorch.

Candice Durand

kan-DESE-e dur-AN

The daughter of Captain Durand, owner of a successful trading fleet that is based in Euticha.

Carmac

KAR-mak

A wide, fast-moving river that flows through the northern wilderness and passes through the Great City of Yorch.

Cinniuint

KIN-you-int

A merchant city south of Yorch in the lands of Gueldrelanne.

Denis Goldarian

DEN-is gol-DAR-ian

Former Kathasiri assassin and companion of Kelly and Dana.

Ederland Forest

ED-er-lund

A dark, old-growth forest in the north of the Kingdom of Gladia.

Eryth Erantress

AIR-ith ear-AND-ress

A mysterious woman with ties to Kelly.

Etherian Gardens

e-THEER-i-an

A famous public garden in northwestern Euticha.

Euticha

YOU-ti-ka

An independent city-state north of Gladia.

Finn O'Seachnasaigh

FIN Oh-SHAWN-a-she

An associate of Eryth.

Garanthet VosMullen

gar-AN-thet vos-MUL-en

The Chief Surgeon of Euticha.

Gladia

GLAY-de-uh

"The Southern Land." A large kingdom at the southern tip of the continent. It maintains a long and close alliance with the Empire of Yorch.

Gobhneh Stormshank

GOV-new STORM-shank

The Captain of the Watch in the palace of Yorch.

Gretchville

gra-VEEL

A village in the unclaimed lands south of Gueldrelanne.

Gueldrelanne

GOUL-dre-lan

A small, vassal kingdom in the Empire of Yorch.

Jaymes Barnangur

james BAR-nan-giur

An agent of the Imperial Raven in years past.

Larissa Coffey

lar-IS-a KOF-e

The Imperial Scribe and chief chamberlain to the Imperial House.

Malatak

MAL-uh-tak

A heavy warhammer gifted to Jaymes by Kelly.

Malazander Pwent

mal-a-ZAHN-der PWENT

The Counselor to the High Regent of Euticha.

Markash

mar-KASH

The dark, assassin's temple of the Kathasiri.

Morden

MOR-den

A mysterious with uncanny properties.

Muiris Baltha

MOY-ris BAL-tha

A former associate of the Imperial Raven, now a civil employee in Yorch.

Na'Sa'Grosh

na-sha-GROSH

The Kathasiri ritual of final judgment.

Niamh Coillte

NEEV KUIL-te

A former associate of the Imperial Raven and innkeeper.

Nicholas Andwen

NIK-oh-las AN-dwen

The captain of the city guard of Euticha.

Preskia

PRES-key-a

The oldest and most prestigious city in the kingdom of Gladia.

Sargeaux

sar-GOI

The formal name given to the kingdom conquered by Willm Steinhargh.

Seoda

sey-OH-da

The capital of the Southern Lands, the kingdom of Gladia.

Tybor al Crolish

TIE-bor al CRO-lish

A chief priest of the assassin's order known as the Kathasiri.

Winter Wyl

WIN-ter WILE

The largest celebration of the year in the Empire of Yorch.

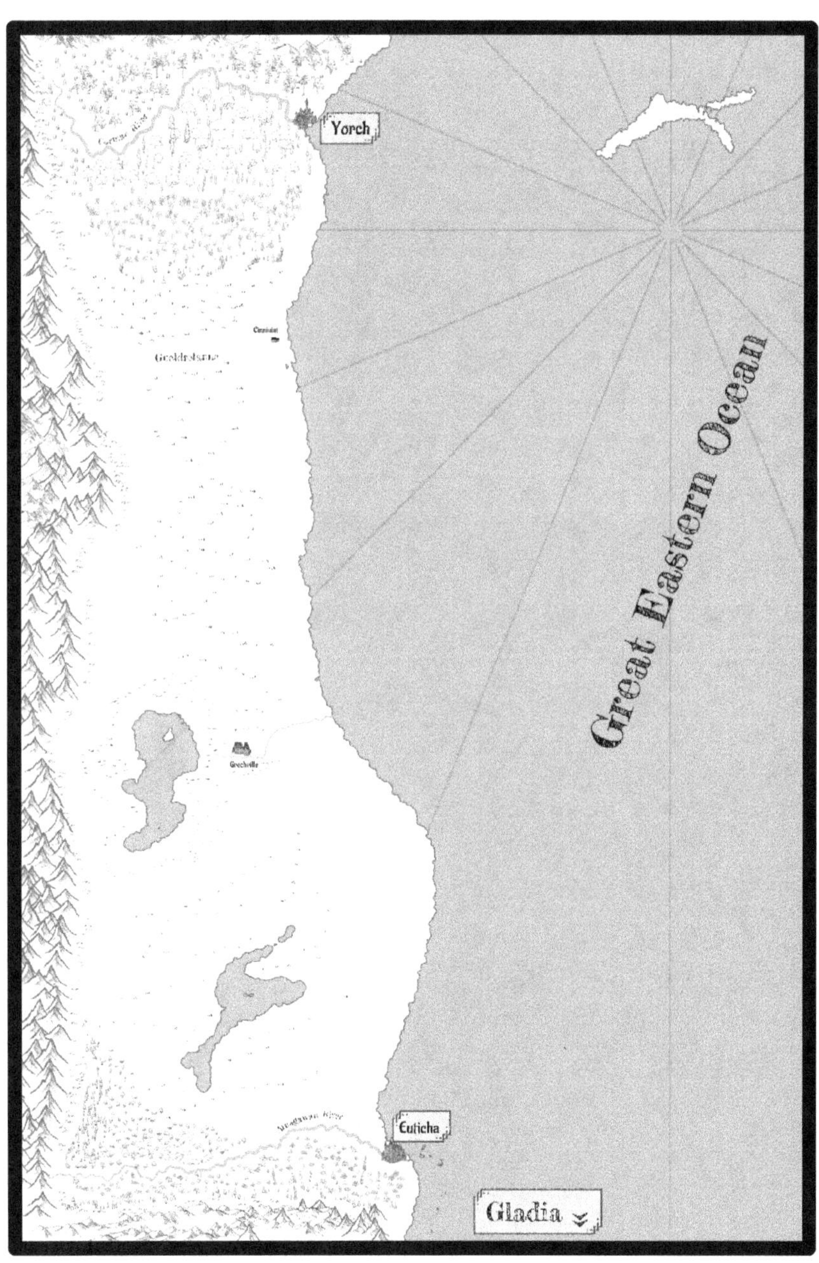
Yorch
Great Eastern Ocean
Euticha
Gladia

www.ingramcontent.com/pod-product-compliance
Lightning Source LLC
Chambersburg PA
CBHW060541310726
48982CB00009B/1330/J

* 9 7 8 1 7 3 3 4 0 8 3 6 3 *